S·W·A·L·L·O·W

It is our intention, with the International Fiction List, to seek out and publish fine fiction – new works as well as classics – by authors from around the world. This on-going series will, we hope, testify that good and even great fiction is still being written and is exciting, relevant, and, above all else, wonderful to read.

S·W·A·L·L·O·W

D. M. Thomas

LESTER
&ORPEN
DENNYS
PUBLISHERS

TEMPTATION by Arthur Freed and Nacio Herb Brown
© 1933 (1961) Metro Goldwyn Mayer Inc.
Assigned to Robbins Music Corporation, New York.
All rights controlled and administered by Robbins Music
Corporation, New York.
International copyright secured.
All rights reserved.

Canadian Cataloguing in Publication Data
Thomas, D. M.
  Swallow.
  ISBN 0-88619-056-8
  I. Title.
  PR6070.H643S9   1984   823'.914   C84-098349-2

Printed in Great Britain

There we caught
The ancient pain
Of swallows . . .
AKHMATOVA

· AUTHOR'S NOTE ·

Swallow is the second in a sequence of improvisational novels, the first of which is *Ararat* (1983). The mysterious way in which a word, an image, a dream, a story, calls up another, connected yet independent, is one of the main themes of *Swallow*. It should be possible for a reader unfamiliar with *Ararat* to read *Swallow* and understand it.

All the characters are purely fictional, apart from those referred to in two autobiographical sections set in Australia.

Part Three includes passages from Sir H. Rider Haggard's *King Solomon's Mines*, scandalously amended.

The Epigraph is from Anna Akhmatova's "Way of All the Earth," and is translated by the author. (*Way of All the Earth*, Secker & Warburg, London, and Ohio UP, Ohio.) The quotation from Pushkin's lyric "For the Shores of your Distant Home" (p. 227) is also translated by the author. (*The Bronze Horseman*, Secker & Warburg, London, and Viking Penguin NY.)

I wish to express my warm thanks to Gay Clifford and Germaine Greer, for their help in obtaining information about the tradition of the improvisatrici in Italy; and to Sita Scheer, for translating that biographical information from Italian into English.

D.M.T.

· CONTENTS ·

P·R·O·L·O·G·U·E

SHE LAY ON THE SHORE OF LEMMINJÄRVI, IN THE WHITE NIGHT of midsummer. The sun was half submerged in the lake. The woman had taken a sauna, and now rested on her back, her eyes closed. Roused by a light sound, she opened her eyes. Before her, over her, stood a Japanese youth in blue swimming-trunks. He was short and slim, but muscular and quite handsome. The muscles of his chest, shoulders, arms and thighs glistened in the sun's glow. He said to her: "Excuse me, but I am desperate. I have nothing to lose by asking. I am the son of the judge Matsushita. He fought bravely in the War, and both my uncles died for the Emperor; but I have done nothing. I am in love with you. Listening to you, I have become crazed with love. Like the lovers in your improvisation, I crave one night of love with you, and then at daybreak I am willing to die."

Covering herself more decorously with her towel, she laughed at his words. "It would hardly be a night," she said. "The sun will be under the water for at most ten minutes."

"That would be enough. I would not ask for more."

"All right, then."

She bared her body and spread her legs. The Japanese youth lay down beside her and started to caress her. She closed her eyes again. She felt for his penis. It was erect, but absurdly small. His fingers and lips were not very skilful. She remained dry. The sun had dipped below the edge of Lake Lemminjärvi, which meant in Finnish the lake of love. The minutes flew by. When he penetrated her she was still dry. It was painful to her. A nightingale sang in the brief dusk. "You haven't got time," she gasped.

"Yes, a *haiku*."

And she felt, indeed, seventeen touches. They were, in turn: feather, eyelid, hammer, wedge, sword, drumstick, grass blade, flower, gong, tusk, open scissors, Antarctica, Australia, Europe, Asia, America, Africa . . . Then the first ray of light broke over the lake, and the young man was standing away from her, panting but calm. He had taken a knife from his discarded swimming-trunks. He knelt before her. "Don't be stupid," she said, gazing at him between her heaving breasts. She had the feeling of lift-off in a plane, and at the same time a kind of shower, *within* her body, expanding her, opening her wide. "I make you this dying prediction," he said. "At Delphi, you were too confident, you offended the gods. But this time you will win." The joyful orgasm went on, as he moved his hand across his belly and a red streak flowered on his skin and on the lake's horizon, the sun's rim appearing. His head pitched forward and struck the ground.

A scream came from his dead lips. She was waking up, fumbling to turn off the alarm. She couldn't find the button and for several seconds the wail went on. Then it stopped. She glanced at her watch. She had ten minutes. The vision of the wailing corpse quickly fading, she felt refreshed from her brief sleep. She sat up, swung off the bed, and fumbled for her shoes. She stood up and straightened her dress. She went to the dressing-table and ran a brush through her hair. Then she opened the door, and walked downstairs.

The sunlight struck her. It sparkled off the lake. The sun looked good for several more hours; though at home, in Italy, dusk would be falling. Passing the Press Centre, she came within sight of the audience, most of whom had taken the opportunity to stretch their legs, stroll about, go to their hotel or guest-house for a drink and a snack. Seeing her striding across the short grass, they started to drift back to their white benches, arranged in a deep semi-circle in front of the platform. Behind the platform was a marquee. When the clouds came over and drops of rain fell—as had happened twice during the afternoon—the proceedings moved into the marquee. The green space on which the marquee and the benches stood was not unlike an English village green, since it was ringed by a plantation of oaks. Behind the oaks, and dominating them, were the more common birch trees, firs and pines. On the lake-side, there were no trees of any kind. That was the great lake, in which the island of Satakieli (Nightingale) lay. Within Satakieli was another lake—a lake inside a lake.

That smaller lake could not be seen from the open-air auditorium. If you walked through the trees on that side, you could just glimpse it in the distance. The ordinary holiday-makers kept to that lake, during this time when the main resort was taken over.

The woman glided, in her long skirt, over the grass, and the audience settled. Most of them put on their head-phones, for hardly anyone could understand Italian. A row of make-shift cubicles, on the side away from Lake Lemminjärvi, housed translators, who did their best to turn fluent Italian into Finnish, English, French, German, and Russian.

The woman reached the platform. There was a scattering of applause. She bowed. She touched the microphone. She closed her eyes to recall how she had ended. The Soviet poet, Rozanov, meditating on the day ahead, after spending an unsatisfactory night with a blind woman in Gorky. They would have breakfast together . . . She opened her eyes. She began to speak. She was interrupted by the arrival of two black limousines, on the rough track behind the translators' cubicles. It was the expected visit of the Minister of Culture from a revolutionary South American state. The newly appointed revolutionary Minister was a famous poet. He was paying a courtesy-call on Finland on his way home from Moscow. There was a ripple of excitement in the audience. Car doors opened. Two large men in dark suits appeared, their jackets bulging. They wore sun-glasses. A Beautiful Lady appeared, elegantly dressed, followed by two more "heavies." Then the Minister of Culture appeared, a little old man in a smock and a black beret: a Picasso-figure. Discreet in the high trees, the television camera, Estonian not Finnish, zoomed in on him. The little old man leapt on to the platform, and his *entourage* filed along the front row of benches which had been reserved for them. The Minister addressed the audience in Spanish, which hardly anyone understood, saying that policemen in his country now wrote poems—and jailors and soldiers too—then he wished the Olympiad well, nodded at the performer who had stepped aside, and jumped off the platform. He headed for the limousines. The four heavies, and the Beautiful Lady, stood up, and filed out again. They got back into their limousines, and were away, heading for the bridge and the highway south to Helsinki. The Italian woman stepped forward, and began where she had left off. She spoke without a pause for two hours: her voice suggesting, by the subtlest of modulations, different emotions, different voices.

O·N·E

· I ·

FEW WHO LISTENED TO CORINNA RIZNICH'S IMPROVISATION understood it well enough to remember it for long; but not one of them (except a single blind man) would ever forget her dress. For the preliminary rounds, she had worn a plain black shift, which had suited her tall, slim form, her delicate face, and the cascade of wavy black hair falling almost to her waist; but for her performance in the finals she had chosen to appear in an extraordinary and extravagant dress which represented the world. Light blue for the oceans and gold for the continents, it had brought gasps of pleasure. Now, as she spoke the last words of her improvisation—some five hours after she had mounted the stage and drawn her theme from the envelope given to her—she uncrossed her arms from her bosom, took a step back, gave a short bow: and the cascade of black hair covered the northern hemisphere as far south as Zaire and Colombia, where the equator was compressed into the narrow span of her waist. As the applause started to unroll—and many listeners got to their feet to show their enthusiasm and stretch their cramped legs—she stood up straight and pushed her hair back from her eyes. She turned to the right, and bowed to the line of expressionless and unclapping jurors. She turned to the left, and bowed towards the five other finalists, who were clapping vigorously. Markov, his mane of brown hair gleaming under the bright evening sun, had stood up from his seat and lifted his hands high above his head to clap. He, alone of the competitors, had not had to use head-phones; he alone knew Italian.

Corinna turned again to the front, and bowed low. Again the wavy hair tumbled over half the world; her broad skirt undulated; Southern Africa and South America rippled like fields of wheat, and a serene storm swept the great southern oceans.

A different storm was agitating the grassy slope behind the benches. A group of women, some in shorts and loose tops, some in overalls, were leaping in the air and brandishing banners proclaiming, in various languages, the rights of women. This group had "adopted" the Italian *improvisatrice* from her very first appearance at the Olympiad. They had, many times, interrupted her performance with shrieks of approval, as they had interrupted several of the male competitors with howls of derision. Now, as the world of Corinna's dress librated, turned aside, and quietly left the stage, the still-leaping women at the back set up a chant in English: "*No more patriarchy! No more shit!*" Murmurs of distaste ran through the audience; an elderly Finnish gentleman tottered on to the stage and appealed for order. Gradually the chanting faded away; the group of demonstrators turned to make their way to their camp-site; the rest of the audience began to babble, gather up rugs, coats and bags, and drift away.

Corinna, meanwhile, had walked swiftly to the small hotel, closed the door of her room, and stretched out on her bed. She closed her eyes. She allowed the turbulence of her improvisation to die down in her mind. Ararat, the blind woman, the feverish voyage, the St Petersburg inn, the shark-men, the Moscow flat—all grew cool, and vanished. In their place, came a bay, under hot summer sunlight; a girl bringing bread and wine to her father in the vineyard. She sees the sun glinting on his scythe, with which he is clearing a patch of long grass; she sees him straighten, on hearing the rustle of her skirt; his toothless smile, his sweat . . . She is pleased because she has pleased the Father with her Greek, and it's a holiday. Then Corinna's closed lids filled with red, and quickly she brought her mind back to her fictional visions. And now, as always happened, she thought of things she ought to have included, but had not; or had included, but ought not to have done . . . That rape didn't quite work . . . The hair-curlers maybe were too much, too farcical . . . And I thought of an extremely good pun for Surkov to say: what was it? *In* Reno *veritas* . . . but it slipped my mind. Was I too long? Did I bore them? A lot of the men in the audience didn't clap; did they find my heroes offensive? Those feminists didn't help.

Screw it, it's all over. I did my best. Were there seven veils, did I get that right? Let's see, there was the *improvisatore*, then Pushkin; Surkov; the Armenian—I've forgotten what I called him; Rozanov, and then myself narrating the end. Shit, that's only six . . . That's really screwed it up. Markov will get it. . . .

She awoke to feel someone softly stroking her dress, just where Brazil was; and opened her eyes to see Cesare's pained, adoring gaze. She granted him a half-smile, rather sly and flirtatious; then, recalling her improvisation, remorseful, she turned her face away and went on to the attack. "Where have you been?" she asked. "What kept you so long?"

She gazed up at him long enough to see that her attack pleased him—his cheeks pink above the greying beard. "I've been having a drink with Igor," he said. "I thought you'd like some time on your own. You usually do."

"Not after an Olympic final. I wanted to be told I was okay."

"You were more than okay, my dearest. You were wonderful. Better than in Tbilisi, even. You will win. Igor thinks so too."

She lifted one shoulder in a shrug, then closed her eyes and gave a tired sigh. She felt his hand lift from her thigh and then, with extreme tentativeness, begin to stroke her silk stocking just above the ankle, under the long skirt. She heard him say, "I should be angry with you. I know too well how everyone sees me. That's humiliating enough, without finding out that you despise me too. And to have to sit and hear you describe our relationship, or non-relationship rather, to everyone."

Opening her eyes, she lifted herself on her elbow and looked him in the eyes, frowning. "What on earth do you mean?"

He took his hand from her leg, and clasped his smooth hands between his white Cosmo slacks. "Don't pretend, Corinna," he said. "That was our Russian trip—you know that. I'm not an idiot."

She chuckled. "Oh, I see! You think you are Findlater! How amusing! . . . But completely ridiculous."

Smiling sadly, he held her gaze. Her lips too, eventually, formed an involuntary smile, but she quickly controlled it and turned away. She ran her hand over her silky hair, and wound a curl round her finger, under her small, shell-like ear. Well, she thought to herself, he *was* kind of heavy and pompous, moving still with that plump decorum—and it might do him no harm to be apprised of it. Besides, she had found herself introducing Cesare—and herself also—without intending to. The god had dictated it.

She took the weight of her body on her elbow, then pitched on to her front, burying her face in the pillow. Why should she feel remorseful? She had never asked him to leave his Order. Never promised him anything. If she made use of his, or rather his family's, money, it was only because he begged to be allowed to accompany her on her trips abroad; besides, quite a lot of business went to Cosmo because she wore their clothes and made it known that she did.

If, at forty-five, he was at last tired of his virginity, he should get another girl. Or go to a Milanese brothel. She had told him so. But he enjoyed being hurt by her. His guilt probably required it.

His hand stroked her back. "You must be hungry," he said gently.

"Ravenous. And thirsty."

"Shall we go to the restaurant?"

"Later, Cesare. I must take a shower; and ring Giulio to thank him for his cable. Wasn't that sweet of him?"

"Yes." Cesare formed an image of the polite, attractive seventeen-year-old boy. She had only allowed him to meet her son once, but he had taken to him immediately. He would enjoy having him as his step-son. Though Corinna, by all the laws he had once held dear, was still married, there had been a divorce in England—her husband had been an English football fan, accompanying his team to Italy.

But Corinna made it clear there was no chance.

Continuing to stroke her back, and her beautiful hair, the reformed black sheep of the wealthy Cosmo family caught sight of his bearded but cherubic face in the mirror of the dressing-table, on which her bottles of make-up stood angularly, like the towers of Manhattan they had seen together that spring. He sighed. He was no match for her. She had had experiences which seemed to have deprived her of the gift to respond to the handsome, powerful men her beauty and her talents deserved. That was both his good luck and his bad luck. Giulio had been the only good fruit of her too-early marriage. Before that, at thirteen or so, her father had died of leukemia, and she gave the impression of seeing his death as a betrayal of her. She would not talk about her family background, and had not allowed him to go with her when she had visited her family in Sorrento. He only knew she had had a poor childhood. Hence, her liking for luxurious clothes; and also, probably, her reserve.

It was most fitting—as well as ironic—that when he had first set eyes on her, and listened to her, at the Santa Maria church in Milan, she had improvised with wonderful purity on *The Cloister*.

She was herself a cloister; though he had not guessed it at first, when he had spoken to her after and she had pressed his fingers with her gloved hand. Then—the delirium, the nights in his cell when all the buried passions of twenty-five years had surged up through him . . . Madness!

She had turned out to be as cold as the Santa Maria. To everyone but those athletic young gods, occasionally after she had performed in public; worshipful young men who refused to believe she was thirty-five, and saw him, Cesare, as her father! What pain she had caused him. Yet he would not wish to return to that other cloister. Let her use him as the punch-bag on which she could unloose her aggressions, if that was what God intended.

Behind his unhappy face in the mirror he caught sight of the bottle he had put on the shelf above her bed. "There's some Armenian cognac," he murmured to the head he was caressing. "Ararat! Sergei bought it for you. Would you like some?"

"I'd prefer some wine," she said drowsily, muffled, into her pillow.

"Shall I go down for some?"

"No, we'll go down and eat." She twisted round on the bed, sat up, and put her feet on the floor. She stood up, swaying. "I'm dreadfully stiff," she said. "Unhook me, will you?"

Offering him her back, she coiled her hair aside. Thanks to a stroke of imagination on the part of the Cosmo designer, the Bering Strait leapt apart as Cesare succeeded in releasing the top-most hook. Clumsy, tremulous fingers unfastened her dress down the light-blue Pacific. The range of her spine appeared. "Thank you," she said; moving away from him, she flexed her shoulder. "I didn't realize how stiff I was."

"It's hardly surprising. Why don't you let *me* massage you?" he offered; and he laughed shakily.

"Yes, if you like."

He stammered in his amazement, at length croaking: "Really?"

"Why, yes. You've never offered before. I love to be massaged. In that, I rather agree with Marie—I could let almost anyone massage me. It's not a sexual feeling, it's just pleasant, relaxing . . . But we've no lotion!" It was her turn to give a light laugh.

"Do we need it?"

"Oh, yes." She walked towards the bathroom, and hesitated in the doorway. She nodded towards the bottle of cognac on the shelf. "We'll use the cognac. It will be a new sensation. I'll just take my clothes off. Would you ring down and get a line to my home? I must speak to Giulio before he goes out to the birthday-party."

"Okay." The bathroom door closed and locked. In dozens of hotels all round the globe, during the two years they had known each other, bathroom doors had locked like that, for her to dress or undress in private. Cesare picked up the phone between their beds and asked the woman to get a Florence number. Above the gurgles of a flushed toilet he heard Corinna's son say hello, and he exchanged a friendly greeting with him. Corinna rushed out, wrapped in a towel, sat on her bed and took the phone from his hand. Cesare, trying to stop himself from trembling, scarcely heard her long, friendly, sisterly conversation with her son, during which she thanked him for his good-luck cable, confessed that her performance had been too long and she was bound to lose, and told him not to drink too much if he was going to be driving his girlfriend's car.

"*Ciao*, my darling!"

She lay on her front, burying her head in the pillow. She pushed the towel down to the cleft of her buttocks. He poured Ararat into his palm, and pummelled, stroked, churned, her back.

"Am I doing it right?" he asked, unable to keep his voice steady.

"Mmm, yes. It's very good."

He leaned back, panting. "Would you mind if I undressed too?"

"Why? Is it necessary?"

"It's making me hot. It would feel better."

"I'd rather you didn't."

He dug his fingers more strongly into the muscles of her neck and shoulders. He gripped her shoulders to turn her over, expecting her to resist, but she did not. For the first time he saw her breasts, the red nipples. He touched her breasts gently, stroked them. Her eyes were closed. He felt joyful, worshipful. Yet how strange she was. Were women. She had never let him see her even in her underclothes before; she appeared to regard a massage as somehow outside of life, as though the bed were a beach . . . His sisters, at the Lido, soon after he had come out into the world—brazenly topless!—though in real life he was sure they were very strait-laced.

And he—when he dressed and undressed openly before her, she never seemed to mind, or even to notice. Yet now, when she lay naked above the towel, she didn't want him to undress. . . .

"I would feel more comfortable if I were undressed," he repeated. "May I?"

"If you must."

He crawled back from her, and stood up, tearing at his shirt buttons. Her lithe, bronze torso, bound at the hips by the white bath-towel, made him think of the Cleopatra she had called up in her improvisation. As he crouched over her again, she slit-opened her eyes and murmured, "I'm not sure this was a good idea; I'm not sure this is good for you." He too looked down at it, so raw, so lustful, so out of control. He poured more cognac on to her belly and breasts, and stroked it in. His lips lowered to a nipple and took it for a moment, but gently she pushed his head away. He inserted his fingers between the tightly wound towel and her skin, and cupped her pubic mount. She caught hold of his wrist, murmuring, but without anger, "I don't need to be massaged there." But he had touched that place in women, for the first time in his life, and he knew he would carry the memory of it through a thousand nights.

But Igor had. . . .

"But you let Igor massage you there," he said, his voice hoarse, his fingers and thumbs digging again into her shoulders, neck, breasts.

"What on earth do you mean? When? Where?"

"In Moscow. You let him make love to you. That night at their flat. You made it quite plain in your performance." His voice jerked to the rhythm of his strokes.

"What! You really think Igor fucked me? With you and his wife in the same room!"

He winced. "I wish you wouldn't use that word, Corinna."

"But that's what you *mean*."

"Well, didn't you? Please don't lie to me. I don't mind as long as I know the truth. I knew about those young men, in London and Athens, and it upset me very much; but I didn't try to stop you."

"And why should you?" she said fiercely. "What right would you have to? I've told you my body is my own, and my soul. I'll give either or both to whom I like, and when I like. Perhaps, one day, to you . . . But I'm not promising; I've never promised."

"But did you? Make love to Igor? Just tell me."

"Is it likely, with you and Anya there, and two teenagers upstairs?"

"But I had passed out, just as you described. And all the others were asleep too."

"Teenagers never sleep. Wives never sleep. You're crazy. We just practised my Russian, and he recited Pushkin to me."

Yes; yes, he thought, they would, they would have done that. . . .

"Okay, I believe you," he said. "I'm sorry. You're so beautiful. I love you so much." He took his hands from her breasts; she sensed that he had turned his attention from her flesh to his own. Why were men such animals? "Do you have to do that?" she said. "I knew this was bad for you. Can't you do it in the bathroom, if you must?"

"No! It's not an act of excretion. It's because I love you."

She heard the bitterness and pain in his voice and, opening her eyes, she stretched up her hand to touch his chest. "It's I who am sorry, Cesare. You really should find yourself a nice girl."

"Only you. Only you."

Her face turned aside; she watched with interest the shadow of his moving hand on the still-bright wall.

"Perhaps I can be nicer to you in time," she murmured. "But I have to take things gently—at long last. Can you understand?"

"Yes, I do understand that." His voice tried to be tender, but an animal panting came through it.

She closed her eyes. The bed moved pleasantly under her.

After a while he said, in the same drugged, panting voice: "He wants you though. Igor."

"Nonsense. He's madly in love with his wife. Not even *you* could imagine he's anything like—who were they?—Rozanov or Surkov?"

"True. But I watched him during your improvisation. He never once took his eyes off you."

"Well, I should hope not! *You* should have had your eyes on me too."

"I did. I watched you both. And your eyes kept straying towards him."

"Rubbish."

For a time there was silence in the room except for Cesare's hoarse breaths. An impulse she did not quite understand made her break the silence by saying: "Nothing at all happened between us in Moscow. But on the train between Tbilisi and Yerevan, during the night, when I went along the corridor with him to have a cigarette. Do you remember? When I broke my resolution?"

"Yes? Well? What happened?"

Her eyes still closed, and her face turned to the wall, she told him what had happened between her and Markov.

"You did that? When anyone might have come along at any moment. . . ."

"Most people were asleep. It was all over in less than a minute."

"Yet you give me nothing!" he said bitterly.

"That's right. Because he was practically a stranger. Because you're closer to me." She turned and looked at him: the eyes closed and seeping tears; the hand fallen away from the raw, erect organ. "I don't pretend to be a nice person," she added.

"No! And I'm not even sure you're telling me the truth now!"

She smiled, turning her face aside. "No, you can't be sure!"

"You're a swallow!"

Her smile widened. "You're right. I'm a swallow. Actually, I'm telling you the truth. I did it like this." She lifted herself up, and her mouth dived at him, as swift as a gull, taking him in for an instant; then she threw herself back on the bed, her eyes closing. After his cry, she felt the warmth spattering her skin. His head sank on to her breasts. His beard tickled her. She ran her fingers through his wiry hair. He was sobbing. "I may never do that to you again," she warned. He continued to sob.

"Let's have a glass of Igor's cognac," she said softly. "I presume it's from Igor. You said Sergei."

· 2 ·

MEANWHILE THE JUDGES WERE BEGINNING TO ASSEMBLE IN THE smart guest-house in which they had lived, secluded, for the past three weeks. The adjudications took place in a large room dominated by a long pinewood table. No pictures hung on the plain white walls; nothing to distract the attention of the judges from the task before them. In front of each of the thirteen chairs had been placed, by a handsome Finnish youth who had assisted efficiently throughout the competition, a fresh sheet of blotting-paper, some sheets of notepaper, a fountain pen, a glass. Carafes of water were disposed around the table. There were no ashtrays: smoking was not allowed.

Each chair bore on its back the name of a country. A set of head-phones rested close at hand, in case one or other of the judges needed to tune in to a translation in his own language of the performance under adjudication. Behind the chairman's seat, at the end of the table furthest from the doors, was a complicated recording system which the assistant, a student of electronics, had set up.

One by one the judges slipped into their places, nodding to

their neighbour or exchanging a whispered word or two. The hushed decorum was a tradition of the Olympiad. For three weeks the judges had kept to themselves, confined almost like prisoners to their plain but comfortable house. Their deliberations were as secret and exclusive as those of the College of Cardinals before the election of a Pope—and lasted much longer. As a matter of fact, the tradition of the Olympiad went back further in time than that of St Peter's chair: at least to the time of Pindar.

As with the College of Cardinals, the Olympic discussions would never be divulged to a soul. The assistant, Matti, had little English, the language in which the discussions took place.

All twelve judges, and their non-voting Finnish chairman, had taken their seats, and were rustling papers or sipping water. Six major languages of the world were represented by judges, as of right, at every Olympiad: English, French, Italian, Spanish, German and Russian. The other six places varied from Olympiad to Olympiad. At Satakieli, there were also a Pole, a Hungarian, an Israeli, a Japanese, an Iranian, a Portuguese. The judges were chosen for their skill in languages as well as for their literary taste, and most of them had at least a rough knowledge of several languages besides their own. Nevertheless, the linguistic problem flared up at every Olympiad, causing tensions and protests. The professional translators were excellent, but it was far from certain that they always produced a fair interpretation of this or that literary improvisation—insofar as *any* translation of literature can do justice to the original work. It could not be denied that *improvisatori* in one of the rarer languages—Bantu, say, or Breton—had little chance of reaching the finals, let alone of being crowned with the laurel and the bays. At Satakieli, what to make of the Pueblo Indian who had improvised an epic poem, without a pause or hesitation, for four whole hours? The melodic rhythms, rising at times to song, had held the audience spellbound; but the translation had sounded uncouth and, not without feelings of guilt, the judges had eliminated him after the heats.

The bane of nationalism held sway even here. Could the judges put their hands on their hearts and swear that the six finalists—two speaking in English, one in Russian, one in Italian, one in Finnish and one in Hebrew—were incontestably better than the Breton, the Gaelic speaker, the Pueblo Indian, the Fijian, the African Bushman? No, they could not. What preserved the Olympiad, decade after decade, and century after century, was the common knowledge that perfect justice was impossible.

Also, that everyone could go home claiming, with some hope of being believed, that he had been robbed.

Twenty-four competitors, convinced they were the best, had already flown out of Finland. They had withdrawn for the most part to a purely local fame; for few *improvisatori* either seek, or have the ability, to have their work set down in print. Of all the victors in the modern Olympiad, only Adam Mickiewicz, twice crowned in the 1820s, had achieved fame also in the more traditional forms of his art. In general the *improvisatore* is content, or has to be content, with the divine gift of spontaneous creation—the seemingly miraculous talent of being able to switch on the power of narrative with the ease of an official switching on a resort's illuminations at the approach of autumn.

A word, or a phrase, on a slip of paper—a closing of the eyes, a clenching of the fists—and the *improvisatori* at Satakieli, Corinna Riznich among them, had "felt the approach of the god", and spoken forth. It was true that the power had sometimes failed. Two competitors had struggled for a few minutes on the stage, and then left without saying a word. It had happened, in fact, during the finals, to the Israeli. No shame attached to such failures, any more than to an athlete who is off form and fails to clear the high-jump bar, at each of his three attempts. The theme, randomly selected, did not strike a spark; or the god did not choose to come.

The early rounds were always in verse. For the finals, the

improvisatori could choose to perform in either verse or prose, or both. The performance might last anywhere from half an hour to five hours; the length of an improvisation carried weight with the judges only if the shorter performances were not perceptibly finer. Should an improvisation go on for longer than three hours—a rare enough event—the competitor was allowed to take a half-hour break. The Pueblo Indian had scorned to take an intermission. Corinna had broken off, at the end of Rozanov's night in Gorky, only because her bladder had insisted.

Her improvisation had been the longest in the whole competition, and by many hours the longest in the finals. The Australian's prose-tale ("A little dog went ambling down the main street of Ballerat . . .") had lasted for an hour and a half; the verse-saga of the Finn had not exceeded the hour, despite the inordinate length of Finnish words; the Russian, Markov, had completed his narrative poem well within the hour, including a break caused by rain; the Englishman's highly personal poem had scarcely reached the minimum of half an hour; the Israeli had simply opened his envelope, announced his theme—*Saint Teresa*—closed his eyes, opened them, bowed, and walked from the stage.

Although it was late in the evening by the time the Italian woman had finished, the judges decided that they were bound to discuss this last improvisation while it was fresh in their minds, just as they had done with all the others. They would then break off for a light supper, and sleep, before re-convening in the morning for their final deliberations. The aged Finn called for the attention of the panel; the rustlings and the whispers ceased. In the customary manner, he asked for a brief, initial assessment from everyone at the table, starting with the English-speaking judge, Coningsby, on his right.

· 3 ·

CONINGSBY, A REFINED AND HANDSOME ANGLO-Argentinian, had not liked the Italian improvisation. It had struck him as little more than a coarse, muddled, seemingly endless, feminist polemic. Every man had been a villain, every woman a victim. It was not surprising it had provoked unseemly demonstrations. The Russian judge, Professor Dibich, small, wrinkled and goldfish-mouthed, agreed with his colleague and complained also of the work's Cold War tones, its anti-Sovietism. On Dibich's right, the chubby, bespectacled Japanese judge, Matsushita, had not found the improvisation muddled; he observed that *The Seven Veils* had contained many layers, like the inwoven petals of a rose: as in a short poem by Lirke.

"Lorca?" asked one of the judges.

The tiny Japanese shook his head. "No, Lirke. The mystical German poet."

"Ah, Rilke!" exclaimed Frau Krüdner.

"Yes, Lirke." But then Matsushita, too, said he had found it brutal.

Signora Rossi could hardly contain herself. She had decided, previously, that she would admit to a childhood friendship with Signora Riznich, but now she changed her mind. Anyway, it was irrelevant. Her thin, nervous body quivered from a mixture of indignation and nicotine-starvation as the Polish judge next to her added to the weight of disapprobation. The tall, sorrowful-looking, soldierly man said, "There were things I liked. It was clever. It was clever, for instance, to set it a year ago, and never for a moment lose sight of that—though I can't, of course, accept her views on Solidarity. But I agree it was hysterical and pornographic. It sounded like the product of a man-hating nymphomaniac."

The Italian judge burst out: "I simply cannot understand this! Have we been listening to the same improvisation? I find these views incomprehensible—"

"Please, Signora," the chairman interrupted her. "A little more temperately." It was a convention of the judging that voices should never verge from a measured tone, however fierce the disagreements.

"I'm sorry," she said, more calmly, "but it's hard for me to sit still and hear Signora Riznich accused of sexism and pornography. . . ."

"Please, no names," interrupted the aged Finn again. It was another convention that the improvisation should never be personalized; the judges referred always to the given theme, or used the neuter pronoun.

"Forgive me. *The Seven Veils* went out of its way, it seems to me, to understand the nature of its male characters. They *were* selfish and superficial, and caused harm to their women; but they also felt guilty about that. And they had a certain quest, a certain vision. In other words, they were portrayed as real people. This is not sexism, not man-hatred. I found the work beautiful, intricate, cunning; a dark tragedy of the human condition. Moreover, pornography is supposed to titillate; the eroticism in *The Seven Veils* was far from that. Was anyone here turned on by an account of a man biting a young woman's genitals and howling like a wolf? I doubt it very much."

Her fingers trembling, she sipped water. After a few moments' silence, the Portuguese woman to her right remarked: "I would not have used the word beautiful about it, but I found it extremely funny. I am surprised that Signora Rossi believes it to be a sombre tragedy. It had its dark shadows certainly; I shuddered during the account of the Armenian massacres: didn't we all? But it was also often very funny, and had a playful form. I thought it was enormous fun."

The chairman nodded at her politely, smiled in his courteous way, and then shifted his gaze to the stout blonde Frau-Professor who sat directly opposite him, at the end of the long table. "Professor Krüdner?"

"It depressed me beyond words. I felt I wanted to vomit. Its so-called humour was extremely crude. When we play some of it back, I suggest we might begin with the bedroom scene of the man's revolting deception of the blind woman. The beginning of the second part. It showed a complete callousness to the feelings of the disabled. There was a blind man in the audience; I can't begin to imagine what he was feeling. And I agree with my male colleagues about its aggressiveness towards men. They were all monsters, except the American—and he was portrayed as an idiot. I think it was an imposture. Clever, yes; and no doubt the Signora's good looks would have had an effect on some of the audience—"

"Please, let us stick to the improvisation."

"Of course. I don't want to say any more at this stage."

Looking slightly abashed, following the reference to the charms of the *improvisatrice*, the Israeli and the Iranian spoke warmly of *The Seven Veils*. Both men—orthodox in their respective religions—had been keen advocates of the Florentine beauty from the first heat. The shy, quietly-spoken Hungarian judge, a woman, expressed mixed feelings. The short, swarthy, moustached Spaniard—also female—conveyed a qualified approval. The aristocratic Frenchman, to the chairman's left, enthused about the work's formidable intelligence.

"For myself," said the aged Finn, "I am particularly bothered by the old man, Finn. I don't know who he was, or what he was doing. At one point, early on, if my memory serves me correctly, the narrator says he saw little of Finn for the rest of the voyage; yet he returned in the improvisation time after time. Well, this can happen, of course, but we should take note of it at this last stage of the contest." The old man, his white hair flashing in the late sun from the window, leaned back in his chair, and bared his yellowish teeth in a thoughtful grimace. He tipped his chair forward, and gazed at his sheet of blotting-paper, on which he had doodled a wolf's head. "More seriously," he continued in his calm, quavery voice, "I was disturbed by the accounts of the massacres. Unlike Signora Rossi and Senhora Casalduero, I was not moved by those accounts. I felt, instead, a kind of intimidation, or even manipulation. It seemed to me pornographic in intent; the pornography of violence. I'm also inclined to agree with Comrade Dibich that the improvisation was crudely anti-Soviet in parts. It disturbed the mood of reconciliation which has always been a feature of the Olympiads—mercifully apart from the Cold War—and a feature also of artistic gatherings of all kinds here at Satakieli." He paused to sip some water. "Unquestionably there was a good deal of verbal skill, a flashy brilliance; but I suspect no more than that. I suspect it was hollow within. However, there is clearly a great deal of disagreement among us. I shall say no more, but try simply to interpret your wishes in these deliberations, and direct the flow of discussion fairly. We must, of course, go over some of the performance. I take it no one would suggest we should play it all?" He flashed again his yellowish teeth; there was a ripple of amusement.

Coningsby, the dark-complexioned, prematurely white-haired Anglo-Argentinian, noticed that he had sketched, quite unconsciously, the face of his friend Pablo, killed on the *General Belgrano* only weeks before. He winced from that pain; but gave no sign of it when he spoke, in his almost too-elegant English: "You see," he said gravely, tapping his pencil-head on the pad, "Signora Rossi asked a good question just now: have we been listening to the same improvisation? And the answer, in a sense, is no. I'm not speaking about the different translations. What I mean is, we each bring to it a different world, a different experience; and so what we hear is different for each of us."

Three or four heads nodded in agreement. All had learned, in the course of their long deliberations, to listen to Coningsby with respect. His judgements were knowledgeable and carefully weighed. They felt sympathy for him too. Everyone was aware of the anguish he must be feeling, with his two countries having waged a horrible, late-colonial war for the Malvinas, a poor, useless lump of rock.

"I can't altogether agree with you," said the ample West German judge. "If you were right, this whole Olympiad would be pointless. We must strive to resolve our differences of opinion; and first of all, as our Chairman says, we shall have to hear some of the improvisation once more. May we perhaps take up my suggestion of hearing the start of the Second Act, as it were? Maybe even all of it from that point, or most of it? I know my attention was wandering by that stage." She glanced around for confirmation. There were murmurs of assent.

Tarkiainen spoke a few words in Finnish to the slim youth who stood patiently behind him. The handsome, blond-haired, pale-skinned youth nodded, and turned to walk to the tape-recorder. Several of the judges, wishing to hear the improvisation in their native tongues, reached for their head-phones.

For those few who understood Italian, the melodious, clear voice of Corinna Riznich came over the loudspeakers. . . .

· 4 ·

UNDER THE IMPRESSION THAT THE WAITER HAD LEFT THEIR
bedroom, Olga had already sat down before a trolley laden with
breakfast dishes and was beginning to eat an omelette. Already
bits of omelette were spilling off her plate: though it was not to be
compared with the havoc of the previous evening's dinner, a
somewhat mushy and liquid chicken dish, when—for all her
fastidiousness—the area in front of her had become like the
overflowing Nile. Rozanov, meeting her for the first time, had
felt the eyes of all the other diners on them, and had been
overcome with embarrassment. It had been bad enough that
Olga was older and plainer than he had imagined; it was worse
that the very thing which had persuaded him to persuade her
to this rendezvous in Gorky—her blindness, his curiosity
about sleeping with a blind woman—merely drew people's attention to his dining alone with a drab and fading woman with
appallingly thin legs. He, so young-looking at fifty, so attractive to women—to be seen, even by strangers in a ghastly
provincial town, with such a companion! His ears had burned
with shame; and he had resolved that they would breakfast in

their room. It was worth the sizeable bribe he had had to pay.

"You haven't told me what you're working on at present, Sergei," Olga said, directing her voice to the point, some distance away, where she believed Rozanov to be exercising.

Grunting, breathing heavily, he replied: "Something pretty big."

"Oh, really? How exciting! Are you going to tell me about it?"

"I'd rather not."

"Oh. I'm disappointed. But of course I understand."

The incredibly fat Mongolian waitress who had brought their breakfast was squatting on Rozanov's lap, on the chair before the dressing-table. Her mouth engulfed his, except when he tore away to reply to Olga; the couple moved in rhythm, their groins grinding together as closely as his jeans and her tracksuit trousers—he had noted them curiously when she had served dinner—permitted. His hand roamed over her fat, oily back, under the loose tunic; and around to her monstrous, bra-less breasts. The woman was unbelievably ugly. The encounter had taken Rozanov by surprise. He had been sitting on the side of the bed as she had brushed against him to arrange the breakfast dishes; her bottom, as she bent forward, had nudged his arm . . . moved away . . . nudged him again. He had felt a perverse excitement, began to desire her because she was so undesirable. He had rested a hand on the inside of her soft, soft-trousered thigh. She had not moved away; she had taken a long time to arrange the dishes. He had run his hand up and down her thigh. He had stood up, turned her expressionless face towards him, and kissed her.

"Your omelette will be getting cold, darling."

He grunted. "I'll be with you in a few moments."

"Do you always exercise before breakfast?"

Rozanov did not reply, except with the sounds of his exertions. He had twisted his arm to run his hand down the front of the waitress's tracksuit trousers. Since she was sitting astride him, groin to groin, it was a strain even to reach her rough pubic hairs under the tight briefs. Suddenly the earth moved under Rozanov: a chair-leg broke, and he found himself hitting the floor, with the Mongolian on top of him. The resounding crash, and a yelp from Rozanov, made Olga spill coffee down her dress; the trolley and her chair shook. "What's happened?" she cried. "Are you all right, Sergei?"

Rozanov rolled free from his companion. He rubbed the aching bone at the base of his spine, then rubbed and flexed his wrist, which had been trapped at a disjointed angle in the waitress's trousers. "I'm okay," he said; "the fucking chair broke while I was doing a hand-stand. Our wonderful Soviet furniture!"

The waitress lay flat on her back, like a beached whale, her round belly rising and falling. A smile lit her impassive oriental features.

"You could have hurt yourself," said Olga. "Do come and eat."

"I must just do my press-ups." Rozanov got on to his knees, and held out his hands to assist the waitress to sit up. Then she too got on to her knees. His pains easing, Sergei placed his hands on the waistband of her tunic, and made to lift it. The woman stopped him, nodding towards Olga as if to say (or so he interpreted it), "That wouldn't be right." He dug into his jeans pocket and produced a twenty-rouble note. He showed it to her. She hesitated, then took it and stuffed it into her breast pocket. Lightly she got to her feet, followed by Rozanov. She pulled her tunic over her head; her huge breasts flopped free. Rozanov unzipped his jeans and worked them off his legs as quietly as possible. The woman, too, undressed silently. Rozanov took her hand, and pulled her down to the carpet. She opened her thighs. It revolted and fascinated him that her thighs hung in folds, like her stomach. He lay on top of her. He thought of offering her a pillow, but assumed her buttocks were fat enough to prevent discomfort. She was already wet, and he slid in easily. She felt warm, liquid, cavernous. "This is how Sonia feels to Kolasky," he thought. The waitress's breasts swung pendulously, under their own slow momentum, like milk-churns. He buried his face between them, his hands pressing them tight against his cheeks. She was breathing quickly but silently; Rozanov's breaths came to Olga as labouring gasps.

"How many press-ups do you do?" she asked.

"Fifty," Rozanov gasped.

"You should take care."

Rozanov came, and eased himself away from the woman. He lay on his back, panting. He stared up at her belly, rising and falling, mountainous. The face still looked as expressionless as when she had served them the chicken last night.

Rozanov went to the bathroom and ran the tap to cover the sounds of their dressing. He kissed the waitress's cheek and squeezed her hand as he quietly opened the door for her and closed it after her. He sat down opposite Olga. The omelette and coffee were cool, but he ate and drank greedily and chatted with Olga briskly. He permitted her gnarled hand to stroke his. A pale light lit the bedroom; the rain of the night had eased to a drizzle. He felt full of good spirits; his penis, under the tight jeans, was still half erect. Weariness, after the sleepless night and the droll encounter with the fat Mongolian, made him feel more, not less, sexually charged.

It was time for Olga to get ready to leave. She asked him if he would share her taxi as far as the station, but he explained that the airport was in a different direction. He replaced the broken chair with one that was intact, and she sat at the dressing-table to comb her hair and apply some powder to her cheeks. It was strange how she preferred to tidy up in front of a mirror, he thought; it was rather touching. Of course, she was used to the ritual; she had gone blind only in her twenties. Her face in the mirror looked sad. She was upset to be leaving him. She called him over to her,

and when he leaned over the back of her chair she seized his hand
and pressed her lips to it. "I love you," she murmured. "Is that
silly of me?"

Feeling overwrought and slightly hysterical from the claus-
trophobic and sleepless night, Rozanov, gazing into the mirror,
twisted his lips into a comic leer, then sucked them in until they
disappeared from sight. He rolled his bloodshot eyes. "I shall
miss you," she continued. "Will you miss me a little?"

"I shall remember last night," he said. "I shan't forget it." He
pulled his mouth into another comic leer. She went on stroking
his hand, which was resting on her shoulder. "But we have our
own lives," he continued. "You have to go home to your
husband."

She gave a sigh. "Yes. And you to your wife."

"Yes."

"It will be hard for me to act in front of Stiva as if nothing has
happened. How about you? Of course, you're more practised at
this sort of thing than I."

Gently he took his hand away and stroked the crown of her
head, then he walked across to the window. "It's important that
you don't give him any cause to suspect," he said. "Be nice to
him. Let this experience be a kind of secret gift for him."

"That's hard. It's so private between us."

Rozanov, gazing down at the puddled street where a few
workers cycled past over the padding of fallen leaves, said: "But
you have to live with him." He felt a momentary pleasure that
Olga's husband, who was also blind, would not know his wife
had been fucked; then he felt remorseful on account of his
pleasure. It was a very wan pleasure—no compensation for his
total lack of pleasure in the actual acts of love with Olga—but it
was awful that he should feel it. Was it just a delight in secrecy, he
wondered? A wish to undercut someone's complacency? Envy
because his marriages had all been fucked up?

She zipped up her overnight bag, put on her coat, and he

carried the bag for her to the lift. She held tight to the emblem of her affliction, the folded-up white stick.

He ordered her taxi from a sullen clerk, then on impulse bought Olga a big bar of chocolate at a kiosk. "You've been so kind to me, Sergei," she said, as he slipped the bar into her coat pocket. "How did you know I love chocolate? I shall think of you when I eat it on the train, though you oughtn't to be tempting me. I have to watch my weight."

Rozanov opened his mouth to say how absurd that was—she was actually much too thin—but closed it again. It was pointless. He knew that a woman's concern for dieting was completely illogical; there were women who would want to slim in Belsen. More to the point, he would never see her again so there was no point in urging her to put on a few kilos. She clutched his sleeve anxiously at that very moment and said: "We shall meet again soon, won't we?"

"I hope so."

"I'll come to Moscow. After all, you're helping me with my dissertation!" She chuckled, then again looked sad and anxious, gazing into space through her dark glasses.

The taxi was a long time coming. Rozanov fidgeted. "Thank you for improvising," she said, after a silence.

"It was a pleasure."

They were silent again. As he waited, keeping his eye on the glass doors, he started to compose his letter to Olga, which she would get some reliable friend to read to her. Their rendezvous had churned him up so much, was so threatening to his marriage, that he was taking the painful decision not to see her again.

"It's here," he said. He took her arm and helped her though the doors. The drizzle and the fresh autumn air were invigorating. She drew his mouth to hers in a fierce, thin-lipped kiss, and said, "Thank you, thank you! It's been so wonderful! Thank you!"

"Goodbye, Olga," he said. She climbed in. He slammed the door. She waved. As the taxi drew away from the kerb, Rozanov took a deep, joyful breath and then leapt in the air: a Nijinsky-leap. Standing then peacefully on the steps, he murmured, "Thank God!" He felt a hand on his shoulder. He turned, and looked into the bloodshot eyes of a heavy man in an ill-fitting navy suit. His heart missed a beat. By instinct, he recognized the hotel's KGB agent. The man was holding out a cassette tape. "I thought you might like this, Comrade Rozanov," the man said. "I couldn't help listening. It wasn't to trap you, you understand? I happen to be a great admirer of your work. I was thrilled when I heard you were going to be staying here. Was she nice?" He winked. "What a marvellous talent you have. I mean, for making up stories! It takes something pretty good to stop me from nodding off."

"I'm glad you enjoyed it," Rozanov said.

"But you should be a little careful, Comrade."

"Thank you. Yes, you're right. Is there any way I can show you my gratitude?"

The burly man spread his hands. "No, no! Unless, perhaps, you have a book I could give my wife? She also is a great fan of yours. She reads a lot of poetry. I'm more for listening. She would love a book of your poems, and especially if you were to sign it for her personally."

Rozanov said he didn't have any copies of his books with him, but would be glad to send one if the man would let him have his address and tell him his wife's name. The man scribbled his address on a piece of paper, and under it wrote "Masha". Rozanov pocketed the slip of paper. The two men shook hands. Rozanov strolled around for a while in the light drizzle, then went back into the hotel to settle his bill and finish packing.

He computed how much he had spent, for a wretched night which also allowed his mistress to have a free evening with his rival, General Kolasky. It didn't bear thinking about: the flight, the room, the meals, the vodka and wine, the taxis, the Mongolian waitress, the clerk for agreeing to send their breakfast up . . .

And for such an awful woman! He groaned. God, what a night!
Well, it should be a lesson to me. . . .

In the taxi, however, he forgot everything else in sheer happiness at leaving the hotel, and Olga, behind him forever. And
Gorky airport, which bristled with guards, which didn't even
exist in foreign Aeroflot timetables, struck Rozanov as a joyous
emblem of freedom.

On the short flight home, he had intended to work on a piece
about Colonel Penkovsky, the spy and traitor; but the moment
he had fastened his seatbelt and felt the plane taxiing towards the
runway, he fell asleep . . . Instead of Colonel Penkovsky, the
subject of his night's improvisation, his friend Surkov, came back
to him.

· 5 ·

THE SUDDEN STEEP DROP TO THE WASHINGTON NATIONAL
Airport deafened Surkov, and made his head feel muzzy. As he
stood up and reached for his lumber-jacket and Castro hat, he lost
his balance and lurched against Abramsohn. Once outside the
terminal, in the cool but brilliant autumn light, he mopped his
brow, uncomfortably hot. His deafness plunged him into a silent,
unreal world where cabs made no sound and his American
agent's lips moved incomprehensibly. Seeing Surkov poke his

ears, Abramsohn shouted that there was time to see a little of the city. Surkov nodded.

Surkov didn't like what he saw. He liked it less than on his only previous visit, in '68, when the crowds had chanted anti-war slogans outside the White House. Even in the depths of winter he had enjoyed the city. But he had been feeling healthy, then.

"I just want to see the Kennedy Memorial and Lincoln's grave," he shouted at Abramsohn. Abramsohn directed the driver to the Lincoln Memorial. At the parking spot, the two men got out and walked to the seated, meditative figure; but Surkov, his legs shaky, headed back for the car almost at once. There wasn't time to drive to Arlington Cemetery, Abramsohn told him. Maybe after the reception.

"Okay. It doesn't matter." Surkov thought of the Kennedys. Marilyn Monroe, whom he had met at a party in Los Angeles. A stab of sorrow.

His left ear had recovered its hearing. "I don't like this fucking city," he growled in his normal voice. "It's all male power. It's like a mausoleum. It's as bad as Moscow." He nodded towards an obelisk, and said, "Why do they have a prick, but no cunt? You have enough fucking feminists in this country—why don't they protest? Why don't they insist on erecting a cunt, in memory of—I don't know—Annie Oakley, Marilyn Monroe, the witches of Salem?" Smiling, Abramsohn pointed out a museum of space flight, outside the cab's gliding window. "Another fucking male symbol," growled Surkov, dabbing his brow with a grubby, sweat-soaked handkerchief.

"Well, I guess," said the bear-like, bald-headed literary agent, "the Capitol is a tit."

"It's full of old women," called the cab-driver over his shoulder, unexpectedly. Abramsohn offered the driver an appreciative chuckle, while the Russian growled: "It's a foam-rubber tit. A prosthesis. And a mastectomy. Where's the other tit? Things have got worse, Dave, since '68. I feel it in my bones.

More dangerous. Dangerous. America is less sure of herself, and more arrogant. I feel it."

"And what about your country, Victor?"

The Russian hesitated. He glanced at the cab-driver's broad, leather-jerkined back. He seemed reassuringly and patriotically American, but you could never tell. The Embassy knew of his unexpected visit. "We just want a quiet time," he said.

Surkov, a glass in hand, listened with his left ear to Senator Hammer, who was explaining to him why he wouldn't be able to watch the Dodgers while he was staying in New York. For some reason the team had moved to California. The Russian murmured his disappointment. Hammer had one hand in a nonchalant pocket of his elegantly-tailored suit, the coat cut away in a vent. His eyes were blood-red and jaundiced. His teeth were very bright.

A woman at Surkov's still-deaf right ear was telling him she went to the dentist every month and he pulled out one of her teeth. Evading the senator, Surkov said with a smile, "Well, your teeth are wonderful. All Americans have wonderful teeth."

The woman with snowcapped teeth clutched the passing arm of Aaron Soupfin, and introduced him to Surkov saying, "You've got a lot to talk about, I guess. Haven't you both written about the Warsaw Ghetto?" Soupfin was a thin, short, Jewish novelist. The reception was in his honour. Soupfin and Surkov shook hands warily, while the woman and the senator glided off in different directions. Soupfin, blinking up through his rimless glasses at the tall, wild-haired Russian, said, "Welcome to the United States."

"Thank you," said Surkov. "Congratulations on the Prize."

"Thank you."

They stood silent, looking intently at different parts of the crowded room. Surkov was thinking of Soupfin's humourless, boring moral seriousness; Soupfin was thinking of Surkov's superficiality: he had even admitted it in the press conference reported in that morning's *Post*. Both knew they had nothing at all in common; each knew that the other knew that.

Surkov made the excuse that he needed a refill, and Soupfin nodded with relief and turned away. Surkov lurched—he felt hot and sick—towards the black-faced penguins who were serving cocktails.

Sipping a Tom Collins, Surkov admired and despised the smooth power of these politicians. How beautiful, how expensive, their suits! So effortlessly disguising burliness. And those handsome gold cufflinks! Those brilliant starched shirts! The hum of powerful men, relaxed and condescending, at an insignificant literary reception. Every moment of their day precisely programmed, Surkov thought, even to their relaxation. It was intolerable, and enviable.

And their elegant, brittle, neurotic, over-exercised, over-dieted wives. Surkov didn't find any of them desirable.

He thought, with rare affection, of Vera, his wife; of Tanya, his mistress. Yes, he would get the hell out. Abramsohn's excited morning call to Donna Zarifian's apartment had fouled up his plans of the night. But he could scarcely have refused the unparalleled invitation to the White House. Not so much the reception as the President's offer to give him an interview for *Pravda*. The Soviet Embassy had approved. Dave, choking with excitement, had said O'Reilly evidently wanted to build up his liberal image, mostly for home consumption. The President's human face. Hence Surkov, a convenient visitor, a poet, a liberal Marxist. It would "make" his tour, Abramsohn predicted. Surkov hadn't had the courage to tell him he planned to get the hell out after Friday's lucrative reading in New York. If possible, with that stylish high school girl he'd met at the JFK press conference. He had wormed her name, and the name of her school, out of Dave.

That place in southern Arizona, he mused, during a merciful solitude in the middle of the buzzing crowd . . . To write up the story he had dreamed overnight . . . To hold the shy, stylish girl in his arms. . . .

Yes, he would get the hell out. That shit Bliudich, the Writers' Union Secretary, would forgive him everything for the coup of an interview with the President. More than that, his slightly tarnished image, on both sides of the Iron Curtain, would be restored, brighter than ever.

One of the political wives slithered up to him and introduced herself as Betty Thresher. Her husband worked in the Justice Department. Wasn't he Victor Surkov, the famous poet? She loved his work. He saw her torso ripple beneath her thin cocktail dress. All the movements of her body and facial muscles were lively and jerkily quick. Her eyes were larger than her weak, friendly mouth. Fighting off his weariness, jet-lag, and the after-effects of feverish illness, Surkov half-heartedly flirted with her while at the same time glancing around. All their eyes, he thought, are like pin-heads, and are stuck on their faces haphazardly . . . Dave was engaged in an intense conversation with a hunchbacked woman who looked like a frog. She was reclining on a sofa, and Dave was leaning over her languid form as if her tiny eyes and hunched back were slowly drawing his bulk down and into her.

"Would you like to sit?" Surkov asked Mrs Thresher.

"No, I'm fine."

"I think I'd better sit down. I haven't been awfully well."

"Oh, I'm sorry. Forgive me. Here, have this chair."

Surkov sat.

A mild, slightly-built man came up, and said to Surkov, "Hi, I'm Henry Requiem." He said it as if he didn't need to say it, as if the whole world knew who he was. He had not heard of Surkov. Surkov had not heard of him. Requiem had been brought from a southern university into the administration. The Russian gathered hazily he was concerned with disarmament negotiations. He asked Surkov about the persecution of Baptists in

SWALLOW   ·   51

Russia. He himself was a Baptist. He was rather afraid Armageddon was at hand, he said. The days of the earth were possibly numbered. But he hoped, personally, to experience the "rapture" of being gathered up into heaven. What, he asked, did Surkov think?

Exhausted, hot one moment, shivering the next, Surkov felt incapable of thought. A commotion at the doors saved him. A royal entry. Surkov caught sight of that famous, amazing head of red hair, surrounded by taller, close-cropped heads. The procession passed swiftly from group to group. Everyone pressed back to let it pass. Soon Requiem was introducing Surkov, and the Russian was staggering to his feet, holding his hand out to take O'Reilly's grasp. So this was the man—referred to informally by Senator Hammer as "Tiger"—who controlled half the world. A blunt head, unusually wide; a huge mouth; the teeth lying on their sides, for some strange reason. A slim but barrel-chested body.

Surkov swayed. He tried to respond to the President's greeting intelligibly, but merely mumbled. It did not seem to matter. Tiger nodded amiably, his eyes already glancing past, and his legs already taking him past, followed by the swift trample of body-guards. Also a young Air Force officer carrying a brown woman's handbag, or a woman's brown handbag. In the wake of the Presidential party, Requiem explained to Surkov that the bag contained the nuclear codes; but the Russian felt too ill to take the information in. Trembling like a leaf, he collapsed into his chair. He heard, somewhere behind him, an exclamation. He turned, and saw blood. A young woman, white-faced—except for a gash on her cheek, from which blood poured—was already surrounded by men and women in white coats, and being steered towards the doors. It was Tiger's daughter, someone near Surkov told him; the President hadn't seen her today, before this reception, and he had kissed her on the cheek. She was thin-skinned; his slight stubble had opened up her cheek. He was affectionate but clumsy, he didn't know his own strength. Fortunately there was always a medical team close at hand.

Surkov swayed on his chair. Abramsohn came up to him. "Are you okay, Victor?"

"I'm okay. My antibiotics."

"Sure. Where are they? In your pocket?"

"Up my arse."

"Okay. You'll be okay. Let me take that glass from you and get you some fresh orange juice."

"Fuck off."

Surkov was with a woman in the back of a car driving through Georgetown. It was dark. Surkov felt muddled, forgetful, yet otherwise fine again. Almost completely well. A middle-aged man with thick rolls of neck-fat was at the wheel in front of Surkov; in the front passenger's seat was his slim peroxided wife. The woman at Surkov's side, her arm slipped through his, was called Thresher. Yes, he remembered now. Betty Thresher. "Tell me, has Abramsohn gone to the hotel?" he enquired humbly. Betty smiled at him, and said, "Yes. It's fine with him. I've promised to get you back safely."

"That's kind." He gazed entranced at the myriad neon signs floating by.

"It's my pleasure." She squeezed his arm. "How do you feel?"

"I feel okay."

"How do you feel, Victor?" their driver asked, in a gravelly voice, his head swivelling slightly on its wedge of fat.

"I'm okay."

The head nodded. "What did you think of Mrs O'Reilly?" it asked. "Betty says she talked to you for several minutes. Did you like her?"

"I guess so," mumbled Surkov, remembering nothing.

"She's very attractive," said the peroxided lady. "It's a shame she's so deaf. Those wonderful earrings she wears are really a hearing-aid, Victor. Did you know that?"

"No."

The blonde head nodded.

"Who are these persons?" whispered Surkov.

Betty Thresher put her mouth to his ear: "They're called Mary and Joseph Spinnaker."

"Ah, yes."

Surkov remembered where they were heading. He had complained to Betty how dead Washington seemed. A mausoleum to male power. She had asked him if he'd like to see how it could swing. Surkov, curious, had said yes. Betty had whispered in her husband's ear, and then gone to phone her friends the Spinnakers. Abramsohn had been reluctant to leave without Surkov, and Surkov had wrestled with him. Surkov also recalled vomiting on to a Persian carpet.

Mary Spinnaker, twisting her shoulders around, said. "Where are you staying in New York, Victor? The Algonquin?"

"No. In Brooklyn. With an Armenian lady. She's very kind."

"Oh, that's good."

"I woke up to Elvis Presley. A poster. I'm sleeping in her daughter's room."

The windscreen wipers whirred. It was starting to drizzle. The male head swivelled slightly again on its fat. It rasped: "Do you have children, Victor?"

"Yes. I have a daughter, Katya, and a son, Petya."

Mary Spinnaker warbled: "How lovely! How old are they?"

"Katya is twenty-three. No, twenty-four, I guess. Petya is five."

"Oh, my!" exclaimed Mary Spinnaker. "So many years apart. That's wonderful! It must be wonderful to have a son so young."

"Yes."

Surkov saw Petya's winsome smile. He had just lost a tooth.

Vera would have put him to bed by now. No, he would be waking up tomorrow, already. It was so confusing.

"We have a daughter. She's living in Houston. Her husband is in oil."

"Uh-huh."

In a quiet residential street Spinnaker, slowing the car, looked for and found a parking-space. "We'll have to walk a couple of blocks," he said. They climbed out to an unfurling of umbrellas. Surkov, scorning the American phobia over a few spots of rain, declined to share an umbrella with Betty. He walked apart. He had a fear of umbrellas—the way they attacked one's eyes. He wondered why capitalist America had never invented a safe umbrella.

After a short brisk walk, they climbed some steps to a discreet building, its porch and windows unlit. Spinnaker turned the door-knob and walked straight in. He led the way along a dimly-lit corridor. At the end, a plump woman sat at a desk, reminding Surkov of a watchful *dezhurnaya* in a Soviet hotel. But she greeted the Spinnakers familiarly, pleasantly, and pushed forward a guest-book to be signed. Spinnaker produced a Parker pen from his breast pocket, and scribbled. The woman exchanged a friendly word with Betty, and smiled at Surkov. "Have a good evening," she told him.

"Thank you."

"You're welcome."

He followed the others through a swing-door. Inside, a plush bar; crowded, humming tables; Sinatra's "My Way" overlaying the conversation. Surkov followed the example of his hosts in removing his lumber-jacket and his Castro hat, and handing them to the cloakroom-attendant, an attractive negress. He thanked her as she gave him a ticket. "You're welcome," she said; "have a good evening." Spinnaker, meanwhile, had negotiated a table. A waiter, clicking his fingers, guided them to a corner. Almost before they were seated he was handing them large menu-cards, and was taking their drinks order. Not for the first time, Surkov admired the American facility for suave living. Even having a crap—he confided to his companions—seemed more dignified, when one did it in a comfort station. They chuckled. Betty Thresher said, wryly, that maybe Americans did make too much use of euphemisms.

"Well, we have a few too," said Surkov, sipping Scotch. He lit a cigarette, and as an afterthought offered his packet around. They declined. Surkov's fingers started tapping as a group sang energetically that they wanted to live forever. "Don't we all?" he remarked ruefully.

"Fame," said Mary Spinnaker.

"Well, it can be double-faced. They can lift you high and then drop you on your head."

Betty Thresher said: "They have such energy. But of course, that's their youth." Surkov, not quite following the course of the conversation, glanced at his companion. Betty's exceptionally large, luminous eyes, her animated movements and her tinted chestnut hair could not hide the years. Brown speckles on her hands. She was possibly even older than Surkov. How could he have got himself into this situation? Yet he watched with curiosity the drift of couples in and out of the bar.

Spinnaker followed his curious, apprehensive gaze. "Now, remember, Victor," he said, "what you do or do not do here is entirely up to you. It's just a nice well-run club. Only legitimate couples are allowed in. We're going through; but you and Betty do whatever you want." He rose from his seat.

"Shall we go with them?" asked Betty.

"Okay." He stood up, swayed for a moment, politely helped Betty with her chair.

They followed the Spinnakers through a door, and were given a key and two large white towels by a coloured attendant. The man held open the door of a cubicle. Surkov closed the door after them. Betty started unfastening her dress; Surkov turned shyly away. He pulled off his check shirt and string vest; unzipped his jeans.

He caught sight of his bony frame and shoulderlength silver hair in the mirror; then the wide gap between Betty's breasts, and their concave slope down to the nipples. He didn't like that kind of pear-shape. She was wrapping her towel around her. He did the same, then turned to her. She ran her hand over the plentiful grey hair on his chest. "Let's go," he said. She opened the door. He padded out after her, clutching his towel in one hand, cigarettes and White House matches in the other. She locked the door and dropped the key in her handbag.

He followed Betty into a large, marble-paved room with a Jacuzzi in the middle. There were about a dozen naked men and women relaxing in it. Round the steps of the Jacuzzi another twenty or thirty people, some naked, others draped in towels, squatted or reclined. The Spinnakers, following closely behind Victor and Betty, removed their towels at once, and squatted on the marble. Victor and Betty squatted near them, but kept their towels on. Spinnaker looked even more revolting out of his clothes than in them. His breasts were plumper than his wife's scrawny pair; plumper than Tanya's, Surkov's mistress, though infinitely less appealing. And that gross belly . . . its size made the tiny circumcised penis look ludicrous. Surkov felt embarrassed that he was uncircumcised. Every man in the room seemed to have that disgustingly animal, yet clinically unerotic, red knob poking out of his flaccid cock. Well, male nakedness was always. unappealing. But, trailing his gaze around, Surkov failed to see a single woman who attracted him. Either they sagged too much, or they had jogged the sexuality out of their flesh.

"Does this inspire you, Victor?" asked Mary Spinnaker, with a smile.

"In a way."

Spinnaker asked his wife if she wanted to go in the Jacuzzi. "Maybe later," she said.

"You want to go straight on up?"

She shrugged. "Okay." The couple lurched to their feet. "We're going upstairs," said Spinnaker, nodding at a staircase beyond the Jacuzzi. Surkov murmured, "*Do svidaniya.*" Hand in hand, the middle-aged couple padded off, and Surkov watched them climb the stairs, exchanging a greeting with a couple passing them on the way down.

"I'm going in," said Betty. "Are you coming?"

"No, I'll watch you and have a smoke."

She stood up, dropped her towel, and scampered to the edge of the Jacuzzi. She stepped down, trailed a foot in the water, squatted, then eased herself in. Floating heads and limbs made a space for her. "It's wonderful!" she called out to Surkov, her small teeth glinting. Surkov nodded, breathed out a cloud of smoke. He scrabbled forward a few feet, awkwardly clutching his towel. Betty's cloven, concave breasts bobbed on the water. "Try it!" she called.

He could see she took naturally to water. She was the best-looking woman in the pool, and the men were watching her. The Muscovite stubbed out his cigarette, undid his wristwatch and laid it beside his cigarettes and White House matches. He stood up, letting his towel slide off, and stepped down to the edge of the Jacuzzi. Carefully he lowered himself in. The water felt warm and surprisingly pleasant. Bobbing gently up and down, he felt his muscles relax. Betty, her breasts bobbing like buoys just in front of him, flashed him a grin, then did a marine somersault, diving head first, rolling over underwater, and surfacing with a gasp, her eyes clenched, her hair and face streaming. She opened her eyes and grinned. She plunged again, and again, like a human water-wheel. The swiftly recurrent surfacing of her breasts, and the brief revelation of her cunt as her buttocks slid underwater, stirred in Surkov a mild desire. Around, he saw floating flaccid penises fatten slightly and lift, in the buoyant water.

After ten minutes or so, Surkov pulled himself out, and Betty followed. They towelled themselves dry. The woman glowed with freshness. "Do you feel like going up?" she asked, nodding towards the staircase.

"Why not?"

He wrapped himself in the towel, put his watch back on and gathered up his cigarettes and matches. She led the way to the stairs. At the top, she pushed open a swing-door. He could at first see nothing. He sensed a huge, high room, like a hangar. Then, as in a cinema, light separated from darkness and he glimpsed a multitude of horizontal forms moving in rhythm. Like turtles on a beach. A whiff of incense. Silence, except for the rustle of laborious forms. The wrestle of laborious forms. Betty took his hand, and they picked their way between mattresses and hump-backed turtles. The turtles grunted, sucked, breathed asthmatically. Betty found, near a wall, a vacant mattress, and they squatted down. By chance, Spinnaker was being fellated on the next mattress. Catching sight of them, Spinnaker rolled his eyes in greeting. On the other side of Surkov and Betty, a skinny, balding man, still wearing his glasses, was locked in a death-throttle with Mary Spinnaker. Mary was too lost in the struggle to notice their presence.

Surkov lit a cigarette.

"I guess all these women would be on the Pill?" he murmured to Betty. "Those who aren't past child-bearing."

"Or they wear IUDs. I wear one. It's safer. But also, a lot of the men would have had a vasectomy."

"I see."

"And how about your country?"

"Lots of abortions."

Spinnaker, watched by Surkov, was gasping; his penis juddering, and almost swallowed whole by the small, wiry brunette. She slid her mouth away; cream spilled. She licked. Surkov jerked his eyes away. He felt the sudden, hurtable weakness of

Spinnaker's circumcised cock. He winced. Spinnaker lay gasping on the mattress, his paunch rising and falling.

The balding man in glasses was grunting, working himself into a lather. Mary Spinnaker hooked her skinny legs around his back, and matched him grunt for grunt.

Betty Thresher put her small, cool hand in Surkov's brawny, sweating hand. "What do you think?" she asked.

"They look kind of desperate . . . But it's interesting."

"Do you want to?"

"I'd rather not, if you don't mind."

"That's okay."

"I'm just a little nervous someone might recognize me. I know you say it's unlikely."

"It's very unlikely. Most of these people are too busy to read any poetry. They're lawyers, or dentists, or in real estate like Joseph. I don't think you need worry. But of course I understand how you feel. Would you like to get dressed? Have a drink?"

"I think I would. I've nowhere to stub my cigarette."

"You could come home with me, except that the children are there. Henry wouldn't mind, but we don't like to involve the children. They're terribly idealistic about their parents, don't you find?"

"I do, yes."

· 6 ·

AT A SIGNAL FROM THE CHAIRMAN, MATTI PRESSED A BUTTON
and Corinna's expressive voice came to a stop. Many of the
judges, less gifted linguistically than the elderly Finn, continued
to listen intently to their head-phones, through which the adven-
tures of the Russian poet were being narrated at a slower pace
than in Corinna's rapid Italian. Signora Rossi took advantage of
the pause to spend a few minutes in the toilet. When she returned,
only the French judge was still listening. Then he, too, took off
his head-phones. Tarkiainen cleared his throat, and invited Professor Krüdner to set the ball rolling.

The large golden-haired Bavarian repeated her criticism of the
Italian improvisation. Where so much was in bad taste, it was
difficult to specify any one moment of outstanding offensiveness:
but probably the reference to women slimming in Belsen, in the
presence of a judge from Israel, marked the summit of insensitiv-
ity.

The Israeli judge—who in fact had lost both his parents at
Auschwitz—let his face fall forward on to his clenched hands.

Tarkiainen, in his quavery voice, said he agreed; but thought there was another summit of tastelessness: Surkov's final remark about using women's vaginas as ashtrays. Not precisely saying that, he added, in response to the protests of the Italian judge, but certainly implying it. Coningsby, on his right, nodded. The French judge, M. Moreau, waved his arms and shook his head vigorously. "That's absurd, absurd!" he exclaimed. The moustached Spanish lady, Señora Menendez, said in a gruff but soothing voice: "We needn't argue too much about details. It's all pretty crude. That scene in the sex club, especially! My stomach churned. But I didn't find the whole improvisation so objectionable. There were, as I said just now, even lyrical moments. We should bear in mind she was starting again, after a break. That's not easy, with people still drifting back in. And don't forget she had to break off again for several minutes."

Two or three of the judges murmured assent. Senhora Casalduero, the Portuguese, cut in with: "But I don't think this scene was so bad! I thought it was very funny in parts! Didn't anyone else think that?" She looked round the table; she smiled faintly, having in her mind's eye a picture of Rozanov and the fat waitress collapsing on to the bedroom floor; but only the French judge met her eyes and smiled back. Her smile vanished, and she blushed.

The tall, sorrowful-looking Pole said that, yes, he had been amused from time to time; but the occasional stroke of vulgar humour was not enough to counteract the man-hating pornography. "When we remember Mickiewicz's Night," he said, referring to the only laurel-winning improvisation, of an earlier epoch, whose majesty and beauty had been preserved for later ages by a listener with a perfect recall, "we really could not consider The Seven Veils as a serious contender. The author has very limited powers of description. Of people, for instance. They are either black-haired or grey, either tall or short . . ." Glancing to his left, he observed the tiny Japanese judge gazing up at him solemnly, and he turned again quickly to the front, to the intense eyes and moustached upper lip of the Spanish lady. "There is no subtlety," he concluded, "no delicate effects. . . ."

The Iranian Shafaq, his eyes glittering sombrely, his fine fingers stroking his short black beard, demanded to be told what was misanthropic or man-hating about the improvisation. The soldierly Pole gathered himself to reply, and Professor Krüdner's heavy bosom also lifted from the table, but Tarkiainen replied rapidly: "From having created such a monstrous hero, or should I say heroes. Who demonstrate nothing but contempt for the women they seduce. Who bite vaginas, or invite their partner to open her legs so that he may flick his ash into it." The old man's hand quavered as it lifted his glass of water and sipped.

"But surely," replied the Iranian, "these women are deserving of contempt? They are fornicators and adulteresses; they have betrayed the modesty of their sex. Surely the males in this story are like avenging swords? In my country, these women would have had their heads cut off." He glanced from side to side challengingly. No one met his eyes; they studied their blotting-papers.

All looked up, and listened with close attention, as Anna Szabó, the Hungarian, shyly and hesitantly intervened. One could see it was almost an agony for her to speak in public; and it was difficult to believe that she had once been an *improvisatrice* herself—the sole judge with that practical experience—and that she had come close to winning the 1966 Olympics, at the tender age of twenty. She had lost her nerve. Yet now, whenever she plucked up the courage to break in, her gentle voice still carried authority. She was not so concerned, she said, with questions of taste. This particular performer, she suspected, needed to shock her audience at regular intervals in order to keep her adrenalin flowing. That was understandable. What she, Szabó, wasn't sure of was the Italian woman's ability to sustain a narrative without shooting off somewhere else, often unnaturally. "Is this poetic flair," she concluded quietly, "or an inability to create at length, slowly, organically, convincingly?" She flushed, dropped her eyes, rubbed her hands nervously together.

"That's very well put," said Señora Menendez; and there were nods and murmurs of agreement. But Moreau waved his arm agitatedly, and proceeded to make an excited analysis of the twists and turns of Riznich's plot: its affinities with Celtic stories in its search for a feminine paradise, the closeness of the realms of the living and the dead, the exotic imagination. The improvisation was a *tour de force*; and not man-hating but certainly male-hating, violence-hating, and therefore profoundly feminist—yes, that was true, but all the better for it. The goal was Ararat, the breasts of women, both sensual and pure.

When he broke off—his eyes lingering for a moment on Frau Krüdner's powerful bosom—Signora Rossi swiftly maintained the counter-attack: "At last we have heard some sense! . . . You are right, I'm sorry; I should not have implied that others have not been sensible. It's just that, so far, we have heard little about the many positive qualities of *The Seven Veils*. I say this not as an Italian. But it was time soneone pointed out how wonderfully original it was. Not only in its overall design, as M. Moreau has argued so eloquently, but in innumerable images and metaphors. Well, just as an example,"—her glance fell to her handbag, which was open, revealing the top of a packet of Kent cigarettes— "where Surkov thought of death in terms of 'Are there any cigarettes left in the packet?'—that was wonderful, I thought . . . Or the whole complex symbolism of Mount Ararat."

"As a matter of fact," interrupted Coningsby, leaning forward, running a long slender hand back over his silvery waves of hair, "both Ararat and the idea of the cigarettes were lifted from *The Crossing*." Into the minds of everyone present sprang a photographic image of the tall, hawk-nosed Russian, Markov, a finalist at both Salzburg and Havana, whose verse improvisation had occupied their deliberations for many hours of the previous night. Everyone followed Coningsby's example in leaning forward; and the Anglo-Argentinian glanced around the table, enjoying the simple pleasure of the slight shock his remark had caused. He continued: "Perhaps you don't remember? I think what I am saying will be clear if we hear *The Crossing* once more."

"It's too early to do that," the chairman interposed.

"I'm not talking about final comparisons," Coningsby explained, "but to deal with this point of originality, which Signora Rossi has brought up. Otherwise I should not have mentioned it. But in my view, *The Seven Veils* was too heavily dependent on the preceding improvisation to be considered truly original."

"My Argentinian colleague is quite correct," remarked Dibich, at Coningsby's right. "I, too, didn't like to mention it. Everything essential in *The Seven Veils* is contained in *The Crossing*. Even the idea for expanding on *Egyptian Nights*. And, incidentally, we should take note that the quotation of Pushkin's story allowed the *improvisatrice* to coast for quite a long time; and I'm not even sure she wasn't breaking the rules. Be that as it may, Professor Coningsby's serious allegations must be investigated. We must hear *The Crossing* again. I think it will convince all but Signora Rossi, who is quite rightly patriotic. It may also convince us of the truth of what I was arguing last night—that we need look no further for the winner."

His small mouth, through which, even when he talked, a drinking-straw could scarcely have been passed, closed completely. Coningsby, the late sunlight flashing off his hair, so startlingly white against his still-youthful, burnished face, remarked, "Please, can't we get away from nationalist interests?" Moreau, sitting opposite, caught the flicker of pain crossing the Argentinian's face, and he nodded sympathetically.

"Exactly," said the Pole at Dibich's right. "And, in fact, *The Crossing* has a major blot on its own originality, as I pointed out last night."

"And I explained last night," said Dibich, "why my compatriot used a Pushkinian stanza-form. Olenin, like Onegin, is a prey to bourgeois negativism. It was an exposure of negativism, as contrasted with the other character, Charsky, who is by no means faultless but doesn't set himself up arrogantly against his fellow Russians."

"I thought we'd demolished that interpretation," remarked the French judge, staring at Dibich, who stared as frostily back. Coningsby said they were straying off the point, which was the question of the originality of *The Seven Veils*. He repeated his request that they hear again the tape of *The Crossing*. The aged Finn asked if it was the wish of the panel and—gathering that it was—turned to the handsome, patient Finnish youth and spoke to him. The youth nodded, stood up from the stool on which he had been sitting, and searched in the box of tapes. Finding the right one, he inserted it in the sound system, and fumbled with the controls which—almost miraculously it seemed to the judges—set going the translated recordings for those who required them. In this instance, all but the Russian and Polish judges, and the chairman Tarkiainen, reached for their headphones. Some of them, however—and noticeably all the women except Anna Szabó—waited a few moments to hear the deep, rhythmic, sonorous voice of Markov before placing the headphones on their ears.

Tarkiainen, Dibich and Wojcicki leaned back in their chairs. While silently, secretly, all round the table, the voices of translators struggled, the voice of Markov rolled in an unbroken stream over the privileged three. Dibich's eyes closed. Tarkiainen's heavy eyelids also quivered shut, after a while, and he began to breathe deeply and nasally. Coningsby, noticing the chairman's flung-back head and open mouth, gave a smiling, sideways glance at the Finnish technician who, also glancing at the relaxed chairman, returned Coningsby's smile.

ALL HAD HEARD, WITHOUT NEED OF TRANSLATION, THE AP-
plause die down, the crackle of an envelope being opened, and
Markov's confident tones exclaiming, "The theme on which I
have been asked to improvise is *The Crossing*." They saw again,
in the ensuing moments of silence, sweat break out on the
Russian's forehead, the sudden glitter of his eyes, the pallor of his
face; they saw him step forward closer to the microphone, cross
his arms on his chest, toss his thick brown hair back from his
eyes, and open his lips to begin.

> Doctor Ivan Olenin, *Stag*
> To those he drank with—soured by life
> Rather than the events in Prague—
> Had forced Tatiana, his mild wife,
> To turn their flat above the Moika
> Into the setting for a *troika*
> Ménage (some said menagerie).
> The third soul in their trinity
> Varied: some slim and long-legged bird.

Yet Tanya loved her hooligan,
Who was, deep down, a gentle man,
And even—though she'd have preferred
Monogamy—saw other men
To please her husband, now and then.

The gentle girl would grow possessive
At other times, and would decline
To play his game; he'd turn aggressive,
Become abusive; she'd resign
Herself to flirting with some rake
And go off with him, for Stag's sake.
To give her husband a free hand
She suffered many a one-night stand.
But mostly—always at weekends,
At home—they'd end a hazy day
Of booze with one girl left . . . They'd play
A languid trio, like good friends,
In their wide bed . . . A long lie-in
Next day . . . champagne and aspirin.

Forever drunk, Stag had the shakes;
In minor surgery his knife
Trembled, yet never made mistakes
When hazarding a patient's life.
Once, though, he all but killed Tatiana,
When, in his most *Stavrogin* manner,
He played the devil's advocate
For suicide; assured her that
He jested in this role of cynic,
"But really, dear, I wonder why
It's not occurred to you to die . . ."
He stayed up drinking . . . In his clinic,
Where she came round, he was deranged,
Wept at her bedside . . . Nothing changed.

Forced once more to be independent,
She felt, one spring, a genuine flame
For Charsky, poet, a descendant
Of Pushkin's hero of that name.
Stag sensed in Tanya that unrest
He felt always in his own breast,
And feared . . . But it died sooner than
The lilac blossom; and Ivan
Later had cause to thank her passion;
So similar, in many ways,
—Rakes, and internal émigrés,
Though Charsky in a modest fashion—
The two men forged an understood
Communion; almost brotherhood.

At times it happens like that. Hunger
For flesh grows stale, then seems absurd,
But turns into a bond that's stronger,
A lifelong *troika*, where the third,
Most awkward, rider is the wife.
Unplagued by love or sexual strife,
The two friends sprawled; the *Ode to Joy*
On loud, they'd talk about Tolstoy,
Tatiana (Eugene Onegin's first,
But then Ivan's, when she had gone
To bed); about Molière's *Don Juan*
Or Mozart's: one's perplexing thirst
To plunge into the sea of love
Knowing it salt; then, that Kirov

Dancer who Stag had found was shaven
And it had turned him off her (he'd
Seen all too many!) . . . Night, a haven
Of comradeship . . . Olenin peed
Out of the window, straight into

The canal, chuckling; Charsky threw
Himself down anywhere to sleep;
Or else at dawn would try to creep
—But halfway down go stumbling, clattering—
Downstairs, and drive back to his pad
On the Gulf side of Leningrad,
His battered Moskvich weaving, shattering
The silence of the well-aligned
Streets a mad architect designed. . . .

That spring when our affairs grew critical. . . .

(At this point in Markov's improvisation his waving hand had accidentally knocked the microphone, and his words had become lost until, realizing the fault, he had rectified it—)

. . . His illness acted like a gag.
He watched Stag's downfall over Prague
(Which was, in part, the fault of Cupid:
He loved a Slovak girl that year)
With jaundiced eyes; and made it clear
He thought him brave, of course, but stupid.
Olenin, asked to quit his post,
Appeared to miss the nurses most;

And he survived. The "pull" or *blat*
Of Charsky saw to it they kept
Tatiana's salary, and their flat.
Stag drank, played records, mostly slept.
But dabbled, too, in poetry:
Parodies, like the letter he
Had sent to *Pravda* about Prague.
Charsky went deathly pale when Stag
Showed him a carbon; even Peter's
Bronze statue quaked—for he'd compared

The Kremlin with the gift prepared
By Pushkin's witch for Tsar Nikita's
Forty imperfect daughters—a box
Of . . . . . without their curly locks

And sweet scent . . . Charsky thought him gifted
With something of a poet's heart;
With talent, even; but Stag drifted
Too much to make his way in art;
Was scarcely able to be lucid
One day in three. His soft, Seleucid,
Ivy League charm he also chose
To dissipate—would scare the crows
With his appearance, soiled, dishevelled;
Which might have passed, if only he
Had been a tramp consistently,
But no—reserved, morose, he revelled
At times in social life, droll, gay,
And dressed up like a popinjay.

Was even, now and then, uxorious;
Between adulteries, he'd creep
Round Tanya's skirts, in an inglorious
Parody of Uriah Heep . . .
So there were many things resented
By Charsky. Yet he liked the scented
(In that warm spring when first he came)
Lilac bush by their house; the game
Of chess with Tanya, who was bright
—A radiologist. They'd dine
On cheese and fruit and Georgian wine;
Vodka and chat into the night . . .
A pleasant haze, their cigarette-
Smoke mingling with a string quartet.

Above all, Charsky, who saw double
—But *saw* himself see double too—
Knew that in any kind of trouble
His friend would take a generous view:
Having himself been "there" before,
Most likely; and one could be sure
No confidence would be revealed
Even to Tanya, but tight-sealed
As in a tomb. And Stag would never
Probe deeper in a wound, unless
He sensed a wish for him to press—
With a heart-surgeon's tact . . . However,
Their serious talk would turn to lewd
Banter about the girls they'd screwed,

Or had an urge to, like the slim
Languages-student Stag had met,
In form and face like Nelli Kim.
She hadn't let him screw her yet;
And Charsky found it entertaining,
Amusing, hearing him complaining
Of her intransigence, the bitch.
She had Mongolian features which
Charsky, on meeting her, found boring;
But to Olenin's face he said
"She's nice." "Too nice!" Stag held his head
And groaned. She knew about his *whoring*
(As she, Natasha, called it) and
Would stoop to nothing underhand.

Although she visited the Moika
Ménage, she was too young, eighteen,
(Half Ivan's age) to join a *troika*;
Too well brought up, too pure, too green;
And—it appeared—too much in love.

Charsky observed the flowering of
An answering passion in his friend
With humour, knowing it would end
In ribaldry. A spring vacation
Tatiana and Ivan had planned,
Staying with friends in Samarkand,
Would do the trick . . . In agitation
The girl called Charsky on the phone:
"Konstantin, could we meet—alone?"

In a brash restaurant, the Red Banner,
Whose décor set off her red hair,
Transparent envy of Tatiana
She tried to cover with an air
Of wanting Stag and his nice wife
To re-cement their married life.
They still cared for each other—that
She had seen clearly at their flat.
Wasn't it true? What did he think?
She wanted his advice: the truth.
What should she do? He knew them both
So well . . . Buying another drink,
The battered connoisseur agreed
With Ivan's shade there were, indeed,

Few lovelier sights in Leningrad
Than those soft globes, the blouse low-cut.
"Well, all advice," he smiled, "is bad,
And good advice is fatal! . . . But
If I were in your shoes I'd treat it
Light-heartedly." Then he repeated,
Guiltily, her hooligan's
List—as Leporello, Juan's.
"That's as I thought. Please take me home."
They kissed and fondled in his car.

Not much—yet Charsky thought too far
For one in a delirium
Of love . . . But she could feel Stag's mouth
Greeting his wife's, in the hot south. . . .

The real Stag, meanwhile, on vacation
To please his wife, who loved to bask
In the sun's blaze, in perturbation
Settled to this unpleasant task.
He got up late, saw minarets
Through a foul haze of cigarettes;
Was sullen, surly, spoke at most
Ten words a day to their kind host
And hostess, who left him alone
After a while. He saw no flowers
Bloom in the desert, but spent hours
Pleading with someone on the phone
Long distance. His wife squeezed his hand
As if to say, "I understand."

She knew the tall, red headed student
Was giving him an awful time;
To interfere would be imprudent;
And also Tanya knew he'd climb
Out of the flood, her shivering stag,
As after that brunette from Prague,
And others. There was still some deep
Connecting current in their sleep,
Even though he cried out in despair,
Dreaming. What he dreamed Ararat,
Or Sheba's Breasts, beyond this flat
And drum-tight desert, was a pair
—He'd see it soon enough—of boobs.
His girls were all like Rubik Cubes

He gave up on. Charsky was staggered
To see his friend so spiritless,
On their return—gaunt-eyed and haggard;
Tatiana, in an ethnic dress
And peasant tan, looked radiant; she
Described to Charsky sparklingly
The miracles of Samarkand;
He sparkled back about a blonde
Student from Bucharest who wrote
Good stories. "You must bring her round!"
"I'd love to!" But Konstantin found
No time . . . And then, one day, a note
Dropped through his door. Sheer disbelief
Struck him at first; then anger, grief.

The very next day brought a visit
From the smug Stag himself. He brought
His brand-new "better-half," exquisite
In a new dress Mama had bought
(She was a widow with some cash);
Olenin also cut a dash
In a blue suit complete with vest
(American) which he confessed
Shyly, yet with a shameless smile,
Had been worn by Natasha's father.
Mama-in-law-to-be would rather
He dressed now in a seemly style . . .
Konstantin infinitely preferred
His former style, when he'd appeared

More like an *improvisatore*,
Unkempt and wild-eyed, sweating, pale,
Stains on his shirt, than like a Tory
Sir Grandison, pink-cheeked and hale,
With a young woman of much charm,

And future assets, on his arm.
It only lacked a trail of neat
Children to make the change complete.
He drank less now, Natasha said,
And smoked less, for her mother's sake . . .
"So bravely taking on a *rake*!
She even brought us tea in bed
This morning!" Stag laughed. It was strange
How Charsky grieved to see the change. . . .

For he—Konstantin—was as ordered
As Peter's streets in their closed ranks;
The tumult of his life was bordered
As Neva by her granite banks;
There where he wrote, his rage was still;
Leda, her nape caught in the bill
Of a wild swan—a statuette—
Stood on a filing cabinet . . .
He'd learned to take her as a dove
(The Muse, that is) not as a swan;
Before he raised his pen, he'd don
A single, tingling, silken glove.
He missed now—what he'd loathed before:
Stag ghastly, swaying, at the door. . . .

(*Finding a natural pause in his story, Markov had broken off. The
pleasant afternoon had turned sour suddenly; rain spurted and a cold wind
blew, distracting the audience—and distracting the performer—with the
flutter of rugs, coats, umbrellas . . . The improvisation had resumed,
several minutes later, in the marquee. The technician, who was following the performance in Finnish, ran the tapes on, to Markov's assured
resumption.*)

· 8 ·

White nights. Then autumn. Charsky, lonely,
Missed his old friend, the dropping round.
He'd call on Tanya, but they'd only
The past to talk about, they found.
Where once the Terrible played God,
Ivan lived now—in Novgorod—
Dependent on the girl, who had
A job with Intourist. How sad
And gaunt looked Tanya—not so pretty;
Lulu the pup, cats, crackling fire,
Neva, the Admiralty Spire,
All the wide vista of the city
Seen through the window, seemed as lost
As his hostess without the host.

Then fate paid Charsky an odd visit
—Fate, or good fortune, or mischance
(God knows, we never know which is it);
At any rate, coincidence:

Novgorod offered a semester
Lecturing to students in the Western
Authors he cared for—Byron, Poe,
Jack London, Alan Sillitoe,
Etc. Hard-pressed of late
For cash, he thought he'd like a change,
And he was taken by the strange
Coincidence or chance or fate.
Stag answered Charsky's cable: "Share
Our flat until you find somewhere."

So, when Neva was iron-shod
Like Peter's horse of bronze upreared,
He took a train to Novgorod
   New Town. Familiar faces peered
Over the barrier; he waved.
Ivan, he noticed, hadn't shaved;
Which rather pleased him. Natasha kissed
Him warmly, said how much they'd missed
Him; and Ivan looked glad. A gander
Past snowy factory sites . . . the shock
Of reaching an apartment-block
More awful than the Stone Commander,
A sombre prison, sad cell doors
Stretching down concrete corridors.

One room, divided by a curtain . . .
Clothes, rubbish, everywhere—and just
One double-bed . . . He grew uncertain . . .
Where would he sleep? A marble bust
Of Dostoievsky he recalled
From Stag's past. But the rest . . . Appalled,
He said how nice it was. Stag shrugged
And barked a laugh. Natasha hugged
Her lover. Vodka and cognac;

Charsky amused them with his blonde
Romanian vixen . . . His hosts yawned,
Excused themselves; Ivan came back
Bringing a towel, a sleeping-bag . . .
And Charsky dreamt a hornless stag.

Next day, a bribed official found him
A room not far from St Sophia;
Student digs really; but around him
A pleasant view of dome and spire.
Three easy months had been his plan—
Sight-seeing—parties—girls—Ivan;
But just as he was settling in,
Just when his lectures should begin,
The Muse tapped on his door to claim him.
Also a girl who never slept
Nor wished to leave. The hostel kept
Strict curfew, though: she couldn't blame him
If, at ten-thirty, he said, "God,
It's almost time . . . You must dress. Sod!"

Charsky was scornful, more than ever,
Of his friend's feckless, drifting ways,
Couldn't begin to think whatever
He did with his long empty days;
He gathered that he wrote a bit,
Watched football, cycled in to sit
In a Museum of Atheism;
He talked with his old cynicism,
Wore always the same ragged sweater,
Drank heavily, chain-smoked again;
Still loved Natasha, that was plain,
Yet often said it would be better,
For her, to get out of his life.
Seemed quite indifferent to his wife

—Tanya, that is. Oh, it was sad,
But still . . . Then the divorce came, and
At once a card from Leningrad
Inviting Charsky to a grand
Wedding. Post-haste came another
From the same source, Natasha's mother,
Calling it off . . . And then Natasha
And Stag burst in one day, with Masha,
Charsky's new girl. Stag seized the pen
From his friend's hand, and made him change
Into a suit. A casual, strange,
Drab little ceremony; then
A drink . . . The happy couple soon
Back in their room   the honeymoon. . . .

For Stag, as he'd explained while swaying
At a urinal, couldn't stand
The notion of her mother paying
With an indecent sleight-of-hand
Some *apparachik* for a job
For him, and flat; she was a snob;
He would not ride in the Moskvich
She'd given them. She'd been a bitch
To poor Natasha . . . Charsky, lying
In Masha's arms that night, felt sad,
Constricted, dead—like Leningrad
When he had been a baby, crying
For food and warmth, while round the doomed
And frozen city the guns boomed.

Full of ill omens for his friend,
Konstantin thought he would drive home
For a short break, that March weekend;
His flat seemed silent as a tomb.
Morosely he recalled his own

Wedding—just when the zest had gone.
They'd missed a train; a tiny cell
Instead of the honeymoon hotel;
Charsky, although his bride was splendid
(Or seemed so now) began to gasp
For air, and slipped out of her clasp;
Said he must take a walk. He'd ended
(He winced to think of it) in some
Cheap prostitute's even dingier room.

Moist-eyed, he rang Tanya Olenin
To cheer her up!—but she seemed bright:
Told him a rude joke about Lenin.
"Come round and see me, Kostya!"—quite
Mae Westerly!. . . She liked his after-
Shave . . . "And *you* look splendid!" Laughter
Behind a door: Bibich, a friend,
Gifted with bonhomie, no end,
Who jovially poured the wine,
Played Ivan's records, played mine host.
Konstantin saw Olenin's ghost
Everywhere; and recalled a line
Of Akhmatova: "And those whom we
Have left, have got on splendidly. . . ."

Then, the Olenins went together
—An Easter break—to Leningrad;
And after, Charsky asked Stag whether
He had seen Tanya. Yes, he had.
"She's fine. We had a pleasant chat;
I took a few things. That was that."
So off-hand, with such cool reserve,
Konstantin tried to probe a nerve,
(And when he tried, he was resourceful).
Bibich he mentioned casually;

Lulu the dog; then stopped, could see
He'd gone too far; became remorseful.
He'd seen his friend in very deep
Waters before, but never weep.

It passed. The bar filled up. Natasha
Joined them, also a student who
Knew Charsky; also Charsky's Masha.
Something got said—nobody knew
Quite what . . . The next thing, Stag was brawling,
Then Charsky's student sent him sprawling.
Konstantin hauled him to a chair;
Coarsely Ivan began to swear:
Her mother's vulgar, bourgeois manners
Passed on to her, the whore, the bitch!
In her tight skirt, a standing itch!
Natasha then: "Who slept at Tanya's
Last week, Ivan? Ah yes, you want
Her still . . ." Ivan: "You childish—slut!"

The scene passed off; and the next night
The Olenins called at Charsky's cell,
Just when . . .

*(The next lines were submerged under a shrill, angry outcry. Markov's
voice emerged again out of the counter-hisses of others in the marquee.)*

. . . With a kind smile, he liked the blue
Suede suit. Natasha liked it too,
Both seemed—especially Ivan—
Serene, replete with happiness.
Stag noticed Charsky's uncut, slim
New book, and complimented him;
"May I just glance at it?" "Why, yes!"

The glance was rather cursory,
Yet with an odd formality.

Tactful as ever, Stag, surmising
From a quick movement of a cuff,
His friend's impatience, murmured, rising,
"We're keeping Kostya. We'll be off.
Must have a pee first." His wife, sad
Suddenly, murmured, "Things are bad.
I'm driving home—just for a break—
Tomorrow; as much for poor Stag's sake
As mine. But may we talk sometime?"
"Of course; in fact, I'm going home too
This weekend. Shall I come with you?"
She blushed, and pushed her hair back. "I'm
Sorry, I may be stopping off
To see my sister in Pskov."

"Oh!—right. Then ring me at my flat?"
"Saturday morning?" "Yes." Ivan
Came back, Charsky said smoothly that
Next week a foreign film was on
Called *Soldier Blue*; he wondered whether
The four of them might go together.
Natasha said yes, eagerly;
Olenin shrugged, and said, "We'll see."
They left, all three; went down the steps;
Charsky turned right, towards the bar
And Masha; they, towards their car;
Though Ivan paused, as if perhaps
A longer route might be okay,
But no. He waved; they strolled away. . . .

(*Some clapping could be heard, followed by three muffled explosions.
Markov had turned away from the microphone and bent forward; several*

of the audience had taken his stoop for a bow, and applauded. Markov
had sneezed, three times; the sporadic clapping had stopped; the Russian,
after taking out his handkerchief and wiping his nose, had turned again to
the microphone and continued. . . .)

Spring seethed at last: the Neva breaking
Her crust of ice; the lilac bloom . . .
Charsky stretched happily on waking;
The sunlight shining in his room
Made the flat seem a pleasant friend;
Thank God his term was near its end.
He ate, with English jam, hot toast,
And waited eagerly for post.
Some bills; one package . . . still—he ripped
The wrappings off, and found inside
A plain, black, home-made book, beside
A letter in Olenin's script.
Since they had met in Novgorod
Only on Thursday, it seemed odd.

And yet he read the letter lightly
Knowing his friend's eccentric ways.
It was couched formally, politely,
And spread an enigmatic haze.
This book he might have heard him mention
Was not worth reading; his intention
Had been to burn it—it was his life.
He'd sent a copy to his wife.
(Sent it? How come?) He might destroy it
Unread, if he so wished; that was
What he would recommend, because
He could not possibly enjoy it.
But if he read it, he might live
To understand, if not forgive.

The poet, who had many a tome
Sent him by amateurs, could see,
Now, why he'd sent this to his home;
Stag was embarrassed, naturally.
He smiled, felt touched; and he would praise
It with the usual turn of phrase,
Not meaning much, but sounding grand . . .
Went to his study, book in hand . . .
Single-space typing, reams of pages
—Oh Lord!—some manuscript, then blanks.
Drily he muttered, "Many thanks!"
Familiar incoherent rages
And Western-style morbid despair
He found, while flicking here and there.

His interest faded. The typed journal
Did not exactly hold the eye:
Self-conscious maunderings, infernal
Abstracts of *tedium vitae*;
The later parts, in ink, were better;
More terse, at least: "Good ballet. Letter
From Tanya." "No word from Leningrad."
"Natasha packed and left me—sad."
"Got married. Dear Natasha splendid . . ."
"Had a bad weekend, here alone."
"Sunless and dreadful day." The tone
Increasingly withdrawn. It ended
On Thursday—when he'd praised a blue
Suede suit, and asked if it was new.

Ended with words which meant, in short,
When one cut through the flowery style
Out of Turgenev—"I depart."
He felt uneasy. All the while
He saw his friend so vividly

It wasn't possible . . . If he
Were on the phone he'd get straight through
Of course; but . . . Tanya: "Kostya, *you*!
How nice!" But he asked urgently
If she'd had any mail—a book,
Perhaps, from Stag. "I'll go and look;
The mail's just come." He waited. She
Spoke with a sob: book, letter—will.
Grief struck him; yet a kind of thrill.

But God! He hoped Ivan was joking
(A funny sort of joke, but still . . .)
Or changed his mind; or was provoking
Someone to notice he was ill.
He walked round, poring through the black
Book. She had promised to ring back
When the police rang *her* . . . The sad
Farewell to Tanya, Leningrad,
Lulu (he'd stayed the night there, being
Too drunk to drive, on a divan);
And on the final page, Ivan
Noted that he was bent on seeing
Once more—that Thursday night—his friend
Kostya . . . Then to the last weekend.

The phone rang . . . Charsky leapt to it;
But it was too soon to have news.
The voice was dull, lethargic. Shit!—
Natasha! He could not refuse
To hear her problems. Charsky stalled,
Advised her cautiously, appalled.
Said he felt sure she could still save
Their marriage, though it did seem grave.
His horror, faced with her calm sadness,
Didn't seem real; he half forgot

The situation now was not
(Most like) depression, drink, or madness,
But something out of all control;
Death—what the ancients called the soul.

When she had let him off the hook,
He dressed, then sleep-walked round the flat
From room to room, the heavy book
Held open in his hands; or sat,
With vodka he could hardly swallow,
On bed or chair or couch. How hollow
And meaningless life was, he read;
Ivan believed that he was dead
At every moment of his living,
Felt he was in a chasm, far
Deeper than ever Babi Yar;
He wrote, two crimes were past forgiving
God for: Stag's own existence, first;
And then—that He did not exist.

Still, in Konstantin's frantic striding
A faint hope struggled against fear,
But also—it was no use hiding
The truth, which would not disappear
(And which proved Stag was right, of course):
He could not quell a powerful force
Of mounting tragedy, a thirst
Almost to hear the very worst;
He tried to fight it down, tormented
By guilt, which added to his grief;
But could no more obtain relief
From that instinctive and demented
Thirst than, amidst a "little death,"
One can control one's heart or breath.

—Or stanch, at Ladoga, the Néva . . .
The phone!—it gathered to a head
That force. He lifted the receiver.
Tatiana, with a groan: "He's dead!"
At once the flood-gates of an ocean,
A vast and fathomless emotion,
Utterly pure, burst in and swept
Everything else away. He wept.
The black contrary tide went foaming
Back down the river to its source,
Leaving a filthy scum, remorse.
Sobs, racking like a child's, kept coming.
No one to comfort him. The one
Who might have comforted was gone. . . .

Tanya had said she'd ring his wife,
Also his parents: once more took,
Through death, the status of her life
With Stag. The phone jumped from its hook
Into Konstantin's shaking hand:
Natasha's hideous sobbings; and
Her mother's strident anger at
Stag's selfishness. An hour he sat
Trying to calm Natasha: she,
So young, could not have sensed a warning
In his wild mood, the previous morning;
Nor yet, the night before, when he
Gave to the youth with whom he'd fought
A cup-tie ticket he had bought

Weeks earlier . . . A living ghost,
Charsky walked round. The radio
Mentioned that Novgorod had lost.
News that Ivan would never know,
Nor wish to know . . . How could one choose

To be indifferent to news?
So casually to wipe the slate?
He went out walking, past the great
Equestrian statue; and saw many
Girls who might offer love or sex;
Of men, though, in those wide prospects
Who might take Ivan's place—not any:
A friend, a confidant, and one
Whose swing was wilder round the sun.

On an embankment seat, the poet
Looked at the black book he had brought.
Seething with rage, he thought to throw it
Into the waters, but did not.
He turned to page one, and began
To draw the black blood of Ivan
Into his arteries again,
Like Nembutal to dull the pain.
He looked for greater understanding,
And found out things he'd but half-known,
Like how unbearably alone
Stag felt, even making love, or standing
Charming and witty at a ball.
Then things he hadn't known at all,

Such as the dreadful agitation
(So strange, that Charsky wept once more),
In the Crimea, on vacation,
Staying with friends, two years before.
Their friends had had an old dog, growing
Infirm; and Ivan took to going
For long walks with her every day;
The bitch became his holiday;
He saw indifferently the Black Sea
Shore, but felt utterly bereft

—Surprising Tanya—when they left
Their friends, and drove off in a taxi.
Tears welled up, right from Ivan's heart,
For a dog, watching him depart. . . .

Was death, Stag wondered, a reversal
Of life, as shamanism said?
Once, he'd conducted a rehearsal,
With Nembutal beside his bed,
In Gorky . . . Thenceforth he stayed near
The icy, mountainous frontier,
Biding his time . . . One desperate night
He'd played, till it was almost light,
The Verdi Requiem—twice (his wife
Trying to sleep). At last he too
Lay down, and for the first time knew
Dreamless oblivion. Yet life,
Its essence, had not disappeared;
So why should deepest sleep be feared?

Charsky went home, but read on, ending,
When it was dark outside, his face
Cupped in his hands, with those heart-rending
Handwritten entries, and blank space.
He fell asleep. But then a thumping
Roused him in bed; the heavy, clumping,
Marble approach of the Stone Guest.
But the noise came from his own breast;
He couldn't breathe; he shot up, certain
It was—at last!—a heart-attack.
His breathing eased, and he fell back.
The Baltic blew against the curtain;
He thought the moonlight through the thin
Drapes was Stag trying to climb in.

Tanya and he went down together
By train, since they agreed their nerves
Were in that state when, if a feather
Blows from the roadside, the car swerves.
They looked, said Tanya, like two *zeks*
Returning from the Gulag—wrecks.
"It's shocked me to the core," he said;
"I knew he'd just as soon be dead,
But thought indifference would save him.
He had to work quite hard to die."
Tanya admitted, with a sigh,
He'd asked to come back; but she gave him
No cause to hope; she'd borne too much;
And had just started with Bibich.

A kind, grey, "Bolshevik Karenin"
(Stag's phrase) who had identified
His son—shocked, shaking, more like Lenin
In the last weeks before he died—
They briefly met; then waited for
Natasha, who'd come down before.
They walked to St Sophia. Stag's will
Said there should be no funeral.
Rightly his father disobeyed him,
And drove to the cremation fire;
The others, under St Sophia,
Huddled, and *in absentia* laid him
To rest; Konstantin spoke a few
Biblical words, a verse or two.

The room by order had been sealed.
The janitor produced a key.
Entering last, Konstantin reeled
Back from its air of mystery.
That was its only air; he panted,

It was as if the corpse had haunted
The room for days after his death,
And gone on drawing its stale breath.
A bedside chair; and on it, Blok's
The Steps of the Commendatore;
And a strange smell, as if some furry
Wild animal, a wolf or fox
Or badger, trapped in this vile tomb,
Had madly dashed about the room.

A crumpled cigarette pack nestled
Beside the book upon the chair.
The women, crying, meshed and wrestled
—Or so it looked—in their despair;
They rocked and stumbled like tired lovers.
Charsky was dying to discover
Whether the packet near the book
Was quite as empty as it looked.
Absurdly, even as he grieved,
And smoked, he felt a vulgar greed
To "lift" the packet—if indeed
There were some left, as he believed.
But with the two wives rocking there,
In such pure grief, he didn't dare.

They read the letters which had waited
For them upon the chest of drawers.
The one addressed to Charsky stated
That no one's act had been the cause
Of this; he took the blame alone.
He had been grateful to have known
Charsky, was thankful for his help . . .
Konstantin swayed. A kind of yelp
Broke through the haze of cigarette-
Smoke and delirium; whimpering,

Natasha cried that Ivan's ring
Hadn't been on his hand, nor yet
In any of the drawers: all three
Groped round the floor then, desperately.

Tanya went off with her ex-father-
In-law to Stag's birthplace, Kiev.
The other two went home together.
Natasha, driving, asked him if
Ivan had sent him a black book
She'd seen him writing in. He shook
His head. The car veered, in her grief.
First love . . . It was beyond belief.
When they reached Leningrad, exhausted
From shared bereavement, she dropped by
To have a drink; the pearly sky
Began to fade; Konstantin lusted
To pay out the dead man—to screw
Natasha; somehow to break through.

She felt too tired to drive. When he
Had driven her home in the Moskvich,
He laughed, at the absurdity
Of life, the enigmatic bitch;
And, on the dark road, Leporello
Spoke at his side: "Did you, old fellow?
Let's sniff your fingers. Yes, like fish!
Now, isn't she a tasty dish?"
Charsky grew agitated, and
Burst into tears; he fumbled round
The glove-compartment till he found
Sobranies, though in his hand
One glowed; sobbed, "Stag, you idiot!"
And lit a second cigarette.

·9·

AT THE AGED FINN'S INVITATION CONINGSBY, GLANCING down occasionally at the notes he had made, led his fellow-judges through the maze of similarities linking the penultimate improvisation, *The Crossing*, with the final one, *The Seven Veils*, "Taking first the major themes," he murmured in his grave, sweet English voice, "we have the theme of frontiers, of crossings, of suicide: whether by Nembutal or a borrowed bottle of aspirins on top of alcohol. It's present, centrally, in the poem. There's also the divided self, divided artist; and that's of course linked very strongly with the theme of *Egyptian Nights*. It's slightly surprising that the author of *The Seven Veils* knew that story by heart; but unquestionably she was reminded of it by her Soviet rival's having called one of his characters Charsky. Her supposed continuation of the Pushkin story was simply a mishmash of the plot of *The Crossing*, only reverting to Pushkin's time. The unhappy marriage, the squalid room; the dog, for whom Ivan weeps. She even kept the same name. Even the sneezing *improvisatore* was probably picked up from those spontaneous sneezes by Mark—by the Soviet contestant! But we shouldn't condemn her for that!"

Pausing, he glanced around the table, inviting disagreement. Heads were bent; the fine hands of Signora Rossi were held over her ears, as if she were unwilling to listen to such painful matters. Coningsby continued: "Elsewhere, there are also innumerable minor details . . . Gorky, the setting, has been borrowed from the poem—the town where Ivan carried out his 'rehearsal' for his suicide. Ararat, too, is mentioned in the Russian work, as I've said. Surkov's study—I believe there was a fragment of Siberian meteorite on the filing cabinet; whereas Charsky had a statuette of Leda and the Swan on his . . . The gymnasts on the ship were picked up from a reference to Nelli Kim. Well, Comaneci or Kim, you take your pick! Personally, I prefer Nelli Kim!" He gave another slight smile. "The references to Don Juan, which was made quite a lot of in *The Seven Veils*. There are—I think I counted at least a dozen references to Don Juan in *The Crossing*. And so, one could go on . . . The shamanist idea, mentioned in the dead man's diary, that things turn into their opposite after death: that gave her the Finnish shamaness. . . ."

Tarkiainen cut in with: "Ah, of course!" Asleep for most of the re-play of Markov's improvisation, he recalled the lines in question from the previous day.

"And the episode of Surkov's lost ring," Coningsby went on, "was a lift from the extremely powerful last part of *The Crossing*. The cigarettes—the image which Signora Rossi found so original. This is all very unpleasant. I've said enough."

There was a long silence, a painful silence. Tarkiainen, with a sigh, said, "Thank you."

M. Moreau, raising his head, sighed too, but did not speak. Signora Rossi fumbled in her handbag for a tissue, and blew her nose, dabbed under her eyes where her mascara had run slightly. Senhora Casalduero said sadly, "I think you've proved your point."

"Yes, yes," murmured the Israeli judge, taking off his glasses and wiping them.

"There are allusions, echoes," admitted Signora Rossi, lifting her chin high, beginning to take a grip on herself; "but surely we were all conscious of them at the time? Not in detail, maybe, but in general? They are so obvious, it's inconceivable that Teresa— that the *improvisatrice* intended to cover them up. But a single reference to Ararat hardly cancels out the originality and power of the later use of that symbol?" She glanced along the table at the refined figure in his navy-blue Olympic blazer with a striped English Club tie. His wavy white hair flashing in the light as he leaned forward and looked askance at her, he nodded, anxious to concede the point. "Oh, yes!" he agreed. "She has made a good deal out of it; and no one would wish to deny her allusions, echoes. You're absolutely right, Signora." He stroked his lean, bronze cheek, and bent over his notes.

"Nevertheless," the Spanish judge remarked, rubbing the heavy down above her lip, "the themes of escape, crossing the frontier, betrayal, division, duplicity . . . I confess I had not seen the very close dependence until Professor Coningsby had pointed them out to us; and they must seriously diminish the originality of the final improvisation."

Dibich: "So much so that the so-called author should be disqualified."

"No, no!" cried several voices.

"That isn't called for," remarked Coningsby. He ran his hand over his hair, and looked weary. "If nothing else, this has enabled us to hear *The Crossing* once more; and I must say it continues to grow in my esteem. With the slight reservation Wojcicki mentioned, concerning its form. But what a powerful, moving poem! It would not be disgraced if it were to appear in print. . . ."

By chance, Corinna Riznich and Igor Markov were also, at that time, discussing their improvisations. Corinna, unable to sleep, had left Cesare snoring in their room and had gone to rouse Markov from his. It had not been necessary to rouse him: she found him already wakeful, reading. He had slept, exhausted, for fourteen hours after his performance, waking only in time to hear Corinna begin. Now he wasn't at all tired. He was happy to stroll with her by the side of the lake, in the brief dusk.

By chance also—and by a curious paradox—he was apologizing to her for having "borrowed" his poem, to a certain extent, from something she had told him in confidence during a train journey the previous autumn.

Until that visit of Corinna's to the Soviet Union they had met only once, at the Salzburg Olympics of 1970. She had been too poor to go to Havana in '74; he had been prevented from going to Delphi in '78. Yet Markov and his wife had been generous hosts when at last she crossed that mysterious border. He had arranged engagements for her.

In the unreal, transitional world of a long-distance journey by night, between Georgia and Armenia, she had told him about her father. An unhappy man, a failed actor bitterly regretting that he had left Corinna's mother, he had poured all his love on to Corinna. And once, meeting her after a long separation, sharing a hotel room in Genoa, he had seemed especially desperate for her affection; at his invitation she had undressed and crept into bed beside him, to cuddle against him as she had done as a child—but she was eighteen. She had found the embrace deepen, turn into something quite different, horrifying and yet also, at least to begin with, not unpleasant, even—she had admitted to the Russian—enjoyable; she had leapt out of the bed, weeping, thrown on her clothes and, ignoring her father's pleas for forgiveness, rushed away.

She had not seen her father for the next three months, by which time she knew she was pregnant. She arranged to meet him in a restaurant in Rome. He wept, he was in despair; she had been hard with him, cruel, hateful—as it seemed to her later. She wouldn't allow him to arrange an abortion for her; she had told him she would cope with it alone. A few days later, she had received a letter from him, begging her to forgive him, and saying goodbye. He had gone to a hotel, in the slum district of Rome, and taken an overdose.

Yet it had not been impulsive. The diaries she discovered showed he had long made "conclusions infinite/Of easy ways to die."

Corinna had decided to go ahead and have the baby. She wanted something of her father to remember. She invented a phantom lover. Her baby had been perfect.

All this she had told Markov, as they puffed clouds of smoke into each other's faces, and swayed against each other in the jolting train. She had never told anyone else, she said: for her son's sake. Perhaps she was "high" on smoke in the confined space at the end of the corridor. Perhaps she was "high" on her triumphant performance in Tbilisi, and was practising for Yerevan. Igor had been moved and also excited, stirred, by her story. When she was thrown against him by an unexpected jolt, he had embraced her. Then, it had happened as she had told Cesare: her impulsive unzipping of him—the sudden swoop—the swallow.

Tonight, strolling by the lake, it all seemed very far away. He could joke about the dress she had worn for her performance— she had put on jeans for this nocturnal stroll—telling her he had gazed up at her on the stage and felt a desperate urge to visit Nigeria! She chuckled; it was just light flirtation again. His real thoughts, as she knew, were back home with his pregnant wife Anya.

But after his joke he became serious and said it had been unforgivable of him to have used her story like that, adapting it freely and bringing in certain experiences of his own. "It was just the theme," he said, "and seeing you there in the front row."

"It was a long time before I saw the connection," she said. "I had forgotten that I'd confided in you. Please keep my confidence: but there's no need to apologize for your poem. It was brilliant, beautiful. It was even probably good for me. To be able to cry. It was almost as if you had known my poor father . . . But of course, I couldn't get it out of my head when it came to my turn. I need to ask your forgiveness for—for bringing you into it."

"Really!" Markov's brown, slant eyes, inherited from Georgian ancestors, twinkled at her. "I didn't notice!"

She smiled back, said, "You're quite right! Anya's a lucky woman, Igor"—and made him break his step to kiss his cheek. They strolled on. "I told Cesare about—when we smoked together in the train. . . ."

"Shit! Why?"

"I had to. After my Moscow scenes. He was assuming the worst."

"Yes, I can understand that. He glared at me pretty hard while we were having a drink."

"He had no reason to," said the Florentine, scowling. "He has no rights over me."

"Still?"

"Still."

He shrugged, and draped a friendly arm round her. "I think tonight," he said, "you should reward him, thrill him—wearing your laurel crown in bed!"

She laughed. "Impossible!—you will win. You deserve to win, Igor."

"No. My first-round piece was my best, when it was thundery and I felt a lot of energy flowing. Yours was astonishingly good . . . But I fancy neither of us will win."

"Why, who do you think will get it? Not—Morrie Blake?"

The Russian poet screwed up his mouth into his comical imitation of an Australian accent: "A little dog went ambling down the main street of Ballerat . . ." he croaked. Corinna laughed, choked on her laugh. Markov cackled. Their laughter echoed round the silent birch-wood. "Too right," he said, in the same rough twang: "Morrie Blake . . ." Their laughter rippled to a halt. "Well, he's very healthy," Markov explained as they strolled on. "You and I are a little crazy."

That was true enough. Both had found their remarkable talent after severe mental illnesses in their youth: Markov, at around the time his father, a political *zek*, had been posthumously rehabilitated; Corinna, in her fourteenth year.

"It's fucking stupid," the Russian went on, "that only one of the judges is an *improvisatore*. Szabó. And she's so shy she's lost her tongue."

"Listen, Igor! A nightingale! . . . *He* has a hundred tongues, in Finland. That's what *Satakieli* means. It's a beautiful language. So many vowels. Do you know what a woman's orgasmic cry is in Finnish? *Hääyöaie!* . . . According to Kauppinen."

"How would he know?"

"I guess by using his tongue."

. . . The mood among the judges, following Coningsby's persuasive assault on the Italian contestant, was moving towards a swift decision on the winner of the laurels: now, tonight, rather than breaking up for sleep and resolving the contest in the morning. Tarkiainen pointed out that this would be against precedent; but the Polish judge, Wojcicki, reminded them that in 1934 the last contestant, an Austrian, had "frozen" as utterly as had the Israeli contestant this time and the judges had proceeded immediately to a decision. Support for *The Seven Veils* had collapsed: only the Italian, the French, and the Iranian judges still spoke up for it, and two of those only falteringly. All but Signora Rossi, in fact, agreed that *The Crossing* would be a worthy winner. Its merits were flashed enthusiastically from voice to voice. Even those who had been able to listen only to a literal translation—the great majority—could feel its controlled energy; and without understanding the Russian they had felt the rhythmic strength and the cunning rhymes of the original.

There was, however, as Dibich rather surprisingly pointed

out, a need to be absolutely fair to the earlier improvisations. They must reconsider their earlier thoughts, as the re-playing of *The Crossing* had caused them to think much more warmly of the Russian poem.

Tarkiainen led the way by defending with vigour the Finnish improvisation, on the theme of *Space-flight*, which had started off the finals. It was, he agreed, a somewhat strained adaptation of a legend from the Kalevala, but he could vouch for its linguistic beauty. Tarkiainen suggested they should listen again to its opening section, but the idea met with little favour and none of the judges could find anything particularly good to say about it. The aged Finn spread his hands and nodded, accepting the negative verdict. "So, what about *First Love?*" he demanded.

The general feeling about the Australian entry was that it had been pleasant to listen to, especially as they all could understand English, but that it was essentially modest. The Australian, Blake, had scraped into the finals. It was pleasing but *banal*, M. Moreau reflected, and his remark was greeted with nods. The Frenchman looked across at Wojcicki and, with a smile, said: "*Ce n'est pas Mickiewicz . . .*" It brought an amused head-shake from the sad Pole, and a ripple of amusement round the table, quickly stilled by Tarkiainen.

"Please! . . . So you don't want to hear it again?" he enquired.

No, it was not necessary. "But he should be complimented," added Dibich, with a glancing-round of his small, goldfish-face; and head-shakes turned to nods.

"Which brings us to the British improvisation," said the aged Finn in his mild, quavering voice. "We had some disagreements, I remember, on *White Nights.*"

Each one formed an image of the middle-aged, sandy-haired Britisher, Southerland, who had barely reached the half-hour— and only by much stumbling and pausing. Yet three or four of the judges had found the autobiographical poem attractive. The Pole, the Spanish lady, and the Israeli judge, spoke up for it again with considerable warmth. Others reminded them that it had been extremely personal, and therefore not in the tradition of improvisations; that its subject-matter had been scarcely, if at all, relevant to the given theme; that technically it left a lot to be desired—the rhymes varying in position, and with one line in each verse, indeed, left without a rhyme. Finally and conclusively, in the opinion of many, so short an improvisation would have to be quite outstanding if its author were to be crowned with the laurel.

Yet its very shortness permitted a second hearing of the tape; also, as usually happens when some long and important process is almost at an end, there was a reluctance to let go. The night was young enough and light enough, and most of the judges happy enough, to sit back in their chairs, without using the tiresome head-phones, and listen to a pleasant voice for a short while. It would satisfy those who still thought highly of *White Nights* that it had had every chance. Then they could proceed to vote, and *The Crossing* would be an almost unanimous winner. . . .

· IO ·

HEARING THE *IMPROVISATORE*'S TENTATIVE BEGINNING, HIS hesitations and his stammers, they recalled that his hands had shaken so much he had scarcely been able to open his envelope. And after he had announced his theme, he had appeared bereft of inspiration. They had feared a repetition of the Israeli contestant's *débâcle*. The English *improvisatore* had seemed to gain courage and inspiration from fixing his gaze on a woman friend in one of the front rows; at one point during his verses he had addressed her by name, to the confusion of the audience. Yet that had been only the most confusing of many confusions, created by an excess of personal details, period details, names: almost as if he had been trying to compose a compressed autobiographical novel . . .

> . . . My pleasure at four weeks away from school,
> Summer in the country of the Don,
> And my friends' envy of me, began to cool
> When we'd sold up the house my father built.
> Driving from "Beverly" to spend our last
> Night at my aunts', I seemed already on
> The endless ocean; home had become the past.
>
> In winter gales, my childhood fell away.
> Seasick, I gulped salt, aching tears of loss.
> Father grieved also; to the gods of Kandy
> He vowed we would go home, after two years;
> And celebrated, daringly, on shandy.
> Dolphins and table-tennis marked each day,
> Calm, humid nights dragged up the Southern Cross.
>
> In the ship's concert, they sang a duet:
> "Wanting You." A young woman let her robe
> Slide softly open in the library
> And her breast spill out to her lover's hand;
> Everything swirled in me: the turning globe,
> Tears for our cat. I didn't understand
> The uprush of a new world, like a jet.
>
> I keep, from our land-fall, only blue gleams
> Of hot sky I'd have changed for English rain,
> A taxi; cornucopias of food

I couldn't eat. I understood the pain
Lois had felt—her Hollywood-fed dreams
Turning, as she left "Beverly," to a flood
Of tears, which deepened till it launched us out.

Father found work, with other immigrants,
At the Royal Melbourne Hospital—high up
On scaffolds, plastering. In one sense, he
Had risen in the world. And mother, for
The first time, took a job, in a dress-shop.
My school next to the hospital, I could see
A speck I loved among the worker ants.

We both had shocks; his, hearing from the lips
Of a White Russian navvie that the Hammer-
And-Sickle wasn't as Sir Stafford Cripps
Had claimed it to be. Stalin lost his glamour,
Though we were Labour still. A revelation
More to his taste was when a woman patient,
Who saw him through the window, calmly stripped

To wash . . . I lied about my batting; shocked,
I found myself float out, as opening bat.
A budding Lindwall thundered up; I blocked
A ball I didn't see; the next knocked flat
My middle stump. I never played again.
Unable entirely to get out of sport,
Learned tennis on a dusty, blood-red court.

Each afternoon, mother brought fish and chips
For me to eat before our meal, a taste
Of home, though greasy, *ersatz*. I grew fat.
I cried still for our ginger cat; and traced,
An inch a month, a red line for our ship's
Slow voyage home, on a world map. A year
Would pass before the first land-mass drew near.

In the first month or two, I mostly slept
With father; but in secret. My own room
I couldn't bear when the dark silence fell:
Far out, and crammed with junk. I saw ghosts loom
And sensed the lurking spiders, though in fact
I never saw one there. And so I crept
To turn my mother out. The canvas cracked

Outside my sister's room. Once, like the ape
At Melbourne Zoo, Ray burst out nude; we rocked
Back on our heels. I said I couldn't sleep.
He swung by, muttering. I guess I lacked
Imagination where it touched the game
Adults could play. My father's snarl, one night,
Was simply restlessness until I came.

In England, when I'd crept in, he would tell
Me stories. Now, his reassuring smell
Was all I got or needed. Eventually
They changed rooms with me—called my bluff, I guess.
Theirs clearly wasn't haunted. Till I saw,
Bathed in the full moon's radiance, the tree;
Then, on the wall, my first tarantula.

It was about the time when I had read
The Haunting of Toby Jugg. The witches sent
A host of spiders into Toby's room
Where he lay paralysed. The full moon's loom
Shuttled a mother-spider; from his bed
He saw her fill the window. Dennis Wheatley
Seemed to have read my tortured mind completely.

Yet I sought solitude. Beside Ray's few
Unreadable books I browsed—*An Analogy
Of Religion*, Shakespeare—Lois had thrillers and
Romances. Thrilled and stirred, I listened to

The dark piano chords that introduced
Popular Classics. But the leafy tree
Outside my window trembled too, and loosed

Tarantulas. A dozen times all told
In our two years in that suburban street
I woke to find one couching there, its hold
On the wall as fragile as a steeplejack's.
Ray would come in to pump insecticide,
Spreading a sweetish odour; horrified,
I'd watch the becalmed creature's grip relax,

Its splayed legs lurch it sideways down the wall.
One such occasion, all the others gone
To work, and I left juddering from the horror,
I sensed—felt—saw a second spider crawl
Out from between my feet into the sun.
I dropped a big book on it—let it go
Like Juliet, straight after Romeo.

It stopped . . . It seemed to wait . . . Elizabeth,
Since then, some horrors have put out the light
And left in me a permanent trace of death,
Yet none with such a strangling shock as that
Coincidence of tarantulas: the one
Appearing customarily in the night,
The other in the morning. Almost none.

I couldn't pick the Bible up to see . . .
The crushed gore . . . and how near its life had got
To safety, cruising with the speed of light,
Luckier than old Gagool, and out of sight,
A secret member of the family.
I left it; shaking, walked out to the calm,
Already sun-drenched street and caught the tram

To school. The spiders settled in my mind.
A fair-skinned country-boy among dark faces
Of brilliant Jews who were polite to me,
I struggled to survive; their squat briefcases
An earnest of their adult earnestness.
But that particular day, in an art class,
I heard the storms of "Francesca da Rimini:"

It crackled on the teacher's gramophone,
Opening a Red Sea into other worlds,
Yet more antipodes. The teacher said,
Drily, they were being tortured on the winds
Of their own passion. In swirls of black and red,
I painted blind. I never talked to girls;
I couldn't conceive of those Italian sins.

I'd crossed the line between the hemispheres
And watched the equatorial baptism,
But nothing marked the splitting of the years
Of innocence and experience, which was
The brutal, unimaginable chasm:
From daddy-longlegs to tarantulas,
From spinning tops to that tormenting joy.

Girls were the other side of the school-fence;
Angelic boaters. I hid my ignorance
When a crude Cypriot said poufters were
Blokes who liked sniffing saddles of girls' bikes.
Why should they want to do that? It seemed mad.
Hearing the rising, falling, chords I had
No violence to go by but the strikes

Of throbbing German bombers on Swanpool,
Lighting the horizon up; the rise and fall
Of warning sirens, though Redruth was safe;
And, though the honing searchlights, like stage-lights,

Wheeled in the Cornish dark, no violence
Threatened my sister, strolling from a dance
Home with an airman, on soft summer nights.

There was a girl, in a green uniform
Like mine, and with the motto *strenue*
ac fideliter over the tender breast,
Fair, close-cropped hair, and eyes immense and blue,
I worshipped ardently and faithfully
At the school tram-stop; after Francesca's storm,
Her vision came quite close, and then withdrew.

(*Southerland had taken a step back, as if to collect his thoughts; a catcall
had come from a group of Finns, who stood at the back with beer glasses in
their hands: "White Nights!" The Englishman, stepping forward
again, had seemed to draw strength from the implied rebuke, for he
resumed more confidently and fluently.*)

Yes, those Australian white nights! My thighs
Spread wide each side the twisted sweatsoaked sheet;
The spiders that were called tarantulas
But only as a tribute to their size;
The garden, rank with green; the nightmare heat.
Mosquitos whining, those unsettled specks
Of bloodlust round the Southern Cross of sex

On which I hung, spreadeagled like the tree
Against the moon. The window open wide,
I dared not sleep, until the dawn moved clear
Around the leaves; a fresher atmosphere
Crept in; I turned my light out, satisfied
The ghosts had gone. The phantom-girl who came
To drench me, then, in ecstasy and shame—

Was she Jean Simmons of *The Blue Lagoon*
Who searched the drowsing ocean for her friend

She believed drowned, and heard some lines of Donne
(I didn't know he wrote them, nor did she);
And vague unrest and wonder stirred in me?
Some other star I cut from *Photoplay*,
Wide-eyed June Allyson or Doris Day—

My sister's generation—fringed hair, fresh
Complexion, good health bursting from her flesh,
Strict as her belted waist, straight as her seams?
Or the girl waiting for a tram? And what
Happened between us, that it brought the chords
Of that concerto crashing into my dreams,
The dreams which woke me to the rustling hordes?

She clearly dated from—or in—the war . . .
One evening, held by the swift silent thresh
As Lois slimmed her thighs, kicked from the floor,
I sensed, in the skirt-rucked, suave violence
Of straps between her nylons and tight pants
A glamour, like the searchlights gliding round
The night-sky—only black against white flesh.

I've come to know Ray from his diary
I've read of late, which he kept faithfully
And privately: his wondering, in mid-ocean,
After the war, if going back for Bluey
Was a mistake. Sad undertows of emotion,
Stuck in the doldrums. But the course was set
That night when, like two vague searchlights, they'd met.

And all proved well. In Melbourne, they still gazed
At one another, almost as when the deep
Snows had held "Beverly," falling in his sleep,
Amazing him. He saw, still more amazed,
My father's prints—he'd fought his way to work.
I too (though in a different way) recall
That Eden after, and before, the fall.

Our second summer. Hot winds scorched my throat
Unspeakably. Life was a continent
As dry, unknown, and pitilessly burning
As the outback we read about in school.
I fell in love with Man Shy—a colt, gaunt
From wandering, stumbling, in the bone-bleached drought;
I longed, like him, to stumble on a pool.

But forest-fires swept through the bush; the winds
Were sultrier than the woman who, each night,
Sang to me that I was born to be kissed,
I was *Temptation*, she could not resist;
I longed to wake one morning to that deep
White night in dunes on fields and granite carn,
Not branches crucified against the sun.

Knowing I would be slaughtered by the Jews,
And half-aware my dream-time had begun,
I stayed away from school, during some tests;
And tried to make up for a desperate night
By sleeping. Out of dreamless oblivion
I rambled in the desert, but caught sight
Of peaks on the horizon, Sheba's Breasts,

A snow-capped, icy, mountainous frontier,
Intangible, the mysteries of love.
I thought there must be ways to bring together
The night of spiders and Rachmaninov
And the harsh, brilliant day . . . to make a sphere,
Male within female, sky embracing earth,
With secret rites move to a second birth.

My sister's room, the curtains drawn, felt cool.
Paolo embraced Francesca; but Gagool,
The black death, stabbed; Foulata in the arms
Of honest Good died, crying that the sun

Could not mate with the moon, nor white with black.
And, as I clasped the girl craved *strenue ac
fideliter*, almost becoming one

With her, I choked on the embrace, enchanted
At being choked, and drowned in her perfume.
Though shivering lest a key grate in the lock
Of the back door, I opened it and led
Her down into the garden's heat . . . The shock
Of a small spider on my wrist . . . I panted,
Flinging it off, and rushed back to my room.

That was the end of adolescent rites;
And I went back to school, with a forged note,
Unborn still, and no dream-song in my throat,
No water-hole in sight; just burnt-out gums,
Ghost-trees, the desert trembling like a drum's
Taut skin, under the pounding sun. I choked
In a school-tie by day, naked at night.

The bloated summer nothing could abort
Nor bring to birth . . . On the school's red-dust court,
I killed all rallies with a vicious drive
Like swotting flies. Then an Antarctic breeze
Fluttered our curtains, as we lolled in shorts
Under the useless fan, scarcely alive,
And the thermometer dropped ten degrees.

Time moved now in a slightly quicker stream.
We'd booked our passage twelve months in advance.
My grief, that winter, was to see my team
(Australian Rules) get to the finals, lose
The trophy by a record sixty points.
Though I'd be glad to see the Reds again,
Rugby again, I knew I'd miss the Blues.

I liked the Saturday ritual with Dad—

The morning film, the frenzied stadium;
But even the schooldays didn't seem so bad,
Now my ghost-ship had reached North Africa;
With gentler teachers than those handlebar-
Moustached war-surplus schoolmasters back home
I edged up through the Aryan pack—not far.

Now jokes about Ray's prudent family-planning
Began to mix with thoughts of how they'd use
The space when we were gone. I had stopped reading,
Unwrapping even, the comics sent from home
By a class-bully who'd stayed touchingly
Faithful to me. Now Malta was receding;
And unexpectedly I beat the Jews.

I fell in love with love and poetry,
And like the sexes in my class, they merged.
Starting our third, short summer, happiness
Consumed me in the shape of a Jewess
Called Sara. Slim and graceful, without taint,
She rarely spoke to me, but I'd grow faint,
Watching the way her short black hair converged

On her pale nape. I lost weight. One weekend
I told my parents they could leave me there.
Hot tears gushed out. Mum and Dad were aghast;
Lois and Ray alarmed. The line I'd traced
On the world map had come to a dead end
Some weeks before, abandoned or becalmed
Between Gibraltar and Cape Finisterre.

The nights, though fearful still, were bearable;
The dawns exquisite: bird-notes, and the cool
Freshness; the leaves appearing mistily
At first, then sharply, dark against a sky
Of deepening brilliance; grey, then moving through

The rainbow from vermilion to bright blue,
Dazzling my eyes. How beautiful the tree.

Ray thought he'd better take my sister off
On holiday before we left: the scars
Might be less deep. I made a joke of that
Painful last hour together in the flat;
At the piano, raised a shaky laugh
By thumping out the Dead March from *Saul*.
But wept for Sara under changing stars.

We moved in with my aunts. One weekend, we
Followed our frozen breaths towards "Beverly,"
But just to see old neighbours. It felt queer
And sad, recalling how, as we drew near,
Father would whistle, and our ginger cat
Bound down to meet us. We'd be seeing her.
I thought of how we'd left her: she had sat,

Puzzled, on our settee, for all the rest
Smelt strange—our neighbours having taken both
Settee and cat. Now, as a mournful joke,
My father whistled, and amazingly
Our ginger cat came bounding down the road.
Either a distant memory awoke,
Or had lived on, ardently and faithfully.

· I I ·

MATTI'S FINGER CUT SHORT THE AUDIENCE'S APPLAUSE FOR the English *improvisatore*: applause which, for all its good nature, had seemed also to say, "Well, that wasn't very long . . . the jazzband will have to be good if we're to get our money's worth today. . . ."

In the relaxed quietness after the tape-recording, Tarkiainen remarked: "It's quite refreshing to hear a contestant who doesn't need to employ bad language—don't you think?" His yellowish smile evoked a wordless murmur. "It was rather a shame," he continued, "that he started so badly. The extraordinary change of direction in the second or third line! One moment we were heading for Russia, the country of the Don, and the next we were *en route* for Australia!"

"Yes, I noticed that!" Coningsby said with a smile, his pen idling on his note-pad.

"But he carried it on extremely well," said the Frenchman.

"Yes, he did," agreed the Spanish lady. "It was very charming."

Again, the wordless murmur of agreement. And the same

murmur when the German judge said it was really a shame it had been so personal, so subjective, because otherwise it might have been a serious contender, in spite of its brevity.

There was silence; the tapping of pencil-heads on blotting-paper. They waited, not impatiently, for the chairman to call for the vote, which would find Igor Markov the winner. Tarkiainen didn't seem to be in any hurry. It was understandable. He had been retired for many years from the Chair of Philology at Helsinki University, and the honour of presiding at the Olympiad was probably the last major event of his life.

Breaking the long silence, Senhora Casalduero remarked: "We've had quite a lot about Australia."

"Yes, and dogs and cats," said Moreau.

The Israeli leaned forward. "I hadn't noticed it before," he said, "but the grief felt by the boy in *White Nights* is echoed in the stanza about the dog, or rather bitch, in *The Crossing* . . . It's of no importance."

There was another restful pause. "It was good, it was extremely good," murmured Coningsby. He fingered his tie, the striped tie of the Mar del Plata English Club. He would not wear it again for a long time. Hostility, anger, the Malvinas stolen back; and few knowing that he had suffered as much as anyone. "The cat, at the end, yes . . . touching. . . ."

Tarkiainen, pressing his hands together as if to pray, said: "Well, shall we move to a vote?"

Coningsby, as though not hearing him, remarked: "There *is* some degree of plagiarism in *The Crossing*, that's undeniable."

A rustle of interest ran round the table. Tarkiainen leaned to his right. "Would you care to explain, Coningsby? You mean, in the sense that Elsberg has just pointed out? But surely, that's of very little significance?"

Coningsby rested his elbows on the table, and briefly pressed his hands against his skull. "No," he said, folding his hands on the table and gazing at the bare wall above M. Moreau's head. "I agree, that isn't significant. No, actual quotation, from *White Nights*."

"Please be specific."

"Yes, please do."

"I didn't notice it until we heard *White Nights* again just now." The austere, scholarly man glanced down at his note-pad. "*White Nights* has the line 'The snow-capped, icy, mountainous frontier;' *The Crossing* has 'The icy, mountainous frontier.' I don't know if this was an accurate translation?" He glanced aside at Dibich.

"*Da, da*," the Russian said, shrugging.

"The English, in the same verse, has 'desperate night' and 'dreamless oblivion,' the Russian makes it 'One desperate night' and 'dreamless oblivion.' And both desperate nights involve music—listening to music. Again, the English has, somewhere else, a reference to the drum's taut skin—the desert; the Russian has a drum-tight desert—and Sheba's Breasts too."

"I didn't understand that," said the Pole.

Coningsby explained it was from a children's book by Rider Haggard.

"This is a red herring," said Dibich. "Markov—the author, rather—has made of it something new, something his own."

"Well, I agree, up to a point," said Coningsby. "But it makes one wonder if he has borrowed anything else."

"As a matter of fact," interposed the Spanish judge, "the Chilean improvisation—you remember? *Remorse?*—told a story, which we felt wasn't a very good one, about a woman waiting by a phone to hear if the man she loved had died in an accident."

The table had come alive now. It concentrated. "Yes, you're quite right," said Signora Rossi, her eyes animated. She nodded gratefully at the moustached woman.

"Well, it wasn't altogether the same," said Coningsby.

"But there was also a drive through city streets at night, at the end of *Remorse*," observed Wojcicki; "and an interfering mother-in-law."

"I think this is absurd," Dibich said, scowling.

"Well, of course, you would!" flashed the Signora. "But, now I think of it, the resemblances between *The Crossing* and *Remorse* are very strong. And all this makes Anton's—Dr Wojcicki's—point about the form—that it's taken from Pushkin—distinctly relevant."

The Israeli and the Iranian nodded.

"It would be most premature to take a vote," said the Italian judge. "We have passed over—dismissed—*The Seven Veils* after almost no discussion of it. After listening again to only a fraction—a fraction of what was, at the very least, a tremendous *tour de force*. Can we seriously maintain that the whole of that immense and imaginative improvisation was taken from *The Crossing*? The interview with the President of the United States? From what? . . . The Armenian massacres? That splendid *Walpurgisnacht* of the finale? . . ." Realizing that she was speaking too rapidly and forcefully, she slowed and quietened. "We should clear our minds of everything we have been discussing in the past hour or so; listen to a great deal more of her performance, followed by further discussions on questions which are relevant, artistic—and only then break off for a few hours' sleep. The final discussion of all the contestants, and the vote, should take place tomorrow, when we are fresh, in accordance with our original intention and with the rules."

"The Signora is right," said Moreau. "We have led ourselves astray, to some degree. *The Seven Veils* was unquestionably a remarkable improvisation."

"But so, I think, was *White Nights*," the Spanish judge observed. "It was admirably direct and honest."

"But feeble in style," said Dibich. "Occasionally he tries to ape Gogol, whom for some reason he describes as the black death. I should like someone to tell me how the Russian navy could be described as 'white'? The adjective is meaningless. And it is even more absurd to talk about the lips of a navy!" His anus-like mouth twitched in an attempt at a smile. "The whole reference was incomprehensible; I assume he was trying somehow or other to get back to his theme."

In the embarrassed silence the mild, shy Hungarian woman surprised everyone by saying faintly, "It was about political illusion and reality, I thought." Seeing Dibich's cold eyes directed at her, she dropped her gaze and added, "It was muddled, yes."

After slopping more water into his glass, drinking, and spilling some down his chin, Tarkiainen said they should not ignore the inventiveness of *Space-flight*. Nor, after all, the touching simplicity of *First Love*, said the German judge. Professor Krüdner was right, said the Pole, glancing pleasantly in her direction. Meeting his eyes she blushed and looked down at her note-pad.

"Professor Krüdner *may* be right," said Signora Rossi, addressing the chair. She noticed that the aged Finn looked exhausted, ill. "The point I am trying to make is that now isn't the time for a general discussion. Let us stick to the precedents, and confine ourselves, tonight, to today's improvisation."

"You are right, Signora. You think we should hear some more?" His voice quavered, his gaze beseeched her to say no.

"What we hear in the quietness of this room is very influential. With all the other finalists, we played back the whole of their improvisations. That would clearly be impossible in this case; but it would be grossly unfair to judge her largely on a short, unrepresentative section when—as M. Moreau remarked—or rather, it was Señora Menendez—she was beginning again, and having to break off once more. Altamira's visit was wonderful, and typical of the man, to come out of his way like that, but it couldn't have come at a worse time for the *improvisatrice*. If we continue from where we stopped the tape, I think we'll find she got better and better. I propose that we do that. But perhaps we should have a short break, to get some fresh air."

Tarkiainen looked at her gratefully. He asked if anyone

dissented. No one either dissented or assented. They were weary. The pale dusk was deceitful. All made haste to get into the fresh air for a few minutes. Signora Rossi had lit up a cigarette before she was quite out of doors. She strolled away, to the lake-side. Most of the others also strolled away, or squatted down on the grass, alone. Coningsby and Matti, sipping coffee they had collected from the bar, chatted near the entrance: the young man frowning and nodding as he wrestled with the barbaric tongue.

When the judges had settled into their chairs again, Matti switched tapes, head-phones were put on—the Israeli and the Iranian waiting until they had enjoyed for several moments the rapid, cool, incomprehensible speech of the beautiful *improvisatrice.*

T·W·O

. . . Swallowed up and lost
In the wide womb of uncreated night.
MILTON

· I ·

A LATE AND HEAVY MEAL WITH MRS THRESHER AND THE
Spinnakers gave Surkov another wretched night. The red snapper seemed alive still, bloating his stomach, snapping and butting
at his lungs and heart. The central heating in the Washington
hotel was even more stifling than at Donna Zarifian's apartment:
he drenched the sheets with sweat. The Harvey Wallbangers
banged in his head; and the man in the next room banged on
the thin wall, and cursed, because the Russian was farting so
loudly, so often. The explosions woke Surkov himself a couple
of times, when he was lapsing into a drowse. There was nothing
he could do about them. Mercifully, Abramsohn in the next
bed slept through them all, snoring lightly.

Then, when the red snapper quietened, about 5 a.m., jet-lag
had the effect of making Surkov feel deceptively wide awake. He
sat up in bed smoking, and churned over in his mind what
questions he wanted to ask the President, and in what order. He
scribbled some questions on a hotel pad. Surkov had never
interviewed anyone in his life before. He believed it should be
possible to plunge beneath the conventional topics, and show the

President of the United States as a real human being. And the President, from what he had been told, seemed to want that. He seemed to want to say to the readers of *Pravda*: "Look, you guys, I'm human!"

But the Wallbangers, though they too had calmed down, resisted ordering, structuring; and Surkov crunched up the page of questions and decided to trust to his instinct—to let the questions come just as they would in ordinary conversation.

He was lying sleepily wakeful when the alarm-call, ordered by the agent, came through at seven-thirty. The telephonist wished him a good day. Abramsohn had come awake with a groan, and looked relieved when he saw his Russian friend and client replacing the receiver.

Now, hardly able to keep his eyes open, Surkov was swaying outside the White House on a cloudy, humid morning, exchanging words with Walter Mako, the Secretary of State. Mako was dressed in a blue track-suit; he had just come from his morning jog. At sixty, Mako was the youthful, up-and-coming star of the Administration. His face glowed with health; his three-mile jog had scarcely raised a sweat, and he was not breathing heavily. Surkov yearned briefly to be on the skating-rink in Moscow; his illness had kept him away from it for several weeks.

"Go easy on the old man, Mr Surkov," Mako was saying, as the sun dazzled off his capped teeth. "His daughter had to have a blood transfusion in the night. You saw what happened. It's been a shock for the President, and his sleep was disturbed. You may also find he takes his time before answering. He prefers to think about a question carefully. So please don't rush him. We're delighted you could come. I'll take you to his office."

Between Marines jumping to attention they entered the White House, and headed for the holy of holies. Surkov felt awed, and proud. He stumbled through corridors after Mako's long swift strides. The Secretary of State knocked at a door, and after a lengthy interval a voice growled, "Come." Mako threw open the door, leaned in and said, "Mr President, I've brought Mr Surkov to see you. You remember—the interview."

Resting his hand on Surkov's shoulder, ushering him into O'Reilly's presence, Mako said, "Good luck. Have a good day now."

"Thank you."

Surkov stumbled in. He grasped the President's hand, thrust at him across the big mahogany desk. The desk was empty of papers. "Please sit down, Mr Surkov. Good of you to come." The President sat, and Surkov collapsed into the low chair in front of the desk.

"I believe we met at the party, Mr Surkov?"

"Yes, we did."

The staggeringly bright red hair, slicked with gleaming lotion; the wide, blunt face; the huge mouth, and the white teeth lying strangely on their sides. The slender, barrel-chested body. The clothes so well tailored, Surkov could not tell where skin ended and fabric began.

"It's a beautiful room, Mr President."

"Yes, I thought we'd met. Then there was that dreadful accident to my daughter."

"Yes, I saw it. How is she?"

"You don't have to call me Mr President. Call me sir if you like. It's easier. I'd like this to be as informal as we can make it, Mr Surkov."

"That's how I see it too—sir. I've no prepared questions. I merely thought . . ."

"She's much better. She's stopped bleeding. But we had a bad night. I didn't get much rest."

That was evident from O'Reilly's bleary, closed-up eyes, and the encircling bags and wrinkles. They alone betrayed his age, the three score years and ten. Yet Surkov felt his own eyes were in no better shape. His lids kept drooping. He wished desperately to be asked if he'd like some coffee; then he recalled that O'Reilly was a Mormon, so the invitation was unlikely to be made.

Out of the blurred corner of his eye he caught sight of a television screen, which faced the President. The otherwise blank screen carried the message "Hope abandoned." Surkov tensed. He had read Nadezhda Mandelstam's work in *samizdat*. But why should its English title be flashed up on a screen in the Oval Office? Was it a subtle trap? Surely the office was not wired for sound, after . . . ? Or, even if it was something quite innocent, had some unknown agent from his Embassy planted a bug on him? Sweat broke out on his brow. Someone brushing past him . . . even the dressing-room attendant at the swingers-club . . . Betty Thresher, even—one could never be absolutely sure. No, it was absurd. He must really be carrying the feverish infection still, if he fell prey to such absurd suspicions. Perhaps it was the beginning of an educational programme; a dramatization, or a political discussion, of the book. He glanced directly at the screen, but the words were still there, frozen, and there was no sound.

"Could I ask you what those words mean, sir?"

"I'm glad," O'Reilly said, "that you've not come with prepared questions. I don't have any prepared answers either."

Aware that he had committed a *gaffe* in questioning the President about the message on the screen, Surkov stammered: "Well, then . . . I was merely curious because I . . . Shall we begin, then?"

"Oh, that? It's saying the Bob Hope Classic in Florida has had to be abandoned because of the storms down there." The "Tiger" gave a throat-clearing chuckle. "You can see I'm human, can't you! Actually, that screen does occasionally bring me important information, the instant something happens that I should know about. Vital information. But when nothing much is going on, I like it to come out with little news items to help keep me in touch with what's going on around the world. Sports items, that kind of thing." As he was speaking, in his rather slow, gruff voice, the words on the screen vanished and were replaced by "Howard Crane dead, automobile accident—confirmed." "Oh, that's too bad!" the President exclaimed, after some desultory chat about the weather. "He was in a picture with me, once. I must send a note of condolence to his wife. She's only twenty-one or two, I guess; a very pretty girl. There was a big difference in their ages. Howard must have been—oh, pretty old. In his late sixties, I guess."

O'Reilly suddenly looked flustered; he hooked a finger under the starched shirt collar, to scratch.

"That's no great age, sir," Surkov remarked. He fumbled in the breast-pocket of his lumber-jacket, and took out a notebook and a pen. He scribbled a few lines.

"Yes, let's begin," the President said. "Fire away."

· 2 ·

Well, speaking of ages, Mr President . . . do you ever feel that you're too old for the Presidency? You're—what?—Seventy-four?
It's not a great age, you're right.

Do you think wisdom comes with age?
No, I don't feel that. I'm in very good shape.

What is your outlook on death, sir?

You'll have to ask my wife! It comes, not with age so much, as from long experience of family life, sharing everything, all the joys, all the sorrows, with a woman you love and who loves you. Having children and grandchildren too, of course. Seeing them grow up, have children, get married. I don't mean in that order!

But those children could be faced with nuclear holocaust. What are your real feelings, as a man not as a President, about the possibility of a third World War?

I'm ready for it when it comes.

You're ready for it? But do you think it can be prevented?

I don't believe that's a serious possibility.

That's very alarming. Your Administration has agreed with ours that neither side could win a nuclear war. Is there any new thinking on this? Do you believe the United States can win an all-out war?

I believe it can. I'm sure it can.

That would seem to cast doubts on your commitment to arms reduction. Are you committed to it?

We're still of the same mind. The answer is no. And it ought to be clear to any sane person, in my country or yours.

I'd like to get on to a lighter note. Do you ever watch your old movies?

Yes, of course. I don't see why you should have to ask. I'd like to think it's what my Presidency will be remembered for.

I've heard you watch television in bed, just before going to sleep. Can I ask a delicate question—do you still have marital relations? A normal married life—do you still sleep with your wife?

No, no, there's no time for that. All that is of no interest to me anymore. Life moves on . . . well, I watch occasionally, mainly when we're at Camp David.

You watch?
Yes, of course. There's life in the old dog yet!

What precisely do you watch?
Well, it's only occasional, as I said. And mainly at Camp David, weekends. A couple of weekends ago I watched *My Wife and Her Lover*. Well, I found it pretty good! A good laugh! A bit daring, considering the period, I guess. Well, it passed an evening. All work and no play makes Jack a dull boy.

Let me get this straight. You watched your wife and her lover?
I enjoy comedies. I also see nothing wrong with a little nostalgia, seeing oneself as one was. But like I said, I don't often watch.

Well, that's fantastic . . . You mentioned something about a period—"Considering the period." I wasn't clear what you meant by that.
Does it surprise you? It really wasn't *that* bad! It was okay; it's harmless! . . . Just a little risky, a little daring, but not far out. Not by today's standards.

But your wife—how old is she?
You know, the forties . . . Well, it was a strange kind of period. Bloody, and terrible—well, you Russians would know —but exhilarating too, looking back. That extra challenge.

Forgive me, I thought I read she was sixty.
She's sixty—but don't you agree she doesn't look it?

She's an attractive woman, Mr President.
I told you, she's sixty. I married her in '44, just after I made *My Favourite Dumb Blonde*. That was kind of fun, too.

I got told off at a press conference for using that phrase. And, of course, I know lots of women, especially in my country, where they have complete equality, who would get mad as hell at a guy saying he had "made" them. Do you think the American woman is equal to the American man?
Well, she tries her best to keep young and attractive. She dresses well, is careful about her make-up.

But is that what equality is all about? Or how would you define it?
Who told you off? What blonde? Well, yes, I think she is. Women are equal but, of course, different.

I know your wife has an important position now; but before you were President, did you encourage her to work? Did she have a job?
Mutual trust. Will that do? Nothing high-flown. Mutual trust.

An insurance firm?
No, she just ensured her children were brought up to be good Americans. That's an important job.

Of course. Which brings us back, in a way, to the arms race, which could wipe out our children. Mutual Assured Destruction. . . .
An insurance firm?

I like your black humour, sir. But of course it's not funny, as you would agree. It's mad. Isn't there anyone, West or East, who could knock some sense into our heads?
I know, I know . . . the children, Russian or American it doesn't matter. The children. . . .

That's very moving. Our people will like that. We must hope that the present generation of women are bringing up our children wisely . . . And speaking of women—is there any woman of note whom you admire particularly?

The Pope, perhaps.

Very funny! But you admire him . . . You are, of course, known to be religious. I'd like to ask you about that. Do you see God? I mean, have you a picture of Him in your head?

I guess, Margaret Thatcher.

Really? You think God is a woman?

No, I don't have any particular image. I just know, when I pray, I'm talking to someone.

You believe in a life after death?

Hell, no! That's just a fashionable feminist idea.

I wouldn't have thought so. Well, there are certain Soviet dissidents, mainly from Leningrad, who call themselves feminists and who are religious. They think women should be the centre of the home, and they're against abortions—that kind of thing. But I'm surprised you know about them, sir. They don't have the support of the masses. But I'd like to come back to your personal life, and your marriage, about which you have been remarkably frank . . . May I quote you on "my favourite dumb blonde," or shall I re-phrase it?

I'm not ashamed to admit it. I'm a Mormon, Mr Sadkov. There is a life beyond the grave.

You truly believe in open marriages?

I've always tried to live honestly, and I'm not going to change this morning. What more do you want to know? Why shouldn't you quote me on *My Favourite Dumb Blonde*? I'm not ashamed to own up to it. It was good honest entertainment. Nothing pretentious, you know. I made it with Irma Fleming. She was very talented, very beautiful. Well, she still is a lovely lady. I had my picture taken with her at a garden party the other week.

But how about the public? Your constituents?
I believe they're crazy. I don't hold with them. What gave you the impression that I might?

So you don't care what they think? About your having had affairs in the past, and your wife having a lover now? This is off the record but I simply can't imagine any of our leaders being so open about their lovers, and their wives' lovers.
Well, I feel very close to them all. Of whatever race, creed, or colour. Black or white, it makes no difference. They're the salt of the earth, and I just do my best not to let them down.

So you've slept with coloured girls, sir?
Jesus Christ! What are you getting at? What sort of a fucking question is that?

I'm sorry. Please accept my apologies.
Is this some sort of a trick?

I'm truly sorry . . . Could we, please, come back, just one more time, to the question of peace in our crazy divided world?
I find it offensive. Why don't you ask me how my wife and I have sustained a happy marriage for over forty years?

Well, okay—gladly. Have you any advice for young Soviets launching into marriage?
Well, okay. It's a very, very difficult business. Sadly, there seems no alternative to a controlled conflict. If there's a build-up of tension, you have to appear willing to go the whole hog. Like the game of Chicken—you know it? Two cars race straight at

each other, and the one who swerves aside is chicken. Well, in the end you *have* to swerve, but you try to do it later than the other. It would be irrational not to swerve; but the other driver knows that, so you've got to give the impression that you *could* behave irrationally, that you might do something crazy. But then, of course, it's not like driving a car. If you think the other party is a little crazy, there's the temptation to get your blow in first. *Wump!* right in the belly. So the other has to be able to respond with an equally devastating blow, to discourage you from that first blow. Well, that's about it. It's sad, but there's no alternative.

A gloomy view, Mr President. Have you anything to say, at the end of our interview, to the Soviet people generally?
I'd tell them, don't think you'll have it all your own way. There must be give and take.

Thank you, Mr President. Is there anything you'd like to add?
God bless you.

Thank you. Oh, one more thing—would you have any objection if someone from the New York Times, say, or the Washington Post, were to persuade Comrade Brezhnev to talk to them in a similar way?
No, I don't think so. Thank you.

Don't mention it.
No, of course not.

· 3 ·

SURKOV WAS CHOKING WITH EXCITEMENT AS HE PUT HIS PEN and note-pad away. He believed he had a "scoop," yet something nagged at him, something vaguely wrong.

"Do you have a family, Mr Surkov?"

"Yes. I have a grown-up daughter, and a small son . . . I agree with your gloomy estimation of marriages in general. It's clearly a great strength to you to have such a happy one, Mr President."

"A family is everything." O'Reilly had stood up, and was propelling his heavy, streamlined body around the Oval Office—not in a circle or an oval but in clumsy, stumbling zig-zags.

"You're right, Mr President. I'm missing my little boy. Thinking of him, I find the threat of nuclear holocaust simply awful."

"Well, we survive. We've survived almost forty years of it. It's important to be able to kiss and make up. A cuddle can do wonders. Over forty years you're bound to have disagreements, but we've never let the sun go down on our wrath."

"That's true, sir."

Surkov liked the President's colourful, homely metaphors and his dry humour. He was not nearly so dull as some of the Western press made out. He saw, on the television screen, the words "Dodgers coach sacked unconfirmed" replaced by "Kabul. Soviet air-raid. Heavy Afghan casualties." He sighed. "But can it last for another forty years, Mr President?" he asked the zig-zagging figure. "Or four hundred? Four thousand?"

"That's unfortunate," said the President. "Beamish was a damn good coach."

"I'm sorry?"

O'Reilly chuckled. "Well, I guess we don't have to worry if it can last that long!"

The Russian stared at the screen. His heart started to beat quickly. The screen read: "Soviets attack Dallas. Nuclear." But it simply couldn't mean what it said. A NATO manoeuvre. At worst, a Warsaw Pact exercise. "What does that mean, Mr President?" he asked, his voice tremulous.

"He was a good coach. Have you ever seen baseball?"

"On the screen now. What does that mean?"

"On the screen, you mean? Yes. Well, you tell Comrade Brezhnev they'd better get the hell out of there . . . Oh, shit! Holy fucking shit!" The President stumbled to his chair, crashed into it, picked up a red telephone. Surkov, standing up, heard a faint double-echo, a rough Russian greeting, translated almost simultaneously into English. He heard O'Reilly growl, "Comrade Brezhnev, have you attacked Dallas?"

A mumble at the end of the line. "Yes, hello, Comrade Brezhnev," growled O'Reilly. "Are you attacking us?"

Surkov gripped the desk top to save himself from collapsing. Nausea swept through him; he thought his heart would burst out of his chest. The President slammed down the phone and sank back in his chair, his face chalk-white. "I can't believe it!" he said. "He joked with me! He said it had nothing to do with him personally, but he recalled something about it in *Izvestia*! But surely it was not important! Why was I phoning! I tell you, the guy was fucking playing with me!"

"I can't believe it! There must be some mistake," mumbled Surkov, dry-mouthed, pulling out a handkerchief and dabbing his sweating face. A terrible pain clenched at his heart; he crashed back into his chair.

"We must keep calm," said the President to himself. He pressed a button. Surkov saw a grave, deeply-lined, grey-haired man in American officer's uniform appear on the screen in place of the innocuous-looking, dreadful message.

"Hello, Vane," rapped the President. "Is there a Red ICBM on its way to Dallas?"

"Hello, Mr President. What can I do for you? We have a slight communications problem here. An electrical storm, interference. I guess we may not have vision for very long." Surkov saw the general glance at his watch.

"Is this a false alarm?"

The general looked puzzled. "No, we've no evidence of it."

"Shit! How long have we got? Is this the big one?"

"I guess it must be, sir."

"How long have we got, Vane?"

"I guess three–four minutes. The big what? The main computer?"

"Then what do you suggest we hit?"

"As I said, Mr President, about three minutes now. But as regards any nuclear threat, we've no indication. . . ."

"Three–four minutes—can't you be more precise?"

"Don't hit anything. As I said, we've no indication of any nuclear attack or preparation for one, Mr President."

"Jesus Christ, three minutes! I'm going for Rostov and Tbilisi. Goodbye, Vane."

O'Reilly pressed the button, and the general blanked out. The fateful words returned. Surkov, who had for a few moments blacked out like the general's worried face, came round hazily to a babble of commands through an intercom . . . where was Mako? . . . Where was the Vice-President? . . . Send for the First Lady . . . the SAC on Red Alert. . . .

Mako, still track-suited, was urging the President to hold back. O'Reilly was not listening. The Russian remembered Mako's advice about the President's slow responses. O'Reilly's brain was trying to keep pace with the second-hands of his watch, but failing. The talk of Rostov and Tbilisi made Surkov undergo another cramp of nausea. His second wife, Yevgeniya, lived in the Georgian capital; and Katya was working in Rostov.

"Not Rostov and Tbilisi, Mr President," he beseeched. "Why not Kiev and Voronezh? Kiev would be a much more terrible blow."

"Fetch my wife, Mako. Ask her what the hell's keeping her." Mako loped out. "Kiev and Voronezh?" said the President. "No, we agreed on Tbilisi, if we ever got into this situation. Fuck, we've got a minute and twenty seconds, roughly." He zig-zagged ponderously around the room again, rubbing his chin. "Maybe Tbilisi and Kiev, that's not a bad idea. Okay."

Surkov heaved a thankful sigh. Katya would be all right. As for Yevgeniya, he had tried. Anyway, she would not pauperize him any more with her demands for maintenance.

The President's wife arrived. She had hair-curlers in. "What's wrong?" she asked, anxious, fumbling nervously with a pearl earring.

"What kept you?" shouted the President. "We've got one hell of a crisis. The Russkies have launched an ICBM on Dallas."

"Oh my God!" Mrs O'Reilly's wrinkled eyes spilled tears.

An officer carrying a handbag—well, it had looked to Surkov like a handbag, though now that he saw it for the second time he realized it was not—stood at attention near the President.

"Mako's looking for you, Wanda," shouted the President. "Why is nobody around when I need them? Where the fuck is

Mako? There has to be two of us. Wanda, you'll have to step in. I guess the First Lady can do in an emergency." He fumbled in a drawer, and produced a key. He dug into a trouser pocket and took out a second key. "Put the bag on the desk," he ordered the young officer. The officer complied. The President's clumsy hand fumbled. "Kiev and Tbilisi," he muttered. "That's it! Wanda, put your key in there and turn it when I've counted to three."

The President and his wife stood side by side behind the desk, their hands together in the case. O'Reilly stared at his wristwatch. Surkov staggered round the office, in a daze. Passing in front of the screen, he saw that the words had changed slightly. They were saying: "Soviets attack Dallas: unclear." Then, even as he stared, the message flickered to: "Soviets attack 'Dallas': confirmed."

"Mr President! Look at the screen!" he screamed, only in Russian; and at that moment Mako, stooping to get through the door, rushed in. "It's a false alarm, Mr President!" he cried, but in a faint, choked voice. "It was just a piece in today's *Izvestia* about our television programmes. Capitalist trash—that kind of thing. No crisis!"

Staring at the President and the First Lady, Surkov recalled none other than Bliudich telling him at Sheremetyevo Airport that he had written a punchy piece on the so-called "freedom" of American television, concentrating on the popular soap-opera *Dallas*.

The First Lady, deaf to Mako's pleas and Surkov's Russian stutters, kissed O'Reilly very delicately on his cheek, and said huskily: "I love you, Tiger!"

"One—two—three!" growled the President, as Mako and Surkov stood transfixed in the centre of the office. The keys turned.

"Jesus Christ!" groaned Mako, subsiding into a chair.

O'Reilly also collapsed into his chair, covering his face with his hands. His wife sat down on his lap, and put her arms around him. Surkov sat. The young officer stood to attention.

"You say they attacked the TV programme, Mako?"

"Yes, sir."

"JR?"

"Yes, sir. It was just a small item in *Izvestia*."

"Fuck."

"You weren't to know," his wife said, smoothing his dishevelled red hair, her scrawny neck quivering, her eyelids wet. Her face sinking against his, her hair-curlers touched his cheek and he jerked away.

The quavery voice of General Vane filled the office: the screen had replaced the "Dallas" message with "NORAD Head-quarters: sound only."

"Mr President, they're hitting Houston, Boston, San Francis-co and Detroit."

"Hello, Vane. What a fuck-up."

"What do we strike, Mr President?"

"Shit! Detroit too? There goes our auto industry . . . and cousin Beth is Boston . . . What do we hit?"

"Hello, Mr President. What do we go for?"

"Moscow and Leningrad."

Surkov leapt to his feet. "No, please, Mr President! Not Moscow! Think of my little boy!"

"I suggest we have to hit Moscow and Leningrad, Mr Presi-dent," said the spectral voice.

"As I said, go for Moscow and Leningrad . . . No, wait a moment—what's that, Mr Surkov? Well, there's something to be said for backing off a little. And then, of course, they wouldn't strike at . . . They'd probably be content with New York. Vane! Just Leningrad."

"I'm glad you agree, Mr President. Moscow and Leningrad."

"Just Moscow, General Vane. I mean, just Leningrad."

"Leningrad. Very well, Mr President. Though it might be

taken as a sign of backing off. But very well. Now take my advice sir, and get your ass out of there pretty damn quick."

Surkov wept with relief. They could have the Hermitage, the Winter Palace, all of it, so long as Petya was spared.

"Now let's get our asses moving!" snapped the President. He eased the First Lady from his lap. "Mako, stop gaping! Wanda, get the medics to prepare Katie for a move, pretty damn quick . . . Mr Surkov, you can see this is where the buck stops. I'm afraid you'll have to take your chance. It's been good talking to you."

· 4 ·

SURKOV TOOK THE PAD AND PENCIL OUT OF THE GIRL'S HANDS, and pulled her down to him. Their mouths met and clung, her thighs opened and he slid into her. He kissed her small breasts, and then her fresh young lips again. It still felt good. After five days in the small hotel in southern Arizona, he still liked making love with her; and only once had he made an excuse, and slipped out for an assignation in the attic-room of the attractive, black-eyed, barefoot Mexican servant.

He had woken Imogen at five, made love to her, drunk some more of the tequila, and then he had made her take down the scenes in the Oval Office, those scenes which had come to him in the night. Her tiny, spidery shorthand had raced across the page.

She had appreciated these scenes much more than the coarse fantasies of the previous evening. As his broken English poured out, she had chuckled a lot; and occasionally, during a pause, she had made complimentary remarks in her well-bred, assured English accent.

But he was teaching her to be less well-bred in her lovemaking. He enjoyed it when she came out with soft cries, almost whimpers: cries which seemed a million miles away from her background—the equine-looking left-wing English politician-mother, whom Surkov had met and disliked; and Hampstead, in London, of which Imogen often spoke.

Imogen's mother, defeated in the elections won by the right-wing Thatcherites, had taken up a year's fellowship at Columbia University, and had brought her daughter with her, to broaden her education. She was attending an American high school, but finding the standards far below those of her Hampstead comprehensive school. So there was no problem about taking a couple of weeks off, to fly south with Surkov. She had jumped at the chance, when he had thrown out the invitation after the big New York reading. Only she would have to tell Mummy. The girl had assured him it would be perfectly all right. It would give Mummy a chance to be alone with her new husband, a Puerto Rican academic. They had got married on the afternoon of Surkov's arrival in New York—which was why Imogen had been dressed in uncomfortable elegance, so appealing to the Muscovite.

And Imogen's mother had indeed said yes—gladly. Surkov, while pleased, was also shocked at the mother's irresponsible tolerance. He would never have let Katya go off, at sixteen, with a man of fifty, especially a hooligan poet. (Well, that was, if Katya had still been in his care at that age.) He was shocked by the air of affected sisterliness between Imogen and her mother. They had even, on the edge of Surkov's hearing, discussed birth-control—whether Imogen needed to get a further supply of the Pill. It offended his deeply conservative Russian spirit.

He was annoyed at having been misled by Imogen's stylish appearance at his Kennedy press conference. She dressed, like her mother, with extreme scruffiness, wishing to minimize her good looks.

Her fashionable, liberal left-wing ideas annoyed him too. He argued with her, sometimes, in their bedroom or strolling in the desert, as though she were grown-up. She behaved as if she were grown-up, except when they were making love.

So arrogantly, so loftily, in his view, she repeated her mother's egalitarian ideas—while mentioning from time to time, as of no moment, the Hampstead mansion, the cottage in Norfolk, the *au pair* girl (but never a servant), the foreign travel, the assumption that she would go to Cambridge, like her two elder brothers, and her barrister-father, and her diplomat-grandfather. As for her school! How snobbishly proud she was that it wasn't a public— that is, a private—school, but took in everybody. Which, Surkov knew from having visited Hampstead ten years before—indeed, he had "holed up" there with English friends when he had been contemplating defection—simply meant that the pupils and their parents could enjoy an élitist education while preserving a snow-white conscience. When she mentioned particular friends, they always seemed to be sons or daughters of leading left-wing politicians, or *Guardian* journalists, or celebrated musicians and writers, etc. No wonder she and her mother believed in State education! sneered Surkov.

He thought of his father, a humble factory-worker, then a sergeant in the Red Army—then a camp-guard at Kolyma. And of his mother, a peasant's daughter. His blood boiled. What the fuck did this girl know about anything? So she regularly met Mr Foot when they walked their dogs on the Heath; so the Benns sometimes came to dinner . . . So what?

Yes, they argued violently; and he thought it served her right when, engrossed in arguing some fashionable point or other, she didn't see the tarantula scuttling across the desert path until she was almost upon it; and she had screamed and flung herself into his arms. After that, she wore shoes, not the open sandals.

Their arguments sometimes turned into a fiercer passion. And, after, Surkov turned the fierce passion into literature. He made her pick up the note-pad and add new passages to what had gone before . . . "Her eyes were clenched tight, her lips drawn back in a grimace; the muscles of her neck and shoulders stood out, as if she were in the act of hurling a javelin. . . ."

She never minded the work he made her do. She had learned shorthand as an optional extra at her exemplary school, because one day she wanted to be a journalist.

Surkov, with a groan of pleasure, slid out of her and fell back. She sighed with contentment, resting her hand on the place where she still felt him to be. The morning-blue light shone through the window, but it was not yet hot. After a few minutes Surkov stirred himself and rang for some breakfast.

While they ate their eggs and drank their coffee, they watched breakfast TV. Surkov, this morning, saw his native city, flakes of snow falling, the Kremlin leaders muffled up and saluting the passing armoury in Red Square. He studied Brezhnev's face carefully to see if it gave any sign of life. "Look at our El Cid," he growled at Imogen. "It's his corpse. They dare not tell the people until they've decided the succession."

"You're joking?"

"No, I'm serious. Or maybe it's a wax model. Like—what is it in London?—Madame Tussaud's."

He found himself, after a while, warmly defending Mrs Thatcher, about whom he knew little, except that she was a tough-minded woman and the daughter of a provincial grocer. Admittedly, she looked a little like a wax-works dummy herself, in the pictures he'd seen of her; but underneath that shell, and the cut-glass English voice, he glimpsed an unpretentious working-class—well, maybe lower middle-class—girl, who would stand no nonsense from the Hampstead Marxists and feminists. She would never have encouraged her daughter to go off with a disreputable fifty-year-old foreigner. She would never have made sure she had a sufficient supply of birth-control pills. If she had smelt that sickly odour of marijuana, she would have thrown her daughter out on to the street. Surkov fumed inwardly again about the mother's irresponsibility, wealth, connections, expensive scruffiness, dislike of privilege.

The girl put her hands on his shoulders and shook him, furious; they wrestled on the bed, she bit him, he laughed, she laughed, he fucked her again.

While she was taking a bath, he managed to put through two laborious calls to Moscow.

He felt sad, depressed, again, after the calls. Is it true what the shamans say, he wondered, that everything turns into its opposite after death? As he sat in the foaming, scented bath, and let Imogen scrub his back, he cheered up; and when he had towelled himself dry he ordered Imogen to pick up her note-pad and pencil, promising a drive in a hired car before lunch. He wanted to re-visit some of the old mining towns, ghost-towns, in the desert.

· 5 ·

FAR UNDER FLATTENED WASHINGTON, O'REILLY WAS LISTEN-
ing to General Vane on a crackly radio, and sipping coffee. Mako,
still in his red track-suit, was pacing agitatedly around the
operations-centre. Other aides were rushing about, looking pur-
poseful. "Blue" White, the famous evangelist, was kneeling,
murmuring prayers.

"Shall I freshen it up?" asked the First Lady, lifting the coffee-
pot in the Tiger's direction.

"Hello, Vane," the President was saying, "how is it going?"

"Can you hear me, Mr President?"

"Shall I freshen up your coffee, dear?"

"Hello, Vane."

"It's not going too badly, Mr President. Their last attack took
out a couple of ghost-towns in Arizona—Pearce and Tomb-
stone—but nobody got killed except a few billion tarantulas.
Frankly, I don't see any point in responding. There's not much to
go for. We'd have to start in on the less friendly Third-World
countries!" General Vane's bleak chuckle mixed with the static.
"Maybe India!"

"Do that. I'm really enjoying this. I've re-acquired a taste for it." The Tiger held out his coffee-cup and the First Lady, holding the coffee-pot in both shaking hands, gratefully obliged.

"Hello, Mr President; did you hear me?"

"Okay, Vane, I don't think Mother Teresa would appreciate that. Call a halt."

"You mean it? Okay, Mr President, if you're quite sure. You're the boss. We'll hit Calcutta and Bombay."

"I hear you, Vane."

The crackle stopped as General Vane switched off his radio. The Tiger said, "You can still make great coffee, sweetheart!" And his wife's face lit up.

Mako strode around with increasing desperation. He could see there was something wrong with the President. His keen Princeton-trained mind had worked it out that the Tiger's slowing-down brain could only respond to the last question but one: a strange condition that had simultaneously affected General Vane. There was even a term for it in the medical encyclopedia Mako had looked up: *logotarditis*. A senile condition, it could be brought on by some shock to the system (such as the injury to the President's daughter), or even by violent atmospheric conditions (the thunderstorm at NORAD). Cormorant, the White House doctor, would have diagnosed it more quickly, probably; and then he, Mako, could have stepped in. But the doctor had been screwing his mistress in Charlottesville when the unreal crisis had blown up, and he had got caught in the crazy exodus of Washingtonians when trying to drive back. He was now, presumably, no more.

Without medical authorization, it was against all the values Mako held dear to incite a mutiny against the Tiger. Especially since the President gave every appearance of firm command. The obsessional way in which he grated two ball-bearings in his hand could scarcely be regarded as evidence of mental derangement; and since General Vane's responses, equally confused, were muddling up the Tiger's confusion, no one else in the team appeared to have noticed anything untoward.

After the Soviets had nuked Alice Springs, and Vane informed them that every single American missile and bomb had been employed or destroyed by the enemy, O'Reilly embraced his wife, shook hands with everyone else, and ordered them into the underground swimming-pool. The O'Reillys, holding hands, jumped in first. In the water they all—the evangelist included—changed into lithe, twisting shapes.

The Tiger nudged with his nose a button on the pool-side; with a rumble, the roof parted, creating an aperture. One after one the great lithe shapes shot out vertically, their jagged-toothed jaws open, straight up through the silo.

They all aimed for small towns or villages, in Africa, Asia, South America, chosen for them by the Tiger, out of the *Reader's Digest* atlas. In mid-flight White, the evangelist, made a self-correction and a few minutes later immolated himself at Bethlehem. Thirty-six of the thirty-eight ICBMs landed in the correct place. The remaining missile, the First Lady, wobbled, went awry, and came down on the site of an ancient Roman town close to an erupting volcano, a flattened coastal city. . . .

"*L'ultimo giorno di Pompeii* . . ." Surkov said, chuckling, stubbing out his cigarette.

Imogen waited, cross-legged on the bed, her pencil poised.

"That's it," said Surkov. "Thank you. We can go now."

Putting aside the note-pad and pencil, the girl held out her arms towards him. "When you've kissed me," she said, "and told me you love me."

"Okay. I love you. But just remember I'm old enough to be your father. I'm ten years *older* than your father."

"Daddy doesn't make love like you do."

"I hope that's your English sense of humour."

"Of course, Victor."

· 6 ·

Towards mid-winter, much later than he had antici-pated, Surkov flew north east, in a homewards direction; but stopped off at Helsinki. Then he headed north, in a hired car, along difficult roads. He found himself in the desolation of northern Finland, at the darkest time of the year, just before the winter solstice. He was in a log house, lost in snow and pines and spruce, at the edge of a frozen lake. He was alone in this wilderness with one old woman.

She was a shamaness. Surkov's friend, Rozanov, had sung her praises.

Although Svetlana, the shamaness, had a round, wrinkled, Mongolian face, she was a cultivated woman. She had been born, seventy years ago, in the extreme north east of Siberia, close to the Bering Straits. Her remote ancestor had been the Great Shaman, so strong he had wrestled with God and almost won. Her father, though weak by comparison, had still been a good shaman. Her own powers, born out of privation, and physical and mental illness, were weaker still, she told Surkov. The Russian Revolution had hardly touched her region, Chukotka, until the '30s. Contact with the American Eskimos, and with English language and habits, was much closer than with Russians. Every winter, in her youth, she and all the Chukchee would camp for several days on the ice off the Diomede Islands with the Eskimos from across the Strait.

"In those days of camping," she told Surkov, "there was much coming and going between tents. I fell in love with someone from the other side. The next winter, I left my parents, and went across the ice with my lover. I married him. We were happy, but there were no children. Then one day my husband drowned. I returned across the ice to my parents, who by now were old. The Soviets came. They broke up the old life, but I learned to read. I developed a hunger for learning. I had the chance to leave Chukotka, and study at Leningrad University. I got a degree in philology. It was a new world for me, but I couldn't see how it fitted in with being a shamaness. I became two people, really. In 1960, I returned to Chukotka to be a teacher, to try to pass on what I had learned, both from the university in Leningrad and from my father. He was by now dead, as was my mother. But I wasn't allowed to pass on the old truths. I became so unhappy I would have crossed the ice again, only you could no longer cross. The Americans had sealed up that little chink in the iron curtain. At least, that was what we were told. As a shaman, if only a very poor one by now, I could still occasionally visit the land of the dead; yet I could not visit one half of the world we live in. This began to torment me. I don't like to think there is anywhere I may not go. I managed to get a permit to live in Leningrad again, and there I went out of my way to meet someone from the West, a French philologist, who was kind enough to marry me, simply so that I could get out. After a long time I was permitted to leave and join him in France. We got an immediate divorce. I began to hunger for cold and snow and white nights. So I moved here, to Finland.

"But now I am old, and I don't like the cold so much. . . ."

That was obvious to Surkov. Clad in heavily stained reindeer-skin trousers and two sweaters, she sat hunched over a fierce stove, which she fed constantly with wood. Surkov would strip to his singlet, yet still the sweat rolled off him. The room, murkily lit by an oil-lamp, was filled with the fumes of her strong cigarettes. Surkov, smoking his way through duty-free Kents, was for the first time in his life troubled by cigarette-fumes. He began to understand how Rozanov had been cured. She would not allow the windows to be opened even an inch. Though the wind howled in the darkness outside, not a tremor of draught crept in by way of the windows or double doors. As hour succeeded hour in the airless, acrid atmosphere, Surkov believed he would pass out. Svetlana would not hear of their going outside; the cold would kill them, she said.

He drank water, copiously. She had not offered him any alcohol. In the three days since his arrival, she had given him no food except yoghourt, bread and cheese. She herself ate hardly anything.

Though interesting enough to talk to, Svetlana was not an attractive figure. She was short and dumpy; her bosom flopped low in the old moth-eaten sweaters; she had thick lips, a flattened nose, horn-rimmed spectacles as round as her face; sparse grey hair, cut raggedly short. What a companion, Surkov thought, for the darkest days of the year! What a successor to Imogen!

Often he longed to escape from the over-heated downstairs room to his cool—even freezing—bedroom. But she would not hear of his going to his bedroom, except to sleep. It was much too cold to sit in, she insisted. He could only escape when it was night, to sleep. But, where darkness ruled all but a grey hour or so, when was night? Night was when the old woman announced its presence, by getting up from her chair, stretching, and declaring it was time to sleep. How grateful he was to escape to his bitter room! He could not sleep, however. He had always been able to sleep only at night, and he could not come to terms with this all-powerful night. He listened to the wind, which had risen as the deep night had fallen. Dreadful, devilish gusts. He thought of the forest-god Tapio. Sibelius had brought Finland to him, long before he had crossed the gulf. Surkov had not listened to *Tapio* for many years, but he could still hear its sinister harmonies; there, with the god himself just outside the double window, and all around him.

Snowy images of Finland had filtered through in his childhood, he told Svetlana. His father had fought in the Finnish campaign, and the newspapers and wireless had been full of heroic victories, or courageous strategic withdrawals, by the Red Army . . . Surkov croaked an ironic laugh, and then said, "I should like to meet my father. To ask him why he served in the Gulag, and why some *zeks* knifed him. To see if there was any good in him. Can you fix it?"

"I'll try."

They ventured at last out of doors. A grey dawn-dusk glimmered above the tall, black, thickly-crowded trees. Snow lay underfoot, but not yet a deep fall. The wind had died down. Surkov felt exhilarated by the cold, but Svetlana's teeth chattered.

Because of the snowfall, the door of her house had been hard to open; and as they trudged between the tree-trunks, over the snow, she told him the shamanic word in her native Chukchee for "opening a door with difficulty." There were, she said, many hundreds of verbs for the act of opening a door. There was a word for opening the door of a room where your lover waited for you eagerly; a word for the same act when he or she was reluctant; for entering a sick-room; entering a room which held a corpse—and this verb varied in its suffix according to whether it was the corpse of a stranger, or friend, or lover, or parent—and whether you loved the friend or lover or parent, etc., very much or hardly at all. The shamanic language was much richer than the ordinary language. Surkov asked, "Is there a word for opening a door hesitantly, for fear of intruding on someone, yet with curiosity?"

Svetlana replied, "Of course," and spoke a word with many vowels, sounding not unlike *kiantijärvi*, the name of the frozen lake which they were skirting.

A howl, far off, made Surkov's flesh creep. "Was that a wolf?"

"Yes," she said. "We still have a few, thank God."

"Are there many words," he asked, "in your shamanic language, for the act of making love?"

"Oh, there are three or four thousand. I have never counted."

"Tell me some of them."

She spoke several words, polysyllabic and many-vowelled, which all sounded beautiful and desirable to the Russian. "There are two basic distinctions," the old woman said, "apart from the distinction of gender. It depends whether your lover is human or a spirit. When my spirit-husband comes to me, he can make love to me in innumerable ways, as could my earthly husband when he was alive. With complete passion, with his mind on a seal-hunt, dreaming of your neighbour's wife, dreaming that you are dreaming of your neighbour's husband . . . tenderly, cruelly, cruelly when you wish him to be cruel, cruelly when you would like him to be tender . . . Beyond number."

"You have a spirit-husband, Svetlana?"

"Yes. He is very jealous. I think he drowned my earthly husband. I can understand it, I have forgiven him. Sometimes, thinking of it, it increases our passion."

When they returned to the house, Svetlana prepared a *séance*. She fetched a drum from her bedroom; the skin was reindeer. The drum, which she called her canoe, would carry her to the underworld and back. She let the fire in the stove dim and go out. She dowsed the lamp. They were in complete darkness except for the flickering of a single candle. The room cooled rapidly, and soon Surkov had to put on his coat, and then his overcoat and gloves. The old woman began to shake her drum and move it about, which she explained as catching the spirits who would help her. She took from a cupboard a bottle of vodka, and sprinkled the liquor on the drum-skin. Surkov stared enviously at the drum-skin. In her harsh, masculine voice, Svetlana started to sing, wordlessly; her song blended with the wind outside.

She stopped singing. "Are you ready?" she asked. Shivering with cold and not a little fear, Surkov said, "Yes." Sitting cross-legged on the floor, the drum and stick beside her, the shamaness pulled off her baggy sweater, then the tighter sweater underneath. In the faint light, her scrawny, low-hanging breasts appeared. She stubbed out a cigarette and placed a wood pipe in her mouth. Already filled with some sort of villainous tobacco, the pipe belched thick smoke as soon as she struck a match and held it to the bowl. Surkov was caught by a strangling coughing-fit; the shamaness went on puffing serenely. Then, when her guest had recovered, she took up the drumstick and beat the drum. She swayed her body. She sang again. She told him later that she never knew what she was going to sing. Surkov lost himself in the endless singing and drumming and smoke-belching. The windows lightened, and again grew black. Then she started to cry out and to jerk her head around. Surkov sat rigidly, shaking; he heard whispered voices coming from the corners of the room, but none that he recognized. He heard the whinny of a horse, a wolf-cry, from inside the room. He saw an elegant modern Finnish coffee-table rise several inches from the carpet, glide towards the window, then settle gently. A picture fell from the wall, smashing the glass. Svetlana's singing changed to a falsetto. Dropping the drum, she leapt to her feet like a young girl, and whirled around in a dance. Suddenly she crashed to the floor, and lay motionless. Everything became silent: even the wind in the trees outside dropped.

Surkov heard a sound like the crashing of some large animal through undergrowth; it got louder and louder; the room shook; the animal seemed to be in the room, he heard its hoarse breaths.

He saw grey antlers hover above Svetlana; she writhed; her spine came off the floor. She collapsed, and was again still. The hoarse breathing stopped; again Surkov heard the sound of crashing through undergrowth, but this time it died away into silence.

An hour or so went by, during which she did not move. And Surkov, from sheer fright, could not move. At last he forced himself to get up and walk across to her. He knelt beside her. She did not appear to be breathing. He felt for her pulse, but there was none. She had told him not to worry. She would be on her journey in the underworld; and perhaps she would meet people whom he loved, such as his mother. And perhaps, his father.

He returned to his chair, and waited in the silence.

The wind rose and gusted around the log-house. The trees sighed and wailed for their dead comrades and lovers. Svetlana stirred, opened her eyes, and raised herself on an elbow. She ran her left hand across her belly and breasts, and stared down, as if searching for something. She sat up and rubbed her eyes. She grasped the chair-arm and pulled herself up to sit in the chair. She reached down, fumbling; found her glasses, which she put back on, and her pipe. She puffed it; it had gone out. She laid it on the dead stove. She picked up one of the discarded sweaters and pulled it on over her head. The second, baggy sweater followed. Only then did she start to shiver and complain—to herself rather than to Surkov—that she was cold.

Turning to her guest, she said in her normal deep voice, "Now I will tell you what I saw in the land of the dead. I followed the shore of the lake till I came to a river. I crossed it by a ford, then followed the river bank. I had to pick my way through the cervical bones of dead shamans. It was very hot weather; I became very tired. I found a birch-wood and I lay down to rest. Then my spirit-husband came along and woke me up. I was happy to see him. He was in the form of a stag. He fucked me cruelly but wishing to be tender. He left me, I got up and walked on. I followed a path through the wood. I came to a clearing where there were people camping. They had lit a fire on which they were roasting a fox. They gathered around me, curious. I found they were people who had died by violence, so that they were not sure if they were dead. They were all naked. There was a woman who gave me a message for your friend Rozanov. Look, I carry the marks of her death on my body . . ." She took hold of her sweaters, and pulled them up over her breasts. He saw scar marks all over her skin. "I asked after your father but they knew nothing of him." The shamaness pulled down her sweaters. "On my way back I met Rozanov. I passed on the message. His spirit has left his body, he is asleep, between Gorky and Moscow. He is in that ghost-land, on the borders between life and death, not unlike Karelia, stolen from the Finns."

The old woman yawned, and rubbed her eyes. "I'll tell you about the rest tomorrow," she said. "I'm feeling tired. Today is the longest darkness. I have a gift for you. A spirit-wife. She will come to you at midnight. Go to bed now."

Surkov went up to his room, undressed by candlelight, and got into bed. He blew out the candle. The sheets were icy; he shivered for a long time. He was naked except for his wristwatch. He saw the luminous hands creep around towards midnight. When the hands were together, and erect, his door opened. A beautiful, tall, statuesque negress stood at the foot of his bed. Though Surkov had never known any negresses, he thought he recognized her, vaguely. It was hard to separate the young spirit-woman from the surrounding darkness. He thought the young woman was naked, but then he heard the rustle of a dress being removed. She came close; she towered above him. He did not feel frightened. He saw in the blackness only the whites of her eyes—and what seemed to be reflections of them further down, towards the top of her naked, ebony thighs. He brought his arm out from under the blankets, and moved his hand slowly to touch those inferior eyes. His delicate fingers were careful not to hurt them; but he found them cold, metallic; he realized she was not naked but still wearing stockings, a suspender-belt, and—his fingers wandering over her soft smooth flesh—pants. The black underclothes and stockings melted into her black skin. He felt his hand being taken gently by hers, and in a moment the young negress was under the bedclothes with him; he was breathing in her warm sweet breath. He looked now into her eyes, and saw the glimmer of her teeth as she smiled. Her features emerged from the blackness, and with a shock he recognized Masha, his first wife. "Masha! You! My darling!" he gasped. "Oh, I didn't know you had died!"

"I died to you a long time ago, Victor," she murmured, in that familiar, soft, beloved voice. "And afterwards a drunken driver completed my death. But don't worry, my darling, I have gone on loving you, and of course I have stayed young. I have taken care of you. It's not been easy, because you seem to be intent on messing up your life."

Surkov began to weep. He gulped his tears, like a small child—while Masha hushed him and soothed him in her arms. His sobs gradually died away; they kissed; he felt that sweet, cheap, tacky lipstick, and warm wet tongue, of those dances at the University, in the last year of the Green Frog; trembling, he pulled a shoulder-strap over her shoulder, hooked his hand into the cup of her brassiere, and released her plump breast; her nipple grew erect to his wondering lips, and her fingers stroked his hair, his nape. He ran his hand down over her belt, under the tight elastic of her pants, to the pubic hair, to the wetness underneath; felt, with a trembling joy, her flesh yield to his fingers. Tears sprang to his eyes again; he murmured, to the breasts his lips kissed gently all round, "Oh my love! No one . . . ever . . ." He could feel her breaths coming more quickly, her heartbeat quickening.

(Victor broke off with an exclamation of pain: Imogen had dropped her pencil and dug her fingers into his groin; she swooped to his chest, clamped her teeth on his left nipple. Then, as Surkov flecked blood from

his chest and cupped his testicles, rocking in pain, she said, "I won't take down any more! You can fucking well write up your fucks yourself!"

"Bitch!" he said, rocking, wincing.

"I don't mind you going home to your wife and child," said the English girl. "But this is too much. Are you really going to Finland? Don't go! Stay here with me, please! Until Christmas. . . ."

Surkov grabbed his cigarettes, and lit one angrily. "I'll go whenever and wherever I like." He stared towards the window. The harsh blue sky began to bore him. "I may leave the day after tomorrow, in fact. I may fly to Hamburg, and then take a boat from there to Helsinki. I don't know." The English girl, sitting up in the bed, had buried her face between her clasped knees. Surkov stroked her sun-peeled arm. "Well, maybe I'll stay another week," he said. She turned her face towards him, brightening. "But only if you don't argue," he added, "and take down what I write."

"I promise." She picked up her pencil and note-pad. She leaned towards him, kissed him. "Go on, please. I'm sorry. Fuck your beautiful ex wife, I don't mind."

"It's too late," he said sadly. "She's gone. She's probably cooking supper for a nice husband and a strapping son in Omsk or Vladivostok. I hope so.")

After his spirit-wife had gone, Surkov could not sleep, but went on with his series of travelogues for *Oktyabr*. The original title, *New York—Mexico—Havana*, had become *New York—Arizona—Hamburg*. Sitting up in bed, his dressing-gown wrapped tightly round him, the candle guttering, he scribbled:

> One midnight, off the Reeperbahn's
> Gaudy blue-cinemas and dives,
> I saw, behind each lit shop-front,
> A bourgeois parlour for neat lives;
> A small interior by Rembrandt;
> Where women, resting on divans,

Engaged in placid, homely tasks,
Looked out at the dark *cul de sac*
And passing stranger, through the glass.
Half nude, in negligés or basques,
Some negligently watched me pass,
Some negligently called me back.

A hired car, next day, and an urge
Part homesickness and part desire
To wander where two worlds converge,
Drove me into the borderland
Where ever-vigilant sentries stand
Guard over stillness and barbed wire.

Diverting from the *autobahn*
For country roads as lost as I;
Villages greyer than the sky,
Unrepaired tracks, I felt the same
Shiver of eagerness and shame
As by the garish Reeperbahn—

A shameful prickling at my nape.
By fields of golden rape, a gate
Marked *Halt!* . . . the road resuming, straight
Ahead; a watch-tower . . . But between,
The way was overgrown with green
Mounds and deep gullies. No escape.

Yet spontaneity and flight
Flourished above the sombre hollows;
Between the true and the false road
Birds sang in complete freedom; swallows
Criss-crossed the border, and in bright
Invisible writing traced a code.

When he had finished the poem, Surkov. . . .

Nudged awake by his neighbour, Sergei Rozanov found to his annoyance that the plane had still not taken off from Gorky, but for some reason was still taxiing slowly down the runway. Then people started unfastening seatbelts, standing up, stretching; and he realized they had landed at Sheremetyevo. The daylight world, dreary Moscow, claimed him. The closeness of his meeting with Sonia came over Rozanov; *had* she and Alexei Kolasky . . . ? His bowels loosened at the thought of her probable infidelity. He was no more aware of the life he had created during his sleep than I, Corinna Riznich, am conscious of the penguin, waddling on Scott Island, directly under my feet. . . .

T·H·R·E·E

Silk-pyjama'd, sleepless, a glossy magazine propped on his updrawn
thighs, Coningsby read, at three in the morning without a lamp. . . .

· I ·

HARK! CRY UPON CRY COMES RINGING UP THE VAULTED PATH.
It is Foulata's voice!

"*Oh, Bougwan! help! help! the rock falls!*"

"Leave go, girl!" Then—

"*Help! help! she has stabbed me!*"

By now we are running down the passage, and this is what the
light from the lamp falls on. The door of rock is slowly closing
down; it is not three feet from the floor. Near it struggle Foulata
and Gagool. The red blood of the former runs to her knee, but
still the brave girl holds the old witch, who fights like a wild cat.
Ah! she is free! Foulata falls, and Gagool throws herself on the
ground to twist herself like a snake through the crack of the
closing stone. She is under—ah, God! too late! too late. The stone
nips her, and she yells in agony. Down, down it comes, all the
thirty tons of it, slowly pressing her old body against the rock
below. Shriek upon shriek, such as we never heard, then a long
sickening *crunch*, and the door was shut just as we, rushing down
the passage, hurled ourselves against it.

It was all done in four seconds.

Then we turned to Foulata. The poor girl was stabbed in the body and could not, I saw, live long.

"Ah! Bougwan, I die!" gasped the beautiful creature. "She crept out—Gagool; I did not see her, I was faint—and the door began to fall; then she came back, and was looking up the path—and I saw her come in through the slowly falling door, and caught her and held her, and she stabbed me, and *I die*, Bougwan."

"Poor girl! poor girl!" Good cried; and then, as he could do nothing else, he fell to kissing her.

"Bougwan," she said, after a pause, "is Macumazahn there? It grows so dark, I cannot see."

"Here I am, Foulata."

"Macumazahn, be my tongue for a moment, I pray thee, for Bougwan cannot understand me, and before I go into the darkness—I would speak a word."

"Say on, Foulata, I will render it."

"Say to my lord, Bougwan, that—I love him, and that I am glad to die because I know that he cannot cumber his life with such as me, for the sun cannot mate with the darkness, nor the white with the black.

"Say that at times I have felt as though there were a bird in my bosom, which would one day fly hence and sing elsewhere. Even now, though I cannot lift my hand, and my brain grows cold, I do not feel as though my heart were dying; it is so full of love that could live a thousand years, and yet be young. Say that if I live again, mayhap I shall see him in the stars, and that—I will search them all, though perchance I should there still be black and he would—still be white. Say—nay, Macumazahn, say no more, save that I love—Oh, hold me closer, Bougwan, I cannot feel thine arms—*Oh! oh!*"

"She is dead—she is dead!" said Good, rising in grief, the tears running down his honest face.

"You need not let that trouble you, old fellow," said Sir Henry.

"Eh!" said Good; "what do you mean?"

"I mean, that you can screw her now; at least while she is still warm. And by the time she is cold, you will be in a position to join her. *Man, don't you see that we are buried alive?*"

· 2 ·

IN MY CHILDHOOD I READ AND RE-READ *KING SOLOMON'S Mines*, never failing to be enchanted by the struggle across the burning desert, the ascent to the icy snow-capped peaks of Sheba's Breasts, from which the travellers saw the lush king- dom of Solomon. I trembled as the black warriors, the regiment of the Greys, drew up in their ranks for the battle in which they must die. I shuddered at old Gagool, the witch. I rejoiced when the lunar eclipse robbed her of her prey; I yearned, like honest Good, stout and monocled, to take the comely black girl, Foulata, in my arms.

But above all, Sheba's Breasts cast a spell on me. The twin cones, capped with snow, shimmered beyond the desert. There was a drawing of them in the book my parents bought for me. Those mountains were probably the first breasts I ever saw: for my mother had not breastfed me. At ten or eleven, they were the first premonition of desire.

When, two years after my sister's departure for Australia with her husband, my parents decided we would join them, a part of my excitement was in following my favourite writers, Haggard and Henty, south, into the unknown. It was in '49. My father was forty-nine. I am forty-nine as I write this.

I think probably my father, besides hungering to see my sister, felt it was almost too late to leave a dead-end job. A fine plasterer who took great pride in his work, he had suffered a recent disappointment. From having been foreman at a small factory making prefab houses, he had been promoted to works manager. He had a little office, and a secretary; and he wore a suit instead of overalls. Then the owners evidently decided that they'd made a mistake in appointing a working-class manager, and brought in someone else. Father went back to his foreman's job on the shop-floor—only now they told the workers he was production manager. They weren't fooled: he wore overalls again. I can remember one of the bosses showing my mother and me over an oil-tanker, in Falmouth harbour; and explaining to my mother in a soft voice how the Plymouth firm they were merging with had insisted on having their own works manager. Neither my mother nor I was interested in the oil-tanker; and we didn't enjoy the lunch. I didn't fully take it in at the time, but I guess my father was humiliated. I don't know if he would have made a good manager. He was intelligent but not educated. He was also gentle and honest. He read, when he came home tired out at night, only the *News Chronicle* and the *National Geographic Magazine*, which came every month from America. It brought back his twenties, the Californian idyll.

My mother, also, kept recalling that idyll. He had come back for her after four years, and they spent their honeymoon on the Atlantic. She was seasick for five days out of six. They returned after six years, because of the depression, and because his youngest brother, Donald, had been killed in a plane-crash soon after joining the Air Corps. My sister, on the ship, told a waiter: "It's not tomatoes, it's tomaytoes."

"Beverly," the small bungalow my father built soon after I was born, had a "breakfast-nook" and a "cooler." I remember a big spider—it must have been a house-spider—crossing our drawing-room carpet, between the piano and my pouffe, while my father was talking very seriously with some friends who had dropped in. They were discussing whether there would be a war. I jumped up, unnoticed by them, and planted my sandal on the spider. I peeled it off and sat down again. My mother must have been making tea and sandwiches in the kitchen. When I went out to the porch with my father, to see the friends off, I held his hand—it is my first memory of his touch—and gazed up at the starry sky—it is my first memory of stars—and asked him, "Is it peace or war, Daddy?" "Peace," he said quietly, and I felt comforted.

Some time during the War, my teacher announced that they wanted books to send to the soldiers. If you brought one, you would be given a lance corporal's badge; if two, a corporal's: and so on up to about twenty, when you would be made a general and you would be given two free tickets for the Gem. There were no books in our house except mine; but when I told my father, he went to the hall cupboard and took out all his old *Geographicals*. There were about a hundred of them. He looked sad as he gave them to me. My school didn't send them to the troops, but kept them. I got a field-marshal's badge, and the two tickets for the Gem. But the Gem was showing *Tarzan* that week, which neither my father nor I wanted to see. We went to the Regal instead, as we usually did, and saw a Bette Davis melodrama. The manager let us use the free tickets.

A stray bomb crumped in a field behind our house, throwing my mother on to her hands and knees in the passage, her bloomered bottom in the air. But mostly the War was distant: the searchlights turning silently, glamorously; the glow from Plymouth, sixty miles to the east; and once, the night sky like a late sunset, when the oil dumps at Swanpool, near Falmouth, were hit.

My sister dolled up every night to go to the Redruth Drill Hall for a dance, or to the Regal. Her hair rivalled the crimson blaze over Swanpool. We hardly saw her. My father would try to give her a hug and a kiss in her tiny bedroom next to mine, but she would fight him off, and my mother would tell her off for being cold. One night, driving home in father's work van, we saw Lois arm-in-arm with a short and stocky youth in an Australian Air Force uniform. My father was angry with her. It is almost the only time I remember him angry. She was much too young. The young Australian flight-sergeant dated her for nine evenings, and then they wrote to each other. But as they wrote, American servicemen were visiting the house; I was given chewing-gum, a baseball bat and ball, and a German helmet I was so proud of I wore it in bed.

There was a Texan major, whom Lois loved and I liked. My parents liked him too—as they liked all Americans—but he was too craggy-faced, too possibly worldly. They urged on Lois the baby-faced, blue-eyed Australian boy whose serious, religious letters impressed them. They became engaged. She worried, though, because the craggy Texan was more romantic than the Australian—in her memory of him.

When, a year after the end of the War, Ray sailed from Melbourne to claim his war-bride, he suffered his own doubts, stuck in the Indian Ocean because of engine-failure. On the train from Liverpool, he fainted in the crush. He was supposed to change trains at Truro, and be met by "Bluey" at Redruth; but my sister was at Truro station, and he saw a familiar camel-coat rushing towards him along the platform. He knew at once it was going to be all right, and so did she. I can remember a lot of laughing and giggling at "Beverly;" and after we'd gone to bed, Lois and Ray danced to the band-music from the American Forces Network, and Bluey, slipping off her high heels, gazed adoringly straight into his blue eyes.

The next day, a Sunday, we took him to Carnkie, the family

home. The tiny, bleak mining village had lost its mines; each side of its single road of terraced granite cottages the crumbling relics of engine-houses and mine-stacks stood, ghostly on moonlit nights; and on up the lower slopes of granite-strewn Carn Brea and Bassett Carn. The village nestled between the carns, as the locket-pictures of dead World War One sweethearts nestled in the droke of my two spinster-aunts' bosoms. We went to Carnkie every Sunday, to have tea with my father's family, to go to the Methodist chapel, then to sing around the piano. My spinster-aunts, and a widowed uncle and his son, lived in a detached Victorian house above the terrace, below the chapel: they were, in a way, the working-class aristocrats of the village. I liked my relatives at Carnkie. They were gentle, kind, humorous. They welcomed Ray warmly, of course, that Sunday in 1946; and there were winks and banter when he and Bluey decided they would not go to chapel, but stay in and play "ping-pong."

Some of this I remember, some I had to learn from Ray's diaries, which my sister sent to me after his death, in middle age, from a heart-attack.

I learned from the diaries that on the summer night before his wedding, when he had walked up to Carnkie in order to avoid the bad luck of seeing his bride before the ceremony, he was overcome by a feeling of unreality. He couldn't feel his feet touching the ground. And when it came to the vows, I saw him half keel over at Lois's side, and one of my uncles had to steady him by murmuring gruffly, "Ray . . ." In Torquay, that first night, he read a little, switched out the light and turned on his side away from Lois, to sleep. He was being considerate. Later, they chuckled a lot about it.

In his diaries I am mentioned only twice: once when they had to take me to Penzance, by train, to see a cricket match; and once, just before they left, when deep snow covered our garden and he helped me to build a snowman. I remember the snowman, his pipe and scarf. It was an amazing January, an amazing snowfall.

My father had still struggled off to work. That had astonished my brother-in-law. My mother, bringing them in their breakfast-tray, had looked anxious.

The snow was still around when the taxi came one morning to take Lois and Ray to the station. We waved from the drawing-room. My sister, full of excited anticipation previously, burst into racking sobs as the taxi drew away from "Beverly;" and for the next two years she scarcely stopped weeping. It wasn't ending like a Hollywood film.

In a poem I wrote some time ago I confused the snows of '47 with the snowless winter of '49, when we prepared to follow my sister. I was as confused then as I am now. My loyalties were muddled. I didn't know which was my country. I had supported England in the War, of course, but now that it was over I liked to see them beaten on the cricket field. I'd probably been the only boy in England to cheer when Don Bradman hit a big score, or Lindwall's thunderbolts demolished our batting, in the Australian triumphs of 1948. Partly because Cornwall juts out into the Atlantic, partly because of our "cooler" and "breakfast-nook," America seemed closer than London. On the other hand, because of my father's Labour beliefs, which I shared, Stalin's Moscow also seemed close. With shining eyes, my father would quote Sir Stafford Cripps, speaking on the BBC after a visit to the Soviet Union: "I said to my guide, 'These people look as if they own the streets;' he replied, 'They do!' "

As my parents and I prepared towards the sailing date—my fourteenth birthday—I looked forward to the extra, long, Christmas holidays: four weeks at sea, then a week or two in Melbourne before they found me a school. I relished the thought of summer. "Beverly" was sold; our neighbours took some of our furniture, and also my cat Ginger. It was only when I saw Ginger sitting uneasily on the familiar sofa in an unfamiliar house, and gazing at me wonderingly, that the first tears prickled in my throat. A taxi took us to Carnkie, where we would spend our last night before taking a train to Southampton. I hadn't slept in that house since infancy. A drizzly wind rattled the window. I grieved. In the house where I had been born, I already felt homesick.

· 3 ·

VENTVÖGEL WAS LIFTING HIS SNUB NOSE, AND SNIFFING THE hot air for all the world like an old Impala ram who scents danger. Presently he spoke again.

"I *smell* water," he said.

Then we felt quite jubilant, for we knew what a wonderful instinct these wild-bred men possess.

Just at that moment the sun came up gloriously, and revealed so grand a sight to our astonished eyes that for a moment or two we even forgot our thirst.

For there, not more than forty or fifty miles from us, glittering like silver in the early rays of the morning sun, were Sheba's Breasts; and stretching away for hundreds of miles on each side of them was the great Suliman Berg. Now that I, sitting here, attempt to describe the extraordinary grandeur and beauty of that sight language seems to fail me. I am impotent even before its memory. There, straight before us, were two enormous mountains, the like of which are not, I believe, to be seen in Africa, if, indeed, there are any other such in the world, measuring each at least fifteen thousand feet in height, standing not more than a dozen miles apart, connected by a precipitous cliff of rock, and towering up in awful white solemnity straight into the sky. These mountains standing thus, like the pillars of a gigantic gateway, are shaped exactly like a woman's breasts. Their bases swelled gently up from the plain, looking, at that distance, perfectly round and smooth; and on the top of each was a vast round hillock covered with snow, exactly corresponding to the nipple on the female breast. The stretch of cliff which connected them appeared to be some thousand feet in height, and perfectly precipitous, and on each side of them, as far as the eye could reach, extended similar lines of cliff, broken only here and there by flat table-topped mountains, something like the world-famed one at Cape Town; a formation, by the way, very common in Africa.

To describe the grandeur of the whole view is beyond my powers. There was something so inexpressibly solemn and over-powering about those huge volcanoes—for doubtless they are extinct volcanoes—that it fairly took our breath away. For a while the morning lights played upon the snow and the brown and swelling masses beneath, and then, as though to veil the majestic sight from our curious eyes, strange mists and clouds gathered and increased around them, till presently we could only trace their pure and gigantic outline swelling ghost-like through the fleecy envelope. Indeed, as we afterwards discovered, they were normally wrapped in this curious gauzy mist, which doubt-less accounted for one not having made them out more clearly before.

The mountains had scarcely vanished into cloud-clad privacy before our thirst—literally a burning question—reasserted itself.

It was all very well for Ventvögel to say he smelt water, but look which way we would we could see no signs of it. So far as the eye could reach there was nothing but arid sweltering sand and karoo scrub. We walked round the hillock and gazed about anxiously on the other side, but it was the same story, not a drop of water was to be seen; there was no indication of a pan, a pool, or a spring.

"You stupid bastard," I said angrily, to Ventvögel; "there is no water."

But still he lifted his ugly snub nose and sniffed.

"I smell it, Baas," (master), he answered; "It is somewhere in the air."

"Yes," I said, "no doubt it is in the clouds, and about two months hence it will fall and wash our bones."

Sir Henry stroked his yellow beard thoughtfully. "Perhaps it is on the top of the hill," he suggested.

"Bollocks," said Good. "Whoever heard of water being found on the top of a hill!"

"Let us go and look," I put in, and hopelessly enough we scrambled up the sandy sides of the hillock, Umbopa leading. Presently he stopped as though he was petrified.

"Nanzia manzie!" (here is water), he cried with a loud voice.

· 4 ·

GREY DUNES OF OCEAN. MY BODY AND SOUL STAGGERING, above an awful emptiness. Seasickness, homesickness; Mulliga-tawny soup and vomit. I gradually got my sea-legs, but my soul never lost its seasickness. In the midst of taking a bath, as my mother came in with fresh underwear for me to put on, I burst into tears. I was weeping for our cat. It would be missing us, missing his home next-door, and it wouldn't understand. You couldn't explain to a pet; you couldn't send it letters. It would simply, I was sure, be feeling lost and grief-stricken. So I wept in the bath, and mother tried to cheer me up.

Small boats clustering around us at Malta, Port Said. The glow of fresh fruit; yellows, oranges; the shouts of barter; baskets hauled up on lines, and coins passed down. Sun. Water's dazzle. Natives leaning on hoes, watching us, as we nosed through the Suez Canal. Aden; broiled under the arid red rock. The cabin, beneath the water-line—father and I shared it with six men—airless, breathless. The immense glaze of the Indian Ocean. Dolphins leaping. Ice-cream on deck at mid-morning. Ping-pong in the games-room. At night, we slept on the boat-deck, to breathe. The sea alive with phosphorescence; the sky held more stars than darkness, and they were brilliant and new.

To my homesickness was added another emotional turbulence, so intense I hardly knew if it was delight or sorrow. In the tiny library below the games-room there were no children's books: I was forced to read some adult books. And one day, somewhere in the middle of the Indian Ocean, I stumbled on a shy young woman who allowed a man to pull the cord of her dressing-gown, and her breasts tumbled out to his hands. Her breasts, shapely and blushed with pink, spilled out of the dressing-gown; he reached for them. She smiled. The shy young woman smiled, and laughed, and was at ease with him. And whatever *nothing* was between her thighs—there where my hair was also growing—lay open to him, revealed. As her breasts spilled out, I felt a surge at my groin: a heavy, thick sweet, aching pressure against my shorts. My shorts were long, but it felt as if my penis would be visible, emerging from a leg of the shorts, if anyone should come into the library. It felt as if my cock was straining to get up to the dazzling sun, the brilliant stars.

Sex, in our house—for all its healthy laughter, jokes, music—

had been an unknown continent, like Australia on early maps. Not long before our voyage, my parents had gone out one evening, leaving a visiting American uncle, a Methodist preacher, to tell me the facts of life. He had drawn diagrams of circles and trajectories, but it had been abstract and rather disgusting. I didn't really believe it when my uncle told me my penis would stiffen, and the white stuff was capable of jetting right across the room.

We spent a day in Ceylon, where my father, homesick also, announced that we would return home at the end of two years. We would have to stay two years, or repay the Australian government for our free passages. The news was like a breath of English air to me, in airless Colombo. My father never drank, but Colombo was so hot he had a glass of lemonade shandy. We took a taxi to Kandy, which was cooler. We looked at a Buddhist temple.

The heat grew still more intense. Several of the passengers didn't mind being dowsed in water to mark the crossing of the equator. By night, the Southern Cross was ablaze. My parents sang "Wanting You" and "We'll Gather Lilacs" in the ship's concert. I can see them now, half turned to each other: my father's adam's apple above the brown suit which didn't quite fit, his wavy auburn hair . . . mother small, plump, smiling, white-haired. Her hair had turned from black to white very early. I would have fallen in love with that small, *gamine*, frizzy-haired beauty of her first voyage, and of California, captured in a thousand snapshots: a black-haired Jean Harlow. I know her only as white-haired, and radiant except when sudden unexpected showers of tears passed across her face—from some sadness remembered or heard about—then vanishing as quickly as they came. I think of her soul as silver. I think of my father's as bronze.

They loved singing together, soprano against baritone, and they liked spreading enjoyment. The captain of the *Asturias* signed their programme.

The man pulled at the belt of the shy young woman's dressing-gown and her breasts, as round and rosy as the fruit on the boats at Malta and Port Said, spilled out freely. Day after day, night after night, they spilled out to his hands, for his delight. And that *nothing* between her thighs . . . Another couple, in another novel, bounced on mattress-springs. I pointed them out to my father, asking what it meant, and he looked embarrassed and didn't answer me clearly.

Perth. Relatives of my brother-in-law entertained us richly. The Great Australian Bight, stormy, but I had my sea-legs now. My body, not my soul. That was still staggering above a chasm. Then Lois and Ray rushing on to the ship almost before we had docked at Melbourne: embraces, tears, giggles. A bewildering taxi-ride. A huge, glowing, pineapple-spiky meal I couldn't eat for grief.

· 5 ·

WHEN THE SUN ROSE AND, FOR A WHILE, CLEARED AWAY THE mysterious mists, Suliman's Berg and the two majestic breasts, now only about twenty miles off, seemed to be towering right above us, and looked grander than ever. At the approach of evening we started on again, and, to cut a long story short, by daylight next morning found ourselves upon the lowest slopes of

Sheba's left breast, for which we had been steadily steering. By this time our water was again exhausted and we were suffering severely from thirst, nor indeed could we see any chance of relieving it till we reached the snow line far far above us. After resting an hour or two, driven to it by our torturing thirst, we went on again, toiling painfully in the burning heat up the lava slopes, for we found that the huge base of the mountain was composed entirely of lava beds belched out in some far past age.

By eleven o'clock we were utterly exhausted, and were, generally speaking, in a very bad way indeed. The lava clinker, over which we had to make our way, though comparatively smooth compared with some clinker I have heard of, such as that on the Island of Ascension for instance, was yet rough enough to make our feet very sore, and this, together with our other miseries, had pretty well finished us. A few hundred yards above us were some large lumps of lava, and towards these we made with the intention of lying down beneath their shade. We reached them, and to our surprise, so far as we had a capacity for surprise left in us, on a little plateau or ridge close by we saw that the lava was covered with a dense green growth. Evidently soil formed from decomposed lava had rested there, and in due course had become the receptacle of seeds deposited by birds. But we did not take much further interest in the green growth, for one cannot live on grass like Nebuchadnezzar. That requires a special dispensation of Providence and peculiar digestive organs. So we sat down under the rocks and groaned, and I for one heartily wished that we had never started on this fool's errand. As we were sitting there I saw Umbopa get up and hobble off towards the patch of green, and a few minutes afterwards, to my great astonishment, I perceived that usually uncommonly dignified individual dancing and shouting like a maniac, and waving something green. Off we all scrambled towards him as fast as our wearied limbs would carry us, hoping that he had found water.

"What is it, Umbopa, you stupid motherfucking bastard?" I shouted in Zulu.

"It is food and water, Macumazahn," and again he waved the green thing.

Then I saw what he had got. It was a melon. We had hit upon a patch of wild melons, thousands of them, and dead ripe.

"Melons!" I yelled to Good, who was next me; and in another second he had his false teeth fixed in one.

I think we ate about six each before we had done, and, poor fruit as they were, I doubt if I ever thought anything nicer.

But melons are not very satisfying, and when we had satisfied our thirst with their pulpy substance, and set a stock to cool by the simple process of cutting them in two and setting them end on in the hot sun to get cold by evaporation, we began to feel exceedingly hungry.

23rd.—Struggled forward once more as soon as the sun was well up, and had thawed our limbs a little. We are now in a dreadful plight, and I fear that unless we get food this will be our last day's journey. But little brandy left. Good, Sir Henry, and Umbopa bear up wonderfully, but Ventvögel is in a very bad way. Like most Hottentots, he cannot stand cold. Pangs of hunger not so bad, but have a sort of numb feeling about the stomach. Others say the same. We are now on a level with the precipitous chain, or wall of lava, connecting the two breasts, and the view is glorious. Behind us the great glowing desert rolls away to the horizon, and before us lies mile upon mile of smooth, hard snow almost level, but swelling gently upwards, out of the centre of which the nipple of the mountain, which appears to be some miles in circumference, rises about four thousand feet into the sky. Not a living thing is to be seen. God help us, for I fear our time has come.

All that day we struggled slowly on up the incline of snow, lying down from time to time to rest. A strange, gaunt crew we must have looked, as, laden as we were, we dragged our weary feet over the dazzling plain, glaring round us with hungry eyes. Not that there was much use in glaring, for there was nothing to eat. We did not do more than seven miles that day. Just before sunset we found ourselves right under the nipple of Sheba's left breast, which towered up thousands of feet into the air above us, a vast, smooth hillock of frozen snow. Bad as we felt we could not but appreciate the wonderful scene, made even more wonderful by the flying rays of light from the setting sun, which here and there stained the snow blood-red, and crowned the towering mass above us with a diadem of glory.

Not very long before dawn I heard the Hottentot, Ventvögel, whose teeth had been chattering all night like castanets, give a deep sigh, and then his teeth stopped chattering. I did not think anything of it at the time, concluding that he had gone to sleep. His back was resting against mine, and it seemed to grow colder and colder, till at last it was like ice.

At last the air began to grow grey with light, then swift, golden arrows came flashing across the snow, and at last the glorious sun peeped up above the lava wall and looked upon our half-frozen forms and upon Ventvögel, sitting there amongst us *stone dead*. No wonder his back had felt cold, poor fellow. He had died when I heard him sigh, and was now almost frozen stiff.

"Starving men must not be fanciful," said Good; "we must eat raw meat."

There was no other way out of the dilemma, and our gnawing hunger made the proposition less distasteful than it would otherwise have been. So we took the heart and liver and buried them for a few minutes in a patch of snow to cool them. Then we washed them in the ice-cold water of a stream, and lastly ate them greedily. It sounds horrible enough, but honestly, I never tasted anything so good as that raw meat. In a quarter of an hour we were changed men. Our life and our vigour came back to us, our feeble pulses grew strong again, and the blood went coursing through our veins. But mindful of the results of over-feeding on starving stomachs, we were careful not to eat too much, stopping whilst we were still hungry.

"Thank God!" said Sir Henry; "that brute has saved our lives."

· 6 ·

MY FATHER'S LEATHERY, TANNED, WEATHERBEATEN FACE broke into a crack-toothed smile one supper-time as he related how a woman had seen him looking in on her, through a window on a high floor of the Royal Melbourne Hospital—yet, pulling off her nightdress, she had calmly washed her breasts in front of him. My father was in his white plasterer's overalls. There were many other immigrants. His White Russian labourer shocked him by telling him how things truly were in the Union of Soviet Socialist Republics.

From the University High School yard, as I ate my lunch-time sandwiches, I could look up at the tall hospital and sometimes catch sight of my father. It was a consolation. Though my new classmates, mostly Jewish I found, were friendly enough, I hated school. I hated my heavy grey double-breasted suit with long trousers, my green cap and tie. They were hot and stuffy, and I was fat. I had put on weight during the last three or four years; at my Cornish grammar school, I had lost my initial fire as a demon fast-bowler: becoming more and more stout and lethargic. I told my new classmates, when they were forming a team to play on games-afternoon, that I was a batsman. They were impressed by my mythical average of fifty. To my horror, I found myself walking out to open the innings, with an athletic, slim, sandy-haired partner, on a silk-smooth, green park oval. I couldn't feel my feet crossing the turf. I took guard; the bowler strode back twenty paces, and came thundering up. I didn't see the lightning-fast delivery, but it struck my bat in the block-hole. The second delivery took my leg stump out of the ground. As I walked back to the pavilion, my suave co-opener walked a few paces with me, advising me how I should have played the delivery. I was not selected for the next match. With three bookish, Aryan class-mates I took to picking up tennis, on a dusty court next to their Church Youth Club.

But almost my first memory after landfall, before I was fitted for the hateful grey suit, was another athletic, sandy-haired boy, the son of friends of Lois and Ray, calling on us one Saturday morning to ask if I'd like to go to the Baths. He carried a white bundle under his arm. I was told to say yes, out of politeness; and we walked through the hot suburban streets together, saying little. He was too polite to ask why I wasn't carrying a towel and swimsuit; and after I'd watched him, and others, swim for an hour or two, we walked in polite silence back to our flat. Unbearably bored and embarrassed, I said I'd enjoyed it. I heard that his parents were amazed that I couldn't swim—especially as they knew I had lived near the sea.

I disliked the earnestness of my classmates, weighed down by bulging briefcases; I refused to give up my satchel. But it was pleasing that they didn't call me Fatty, as my English schoolmates had done; and pleasing that the teachers, some of them women, didn't call me by my surname, in that dehumanizing British way. A nice maths teacher asked me my name, on the first day, and I said "Thomas." When she asked if she could call me "Tom," I blushed and told her my first name was Donald. She shortened this to Don, which I found I liked. It was also nice that I wasn't forced to change, amid sweaty bodies, for gym and team games, but could read a book during gym lessons, and take the tram, past my home-stop, to the Church tennis court. But these were small consolations in the desert of homesickness.

I traced a map of the world, and drew on it the course of our voyage home, in two years' time: Perth, Ceylon, Aden, Port Said, Malta, Gibraltar, then wonderful Southampton. I divided it into twenty-four sections. At the end of the first month, I coloured the first section in with a red pencil. Our ship had hardly left Melbourne, was still moving south, into the Bight; but at least we were on our way, I felt.

All the grownups had jobs. My sister was a secretary, my brother-in-law worked at the linen business he had learned—in Belfast—during his year in Britain. My mother, for the first time in her life, found a part-time job, in a nearby hosiery factory, Holeproof. I would get home first, in the stifling mid-afternoon, and rip off my suit and tie, then sprawl in shorts on my bed. A bundle of comics arrived—*Beano* and *Hotspur*—sent by a neigh-bouring boy who had bullied me all through primary school. But he sent the bundles of comics faithfully. I lay and read them over and over, yearning.

My mother would come home next, bringing me every day a packet of fat, gluey fish and chips. They weren't anything like the crisp fish and chips we had at home, but they bore the same name. They kept me going till supper-time: usually a roast, since we didn't take to salads, paw-paws and passion-fruit. I grew even stouter. My sister and mother were also plump, but in a shapely way. My sister, lying flat, kicked high from the lounge floor one evening, and I ogled her rucked-back skirt above her nylons. I didn't realize I was staring—and everyone else, Lois included, was in a jolly mood; but Ray spotted me and shooed me from the room. I slunk out, feeling my face burn with shame, and with a sense of unfairness that my father had been allowed to stay.

There were girls at University High, but I could glimpse only their straw hats above the fence at break-times. I was still, despite my uncle's lesson, ignorant. A tall, twinkling-eyed Maltese immigrant—the only crude boy in the class—said a *poufter* was someone who sniffed the saddles of girls' bicycles. I didn't know what he meant. But my penis would fatten and strain against my grey trousers, in the tram coming home, just from watching the slim Uni High girls in their straw boaters and green and white striped dresses, stretching up to strap-hang. They were so cool, so infinitely far; their bosoms swelled and strained against their cool frocks, tenderly, innocently, driving me wild.

And there was a girl waiting at the school tram-stop one day—but she was waiting for a different tram—who didn't make me erect but made me yearn, as I yearned for England. She had fair hair, cut close to her head, with a fringe; flawless fair skin; and big, candid, intense blue eyes. She didn't notice me, or she disdained the awkward lumpish boy swinging a satchel. I saw her, perhaps, twice more, over the school fence; but her image went home with me every afternoon. The crude Maltese boy told me, with a chuckle, she was called "Freeza." I wonder, looking back, if it was because she came on or stood off. Painfully shy, I never thought of getting early to the tram-stop and waiting for her, saying hello to her.

Turning in on myself, I glanced at Ray's books, which were few and boring—yet, in a way, interesting. *An Analogy of Religion*, Lin Yu Tang, Roget's *Thesaurus*; these are the titles that come back to me. And there was a line of red book club novels, which my sister read. I remember Peter de Polnay; and an Ethel Mannin which took its title from a sentence of St Augustine which moved me: "Late have I loved thee, O Beauty most ancient and most new, Late loved I thee." There were also *Photoplay* magazines, with the stars I adored: June Allyson, Doris Day, Jean Simmons, Kathryn Grayson, and Janet Leigh—who needed a D-cup brassiere because her back was broad.

· 7 ·

"HEAR HIM! HEAR HIM!" PIPED GAGOOL; "HEAR THE LIAR WHO says he will put out the moon like a lamp. Let him do it, and the girl shall be spared. Yes, let him do it, or die with the girl, he and those with him."

I glanced up at the moon, and to my intense joy and relief saw that we had made no mistake. On the edge of the great orb was a faint rim of shadow, while a smoky hue grew and gathered on its bright surface.

I lifted my hand solemnly towards the sky, an example which Sir Henry and Good followed, and quoted a line or two of the *Ingoldsby Legends* at it in the most impressive tones I could command. Sir Henry followed suit with a verse out of the Old Testament, whilst Good addressed the Queen of Night in a volume of the most classical bad language that he could think of: yet in a way so innocently, as always, as to make those later suspicions and innuendoes, which were to damage his reputation so gravely, appear all the more absurd. Sir Henry Curtis and I are as certain of John Good's innocence of those appalling murders in the East End of London as we are of our own innocence. And

SWALLOW   •   183

what, after all, was the *evidence?*—that he had an unusual knowledge of surgery! that with his monocle and plump clean-shaven
face he would have *appeared* harmless!

Slowly the penumbra, the shadow of a shadow, crept on over
the bright surface, and as it did so I heard a deep gasp of fear rise
from the multitude around.

"Look, O king!" I cried; "look, Gagool! Look, chiefs and
people and women, and see if the white men from the stars keep
their word, or if they be but empty liars!

"The moon grows dark before your eyes; soon there will be
darkness—ay, darkness in the hour of the full moon. Ye have
asked for a sign; it is given to you. Grow dark, O moon!
withdraw thy light, thou pure and holy one; bring the proud
heart to the dust, and eat up the world with shadows!"

A groan of terror rose from the onlookers. Some stood petrified with fear, others threw themselves upon their knees, and
cried out. As for the king, he sat still and turned pale beneath his
dusky skin. Only Gagool kept her courage.

"It will pass," she cried; "I have seen the like before; no man
can put out the moon; lose not heart; sit still—the shadow will
pass."

"Wait, and ye shall see," I replied, hopping with excitement.

"Keep it up, Good, I can't remember any more poetry. Curse
away, there's a good fellow."

Good responded nobly to the tax upon his inventive faculties.
Never before had I the faintest conception of the breadth and
depth and height of a naval officer's objurgatory powers: "You
celestial cunt, vanish! Be wiped clean, you arsehole of the night!
Twat, stuff yourself with earth's jamrag! Bugger off, like a shitty
prick, like a cock in hock! Swallow yourself, like a double-jointed
wanker! Blow yourself off, you Chinese tart's fart! Fuck your
father, you one-balled fairy! Plop off, you squelchy turd! Close
your one eye, you shagged-out Singapore whore! Get lost like a
swimmer's piss! Jerk off in earth's mouth! . . ." For ten minutes

he went on without stopping, and he scarcely ever repeated himself.

Meanwhile the dark ring crept on, and that whole great assembly fixed their eyes upon the sky and stared and stared in fascinated silence. Strange and unholy shadows encroached upon the moonlight, an ominous quiet filled the place, everything grew still as death.

· 8 ·

THOUGH THE DAYS WERE AWFUL, ENDLESS, A CONSTANT gnawing hollow under my heart, the nights were worse. My bedroom was the box-room, at the end of the second-floor flat, close to the back door and the wooden steps leading down to the jungly back garden. The junk of boxes, crates, trunks, pressing round my bed seemed a natural nesting-place for spiders and other jungle creatures: though, to be honest, I never saw one in that room. Separated from the two other bedrooms by the bathroom and a gloomy passage, my room also struck me as a natural place for ghosts to haunt: though again I never actually saw one.

Night after night, terror strangled me as lights were switched out, doors closed, silence fell. My heart thumping, I would wait till I thought Lois and Ray must be asleep; then I would get out of bed, and creep barefoot along the corridor. I had to pass my sister's room to reach my parents'. The floorboards, the cracked canvas, always creaked just outside Lois and Ray's door, and I would freeze before creeping on. At last I could breathe more easily: I'd push open the door of my parents' bedroom, and they would rarely complain, beyond a few mutters. I thought it was quite natural for my mother to get out and take my place in the box-room. Often I had slept with father back home, when I was younger: telling them I'd seen a ghost in the front door-way, though you couldn't see the front door from my bedroom. I would cuddle up close to my father's hot skin, and relish his comfortable, sharp, saffrony tang. He had lulled me asleep with stories he made up. In Melbourne there were no more stories— simply the huge relief of being safe from ghosts for another night.

I have no memory of changing rooms again in the morning; and I guess my sister and her husband must have known what was happening, and I must have known that they knew. But I persuaded myself that my embarrassing nocturnal journey was a secret from them. One night, however, as the canvas creaked and I froze, the door burst open and my stocky brother-in-law burst out, stark naked. Stunned, we both recoiled. I mumbled something about going to fetch a magazine. He pushed past towards the bathroom, muttering something; I found a *Sporting World* in the lounge, and returned to my bedroom. I had to wait a ghost-haunted, spider-threatened eternity before creeping out again, and turning my mother out of bed.

Ray and I rubbed each other up the wrong way. I didn't take to his colonial cockiness; I did my best to irritate him and Lois too. Thus, when they both enthused about Australian Rules Football, I persuaded my father that we should follow Carlton, the Blues, rather than their team, the Redlegs. The Carlton Stadium was close to where we lived, so it was sensible; but my aim was simply to create a bone of contention. On many a weekend, when winter came, Ray and I glared ferociously at each other, felt like strangling each other. I also found that Australian Rules, as they had predicted, would be a reasonable substitute for rugby, till I could watch my beloved Redruth, the Reds, again. I did see one exhibition rugby match, at the Melbourne Cricket Ground; but in the vast stadium, with only a handful of spectators, it was hopeless.

With the arrival of our second summer, came the English cricket team. I supported them as passionately as I had cheered Bradman's touring team in 1948. I waved a Union Jack, and again glowered eyeball to eyeball with Ray. Unfortunately the English team was demolished. I couldn't bear to go with my father and Lois to the MCG on the last day of the Melbourne Test, because we had a faint chance of winning. I lay on my bed all day, listening to the commentary on the wireless.

By now, "my bed" was my parents' abandoned double-bed, for they had decided to change rooms with me. There was no space in the box-room for clothes, so they had left those behind. When I opened the wardrobe-door, to move the red line an inch nearer Ceylon, I was faced with my mother's floral dresses, my father's brown Sunday-suit. And one drawer of the old chest-of-drawers, under the old wireless, was crammed with mother's corsets and brassieres and long pink elastic-kneed bloomers. The change, far from being pleasant, brought deeper horrors, deadlier nightmares. For one garish morning I woke to see a palm-size, black tarantula on the wall between the open window and my bed. All my hairs stood on end; I leapt out, and backed away to the door, never letting my gaze stray from the loathsome creature. I hammered on Ray's door. Chuckling, he brought a spray-gun; while I cowered near the door, he pumped a sick-sweet gas up at the gigantic spider. Slowly it stirred, sidled, lurched down the wall in a diagonal line.

From that morning my imagination was never free of tarantulas. They swarmed into my bedroom every night, as the spiders in a Dennis Wheatley novel—one of the red books—swarmed over Toby Jugg, paralysed, the victim of a coven. I expected, whenever the moon was at full, framing the tree of jagged leaves outside my window, the mother-spider of all spiders to crawl in, as it did for Toby. In a quiet suburban street, with a neat park or "paddock" across the road, I felt surrounded by a jungle. The sweat that poured off me, that indecent summer of 1950, both from heat and fear, could have washed us back to England.

Ray and Lois hinted that we might settle down better if we had a flat of our own, but father and I had no intention of settling. Perhaps my chameleon-mother, happy wherever her family was, could have settled; but my father killed off all discussion by riding into the city one Saturday morning and booking our passages a year in advance. Then he and I saw a film, as we always did on Saturday mornings, followed by a cricket match, or football match in winter, at the Carlton Oval. I liked Saturdays, and especially that one, when our return was made certain.

Yet every inch, every month, on my world-map stretched out like a year. I was becalmed. Every day lasted a week—and every night too. Only the evenings were tolerable, when I shut myself up after supper in my room, sprawled out on my bed. The tree was harmless while the light lasted, but dragged my eyes towards it as dusk passed into darkness. I knew the tarantulas and the ghosts were preparing. Dread swept over me when the wireless in the lounge was switched off, or when Lois stopped playing "The Rustle of Spring" on the piano and I heard the piano lid being closed. Mother would come in to take fresh clothes, and to give me a goodnight hug. Lights went off; bedroom doors closed; tarantulas rustled in the silence. I kept the light on, though the glare added to the intolerable heat and stuffiness. I lay naked, drenched in sweat, and opened my eyes every minute or so to see if a tarantula had come in. A mosquito whined; I searched for it, clapped my hands and it died. I drowsed fitfully; every time I woke I turned my head to the white wall, by the window. My greatest nightmare, though, was to find a tarantula poised right above my head. That never happened. Indeed, very rarely did a spider come in at all.

If I survived until sunrise, I could relax a little, turn out the light, and drift asleep in the fresher early-morning atmosphere. Somehow I expected the tarantulas, as well as the ghosts, to come in the darkness, not at dawn. Yet in reality, dawn was when they came, if they came at all. I never saw one enter, never saw black legs appear round the window-frame. They were either there, or not there, when I woke finally to the radiant, already hot, light.

The second or third time when my nightmare became real, I sat on the lounge sofa, recovering, yet knowing I would see that spider all day and into the next night. The sun poured through the window and burned through my white shirt into my back. The others had left for work. I would soon have to walk down to the tram-stop at the end of the avenue. I felt, or saw, a shadowy creature emerge between my black shoes . . . looked down, and jumped out of my skin. It was not the ghost of the first tarantula, but another, immense, evil, walking out into the light of the fawn-coloured carpet. It crossed the room almost to the gas-fire, then stopped. I wanted to rush out of the house, but dared not leave it in possession, to vanish. Shuddering, panting, I took the biggest book I could find, approached the spider, and held the book a couple of feet over it. The book dropped with a thud—a flash of movement but not quick enough, thank God. I left the book there for someone else to take care of.

I shuddered, all the way to school. Surrounded by green blazers—happily we had been permitted to discard our grey suits—I still saw the two tarantulas.

Yet some English friends of my parents had a flat infested with tarantulas, and didn't mind. They—the spiders—were, of course, harmless, unlike the true tarantulas of Arizona and Mexico. We played mah-jong with these friends one evening, and three tarantulas played their own carefree game in a corner of the high room. That flat—my sister told me only recently—had been intended for us, but the others had taken possession. I could not have endured living there.

The ground-floor flat in our house was murky and dank, and suitable for spiders. An elderly housebound lady lived there, tapping about on a stick. One afternoon, engaged in a kind of sexual puberty rite, I felt my way down the stairs, courting the danger of meeting her in her gloomy hall. But something tickled on the back of my hand; it was a very tiny spider, but a strangled cry came from me as I shook the thing off and raced back up the stairs.

· 9 ·

WE ATE AND SIPPED SOME WATER, AND ANOTHER PERIOD OF time passed, when somebody suggested that it might be as well to get as near to the door as possible, and halloa, on the faint chance of somebody catching a sound outside. Accordingly Good, who, from long practice at sea, has a fine piercing note, groped his way down the passage and began, and I must say he made a most diabolical noise. I never heard such yells; but it might have been a mosquito buzzing for all the effect it produced.

After a while he gave it up, and came back very thirsty, and had to have some water. After that we gave up yelling, as it encroached on the supply of water.

So we all sat down once more against our chests of useless diamonds in that dreadful inaction, which was one of the hardest circumstances of our fate; and I am bound to say that, for my part, I gave way to despair. Laying my head against Sir Henry's broad shoulder I burst into tears; and I think I heard Good gulping away on the other side, and swearing hoarsely to himself for doing so.

Ah, how good and brave that great man was! Had we been two of his prep-school boys, he could not have treated us more tenderly. Forgetting his own share of miseries, he did all he could to soothe our broken nerves, telling stories of men who had been in somewhat similar circumstances, and miraculously escaped; and when these failed to cheer us, pointing out how, after all, it was only anticipating an end that must come to us all, that it would soon be over, and that death from exhaustion was a merciful one (which is not true). Then in a diffident sort of a way, as I had once before heard him do, he suggested that we should throw ourselves on the mercy of a higher Power, which for my part I did with great vigour.

His is a beautiful character, very quiet, but very strong.

And so somehow the day went as the night had gone (if, indeed, one can use the term where all was densest night) and when I lit a match to see the time it was seven o'clock.

Once more we ate and drank, and as we did so an idea occurred to me.

"How is it," said I, "that the air in this place keeps fresh? It is thick and heavy, but it is perfectly fresh."

"Christ!" said Good, starting up, "I never thought of that. It can't come through the stone door, for it is air-tight, if ever a door was. It must come from somewhere. If there were no current of air in the place we should have been stifled when we first came in. Let us have a look."

It was wonderful what a change this mere spark of hope wrought in us. In a moment we were all three groping about the place on our hands and knees, feeling for the slightest indication of a draught. Presently my ardour received a check. I put my hand on something cold. It was poor Foulata's belly.

For an hour or more we went on feeling about, till at last Sir Henry and I gave it up in despair. But Good still persevered, saying, with an approach to cheerfulness, that it was better than doing nothing.

Resting my hand on poor Foulata's cold breast, I said to Good and Sir Henry, "It will not have escaped you that we are, very literally, in the *bowels* of the mountain; and no one could be blind to the significance of the great hole into which Gagool led us, nor of the cavern where the dead kings sit."

"You are right," replied Good. "This cursed mine has been cut out of the mountain. But what of it?"

"*What of it!*" Sir Henry broke in. "Why, of course! Why did we not think of this before? Because we are not so clever as *Macuma-zahn* here!" He gave as near to a laugh as any of us had managed in that accursed place. "What Quatermain means is, there must be at least *one other exit.*"

"Shit, yes!" exclaimed Good.

"With your knowledge of female anatomy, my dear fellow," Sir Henry went on, "you ought also to be able to point us roughly in the right direction."

"Well, I will do my best. Let me see, we entered the cavern of the kings from *this* angle, as I recall." He made motions in the air, and then proceeded to crawl along the wall into a corner.

"I say, you fellows," he said, presently, in a constrained sort of voice, "come here."

Needless to say, we scrambled over towards him quick enough.

"Quatermain, put your hand here where mine is. Now, do you feel anything?"

"Yes. But she is yours, Good. . . ."

"—No, no. My right hand . . . That's it. Now, listen." He rose and stamped upon the place, and a flame of hope shot up in our hearts. *It rang hollow.*

· 10 ·

SEXUAL CRAVING—OR RATHER, CRAVING FOR WOMAN, GIRL, her touch, feel, scent—burned me up, like the forests of ghost-trees in that summer of bush-fires. Unlike the colt, Man Shy, I read of in class at about that time, I was fat, yet I also stumbled through a desert, parched. I found only the salt water of images: the tight belts and straining sweaters of the page-boyed young women on celluloid or in film magazines; the slenderer bosoms of the summer-dressed, straw-hatted girls on the tram, who never appeared to sweat, and who never looked in my direction; even the matronly models, almost as old as my mother, advertising Berlei or Gossard girdles in the conservative *Age*; even Corky, a good-looking young housewife, who attached a milometer to her suspender, for the *Australasian*, to find out how far a house-wife walked in a day—it was, I think, seven miles. And, once, a chance revelation of my sister, her red hair trapped in her slip. I rushed from her room, which I had expected to be empty, and threw myself on my bed, embarrassed, shocked, my face aflame. She came in to see me, when she was clothed: blushing a little too, but also smiling, generous in wanting to make light of it. She asked me if anyone had told me about sex, and I said yes. She nodded, and went out. We were alone in the house, and I recall thinking, momentarily, that she ought to teach me about sex; show me what it was all about. It was a confused, vague, stray thought, soon banished.

I spent quite a lot of time in her room, during the long holiday, or after school before mother came with the fish and chips. Then I started to "minch," or play hookey, from school. I was still terribly unhappy there. I had fiddled my end-of-year report to make it look as if I was high up in the class, but I was far behind the serious and intelligent Jews, who had ambitions to be barristers and brain-surgeons. I refused to sing, at assembly, an oath to serve the school *strenue ac fideliter*: with zeal and loyalty. So I stayed away from school; or else—on mornings when my mother left later than I—hovered in a lane behind the house, and then crept back in through the rank, tarantula-filled garden. I carried out secret puberty rites in my sister's room which, with the curtains drawn, was cooler than mine, and impregnated with woman-scents. It was my dream-time. Man Shy, who brought tears to my eyes, was my totem. But these rites, too, were salt water, and I went on burning. My only orgasms came at night, in entanglements with some unknown woman or girl. They woke me, drenched in sperm and sweat, and I turned my eyes to the white wall by the window.

One morning my sister, unknown to me, had stayed in bed, nursing a cold. She heard the back window scrape open, then steps coming heavily up the passage; she saw the knob turn and the door slowly open towards her; she lay paralysed with terror. I, too, was horrified when I saw her in the bed. The encounter brought to an end my minching from school, my forged absence notes. And, now, I think it was on that day that she asked me if I had been told about sex, and I briefly considered asking her if she would teach me. I was not hung up on my sister; she just happened to be there. I craved the blue-eyed girl whom I never saw; I wanted Doris Day and June Allyson; the cool girls straphanging on the tram, UHS emblazoned on their blazers; the husky-voiced woman who, evening by evening on the Top Ten, sang "Temptation": "You were—born to be kissed—I can't resist; you are temptation, and I—am yours!"

After the Popular Top Ten there was sometimes a Classical Top Ten: always with the Warsaw Concerto and "Claire de Lune." The programme was introduced by the solo opening of Rachmaninov's Second Piano Concerto. Those slow, sombre, wide-spaced chords, gradually growing louder, made the hairs stand on my nape, like the night-tree.

I listened to these programmes alone in my bedroom. I had withdrawn into myself entirely, enjoying solitude until night fell. I did my homework—a little more keenly as time went on; glanced through comics—though I no longer read them avidly; carried on with my scrapbooks of filmstars and sporting heroes: longing for autumn and sight of the Blues again. But the temperature went on rising still higher; for weeks it was over the hundred. Fierce, hot winds blew the dust of the tennis court into my eyes, once every week. My friends and I moved around the court lethargically; I had one good stroke, a left-handed forehand drive, which they could not live with.

The heatwave ended with wonderful suddenness. A forecast one Sunday morning of a breeze from the Antarctic, reaching the city at four—and within minutes of that hour we felt a coolness touch our bare legs and red-hot faces, saw the curtains blow. Energy flowed back into us; we chuckled, went to the balcony to fill our lungs with cooling air. In no time, the mercury had dropped ten or fifteen degrees.

I was starting to do better in school. An acerbic art teacher played us a record of Tchaikovsky's "Francesca da Rimini" tone-poem and, without fully understanding what it represented, I painted a flamboyant picture which impressed him.

A resonant, thrilling voice-over, in *The Blue Lagoon*, expressed Jean Simmons' newly-discovered emotions as she feared that her fellow-castaway was drowned . . .

> *I wonder, by my troth, what thou and I*
> *Did, till we loved: were we not weaned till then,*
> *But sucked on country-pleasures, childishly?*
> *Or snorted we in the seven sleepers' den? . . .*

So this, I thought, is poetry . . . So this is love . . . And I was stirred, equally without understanding, when a student teacher from the University struggled through "Pied Beauty" and "The Windhover" with us. I must have said something sensible, too, because I heard she was asking who the American boy was. Well, a Cornish accent is not so far from an American.

Another bundle of comics came, but I didn't open it.

Time moved more quickly, once the Blues took the field again, amid roars of forty thousand fans. Sitting by father, I was in an ecstasy of excitement. The way they flew high to bring down the mark! Then the huge punt, taking the ball between the centre-posts! Every Saturday, almost, through the too-short season, Carlton won. They came out on top, and the Grand Final against Essendon seemed a formality. It was the most thrilling day of my life, among a hundred thousand at the MCG; and also the bitterest disappointment. No one could remember a final won and lost by seventy-two points. I cried. My brother-in-law, to his credit, didn't rub it in.

· I I ·

"I SAY, YOU FELLOWS," I SANG OUT, "WON'T YOU TAKE SOME diamonds with you? I've filled my pockets."

"Oh! bugger the diamonds!" said Sir Henry. "I hope that I may never see another."

As for Good, he made no answer. He was, I think, screwing for the last time the poor girl who loved him so well. And, curious as it may seem to you, my reader, sitting at home at ease and reflecting on the vast, indeed the immeasurable, wealth which we were thus abandoning, I can assure you that if you had passed some twenty-four hours with next to nothing to eat and drink in that place, you would not have cared to cumber your-self with diamonds whilst plunging down into the unknown bowels of the earth, in the wild hope of escape from an agonizing death. If it had not, from the habits of a lifetime, become a sort of second nature with me never to leave anything worth hav-ing behind, if there was the slightest chance of my being able to carry it away, I am sure I should not have bothered to fill my pockets.

"Come on, Quatermain," said Sir Henry, who was already

standing on the first step of the stone stair. "Steady, I will go first."

"Mind where you put your feet; there may be some awful hole underneath," said I.

Feeling along the wall with the hand, whilst trying the ground before us at every step, we departed from that accursed treasure chamber on our terrible quest. If ever it should be entered again by living man, which I do not think it will be, he will find a token of our presence in the open chests of jewels, the empty lamp, and the white bones of poor Foulata.

When we had groped our way for about a quarter of an hour along the passage, it suddenly took a sharp turn, or else was bisected by another, which we followed, only in course of time to be led into a third. And so it went on for some hours. We seemed to be in a stone labyrinth which led nowhere. What all these passages are, of course I cannot say, but we thought that they must be the ancient workings of a mine, of which the various shafts travelled hither and thither as the ore led them. This is the only way in which we could account for such a multitude of passages as distinct from the two (apart from the entrance) which we could have expected.

At length we halted, thoroughly worn out with fatigue, and with that hope deferred which maketh the heart sick, and ate up our poor remaining piece of biltong, and drank our last sup of water, for our throats were like lime-kilns. It seemed to us that we had escaped Death in the darkness of the chamber only to meet him in the darkness of the tunnels.

As we stood, once more utterly depressed, I thought I caught a sound, to which I called the attention of the others. It was very faint and very far off, but it *was* a sound, a faint, murmuring sound, for the others heard it too, and no words can describe the blessedness of it after all those hours of utter, awful stillness.

"Sheba is pissing," joked Good. "Come on."

Off we started again in the direction from which the faint

murmur seemed to come, groping our way as before along the rocky walls. As we went it got more and more audible, till at last it seemed quite loud in the quiet. On, yet on; now we could distinctly make out the unmistakable swirl of rushing water. And yet how could there be running water in the bowels of the earth? Now we were quite near to it, and Good, who was leading, swore that he could smell it.

"Go gently, Good," said Sir Henry, "we must be close." *Splash!* and a cry from Good.

He had fallen in.

"Good! Good! where are you?" we shouted, in terrified distress. To our intense relief, an answer came back in a choky voice.

"All right; I've got hold of a rock. Strike a light to show me where you are."

Hastily I lit the last remaining match. Its faint gleam discovered to us a dark mass of water running at our feet. How wide it was we could not see, but there, some way out, was the dark form of our companion hanging on to a projecting rock.

"Stand clear to catch me," sung out Good. "I must swim for it."

Then we heard a splash, and a great struggle. Another minute and he had grabbed at and caught Sir Henry's outstretched hand, and we had pulled him up high and dry into the tunnel.

"Christ!" he said, between his gasps, "that was touch and go. If I hadn't caught that rock, and known how to swim, I should have been done. It runs like a mill-race, and I could feel no bottom."

It was clear that this would not do; so after Good had rested a little, and we had drunk our fill from the water of the subterranean river, which was sweet and fresh despite Good's jocular interpretation of its cause, and washed our faces, which sadly needed it, as well as we could, we started from the banks of this African Styx, and began to retrace our steps along the tunnel, Good dripping unpleasantly in front of us. At length we came to another tunnel leading to our right.

"We may as well take it," said Sir Henry, wearily; "all roads are alike here; we can only go on till we drop."

Slowly, for a long, long while, we stumbled, utterly weary, along this new tunnel, Sir Henry leading now.

Suddenly he stopped, and we bumped up against him.

"Look!" he whispered, "is my brain going, or is that light?"

We stared with all our eyes, and there, yes, there, far ahead of us, was a faint, glimmering spot, no larger than a cottage window pane. It was so faint that I doubt if any eyes, except those which, like ours, had for days seen nothing but blackness, could have perceived it at all.

With a sort of gasp of hope we pushed on. In five minutes there was no longer any doubt; it *was* a patch of faint light. A minute more and a breath of real live air was fanning us. On we struggled. All at once the tunnel narrowed. Sir Henry went on his knees. Smaller yet it grew, till it was only the size of a large fox's earth—it was *earth* now, mind you; the rock had ceased.

A squeeze, a struggle, and Sir Henry was out, and so was Good, and so was I, and there above us were the blessed stars, and in our nostrils was the sweet air; then suddenly something gave, and we were all rolling over and over through grass and bushes, and soft, wet soil.

I caught at something and stopped. Sitting up I hallooed lustily. An answering shout came from just below, where Sir Henry's wild career had been stopped by some level ground. I scrambled for him, and found him unhurt, though breathless. Then we looked for Good. A little way off we found him too, jammed in a forked root. He was a good deal knocked about, but soon came to.

We sat down together there on the grass, and the revulsion of feeling was so great, that I really think we cried for joy. We had escaped from that awful dungeon, that was so near to becoming our grave. Surely some merciful Power must have guided our footsteps to the jackal hole at the termination of the tunnel (for that is what it must have been). And see, there on the mountains called Sheba's Buttocks, the dawn we had never thought to look upon again was blushing rosy red.

Presently the grey light stole down the slopes, and we saw that we were at the bottom, or rather, nearly at the bottom, of the vast pit in front of the entrance to the cave. Now we could make out the dim forms of the three colossi who sat upon its verge. Doubtless those awful passages, along which we had wandered the livelong night, had originally been, in some way, connected with the great diamond mine. As for the subterranean river in the bowels of the mountain, Heaven only knows what it was, or whence it flows, or whither it goes. I for one have no anxiety to trace its course.

· 12 ·

OUR SHIP HAD SQUEEZED THROUGH THE SUEZ CANAL; THE journey ahead was so short I no longer bothered to extend the red line on the first of every month.

Spring passed into summer again. The nights were warm, but not yet unbearable. Though I still kept the light on, I found it easier to sleep. If I was woken at dawn by a wet dream, I was happy—once I had checked that there was no tarantula—to lie peacefully watching the light brighten around the tree: grey at first, then pink, then a kind of green, till the sun burst into my room, filling it with another day's warmth. I could see that the picture I had drawn, after "Francesca da Rimini," had been a representation of the tree.

There were no tarantulas in that last, shortened summer.

I surprised everyone by coming first in my class, the only foreskinned boy in the first ten. The Jews took it good naturedly. And after the long vacation came another pleasant surprise: the straw-hatted girls from over the fence were now sitting in my classroom. A tremulous, respectful silence fell on us boys when one of the girls bravely said, "Come to my woman's breasts. . . ."

I fell hopelessly in love with a graceful, slim, light-footed girl called Sara. She appeared in only two or three of my classes, each day; was often absent through sickness; and spoke to me only two or three times during those few weeks—to ask if she could borrow my biology notebook to copy up notes she had missed, and to thank me on returning it. But her shapely, animated face, her gay smile, her step which did not seem to touch the ground, filled my days and nights. If she happened to sit in front of me, the sight of her short black hair converging to a point on her slim nape made me feel weak. I could hardly guide my pen over the paper. During the arid classes we did not share, there were moments of pure grace when she appeared unexpectedly, walking along the windowed corridor; and one weekend—the weekends were unbearably long—her picture, to my amazement and joy, was on the front page of the *Age*, with a caption saying that she loved snow and was skiing in the mountains. I pretended she was my girlfriend, and Ray teased me amiably.

I was blind to everyone else's emotions. The family began to talk, in a kind of tearful, cheerful way of how my/my parents' room might become a nursery after we had gone. I burst into tears over the passion-fruit one evening, and said I'd changed my mind about going home. I wanted to stay; they could leave me there. They were alarmed, disconcerted; mother mumbling that perhaps I could live with Ray's parents. But I didn't fancy that; and of course it was impossible, I knew I would have to go. On my last day at school I summoned up enough courage to speak to Sara, saying I was going back to England. We shook hands politely, while my heart was breaking. I thought to ask if she would mind my writing to her, but was too shy. With the help of an Australian friend I made contact with her again, a few years ago. She was clearly recognizable, and still attractive, in the photo she sent. She was married, and had two grown-up children. She did not remember me; did not remember a plump English boy who loaned her his biology notebook once or twice.

Before we left, Ray was going to take Bluey for a short holiday up-country. It would provide a distraction for her. To break the gloomy atmosphere, as they waited for the taxi, I played a lugubrious piece on the piano. But an ache of grief gathered in my throat when we ourselves, the next day, passed in a taxi along by the Blues' stadium, desolate in the bright, midsummer sunshine; and passed the tram-stop near my school. Sara was in there. . . .

I stared down from the deck of our ship at the swaying mass of people who were waving goodbye to friends or relations. To my surprise I caught sight of the three schoolfriends with whom I had played tennis. Their spectacles flashed in the late-afternoon sun. I was touched that they had come to see me off. We waved at each other. Sirens blared; streamers tore apart; the ship moved off.

Dolphins, and table-tennis. A girl who sat at the next table in the dining-room seemed to want my company, but she didn't appeal to me. I was dazzled by a blue-eyed, corn-haired New Zealand girl called Pat. She was eighteen, travelling with her mother. She was much too old for me, of course, and was in fact going to meet her fiancé in London. I ignored her courteous indifference, and haunted her and her mother. I would squat with my copy of Shakespeare's Tragedies, which I couldn't understand, close to her deck-chair. I persuaded my parents that we should go with them on our afternoon's sightseeing in Gibraltar. From heat, tennis, Sara, the abandonment of fish and chips, and now Pat and strenuous table-tennis, I grew slimmer.

By a happy chance, as it seemed to me, Pat and her mother were going to be staying with relatives in Cornwall, not far from us. They promised to visit. I told her how romantic Carn Brea was, dimly aware I was embarrassing her.

We landed at Tilbury. We were met by my Uncle Willie, in sad exile at Muswell Hill with his hypochondriac wife; and by my uncle and cousin who had travelled up from Cornwall. We watched, that evening, a dreary modern opera on a machine I had never heard of, television.

Strangely perhaps, I remember nothing of our journey home in the train, over the Tamar, the Brunel Bridge. Twenty years earlier, my youngest uncle, who gave me my name and (in a way) my birth, had been borne in a coffin over that bridge, towards my grief-stricken grandmother. We went to live in the family house at Carnkie. There were plenty of rooms, and my father planned to build on an extension. Drizzle rolled across mine-pitted Carn Brea, across the grey and ghostly mine-stacks and engine-houses, from the sea; bitter winds rattled my bedroom window. I mourned for warmth, Melbourne, Sara. I was playing billiards at the Men's Institute when a message came that Pat and her mother had called. I strolled down the road and slipped into the house; but from outside the living-room door I heard my mother say that I was very fond of Pat, and one of my aunts say, after an embarrassed silence, "Well, of course he's very young . . ." Ashamed, I tiptoed away, ran out, and hid behind the chapel hedge for an hour until our visitors had left. Afterwards I wrote her an apologetic note.

A week or two after our arrival, we walked the familiar, hilly, winding road towards "Beverly," to call on our former neighbours. I recalled Ginger, our cat. We talked about her. A hundred yards or so before "Beverly," my father whistled—and to our amazement our old cat came bounding down to meet him, as she had always done.

Father went to work with a couple of friends who had started a small firm. He put what little money he had into the business, but they declined to add his name to theirs. This grieved him. Mother persuaded him to give up his cloth cap for a trilby. I went back to my old school again, and loathed it. I loathed being called "Thomas," by moustached, tweed-jacketed, slightly brain-damaged relics of the war. I loathed the total, juvenile maleness, and longed for Sara's sunburnt nape above her clean white collar. I loathed being made to change for gym, once more, in the jockstrapped, urinous changing-rooms. I refused to join the Air Training Corps.

I couldn't wait for four o'clock, when I could stroll, homesick, towards the house where I was born: through the coombe of daffodils and gorse, past the churchyard where my parents now lie, under the drizzled, granite carn. Nimbly I avoided the apple-cheeked, blousy girl who would see me coming from the window of a carn-sloped farmhouse, and hurry down the lane to intercept me; I would stride on ahead of her, imagining Sara's face.

· 13 ·

"AND NOW, IGNOSI, THE TIME HAS COME FOR US TO BID THEE farewell, and start to seek once more our own land. Behold, Ignosi, with us thou camest a servant, and now we leave thee a mighty king. If thou art grateful to us, remember to do even as thou didst promise: to rule justly, to respect the law, and to put none to death without a cause. So shalt thou prosper. Tomorrow, at break of day, Ignosi, wilt thou give us an escort who shall lead us across the mountains? Is it not so, O King?"

Ignosi covered his face with his hands for a while before answering.

"My heart is sore," he said at last; "your words split my heart in twain. What have I done to ye, Incubu, Macumazahn, and Bougwan, that ye should leave me desolate? Ye who stood by me in rebellion and in battle, will ye leave me in the day of peace and victory? What will ye—wives? Choose from out the land! A place to live in? Behold, the land is yours as far as ye can see. The white man's houses? Ye shall teach my people how to build them. Cattle for beef and milk? Every married man shall bring ye an ox or a cow. Wild game to hunt? Does not the elephant walk through my forests, and the river-horse sleep in the reeds? Would ye make war? My Impis (regiments) wait your word. If there is anything more that I can give, that will I give ye."

"Nay, Ignosi, we want not these things," I answered; "we would seek our own place."

"Now do I perceive," said Ignosi bitterly, and with flashing eyes, "that it is the bright stones that ye love more than me, your friend. Ye have the stones; now would ye go to Natal and across the moving black water and sell them, and be rich."

I laid my hand upon his arm. "It is not altogether so, Ignosi," I said. "That which flies in the air loves not to run along the ground; the white man loves not to live on the level of the black."

"I do perceive that thy words are, now as ever, wise and full of reason, Macumazahn. And ye would go, Infadoos, my uncle, and my Induna, shall take thee by the hand and guide thee, with a regiment. There is, as I have learnt, another way across the mountains that he shall show ye. Farewell, my brothers, brave white men. See me no more, for I have no heart to bear it. Behold, I make a decree, and it shall be published from the mountains to the mountains, your names, Incubu, Macumazahn, and Bougwan, shall be as the names of dead kings, and he who speaks them shall die. So shall your memory be preserved in the land for ever.

"Go now, ere my eyes rain tears like a woman's. At times when ye look back down the path of life, or when ye are old and gather yourselves together to crouch before the fire, because the sun has no more heat, ye will think of how we stood shoulder to shoulder in that great battle that thy wise words planned, Macumazahn, of how thou wast the point of that horn that galled Twala's flank, Bougwan; whilst thou stoodst in the ring of the Greys, Incubu, and men went down before thine axe like corn before a sickle; ay, and how thou didst break the wild bull's (Twala's) strength, and bring his pride to dust. Fare ye well for ever, Incubu, Macumazahn, and Bougwan, my lords and my friends."

When he had finished speaking, the king gazed at us. It was clear that he expected an equally eloquent peroration. Now, I am just a Natal elephant-hunter, as my reader will know, and not much given to speech-making. I was casting about for something to say, but Sir Henry, to my relief, forestalled me, drawing himself up to his full height, and giving vent to an eloquent torrent in, as I thought, Greek or Latin. I knew that Sir Henry was a scholar, having taken a high degree in classics at college, but until that moment I did not dream that his mastery of the old tongues was so complete. He gazed at Ignosi with that Nordic candour and intensity, which can be fearful if one is on the wrong side of him, but which now shone with gratitude and affection. At the end, he gave a short bow. Ignosi inclined his head, looked earnestly at us for a few seconds, and then threw the corner of his kaross over his head, so as to cover his face from us.

We went in silence. When we were in the privacy of our quarters, Good and I rounded on our friend, demanding to know what he had said. Sir Henry, his eyes twinkling, replied: "I told him that he was an old fart, a no-good Kaffir, riddled probably with tapeworms and the pox, and we were glad to be leaving him behind! Well, of course, it is not completely true; but I confess he did rile me a little with his long-windedness, and his arrogant presumption in calling us his brothers. Anyway, I could think of nothing else to say at the time; I had a sudden whim to try to emulate *you*, Good, in obscene invective! And I happened to remember some of my Catullus from college days!"

We laughed, smoked our pipes, and passed quietly our last evening in Kukuanaland.

Next day at dawn we left Loo, escorted by our old friend Infadoos, who was heart-broken at our departure, and the regiment of Buffaloes. Early as the hour was, all the main street of the town was lined with multitudes of people, who gave us the royal salute as we passed at the head of the regiment, while the women blessed us as having rid the land of Twala, throwing flowers before us as we went. It really was very affecting, and not the sort of thing one is accustomed to meet with from natives.

One very ludicrous incident occurred, however, which I rather welcomed, as it gave us something to laugh at.

Just before we got to the confines of the town, a pretty young girl, with some beautiful lilies in her hand, came running forward and presented them to Good (somehow they all seemed to like Good; I think his eyeglass and solitary whisker gave him a fictitious value), and then said she had a boon to ask.

"Speak on."

"Let my lord show his servant his beautiful white cock, that his servant may look on it, and remember it all her days, and tell of it to her children; his servant has travelled four days' journey to see it, for the fame of it has gone throughout the land."

"I'll be buggered if I will!" said Good, excitedly.

"Come, come, my dear fellow," said Sir Henry, "you can't refuse to oblige a lady."

"*You* oblige her," said Good, obstinately.

"You know very well my inclinations don't run in that direction," Sir Henry said. "No, it's yours she wishes to see."

So, in the end, Good consented to open his flies and take out his penis, amidst notes of rapturous admiration from all the women present, especially the gratified young lady, and in this guise he had to walk till we got clear of the town.

Good's penis will, I fear, never be so greatly admired again. Of his melting teeth, and even of his "transparent eye," they wearied more or less, but of his penis, never.

Travelling easily, on the night of the fourth day's journey we found ourselves once more on the crest of the mountains that separate Kukuanaland from the desert, which rolled away in sandy billows at our feet, and about twenty-five miles to the north of Sheba's Breasts.

At dawn on the following day, we were led to the commencement of a precipitous descent, by which we were to descend the precipice and gain the desert two thousand and more feet below.

Here we bade farewell to that true friend and sturdy old warrior, Infadoos, who solemnly wished all good upon us, and nearly wept with grief. "Never, my lords," he said, "shall mine old eyes see the like of ye again. Ah! the way that Incubu cut his men down in the battle! Ah! for the sight of that stroke with which he swept off my brother Twala's head! It was beautiful— beautiful! I may never hope to see such another, except perchance in happy dreams."

We were very sorry to part from him; indeed, Good was so moved that he gave him as a souvenir—what do you think?—a *French letter!* (Afterwards we discovered that it was a spare one.) Infadoos was delighted, foreseeing that the possession of such an article would enormously increase his prestige. After he had made several vain attempts to reach an erection, Sir Henry assisted the aged warrior by stooping and giving his tool a few deft strokes with his mouth. Infadoos finally succeeded in getting the French letter in position. Anything more incongruous than the old warrior looked with a French letter I never saw. Tartan-coloured French letters don't go well with leopard-skin cloaks and black ostrich plumes.

Then, having seen that our guides were well laden with water and provisions, and having received a thundering farewell salute from the Buffaloes, we squeezed the old warrior's testicles (the usual form of farewell among the Kukuana warriors), and began our downward climb. A very arduous business it proved to be, but somehow that evening we found ourselves at the bottom without accident.

By midday of the third day's journey we could see the trees of the oasis of which the guides spoke, and by an hour before sundown we were once more walking upon grass and listening to the sound of running water.

F·O·U·R

FOUR

· I ·

As Coningsby observed to Tarkiainen gravely, only by the merest good luck, the most amazing chance, had he read the tasteless story, or memoir, which exposed the English finalist, Southerland, as a fraud. After the jury had listened to a good deal more of the Italian entry, and discussed it further, Coningsby had gone almost straight to bed to get a few hours' sleep before the final judging. But his brain was still active, the white night unsettling, and he had picked up an American magazine to browse through. Coningsby possessed it only because its cover had featured the Falklands conflict; changing flights at Madrid, he had spotted the magazine and thought it would be interesting to get an American-eye view. He hadn't bothered to read anything else—until tonight, in bed.

Drawn by the apparent coincidence of a title—*Sheba's Breasts*—within a few minutes he had realized, horror-struck, that *White Nights*, which had been so well received by the judges—which might even be in the running for the laurels—was nothing more than a carbon copy of a work by another author.

Clearly Southerland had been relying on the notable indiffer-

ence of judges and contestants alike to glossy American magazines.

Coningsby had thought it right to rouse Tarkiainen. Tarkiainen had not been at all pleased to be woken by a shrill
telephone when he felt exhausted and sick; but the evidence
which Coningsby brought along to his room fully justified
the judge's action, and also justified the chairman in telephon-
ing Southerland, waking him up too, and requesting that he
present himself straightaway to the judges' quarters.

Southerland, a short, plump man in middle age, with a shock
of unruly fair hair, now sat in jeans and a roll-neck sweater,
white-faced and traumatized before Coningsby and Tarkiainen,
who were in dressing-gowns and pyjamas. At half-past four of
the morning, a streak of bright Finnish sunlight shone on his
yellow hair, showing up dandruff. He was an experienced *improvisatore*, a semi-finalist in two previous Olympiads. Yet he had
no answer to the sorrowful accusations of the chairman of
judges and the austere, refined Anglo-Argentinian. Yes, he had
read the piece, just before leaving England. He had not particularly liked it; it was childishly offensive in parts; yet somehow
it had affected him, struck a chord: perhaps because it had reminded him of his experience during the War, as a refugee from
the London blitz, sent off to a strange family in Devon. When
he had read the theme he had been given, *White Nights*, he had
"died" at first; and then, strangely, the memoir of adolescent
nights in Australia had come to him. He was blessed or cursed
with a photographic memory. He believed—continued to believe—his verses were in some sense original. He believed
he had changed many details. He had not intended to deceive anyone.

"But you should have told us of your source, Mr Southerland," said Tarkiainen in his soft, courteous voice. The Finn's
face, above a scarlet dressing-gown, was paler than the Englishman's. The old man was slumped in his armchair, gaunt,

exhausted. His hand shook as he picked up a glass of water from the coffee-table.

"Yes, of course," Southerland mumbled. "I'm sorry . . . I meant to, but I was overcome at the end. But that's no excuse . . ." He glanced at the blue-gowned, El Greco-like figure, standing silent and sombre by the window; then back at the chairman. "I withdraw from the contest, of course."

"Thank you. But it may not end there. You understand that?"

"Yes—yes I do."

"If you'd even changed the names, the places . . . Well, you may go. I'm sorry we've broken your sleep."

The Englishman mumbled a reply, rose from his seat and stumbled from the room. He tried to close the door, but it swung open again; Southerland mumbled another apology, and this time shut the door after him.

"So that's it, Coningsby. Most unpleasant," sighed the Finn.

"Yes, yes . . . Well, I'll leave you. I'm sorry to have woken you."

"You did the right thing. Goodnight."

"Goodnight."

Coningsby raised his hand in a sympathetic, farewell gesture before closing the door on the old man; he climbed the stairs and padded barefoot along the corridor towards his room. He paused outside Matti's door, wondering if he should wake the young man up, talk to him again, try to make him take a more reasonable view. The "scene," earlier, had shaken Coningsby. That was why he had been unable to sleep. The brief, consoling relationship had not concluded as he had hoped, calmly and sweetly, with mutual goodwill. Matti, after they had made love, had shown a disturbed, irrational streak, blaming the older man for what—only two weeks before—he had been happy about: the knowledge, beyond all doubts, that he really was gay.

If anyone should have been upset, it was he, Coningsby. The youth's reaction when he had mentioned those disquieting rumours from the United States (as a friendly warning against promiscuity) had been deeply insulting. Yet he had swallowed his anger and simply reassured the agitated boy there was no possibility of any disease.

Matti had seemed well balanced, but now Coningsby wasn't so sure. He had left the room abruptly—not because he wasn't sympathetic, but he had wept too much himself, lately, drowning in the icy waters that had closed over the *General Belgrano*.

He swayed from exhaustion outside Matti's door. His eyes closed. He heard Pablo's voice, submarine echoes. It had been a mistake to think he could forget him in a diversion. Every time he had penetrated the sweet young flesh it was the athletic, energetic sailor he had entered. It would be pointless to waken Matti. He opened his eyes, and stumbled on to his own room. He slipped off his dressing-gown and threw himself on his bed. He fell asleep.

· 2 ·

NOT ALL THE JUDGES WERE ASLEEP. MATSUSHITA, HIS CHUBBY body perched nude and cross-legged on his bed, his glasses off, had plugged in to the Japanese translation of *First Love*, the Australian entry. All the rooms had access to any tape, at any time. Matsushita was troubled because *First Love*, the story of a dog falling in love with a teddy-bear, a koala, was so transparently simple. Moreau had called it "banal," but others had referred to it with increasing warmth. Matsushita tried to discover depths in it, but it remained utterly simple.

The Pole, Wojcicki, was awake, and lying beside Professor Krüdner in the German's room. In the background, faintly, were the Goldberg Variations they had found on an Estonian programme for nightshift workers. Wojcicki's hand straying languidly around her fat breasts, the couple talked quietly about the episode in Signora Riznich's improvisation in which the antihero, Surkov, had bitten his bride's vulva, and howled like a wolf.

"No, I think his mouth was open wide, as far as he could stretch it," said the tall, soldierly Pole. "Like this." He opened his mouth wide.

"Really?" whispered the blonde frau. "Oh, I assumed he just nipped it."

Wojcicki shook his head. "It definitely said he stretched his mouth as wide as it could go."

"M'mm." Her eyes closed, and he saw her stout thighs relax, part. He took his hand from her breast and laid it between her thighs. "God, you're still wet," he murmured.

"Show me, Anton. Show me what he did." Her torso rose and fell, agitatedly.

"Should I?"

"Yes!"

The Pole got up on his knees, crawled lower in the bed to stare up between her legs. He pulled her legs wide apart. The pink labia glistened, wet, below a coarse tangle of hair. He let his tongue stray around, touching her softly here and there, then moving away again, tantalizing. He nipped with his teeth a wet, matted strand of hair, pulling. He heard her wince.

"You really want me to?" he murmured. "For the death-camps?"

Her plump torso rose and fell still more rapidly. "Yes, yes. . . ."

"Not yet." He tongued her again, a canine lick from the small brown hole to the clitoris.

Three rooms away, Señora Menendez was troubled by desires. All through the Olympiad, she had found her eyes straying towards the austere, blue-eyed Finnish boy who acted as their technician, and she believed that he responded to her interest. True, she was almost old enough to be his mother . . . Yet Matti looked as though he would be attracted to older women. He appeared gentle and vulnerable, and not very experienced. Night after night, Señora Menendez had lain in bed fantasizing a love-affair with the young Finn, in which she would teach him the technicalities of passion.

Now, it was almost too late. She was sure he had looked at her tonight, in that unmistakable way. She brought her hand from under the sheet to touch her upper lip. How she wished she could get rid of that unsightly hair; yet not everyone was turned off by it. There was something ambiguous about Matti, she thought—which might complement her own ambiguous nature.

She ran her tongue over her lips. Yes, she ought to have made a move; he wanted her but was naturally too shy to make his desire known openly, to an older woman, a distinguished woman. He would love her to mount him, bear down on him, press her strong fingers into his slim neck, bite him, treat him a little roughly, eat him. . . .

But perhaps she was mistaken . . . ? If she went to his room, she invited a hurtful rebuff. On the other hand, wasn't she too old to be afraid of that? Wouldn't it be much worse if she left Satakieli tomorrow never having tried?

Señora Menendez made up her mind. She got out of bed, stripped off her pink pyjamas, put on her dressing-gown. She sat before the mirror, applying make-up, and ran a brush through her short, stubbly hair. She dabbed some Givenchy between her breasts, behind her ears. She had bought the perfume at Madrid airport—at about the time, as it happens, that Coningsby was buying his glossy American magazine.

She went out, closing the door softly behind her.

Wojcicki and Professor Krüdner heard the faint rustle of steps past their room. Wojcicki lifted his head for a moment, listening; then again dived to that beautiful ferned swamp. He opened his mouth as wide as it would go, but did not press his teeth into her. His nose, buried in her vulva just under the pubic mount, breathed in her sharp, sweet scent of sopping hairs and flesh; his lips and tongue slithered against her spread vulva. He enjoyed resting there; he liked feeling her tension. Her fingers ran, distraught, through his hair.

Just as Matsushita, on the floor below, was listening again to the opening phrase of *First Love*—"A little dog went ambling down the main street of Ballerat"—he heard a scream, a cry, a howl, from somewhere above his head. Though quite faint, it curdled his blood. He wasn't sure if a woman had cried out, or a man—or even both. He jumped off the bed, silenced the tape, and listened intently, his heart racing. He put on his glasses to glance at his watch. It was five o'clock. There were no further screams, but he heard the sound of rapid footsteps. He wondered if he should dress and go upstairs, but decided it was best not to interfere. He took off his glasses, lay down, and closed his eyes. He had changed his mind about running through *First Love* again; it was, simply, absolutely clear, and therefore incomprehensible.

Others had heard the scream, or cry, or howl, in their sleep, and in various ways it changed their dreams.

Jacob Elsberg, from being on a kibbutz tractor, was suddenly standing in a ring of Israeli soldiers watching Palestinians being gunned down. A woman screamed as the child in her arms was cut to ribbons. She started shrieking that they had killed the Messiah. Elsberg was distraught with grief and remorse, because he saw the woman had a number tattooed on her arm, and he recognized her as a woman from the street in Warsaw where he had lived as a child. He wanted to ask the woman if she had been with his parents when they died in Auschwitz, but didn't dare intrude on her grief.

Ivan Dibich was with his wife, removing some valuable furniture and pictures from her dead mother's flat. (In reality his wife's mother was alive and well.) His wife, rummaging in a cupboard, screamed, and then showed him a loosely-wrapped brown paper parcel. Inside it was a mummified, newborn baby. The sight quite spoiled Dibich's pleasure over the attractive heirlooms. Her mother must have had a bastard child, sixty or more years ago, and she had let it die. There followed a nightmarish car journey from Moscow to Leningrad, with the mummy hidden in the boot. In the middle of the night he dropped the tiny corpse into the Gulf of Finland.

Maria Casalduero was breakfasting at a hotel with her husband and a noted woman gymnast. She and her husband were naked, the gymnast was in a track-suit. The famous athlete was teaching her what exercises to do in the mornings to help solve her weight problem; but while standing on her head, on a chair, the slim gymnast over-toppled, went crashing through the window, and had to cling on to the sill four floors above the street. Maria's husband managed to claw the woman back in, luckily: yet Maria was unhappy at the way he made a meal of it, clutching the gymnast's breast and also holding her between the thighs, and lifting her high in the room as if he were Nureyev.

The black-bearded Iranian, Shafaq, was actually saved from a desperate situation by that cry in the white night. With his girlfriend (who looked like Corinna Riznich, but with the massive bosom of a call-girl Shafaq had once visited in Paris), he was kneeling in a square, waiting to be beheaded. A wolf came rushing in, howling, and scattered the executioner and all the spectators. Shafaq and the girl stood up; the wolf smiled at them and wagged its tail; all three of them walked away peacefully.

Jean Moreau was playing in a chess championship, under the

standing stones of Carnac. His opponent, a Russian grand-master called Charsky, had boasted that he could beat Moreau with his eyes closed, and was doing just that. A gross, hairy spider wandered on to the board, which was resting on a granite rock. Moreau knew he should warn his opponent, whose hands were moving blindly; but he remained silent. Charsky picked up the spider instead of a chess piece. The spider bit him and he fell back stone dead. There was a discussion among the adjudicators about the outcome of the match. Was it a draw, or a win for Moreau? They declared for Moreau, and he went through to the semi-finals.

Coningsby was sailing, with his young friend Pablo, off the Dorset coast. It was a warm and peaceful summer's day, and they were happy. Then they saw the shadow of a torpedo tracking them through the water, like a shark. There was no way they could avoid the impact; they stood petrified, hand in hand, waiting. But then they heard a wailing noise, and saw the torpedo leap out of the water and fly safely over their heads. "It's all right!" Coningsby heard himself shouting. "It's an Exocet!" The missile vanished. They heard an explosion, and saw a cloud of smoke rise above the limestone cliffs. Coningsby felt a mixture of sorrow and relief.

Tarkiainen did not hear the scream.

Russian tanks were in Budapest. A brutal sergeant had interfered with Anna Szabó, and her mother took her to the local police station, but the girl was too shy, in the presence of men, to say what had happened. But she pointed, through the window, at the Red Army soldier who had done it. He was standing in a tank, which was moving. The tank ran over a pigeon, and the girl found herself screaming. Her mother stopped scolding her for refusing to say what exactly had happened to her; she comforted her daughter, and let her wipe her nose in her skirt.

Signora Rossi, strolling in the deep forests, gulping down fresh air and nicotine, heard a cry, at about the same time, but it was actually a wild animal howling.

· 3 ·

AT THAT TIME, CORINNA RIZNICH WAS GIVING AN IMPROMPTU interview in English to a cub journalist who had caught sight of her and Markov strolling by the lake. The young reporter, who was tall, blond-haired and good-looking in a rather Swedish way, had overcome his shyness and begged her to answer a few questions. Corinna, liking his looks, had readily agreed, inviting him to squat down beside her on the grass. Markov, amused by the young man's evident adoration of the Italian beauty, stretched out a little way off, chewing a blade of grass, enjoying the sun—which was by now warm—and half attending to the interview.

". . . No, of course my improvisation wasn't sexist," she was saying. "It wasn't a put-down of men. Believe me, I *like* men . . ." Markov saw her gaze intently in the young man's eyes, making him drop his gaze and become flustered. He pressed too hard on his notebook, broke the pencil lead, and had to fumble through his pockets for another. Corinna went on: "I know my Russian heroes—what did I call them?—Sadkov and Romanov?—were shits; but that isn't to say I think all men are like them

. . . I was trying to depict a type of person—it could be male or female—who is subjected to pretty intolerable pressures. But then, it's wrong to say *I* was trying to depict such a person. *Something* was trying to depict him: some impersonal power which merely made use of me. . . .

"No, I can't say anything about that power. It's behind the seventh veil. Igor, there, would say it was the Muse; and it's perfectly true that I, too, have an image in my head of a man, a disembodied man, when I am improvising. A *young* man . . ."
Markov again saw the young man lower his gaze, confused. Corinna was running her slender fingers through her long black locks, and also at times cupping her chin in an odd way—as if she was presenting to the watcher the delicacy, the fragility, of her lovely face, framing it for him so to speak. The stroking of her hair, and the cupping of her chin, were mannerisms that seemed simultaneously to suggest narcissism and self-doubt. I am very beautiful, don't you think? she was saying; but also: I don't really exist.

She had captured those ambiguities, with wonderful self-knowledge and self-irony, in the portrait of Marie, in the last part of her improvisation.

". . . I can't imagine what is going on in the judges' minds. I would guess they found my improvisation too long and too confused. I don't think it was one of my best. Igor's was marvellously compact and powerful, don't you think? My Petersburg variations were a tribute to him, to his skill and courage. He should win, if there is any justice. He pretends he doesn't agree! Well, we'll see. I also liked the English contestant's performance. A fine exercise of memory and imagination and technical skill. I'm not too keen on space epics, but Kauppinen's effort was undoubtedly fine—you must be hoping he'll win. No?
. . . Well, you flatter me . . . Or they could go for the simplicity of Mr Blake's story. The little dog in—where was it?—an Australian township. It's pointless trying to look into the judges' minds.

We shall know soon enough. And what is important is not the winning but the taking part . . . Truly, I mean that. Isn't that so, Igor? . . . At my first Olympiad, twelve years ago in Salzburg, I was eliminated in the opening round; but it was still a great honour . . . I'm quite relaxed because I'm sure I won't win the laurels . . . Well, it's very kind of you to say so, but. . . ."

Markov, from his prone position, saw Corinna's travelling companion, Cesare Cosmo, approaching from afar, striding towards them through the triangle formed by Corinna's bent arm and cupped chin. Eye to eye with the blond youth, she did not seem to become aware of her friend's approach until he was almost on top of her; and then, she merely glanced towards him with a brief, indifferent smile, and turned again to the youth. Cosmo settled on the grass, where he could watch Corinna's face. The Russian was puzzled by their relationship, as he had been on meeting her again in Moscow, the previous year. It was such a misalliance—the beautiful, young-looking *improvisatrice*, and the slow-moving, ponderous, grey-bearded rogue-priest. He was clearly mad about her; and Markov could see jealousy written all over his face, now, whether of him—Markov—or of the young reporter. But Corinna said she didn't sleep with him, and Igor believed her. She treated him, most of the time, condescendingly, almost sadistically. Was she with him just for his family fortune—that he could finance her tours? Or was he—but this was a Freudian interpretation, and Markov didn't go for Freud—an image of her father, needful and hated? And was that story she had spun, about incest and suicide, true? Like all *improvisatori*, including himself, she struck the Russian as an inhabitant of the borderlands between fact and fiction, uncertain where the boundary was. She was speaking about her parents. . . .

"My mother is still alive. My father died when I was young. His death affected me very badly. I had a depressive illness, soon after his death, and began to make up stories and poems for the other patients in the nursing-home where I—which I attended for

a while. I suppose that was the beginning of my career. Though
there were signs of my *disease* in my childhood—I found I could
remember easily the nursery-rhymes and verses my mother sang
to me; and also I could make up little verses, when I was five or
six. But then my talent, or illness, went to ground . . . There are
only two activities in which I can lose myself: improvising
stories, and making love. My improvisation was much longer
than Igor's because I have more staying power when I fuck than a
man has. Naturally. I hope I'm not embarrassing you . . ."
(Markov, at the reference to himself in connection with the act of
love, saw a look of pain and embarrassment pass across the face of
Cosmo, who had squatted down close to Corinna.—How skil-
fully and cruelly she had "caught" him too, in her portrait of the
ponderous Findlater.) ". . . Improvisation *is* sex, and sex is
improvisation. When I improvise I embrace the unknown, the
dark. Romanov—Rozanov, thank you—didn't enjoy fucking
Olga, so he fucked the darkness instead: which was infinitely
richer, more mysterious, more rewarding. As I do, he found it
difficult to be sexually turned on by someone older than he, or as
old. It is a terrible misfortune. I know all about it. Have you seen
the film *The Roman Spring of Mrs Stone*? . . ."

Corinna was leaning forward; and the blond youth was leaning
towards her. He had forgotten that he was meant to be writing.
His gaze never left hers, she would not permit it.

". . . He fucked the night, the young negress, the black
Madonna. . . ."

She was silent. The young man was silent. Their faces were
only inches apart. Then, with a smile, she leaned back, and turned
her face aside and downwards towards the grass. The cub reporter blushed, and bent concentratedly over his notebook. Markov
glanced at Cesare—then looked away quickly. The face wore an
expression of torment, yet also fascination.

". . . I have one son. I feel rather guilty, because most of the
time I'm not with him. But we are good friends . . . No, I won't

tell you anything about his father. My private life is my own affair. If you are assuming that I and he"—she glanced aside at Cosmo, who bent his head in shame—"are anything but friends, you are mistaken. I am a free spirit. I make what relationships I like. I choose whom I like." She had leaned forward again, and again the young man became flustered.

"A priest, from my home town, helped me to get a decent education, in return for a few hugs and kisses. I was too young to see any harm in this, but when I told my *earthly* father, in all innocence, he . . ." She seemed to lose the track of what she was saying, staring through the young reporter; then she concluded: ". . . became very angry. Anyway I had very little formal education after my breakdown. Since then, I've done everything from A to Z. I was an air-hostess, till I got caught trying to join the mile-high club with a passenger—you know, screwing a mile up. And I was a zoo-attendant till I got sorry for some of the animals in small cages, and let them loose. My son and I have never starved, but it hasn't always been easy. . . .

". . . No. Why should I want to do that? What is the point of having one's work set down for ever more in black type? That would mean I would have to revise my work, which I would find excruciatingly boring. It would be like—like you and I screwing and having it recorded on film. I'm not interested in that. Much better to go into the trees and make love spontaneously, and then it's over. Don't you think? What's your name?—I'm sorry, I didn't catch it . . . Ah, I like that. Have you a girlfriend? You're extremely nice looking; your girlfriend is lucky.

". . . Well, I had an ancestress who was an *improvisatrice*. She was called Amalia Riznich. She was part German, part Italian. She married a Russian merchant, and lived in Odessa. There she met Pushkin, and they fell in love. But she had other lovers too. She drove Pushkin wild; he was so crazy about her that one day he went running in the desert, on and on, until he collapsed from exhaustion. Just to relieve himself of his frustration. A kind of masturbation, I guess. To go running in the desert. It's not mentioned in the biographies that she was an *improvisatrice* because she didn't make a song and dance about it. She kept it quiet. When she had to return to Italy, pregnant and also suffering from tuberculosis, Pushkin forgot all about her. Until, years later, he heard that she had died, in great suffering and great poverty. And alone. That's the fate of us all. Then he wrote a famous poem, about the kiss she had promised him when they should be reunited in Italy. How does it go? Do you remember it, Igor?"

". . . I can remember how it ends," the Russian murmured. . . .

> "But there, alas, where the sky's
> Vault shines with blue radiance,
> Where the shadow of olives lies
> On the waters, you have fallen asleep
> Forever. Your beauty, your suffering,
> Have vanished in the grave—
> But the sweet kiss of our meeting . . .
> I wait for it; you owe it me. . . ."

" '. . . You owe it me.' Perfect. So, of course, I've always been interested in Pushkin; and it was wonderful to visit Russia last year. But I'll travel anywhere—anywhere I'm invited. It's a part of the tradition of *improvisatori* to go from place to place. In my country, we have a proud tradition of the *improvisatrici*. You should have asked me about them . . . Ask me about the great *improvisatrici*. . . .

"That's a very good question, Ingmar . . . Yes, I have many famous predecessors in my country—women with a gift far greater than mine. Actually, one of the most famous was also related to me: Giannina Milli. She was, I think, my great-great-great-great aunt. Or I may have missed out one of the greats. She came of a poor family of Abruzzia. Born in 1825 or 6; died around 1880. They say she became feverish before a performance, and after; and was painfully shy. But when she was actually perform-ing, the adrenalin flowed. Well, she would not have known about adrenalin, but it flowed. Her first public appearance was in Naples, when she was about twenty. No one had heard of her, of course, and an audience of about forty had to be lured in by not charging anything. She was beautiful—black hair, black eyes, made more dramatic by a white dress. Beauty is never a draw-back in improvisation, though it can be a great burden in relation-ships. It was a cloudy, rainy day, and she was asked to improvise about the weather. Well, as she composed, the weather bright-ened, and a ray of sunlight shone in through the window. She caught the ray of sunlight, so to speak, in her improvisation: verse by verse, phrase by phrase, her improvisation reflected the changing atmosphere. She completely won the audience over, and from that day her reputation was made.

". . . Yes, I suppose it was dull and miserable when I made my character speak of the Armenian massacres. I guess I am affected too. . . .

". . . I have some of her letters, and some sketches made of her. You may think I am beautiful, but I can tell you you wouldn't give me a second glance if Milli were sitting here beside me . . . She often composed upon contemporary themes, whereas most *improvisatori* chose classical and religious subjects—or preferred them, I should say, for one cannot choose. I guess I tend to follow her in that respect. But I am much less lyrical; and of course most of my improvisation is in prose."

Markov noticed how the Italian beauty had lost much of her self-regarding air; her hands were clasped in her lap, and her eyes were bright with enthusiasm. The fingers of the young journalist raced over the notebook, unable to keep up with her, though doubtless he was not very interested in the long-dead Italian lady. But Markov himself followed her remarks attentively; he was reminded of certain hallowed figures in the tradition of Georgia, his mother's ancestral land.

"Milli was rather late in the improvisational tradition," Corinna resumed. "The eighteenth century was the great period. One of the greatest and most famous was Maddalena Morelli, better known to us as Corilla Olimpica. She was only seven when her gift appeared. She improvised with astonishing speed—the violins could not keep up with her, they say. Her greatest triumph was in Rome, where the Arcadian Society tested her with twelve themes chosen by twelve judges. Inspired by a friend in the congregation, she sailed through the tests, and the Pope himself adorned her with the Capitoline crown and placed her on the throne. She was tall and fair, with loose-flowing, unpowdered hair; and for her Roman triumph she wore a dress of white satin, and a velvet coat sprinkled with silvery stars. Can you imagine the scene? Somehow I can't see myself being crowned by our present Holy Father, can you? Cannons were fired in St Peter's Square, and the musicians played. That was when she was re-named Corilla Olimpica. She was probably thinking of Corinna, the famous Theban *improvisatrice*, who five times defeated Pindar in public competition . . . Yes, I have taken my name from her, and from Amalia Riznich—which isn't my family name. No, I won't tell you my real name. It's not important. . . .

"Well, there were many slanders spread against her. She didn't live with her husband, a Spaniard. People said she fucked around. Well, she may have done. So what? Maybe she spent many a night like Rozanov, bored out of her mind. She loved Apollo. There is a sonnet of hers which has survived. Let me see if I can recall it . . . Well, here is the sestet. . . .

> "*Ma fin d'allora, il biondo Apollo amai,*
> *E in Elicona, ove talvolta ascesi,*
> *Qualche foglia di lauro anch'io spiccai;*

E fin d'allora a sciorre il canto appresi
All'improvviso, e sieguo improvvisando
L'estro, ond'ho i vanni della mente accesi."

The young, blond Finn interrupted his frantic scribbling to ask
her to translate into English.

"I would hate to translate it literally. It would sound banal.
And my English is not so good that I can easily turn it into verse.
But I will try. Let me see. . . ."

Corinna hunched over her blue-jeaned legs, frowning, and
after a few moments she recited:

"From my first years, I've loved the fair Apollo,
    And loved to climb the slopes of Helicon;
        By improvising, I have sought to find

A laurel leaf; like the free-darting swallow
    I've turned a burning glass against the sun
        And set fire to the spaces in my mind."

Markov stretched out his arms in front of him on the grass, and
clapped. Cesare followed suit. The young man scribbled his
shorthand.

"Well, it is rather free," Corinna said apologetically. "But I
hope it gives you a glimpse of her talent, which was clearly far
superior to mine. And that, of course, made people jealous. They
abused her for her free living and free loving . . . Yet can a
swallow be expected to stay faithful to a budgerigar? That's what
most men are. And the same critics accused Corilla of making up
her verses in advance . . . Yes, I suppose I had her in mind in my
continuation of *Egyptian Nights*. But it's a common accusation.
Budgerigars don't like you to fly. When she died unexpectedly,
of an apoplectic stroke, someone commented venomously that it
was the first time she had improvised. . . .

"In fact, not many friends stayed faithful to her. She retired to

Florence, in her last years, and her final verses were inspired by a
visit from a rising star, Teresa Bandettini Landucci, who took the
name of Amarilli Etrusca. She was another amazing woman—
but I can tell you're bored. She won the Olympic crown in
Mantua, in I think 1773. Again, her family was very poor, and
she had to earn her living as a ballerina, while studying by night;
and also she had to look after a husband and children. Some of
whom died. Shit! What a life! And she dragged herself around
from place to place, performing. She taught herself Latin, Phy-
sics, French, Greek . . . She inspired me to try to learn as many
languages as possible . . . Oh, I guess I have a smattering of about
two dozen or so, but only four or five do I know quite well. The
travel exhausted her. And just think of it in those days, before cars
and planes—dragging from Naples to Florence to Venice to
Milan to Vienna . . . and the little towns in between. One-night
stands . . . I have it much easier. This past year, for example, I've
performed in London, Lima, Madras, New York, Leningrad,
Moscow, Tbilisi, Yerevan, Toronto, Athens, Munich . . . where
else have we been, Cesare? Yes, Oslo, Dresden, Alexandria . . .
as well as most parts of Italy. But with planes and modern hotels
it's not so bad. . . .

"You liked it, did you? Not too flamboyant? Well, thank you.
It was designed and made for me specially by Cosmo in Milan—
the best clothes designers in Europe. Would you mention that,
please? It's the theatrical element, you see. One can't ignore it. I
like to look good as well. I'm not sure what I shall wear for the
award ceremony. Anything too flamboyant and it might seem as
if I was expecting to win. Last time, in Delphi, I wore a scarlet
dress, because I had fairly high hopes—Markov wasn't able to
come, you see!—but of course I didn't win. I felt over-dressed. I
think I'll wear white, like Corilla Olimpica, but not satin. In six
hours or so, we shall know the worst, Igor. . . .

"Oh, really? It was blue at first? Well, I must say, you're
extremely attentive. To have noticed such a triviality."

The young man flushed and she turned her eyes away over the lake. He rubbed his wrist; then, after a long silence, stammered another question. "Well, no," she murmured, pleasantly again, "I don't find it at all difficult to assume a male personality. Why should I? I observe men much more intently than I observe other women. Especially in the bedroom . . . And of course there's a man inside me, as there is a woman inside you." They heard the distant wail of sirens and—glancing in the direction of the track, some three hundred yards away—they saw a police car followed by an ambulance racing along, their beacons flashing. "I wonder what's happened?" said Corinna.

"They seem to have stopped outside the judges' house," Markov observed. "The chairman has had a heart-attack . . . Your improvisation was too much for him, Corinna!"

Corinna smiled, and stroked her hair. "It's not quite a trance," she corrected the young reporter, "but like dreaming-awake. Like a swallow's flight; like leaping from stone to stone across a river in flood—the excitement and danger of not daring to miss your footing or else jumping on to a stone leading nowhere; it's like, as I said, creating an act of love, caressing by instinct . . . Who guides the fingers and lips of a Cleopatra or a Don Giovanni? . . ." She began to talk to him in a quieter voice. Markov could see him losing touch with his surroundings, as though drugged by Corinna's voice and penetrating gaze. The Russian glanced again at Cesare Cosmo; he was staring at the couple with anguished eyes. Corinna said to him, in a casual voice, that she and the young man were going to take a stroll in the woods. The young Finn, his pale face flushed again, stood up and helped her to her feet. They strolled off together towards the trees.

· 4 ·

CONINGSBY WAS WRENCHED OUT OF DEEP, DREAMLESS SLEEP BY a ringing phone. Three-quarters asleep still, he mumbled his name. His stupefied brain took in that someone from the police was calling him; that there had been a death in the Olympic village; a hanging—presumably a suicide, and that a letter, left behind, implicated him in some way. Coningsby unglued his eyes and struggled to sit up in bed. He was being asked if he would come to the administrative office, to make a statement. "But I don't understand it," he mumbled down the phone; "it was absurd to do that. Out of all proportion. I know it was a shock for him, but it had to be done. It was necessary. The chairman and I were reasonably gentle with him."

"The chairman?" asked the voice, evidently puzzled. "Professor Tarkiainen? Do you mean, he was present while you . . . ?"

"Of course," Coningsby mumbled. "He took the lead, naturally. You don't imagine I would do anything like that without his authorization? I was only there for moral support."

"Authorization? Moral support? I don't understand. All right,

I'll call him too. Come downstairs, can you?" His voice sounded cold.

"Yes, of course." The Argentinian put down the phone, hauled himself out of bed, and began to pull on his shirt. "What a mess," he muttered to himself. Striking his forehead against a shelf, and dry-mouthed, he felt an ache of homesickness—not for Buenos Aires, where he lived, but for the rolling pampas.

"Stupid, stupid!" he muttered; a flabby Englishman, killing himself over a reprimand—while Pablo, that graceful, bright-eyed youth, who so desperately wanted to live, had had no choice, screaming as the icy South Atlantic waters closed over him.

Signora Rossi, strolling back through the woods towards the house, was not thinking of the contest. She was meditating on the problems of the Italian Communist Party: ought they to move closer to Moscow, or further away? They were going to have to make crucial decisions soon. She could not make up her mind which way to vote. . . .

She was looking down at her feet as she walked, in deep thought and taking care where she stepped in the undergrowth. Somehow she had lost the path. She stumbled on the naked couple before she was aware of them; her sandal was within a few inches of the young man's heaving buttocks. She took a step back. The distraught face whirled around and gasped. She saw then, beneath him, the face of her countrywoman, her eyes wild, her mouth open, her hair dishevelled. "Lucia!" Corinna gasped; then she smiled, amused.

"Teresa!" Signora Rossi exclaimed. "I'm sorry! Forgive me!" She stepped quickly round the couple and hurried on, ignoring the thorns and brambles cutting her legs. By the time she paused in a clearing, to catch her breath and light up a cigarette, the encounter seemed unreal, like a dream. Well, it had happened; yet she felt unusually calm about it. Normally it took very little to agitate her and make her nervous. Had she, merely, stumbled like that on any other couple, not even making love but just sitting together, she would now be shaking all over from the shock. Why was this different, she asked herself? Because it was so familiar, yet long-forgotten; because Corinna's face, that first moment, had been the face of the child with whom Lucia Rossi had played in the school playground under the flanks of Vesuvius. When they used to play hide-and-seek, and little Teresa, discovered in her hiding-place, had looked just like that—caught out, open-mouthed. And then—just like that—had smiled.

But there's more to it than that, thought the Italian woman, as she leaned against a birch tree and puffed her cigarette. It's extremely curious. I've never seen anyone making love before, and yet—compared with the naked intimacy of her improvisation, for so many hours—it seemed decent, unexceptionable. But, heavens! I must have given them a shock! Him especially—I wonder who he is. His face, when he turned and looked up! . . .

She stubbed the cigarette in the bracken, and walked on. "Oh, she simply *must* win," she murmured aloud.

"Don't tell me it's upset you so much? You disappoint me, Ingmar. Is there *nothing* I can do? . . . Not even this?"

"I'm sorry, Corinna.'

"She won't tell anyone, I promise you. I know her. She's one of my oldest friends, though our paths haven't crossed for over twenty years. But we were kids together, in Sorrento. We sat together in class. She's okay. You mustn't print that, of course—it would be ruinous. You promise?"

"Of course I promise."

"I trust you. You look like my son. You're really beautiful. I love your eyes, and your lips. And these muscles . . . wonderful! I was enjoying it so much—and now I see you're a budgerigar. I bet this doesn't ever happen when you're with your girlfriend."

"This is the first time. I mean, the first time I've made love to anyone."

"Really? Oh, that's marvellous! I don't care if I don't win the laurel crown!"

"You're beautiful, Corinna. I love you."

"Then prove it to me. I'm longing for you. Let me suck your sweet little cock. Come, my sweet. . . ."

"I just can't. . . ."

"You can't! My little budgerigar! Well, it was nice while it lasted . . . You probably think I'm very experienced, don't you? Well, I'm not. I have problems with sex. I usually let a man go so far, then I stop him. So you're very privileged, and now you don't want to take advantage of it. Shall I tell you something that will shock you? That I've never told anyone else? But it's off the record . . . I've only ever been properly fucked twice in my whole life."

"I can't believe that."

"It's true. This would have been only the third time. But that's not all; not by any means. The worst is yet to come. The first man was my father. That fucked me up. The other time was with my son, when he was sixteen—a year ago. He doesn't know I made love to him. It was a masked party at my apartment. My son shouldn't have been there at all, but he brought some of his friends along and got blind drunk for the first time in his life. There were a lot of wild goings-on. I saw him necking with a girlfriend of mine on his bed. When she slipped away, I took her place. He didn't know me in the mask, and anyway, as I said, he was drunk. I don't know why I did such a thing, except that I, too, was pretty tight, and I thought of his—I thought of my father.

"Do you think I'm an evil woman, Ingmar? Wait—why are you dressing? Wait? . . . Ah, I can see, you're just a budgerigar. Budgerigars shouldn't mate with swallows. Go home, then, little boy. Go home to mama. . . ."

★

Signora Rossi, emerging from the trees not far from the house, saw an ambulance and a police car standing outside. She felt a prickling of curiosity and excitement, but there was no one in that house for whom she would feel more than a mild regret, a passing sympathy, if something bad had happened to them. A police car on its own would have frightened her; for she always carried the fear that one of her children would get knocked down while she was away. Thank God she would soon be with them again. She recalled the ambulance in Corinna's improvisation, and Rozanov's fear. How truly observed that was: the natural selfishness of people!

She calculated the hours between Satakieli and Rome. She would ring before the final judging, to make sure Pietro and Angelica were okay.

Several people were in the hall, standing in their dressing-gowns. They whispered the shocking news to her. Once in her room, and in bed, she found her thoughts drifting away from the sordid, painful present to her Arcadian childhood by the Bay of Naples. And to her playmate, Teresa, so ragged, like all her brothers and sisters. Her parents, loving but terribly poor— peasants. The priest had befriended Teresa, thinking her talented. Lucia and she had been friends across a social chasm; then Lucia had moved to Rome with her parents, and lost touch. It had astonished her when she read about Teresa, years later. How well she had done. . . .

"How happy we were. . . ."

She sighed. Set the alarm. Lay back on the pillow.

"She *must* win. . . ."

"That ambulance . . . such mad drivers, the Romans . . . Pietro, Angelica . . ." She whispered a prayer.

Markov lay fully dressed on his bed, watching Estonian television. The early-morning news, composed several days earlier, dissolved into *Good Morning, Finland!*, the daily report from the

Olympiad. Igor had watched it almost every morning: not only for the obvious reason, but also because the producer and presenter, Boris Troshin, was a friend of his. Troshin had once been one of the star producers in Moscow, but certain mistakes during the Moscow Olympics had cost him his job and he had been sent into provincial exile. During the Satakieli Olympiad, he had kept to the strict ideological line; the extracts from Kauppinen, for instance, had been dubbed over in Russian even though Estonians could easily have understood the original. Yet Markov was sure Troshin had been responsible for choosing a few bars of Sibelius's Karelia Suite as the theme music. Since Karelia had been annexed by the Soviet Union (as had Estonia, of course), the choice was provocative, even though the music was never identified by name.

There was unquestionably a self-destructive streak in Troshin. Why else would he have permitted a shot of the Olympic flag after a British victory in the Moscow Games? He had been much in Markov's mind, at Satakieli; Igor wondered if he had caught a few glimpses of his own face in the portrait of the suicidal Olenin. That had been one morning when Igor had slept on and on, exhausted from his performance, and missed the report from Tallinn.

After the brass fanfare from the Karelia Suite, against a still of Lake Lemminjärvi, Gaevsky, Moscow's illiterate reporter in Finland, conveyed the mood of excitement and tension at Satakieli, hours before the winner would be announced. Then Troshin, in the Tallinn studio, took over. Against silent images of the contestants on stage, he summed up their chances. The ageing, cherub-faced Kauppinen (*Space-flight*) had home advantage, Troshin said, and had also had the good fortune, as a specialist in SF stories, of having been given the perfect theme. Troshin hastened to add that there was no suggestion of malpractice on the part of the Finns, the selection process being entirely random. However, Kauppinen's improvisation had been a disappointment to his fellow countrymen. "On the whole," said Troshin drily, "I preferred the contestant from Israel . . ." There followed the comedy of the black-bearded Barash announcing his theme, *Saint Teresa*, hesitating, bowing, then striding from the stage. "If Barash wins," said Troshin, "it will be a controversial decision. It is unlikely, especially as there is no American on the panel of judges to back up the Israeli."

Markov closed his eyes and shook his head, in pain at his friend's cheap though politic jibe.

The youngish, pleasant-faced, pock-marked Australian appeared. "*First Love* undoubtedly went down well with the audience," said Troshin; "but I prefer Turgenev's version to Maurice Blake's. Still, he might win, as a compromise choice. It was a rather touching story."

"Holy shit, Borya," Markov muttered.

The pale, flabby, sandy-haired Englishman appeared. "Southerland's *White Nights* was, as you will recall if you've been watching us regularly, a very personal memoir, set in Blake's homeland. It was a good performance, after a shaky start. He must be in the running. But it somehow lacked that final, indefinable, note of authority. Which cannot be said of the Soviet contestant, Igor Markov." Markov saw his face fill the screen, and winced. Who was that stranger? "Markov's *The Crossing*, as you will know if you watched *Good Morning, Finland!* yesterday, was a wonderfully convincing demolition of bourgeois values, an exposure of *refusniks*." The camera moved aside to a mountain of letters. "These letters have been flowing into the studios ever since we showed the extracts from his poem. They express pride in their countryman's performance. Let me read to you just one of those letters." He fished in the breast pocket of his neat navy suit, and came out with a sheet of blue notepaper. "It comes from ten-year-old Arno Kampmaa. This is what he writes." The childish Russian script came into close-up, as Troshin read: "This Igor Markov—how does he do it? It's magic! I've wanted to be a

magician when I grow up, but now I think I'll be a poet instead."
Troshin's platinum-teethed smile remarked: "Well, Arno, I wish
I knew how he does it—because then I'd do it myself and win the
Olympic laurel!" He composed his smile for Arno into a serious
yet lively public face, adding: "Markov should win, if there is any
justice."

Markov could not suppress a naïve feeling of pleasure at his
friend's empty praise.

Corinna Riznich's beautiful face appeared on the screen. She
was touching her shell-like little ear, pausing between sections of
her story.

"Yesterday," said Troshin's voice-over, "we heard the last of
the finalists, Signora Riznich from Florence. Now, Signora
Riznich is not without talent. Far from it. We played you some of
her improvisation in the semi-finals. Listen again to some of her
verses." Signora Riznich's lips moved, but Markov heard the
gravelly accents of Serge Dmitriev, the Soviet translator. "Marvellous, didn't you think? Marvellous in the Italian too, I assure
you. But yesterday, she gave the worst, the most repellent,
performance of the finals." Markov, shaking his head sadly
again, pulled himself up on to his elbow. "Her theme was *The
Seven Veils*, but it might just as well have been *Genghis Khan*, for
all the sense she made. It was not even a short-lived senselessness;
her nonsensical ramblings went on—believe it or not—for five
hours! It's a wonder if all our Finnish friends are not shell-
shocked. Furthermore, she indulged herself in the most crude,
virulent, pathetic, anti-Soviet propaganda. To show you just
how vile, how pathetic, it was, you are going to hear the last part
of her improvisation, unedited, straight as it comes. . . ."

"Jesus Christ!" Markov hissed.

"Incidentally," continued Troshin, "the Canadian woman in
this extract bears a remarkable resemblance to the Signora herself—who, as you can see, is extremely attractive, though not so
attractive as she evidently thinks she is. It is very crude stuff, I

warn you; the language is pornographic in parts." Troshin leered
for a moment through his thick-rimmed glasses. "But even that
is not so offensive as the Cold War rhetoric. Listen out particularly for a passage which purports to be a Soviet poet's improvisation—her work has improvisations within improvisations, to
add to its chaos—an improvisation purporting to be a speech in
Decembrists' Square, Leningrad, last December, the month of
the restoration of socialist legality in Poland."

Markov shot up straight on the bed, exclaiming, "This is
suicide!"

F·I·V·E

This will last out a night in Russia.
SHAKESPEARE

· I ·

DARKNESS HAD FALLEN BY THE TIME ROZANOV LEFT SONIA'S apartment to drive home to Peredelkino. It was raining; and the mesmeric windscreen wipers added to the effect of insomnia, alcohol, and a vicious row. His eyelids kept drooping during his erratic drive. On the approach to the writers' colony he actually found himself jerking awake; and a glance at his surroundings told him he had been asleep for the past mile or so. He had been driving on automatic pilot. It was lucky the traffic was light. What had woken him—and (who knows?) saved him from a crash—was the throb in his right arm where Sonia had bitten him. It had been one of their very worst scenes. Attack, after he had found the Polish cigarette-stubs in the ashtray in her bedroom, had very soon changed to defence, as usually happened. Sonia had screamed, thrown a plate, bitten him, wept. A sick, exhausted depression swept over Rozanov, as he turned into the rough, tree-shrouded road leading to his *dacha*. Life could not be worse.

He would get it in the neck from Nina too, since he had promised to be home in time to give Sasha his bed-time story.

The child, disappointed, would be in bed asleep. And there would be the torture, all evening, of knowing that Kolasky was still in Moscow, and visiting Sonia—no doubt staying the night, before his return to his tank regiment on the Polish border.

Turning the corner, slowing, preparing to stop outside the *dacha*, he saw an ambulance drawn up, its doors open, and the front door of his house thrown wide, the hall light radiating out. Griped in the pit of his stomach, Rozanov prayed, "Please God, if it has to be, let it be Nina! Not Sasha! I'll be entirely good! I'll give up Sonia, all women, only please . . ." But his wife appeared in the doorway, looking distraught; and after her came an ambulance man, backing out, holding one end of a stretcher. Rozanov stalled the car and leapt out. He ran to the entrance. The body on the stretcher seemed short, yet hardly childlike. He looked at the face: it was old. It was old, white-haired Agafya from the village, who cleaned for them and helped out generally. "Thank God!" he breathed. "Oh, thank God!" The pain in his gut vanished; the nightmare lifted; he did not feel the drizzle. "What happened?" he asked his wife.

"What kept you? She's had a heart-attack. I was putting Sasha to bed, and I heard a crash; she knocked over a soup-pan as she fell."

"Will she be all right?"

"They don't know. I think it's pretty serious." Nina took a handkerchief from her cuff, and wiped her rainy cheeks.

"Poor old soul," he murmured, at the same time as his heart expanded with relief and happiness. The ambulance doors were slammed shut; the driver jumped into his cab, started the engine, turned in the clearing outside the *dacha*, and accelerated away. Soon there was only the swish of rain falling through the trees. Rozanov draped an arm round his wife's shoulders.

"I've phoned her daughter," she said.

"Good. But what was she doing here? She doesn't usually come on a Tuesday."

"She was helping me get a meal," said Nina. "We've got visitors. You didn't tell me. Why didn't you tell me? And why are you late? I was worried."

"What visitors?"

"Ssh! Keep your voice down . . . You should know. Some American called Ben, and his girl. He rang me from his hotel this morning, asked if it was still all right to come. Apparently he'd written to you and you'd said to come to supper—tonight. I pretended I knew. I didn't know what to do."

"Jesus Christ!" Rozanov groaned. "I remember now. Find-laker, or Findlater. He works in an advertising agency."

"He says he's translated you."

"Two or three poems; and on the strength of that he wrote to me and asked if he could call. I completely forgot. Fuck! Oh, I'm sorry, Nina. You should have said it wasn't convenient."

"Well, I didn't know, did I? Don't blame me!" She squirmed away from his arm.

"Okay, okay. I'm really sorry. And I got here as quickly as I could. The plane was held up. It was a fucking awful trip, a lousy audience, a terrible hotel. I hardly slept a wink."

"Well, they're your guests. You'd better take over. The meal is ruined."

"Okay."

"We'd better go in."

He followed her into the hall and closed the door behind him. He took off his overcoat and fur hat, and mentally straightened himself. He remembered that Sasha was all right, and prepared to pay the small price of an evening's boredom. He followed Nina into the living-room. A burly, grey-haired man in horn-rimmed glasses stood up; seated beside him was a young woman of startling beauty: slender-faced and raven-haired. The Russian poet had often dreamed of meeting such a woman—indeed, he now recalled that he had improvised this extravagant beauty only hours previously: in the person of Countess Agrippina

Zakrevsky, a veritable Cleopatra, a copper Venus—but he had never met one in real life.

Rozanov spread his arms, beaming, and sprang forward to grasp an awkward, surprised Findlater in a bear-hug. "So!" he exclaimed, as he released him and held him at arm's length, yet still holding him in his warm gaze as though he were a long-lost brother—"So! you have come to share our tragedy!"

"We feel terrible," said the American; "to visit you like this, and have such a dreadful thing happen. We ought to leave you in peace."

"No, no!" Rozanov said, smiling. "Of *course* you must stay! We've been looking forward to your visit—haven't we, Nina? It's awful this should have happened; but there's nothing we can do and she'll be in the right hands." He sighed dolefully—and rubbed his hands. He did, genuinely, feel sad about "Aunt" Agafya; and the glimpse of her wan, wrinkled old face had reminded him of his mother. He would visit his mother tomorrow, and then go to the hospital to enquire after Agafya. He would pay whatever bribes were necessary to ensure she was treated decently. While determining those duties of the morrow, he turned his hazel eyes towards the copper Venus, caressing her with his smile. "So! You have brought a friend. . . ."

"This is Marie," said Findlater.

"Hello, Marie!" Rozanov leaned over her, and took her hand. "How wonderful! A real beauty!"

She reddened, and turned her gaze aside. She was from New York too? . . . Ah, Montreal! A lovely city, a city as beautiful as she! . . . Rozanov asked her what she did, what was her profession. She looked hesitant; and Findlater replied, on her behalf: "Beauty."

"Of course!" Rozanov chuckled. "Beauty! Beauty is her profession! Pushkin was once asked by a great beauty of his time to sign her album. He declined, saying he wrote his best signature in white ink." The copywriter, after a moment's hesitation, smiled;

the raven-haired woman glanced aside at him, her brow fur-
rowed; then she laughed. "Yes, I see!" she murmured.

Rozanov's wife had been quietly filling the table with plates of
zakuski. "Come and eat," she said.

"Yes, come and eat," echoed Rozanov, pulling back chairs for
them, then pouring wine from a pitcher into jade-green glasses.
"Poor Agafya wouldn't thank us if we didn't eat the food she's
prepared." When they were all seated, he clinked glasses with
Findlater, who was opposite, and with Marie. "To your visit,"
he said; "to your coming to share our tragedy. Actually I wasn't
thinking of poor Agafya. I was thinking of—of our dead commander. Comrade Brezhnev!"

"He's *dead*?" exclaimed the American, his thick-framed lenses
flashing as his head jerked.

"Dead," confirmed Rozanov. "But the Politburo isn't prepared to admit it yet. They send him out on his horse still, like El
Cid. But yes, he's gone to his ancestors . . ." His brain working
swiftly and playfully, Rozanov was also dimly aware of a *déjà-vu*.
He had said this before, today, or someone else had said it. He
couldn't remember. Stabbing a piece of fish with his fork, he
continued: "I think we should compose an elegy for him. Perhaps
in the style of Zbigniew Herbert's *Elegy of Fortinbras*. Do you
know it, Ben? You should read it; a wonderful poem. Let's
see . . ." He chewed, his head bent forward thoughtfully.
He swallowed, and glanced up, chanting:

> "Adieu prince
> adieu Leonid falling like a meteorite
> in this mild autumn
> you have been gathered to the circle of the blessed
> to Lenin and the Green Frog and Nikita Khrushchev your
> > heart
> gave out from too much travel to your various *dachas*
> and from planning too many sewer projects

from taking the strain
to prevent the hundred-ton truck from moving
and now the rest is silence adieu prince. . . ."

"Did you just make that up?" asked Marie: adding, when
Rozanov shrugged his shoulders, "How wonderful! Ben, isn't
that amazing?"

Findlater nodded; then turned his nod to a headshake, as Nina
held out to him a plate of dumplings. "Marie tells me I'm
overweight," he said. "I must watch what I eat." He patted his
ample stomach.

"That's nonsense," Rozanov said. "It suits you, being a little
portly. You have a kind of dignified manner, my friend. Not
heavy or solemn, I don't mean that; but a certain dignity.
You're—what?—early fifties?"

"Forty-five."

"Really? I should have thought you were older than I. I'm
fifty." He ran his hand over his slightly thinning, but still
jet-black, hair.

"You don't *look* as old as Ben," Marie said, glancing from one
to the other. "You look a good five years younger. Wouldn't you
agree, Nina?"

Nina Rozanov looked embarrassed, and did not reply. Findlater's leathery, lined face had turned red. Marie added, hastily,
"Not that you look older than you are, Ben, but that he—
Sergei?—looks so incredibly young." She gazed at the Russian
with frank admiration, as she had gazed at the Greek youths in the
classical collection at the Hermitage. She had stroked the bronze
and marble figures, and looked as if she would like to do the same
to the tall, gaunt, red-eyed Russian poet. Likewise, his hands
swayed about expressively, to the rhythms of his broken English—the tongue they all had in common—at the level of her
breasts.

"But you are so *right* for each other!" Rozanov exclaimed

warmly. "Because you are so *un*like! Don't you agree, Nina?"

"Yes, I do."

"Really?" exclaimed Marie, surprised, but also giving the impression of being pleased, as she turned her intense gaze towards Findlater. The American felt his anger melt; he dropped his gaze from hers, after a few moments, to his wine glass; his fingers trembled as they took hold of the glass. Her affectionate, perhaps even seductive, glance, after such vulgar cruelty, brought a lump to his throat, made him feel close to tears.

"You are like this," Rozanov explained, tapping his fork on his plate, where a piece of mutton lay beside two pickled onions. "Meat and relish. Truly, you go perfectly together!"

"Isn't that amazing?" she exclaimed, her gaze dragging Findlater's up from his wine glass to meet hers. He smiled wanly. "Yes."

No amount of pain and humiliation—such as hearing Marie, across his conversation with Sergei, telling Nina in French about her handsome Montreal boyfriend—could prevent Findlater from feeling that this evening was one of the high moments of his life. It had astounded him when Marie, following the briefest of acquaintances during his business trip to Canada, had accepted his invitation to join him on this short Russian visit. Though she had made it clear he wasn't to expect anything beyond companionship—and had stuck to it—it was still a delight, a delicious pleasure, to be envied by every man they met; and, what was more important, to feel in middle age the shy, vulnerable emotions of adolescence. He had not experienced these agitations since courting his wife, twenty years earlier. Findlater's wife had died of cancer; in the years of loneliness (there were no children) he had had several love affairs but no love. He knew he loved Marie, because she made him tremble.

And Rozanov had been a god to him since, in the late 1960s, he had attended a reading at which Yevtushenko, Vosnesensky and

Rozanov had held five thousand New Yorkers in the palms of their hands for five hours, without once having to refer to their books. Findlater's own poetry had proved not be worth very much—his work in advertising had probably extinguished what tiny spark he had—but he had never forgotten that evening of the reading. It had inspired him, among much else, to teach himself some Russian: just enough to translate those few poems of Rozanov's, and thereby to earn an invitation to Pere- delkino.

Tomorrow he would fly back to New York and solitude; Marie would fly on to Montreal and her boyfriend, and all would be over. Probably he would never see her again. Any slight regard she had for him would dissolve on the Caribbean cruise she was exuberantly describing in advance to Nina. Yet one should live for the moment. And he still nursed the hope that she would "come round", at this climax of their trip. She would be tipsy, as he was; and impressed by having met a famous Russian poet, thanks to him . . . She never *completely* discouraged him. When, for example, she had asked, at the Hotel Intourist, if she could put her wallet and travel documents in the drawer with his, and he had replied, with a touch of bitterness, "Yes, let *them* sleep together," she hadn't fought off his embrace; and in her words, "You think I should yield to you, don't you?" there had been a kind of challenge which had thrilled him. Of course, he had said, "No."

And again, when she had upset him by accepting the only ticket available to them for the Bolshoi, and gone off without even pecking him on the cheek, she had actually been in the room waiting for him, still not quite asleep, when he came up drunk at midnight from the bar. She hadn't seemed to mind his kneeling by her bed, whispering that he loved her, kissing her brow, her cheek. She said the opera was boring; appeared to have missed him.

Findlater remembered such moments as hopeful signs while

trying to follow Sergei's histrionic Russian . . . how everything was *blat*, influence . . . how, if only they were staying longer, he could get them tickets for the Taganka Theatre . . . how it was tough to be attacked by some for being too soft about the régime, and by others for being too hard . . . how it was sad there were no good young poets coming along—he, Vosnesensky and Yevtushenko still had no successors.

The two women had cruised from the Caribbean to love and children . . . and from there to the Hermitage (the Greek youths). Nina, who struck Findlater as surprisingly drab for the wife of such a man, spoke knowledgeably about art, and also about music: she was a harpist. Her harp stood in a corner of the plainly furnished room: golden, as her long straight hair might once have been, but now it was almost as grey as Findlater's.

"I kept wanting to fill the spaces in Leningrad with splendid advertisements," Findlater said in slurred Anglo-Russian to Rozanov, who flashed his brilliant teeth appreciatively. "We're marketing a new lipstick called Gloss; I'd like to stretch a pair of beautiful lips, glistening crimson lips, across the Hermitage, with the word GLOSS above them. Nothing cheap—perhaps the lips could be from some painting by Renoir or Titian . . ." Rozanov, munching, smiling, nodded and poured out more wine. "And the same with Red Square. We had an awful Intourist guide today: rapping out propaganda like a machine-gun; and so drably dressed. Though our fellow tourists weren't much better in that respect. And the Square itself—so ugly. I could see a hosiery ad, bestriding it, so to speak—a gorgeous slim pair of legs in black pantihose. Yes, and across the KGB building, the words HAPPINESS IS A CIGAR NAMED HAMLET."

"Wonderful!" exclaimed Rozanov in delight. "Is that a real slogan?"

"Oh, yes. In Great Britain, it's been very influential."

"You must tell Son—Nina." He nudged his wife; and Findlater repeated, in English, his witty suggestion. Nina's rather solemn, horsey face smiled, and the conversation continued in English.

"I could do a lot to make the Party more popular," Findlater resumed. "My company got Reagan elected. Your slogans are awful—totally unpersuasive."

"We just don't see them anymore," said Nina. "Do have some more fish."

"It's very good. Thank you."

"It's beautiful!" Marie agreed, also helping herself. She recounted an anecdote of their visit to the Lenin Museum: an old, deaf lady from Brooklyn had refused to believe that Lenin was dead. "Lenin is immortal!" she had corrected the bemused Russian guide in ringing tones. The raven-haired beauty asked why there were more cats in Leningrad than in Moscow. In fact, she hadn't seen a single one on the streets of Moscow. The Muscovites, whose own cat had died recently, couldn't explain it. She spoke of the rudeness of German tourists in Leningrad—how they pushed past one in the elevator, as though they had won the War and the Hotel Karelia were their headquarters. Of the hideous clothes at GUM.

That was where they had searched for body-lotion, but not found any. Findlater's business trip *cum* holiday (he had had a meeting with a representative of Stolichnaya Vodka concerning a projected promotion of it in the States) had been haunted by body-lotion. On their second night in Leningrad, Marie had surprised and thrilled him by allowing him to massage her. She claimed that she would allow almost anyone to massage her since it wasn't a sexual pleasure—simply enjoyable and relaxing. Nude to the waist, she had started by lying on her stomach, but later she turned over; her nipples had been the only colour in Leningrad, except for the red slogans.

Surely she had not been indifferent to his stroking. Once, as his fingers dug into her back, she had made a purring sound, and said she couldn't believe he hadn't massaged anyone before. But it was true. She agreed to massage him one night; and to let him massage her again. *That* was something she certainly didn't mind doing.

Findlater had been in a delirium of anticipation. *"For the moments of almost too much bliss . . ."* as he had conjured up for a cigarette advert, with a picture of two cigarettes burning away in an ashtray. Black Sobranie. His success with that campaign, in the maelstrom of the stampede away from lung cancer, had won the vodka contract. Well, to massage again, to be massaged by, Marie would be like that: quite apart from the deepening of intimacy it would bring, the gradual encroachments until—very possibly—she would allow him the final, most intimate, stroke. . . .

The trouble was, she had run out of body-lotion. And they found—or rather, he found—the Hotel Karelia didn't have any. Findlater passed up a coach tour to the Peter-and-Paul Fortress to scour the city; but without success. He had even asked a currency tout, offering the man a fifty-dollar bill; but he had shaken his head, baffled. There was no body-lotion in Leningrad.

They would have to wait for Moscow. The days and nights slipped by, and Marie had withdrawn into her emotional seclusion, continuing to dress and undress in the bathroom.

Body-lotion. It had dominated everything.

They were relating to the Rozanovs their visit to Leningrad's Nikolski Cathedral, on Sunday morning. Ben and Marie disagreed about it. For Findlater, the faint, growing harmonies of the Orthodox choir, as they climbed the stairs from the bazaar-like confusion of the ground floor, had ushered in a revelation. To emerge into a dense mass of worshippers, standing shoulder to shoulder, crossing themselves with such dignity, weeping; to hear the dramatic chants of the priests and the divine harmonies of an unseen choir—he could find no adequate words to convey the effect it had had on him. But for Marie, who had continued to stroke her hair in that anxious, self-conscious way of hers, and who had been agitated by what seemed to her the venomous, envious stares of the old and poorly clad women, the experience had been dreadful. What to him had appeared tears of joy and wonder were to her the tears of agony.

"They were desperate, Nina, desperate."

"I believe you."

"No," said Rozanov, "I think Ben is right. They're caught up in the ritual, the music; they become ecstatic . . . You should bite the tomato, Marie, and then suck it out: like this."

"I felt it myself," said Findlater. "For more than two hours, I was lost to myself and everything."

Yet he knew it wasn't completely true. During the second hour, at least, dreams of body-lotion had mingled with the wonderful choir singing *Gospodi pomilui*, Lord, have mercy. . . .

Moscow, too, had turned out to be lotionless.

He had not so much as touched her bare skin again until this evening, when they were getting ready to go out. The seams of her tight black dress had split, unknown to her—jobless by choice, she always bought good clothes, but second hand—and he had slipped his hand in around her thigh. She had slid away gracefully. She wouldn't even kiss, or hold hands. She was very strange. At their first meeting he had asked her for a photograph to remember her by. She had given him a nude photo, cut off at the neck: she occasionally bolstered her social security with modelling work. Yet the truncated torso, the breasts and pubic hair, had actually disappointed him. He hadn't seen her body; he had wanted her beautiful face to remember. Now, when he craved her body, she gave him only her face.

The evening was growing late. Sergei's ebullience was waning; he looked exhausted. "Yes, I'm pretty shagged out," he admitted—it was his deplorable, sleepless night at Slepnevo. And in the morning—he added as an afterthought, surprising Nina—he had to have breakfast in the city with a TV producer, who was anxious to film one of his stories. But he insisted on driving the couple to their hotel. It wasn't so easy to get a cab after midnight.

They protested; he insisted. First, though, he would take them to
see Pasternak's grave. They must put on rubber boots, because
the graveyard would be muddy.

Findlater staggered upstairs to the bathroom. A night-light
burning, he glimpsed through a half-open door a wall decorated
with Disney characters. After he had used the toilet, he had a flash
of inspiration: opening the bathroom cabinet, he found, as he had
hoped, a medley of expensive Western toiletries. And among
them, to his joy, a bottle of body-lotion. Having washed out a
small, almost empty bottle of cough mixture, he filled it with
lotion, and put it in his suit pocket. He walked giddily downstairs. Marie had put on heavy boots under her long black coat.
Refusing offers of help, Nina was taking plates and dishes
through to the kitchen. Sergei picked up two mandarins and
handed them to his guests. "To give to Boris," he explained;
"they come from Georgia. He loved Georgia." He grabbed a
bottle of cognac called Ararat. Findlater hauled on Sergei's spare
boots, and put on his new fur coat and hat, bought at the Hotel
Intourist *beriozhka*.

· 2 ·

"FUCK! I FORGOT MY LIGHTS!" EXCLAIMED SERGEI. "IT PROB-
ably won't start."

"Take mine, if it won't," his wife said.

But the Volga responded; it jumped forward and stalled. Sergei restarted the engine, switched off the wipers. In the light from the hall, Nina, her arms folded, saw them off, then turned and went into the house.

"You're lucky to have two cars, Sergei," Marie observed.

"I guess so. But Nina had to wait a hell of a long time for hers. Cars are in awfully short supply. A friend of mine has been waiting eight years. He's just had a phone-call to say the engine has come in, and he'd better pick it up!" He chuckled at her over his shoulder. The car ran down a bumpy lane, between birches.

He stopped the car. They clambered out. Silence enfolded them. The drizzle had stopped, and there were patches of bright stars visible above the still trees. After the brightness of the *dacha*, everything was pitch black. Rozanov clicked on a large torch. The beam lit up a muddy path. The heavy-booted intruders plodded after the Russian. It was a cold night, but the wine they had drunk made them feel warm.

The torchlight picked out a white headstone; carved on it, a boyish face. They stood around it, silent. Findlater and Marie stooped and laid their mandarins before the stone. There were other fruits there. Rozanov unplugged the cognac bottle, drank, and passed it to Marie. The Russian poet then recited some verses.

"Isn't that from *Zhivago*?" Findlater asked, swaying a little. Rozanov also swayed. "Yes. It's *Hamlet*. It was read at his funeral. 'Life is not so simple as to cross a field.' You know, it's never been published under Pasternak's name in this country; but Andrei—Voznesensky—inserted it in his translation of *Hamlet*, so it's appeared under Shakespeare's name! Andrei's *dacha* is over beyond those trees." He pointed into the darkness. "It's a pity he's away right now; and Zhenia too. I'm sure they'd have loved to meet you . . . They'd have loved to meet you too, darling!" he said, putting his arm round Marie. She slid out of his clasp, stood on tiptoe in Nina's gumboots, then leapt over the grave. "That's blasphemy," Rozanov said. "You've broken a taboo."

"Forgive her," Findlater mumbled. "She hasn't even seen the film of *Zhivago*."

"I *have!*" she protested.

"Well, I *knew* him," Rozanov said quietly. (And yet, he thought to himself, he had not wept for his old friend and hero as he had wept for poor Sputnik, a cat: so beautiful, so indomitable, such a survivor, a bridge between wives: almost the spirit of the *dacha* . . . He saw her, one-eyed, grey-furred, gazing at him, lifting her head to be stroked. He sighed . . . under the cherry tree where she had played . . .) He took the cognac bottle from the bulky New Yorker, and swigged.

"Wouldn't he have liked it?" Findlater demanded. "A beautiful young woman jumping over him? A glimpse up her skirt? Didn't he love beauty too?"

"Of course. *All* poets love beautiful women. Yes, he would have liked it, but his wife—Zina—is jealous." He flashed his torch at a headstone behind and to the right of the poet's. "And maybe so is Lyonya, their son." He flashed the torch to the left of the grave.

"I didn't know he was dead."

"The younger son. He had a heart-attack on the very street where Zhivago had his fatal attack. Isn't that intriguing?"

Marie gave a shudder. "It's spooky."

"Maybe so. But did Boris have a premonition, or was Lyonya influenced? Eh?"

"Or just a coincidence," said Findlater.

"No."

He turned aside, and they followed him slowly back to the car. His wheels churned in the mud, on a slope, and the visitors had to climb out again, and push. At last the car gathered momentum and cleared the knoll. They climbed back in.

At the *dacha*, Nina was wiping tears from her eyes. She had rung the hospital. Poor old "Aunt" Agafya was dead. Rozanov kissed his wife on the forehead, and mumbled his regret and sadness. But her time had come. At least she had not suffered.

Silent, chastened, they changed back into their shoes. Nina awkwardly embraced her guests, and they thanked her for a wonderful evening. Rozanov said she shouldn't wait up for him: if he felt very tired at the end of the drive, he might stay at his mother's. He ought to pay her a visit anyway, and it would save him another drive in the morning. Nina reminded him of her flight to Leningrad for a concert, and to be back in time to collect Sasha from school.

They got back in the car. Nina waved them off.

"Nina's really nice," said Marie, as they turned into the main road and sped towards the city. "I really liked her."

"Good."

"She's very quiet, isn't she? Quieter than you."

"She's quiet now," Rozanov muttered. "Sasha's quietened her. Kids do that. When I first knew her, she wasn't so quiet; and she was also very good-looking, very seductive. In fact, she was a swallow."

"How do you mean?" asked Findlater. He sprawled against Marie in the back seat, clutching her gloved hand.

"I mean, she slept with foreigners to get them into trouble."

"You're joking!" exclaimed Marie, removing her hand, jerking forward so that her face was almost brushing Sergei's nape.

"I'm not joking. She was very good-looking, and quite sexy. Girls in the sort of professions where they can make contact with foreigners—like an orchestra player—are often recruited by the KGB. There's a school outside the city where swallows are trained. Nina was trained there. A kind of advanced diploma in seduction."

"Jesus," Findlater murmured.

"You were lucky, Ben!" The Russian grinned over his shoulder. "No, she didn't work for them long. Her conscience played up."

"I think that's absolutely fascinating," Marie said, still breathing down his neck. "Don't you, Ben? I'd liked to have asked her about it."

"She wouldn't have answered."

"I suppose not. But *why* did she do it?"

"I guess, partly for the privileges it brought. But there again, some girls do it as one way of rebelling against the fucking awful male power structure. I'm not talking about women's liberation in the obvious sense, in the West; but the way everything, in our society and yours, is an assertion of crude maleness. Washington and the Vatican, as well as Red Square. Isn't that what you were saying, Ben? You're completely right. We need those legs over Red Square."

"And that's why Nina did it?" asked the Québecoise.

The car swerved violently, throwing the passengers to their right. "I'm sorry," said Rozanov; "it was probably only a rat, but they're among the more innocent creatures in this fucking country . . . What did you say? Is that why she did it? Well, I guess, to open your legs and get stuffed, getting pleasure from it and giving pleasure, seemed a more feminine, more subtle, way of taking revenge for that"—he nodded towards the complex of tower-blocks they were passing—"than donning overalls and bawling through a loud-hailer: as your feminists do, I understand. You can't fight against -*isms* with another -*ism*. But maybe you don't agree with me, Marie?"

"No, I agree with you. I'm not a feminist."

"What happened to the men she slept with?" asked Findlater.

"Nothing too unpleasant. A little mild persuasion to be nice to the Soviet Union, I guess."

Marie asked how he, Sergei, had come to meet her.

"Well, I'm afraid I met her at the school where she was trained. I was a kind of—how do you say?—extra-mural lecturer. Erotic verse from Pushkin to Bella Akhmadulina. Some Westerners are more charmed by a few lines of love poetry than by a blatant sexual approach. But I also—did other things, now and then."

"What a job!" said Marie, admiringly.

"We are all corrupt," Rozanov said, with a sigh. "In this country. Even the saints, like Pasternak, were not completely unsullied. There are no Hamlets here. People who would be decent men or women in any normal society turn into Rosencrantz and Guildenstern—or Fedin and Fadeyev. Have you heard of them, Ben?"

"No."

Rozanov concentrated on avoiding a lorry's blinding headlights, then explained:

"They were both neighbours of Pasternak's. High officials in the Writers' Union. They liked him, they even revered him. Fadeyev used to repeat verse after verse of Boris's when he was drunk, his eyes spilling tears. He may even have helped Borya survive—it's quite possible Borya was depicting him in the figure of Yevgraf in *Zhivago*; the half-brother who keeps dropping out of the blue to save him. You remember Yevgraf? But Fadeyev was also obliged to threaten and accuse him in public; and so was Fedin. And they were responsible for countless deaths. What I'm trying to say, Ben, is—they weren't wicked by nature. They were friendly neighbours. Fedin liked Zina's strawberry pies, and Fadeyev liked her baked potatoes. But they couldn't resist evil. Fadeyev had the grace to commit suicide after Stalin's death; and Borya—I was there when he said it—Borya stood over his neighbour's coffin and said loudly, for all to hear: 'Alexander Alexandrovich has made amends.' Wasn't that wonderful? . . . Fedin led the attack on Boris after he won the Nobel Prize, and harried him into his grave. The day of the funeral, he pretended to have flu and hung blankets over his windows to avoid seeing the crowds of mourners. . . .

"Am I talking too much?" he asked.

"No, please, go on," Marie said.

"The fresh air at the graveyard has woken me up. But anyway, my mind always becomes active at this time of the day, or night. Are you tired?"

"Pretty tired," Findlater said.

"If you're not too tired, I'd like you to meet a friend of mine. Well, actually, she's my closest friend. She has a flat not too far from your hotel. Would you like to stop by and have another drink? One for the road?"

"We have to pack . . ." Findlater began; but Marie cut in with, "We'd love to! I don't feel in the least tired."

"Good!" Rozanov exclaimed. "She never goes to bed early. She may possibly have a friend with her. An interesting guy. He's a Red Army general."

Findlater released Marie's hand and sank back in the corner, brooding. The bottle of body-lotion was jogging in his pocket.

Rozanov turned down a side street, with a screech and slush of tyres. "Sonia lives in one of those grey ice-cream cakes, built in the thirties, with a kind of cherry stuck on the top. You must have seen them today, on your tour."

"Yes," Marie said. "Our Intourist guide pointed every single one of them out, as though they were the Parthenon."

"I can imagine that! Sonia works for Intourist, as a matter of fact, but don't be put off by that. She isn't . . . Meyerhold lived there," he said, nodding out of his window. "You've heard of him? No? A great theatrical director. The greatest. All his life, he wanted to direct *Hamlet*—but he hesitated too long!"

He slowed, drew in to the kerb, and stopped. After a while, he switched off the engine. He slumped back in his seat, still resting his hands on the wheel.

Then he broke the silence by barking a laugh. Marie asked him why he was laughing.

"Happiness is a cigar called Hamlet!"

· 3 ·

THE ATMOSPHERE, IN THE SURPRISINGLY ELEGANT AND SPA-
cious flat high up towards the cherry-star, was strained. It had
been clear from the start that Sonia, alone and preparing to go to
bed, was angry with Sergei for bringing *himself*, not to mention
two strangers, foreigners. She had spread herself on the sofa, in
her pink housecoat and fur-rimmed slippers, her feet tucked up
under her; she was reading a book, distancing herself. She spoke
little and sullenly, in almost faultless English. Aged about thirty
she looked, to Findlater, even more unprepossessing than the
guide who had taken them round the Kremlin: with a square,
surly face under a ragged mop of dull brown hair, thin lips drawn
down, a heavy reddish nose, colourless eyes behind rimless
spectacles; her bare legs thick as hams. If Nina was a rather refined
horse, Sonia was a pig. Findlater was staggered that Rozanov had
chosen her for his mistress.

Findlater spoke as little as Sonia. From time to time he felt the
shape of the bottle of lotion in his pocket. Yet if they stayed much
longer he would be too exhausted to do anything but collapse on
to his bed. In any case, did he really *want* to massage her any

more? She was a bitch, a man-hater. She enjoyed tormenting him. When Rozanov had gone up in the elevator, alone, to check that his friend was in a state to welcome visitors, Marie had exclaimed, with a sly, sadistic look in her eyes, "He's marvellous! Now, I could really fall in love with *him*!" It had struck Findlater as childish and insulting; he had been hurt by it.

Sipping vodka, he stood at the window, staring gloomily out at rainy, darkened Moscow.

Rozanov slumped at the table, knocking back the vodka, and talking with a desperate zest to cover Sonia's silence. Marie was standing glancing at books and pictures, many of which related to the theatre. Sonia's mother had been an actress. Sergei had pointed her out, in a still from Meyerhold's production of *The Government Inspector*—a pretty young woman in an Empire dress. The photograph had been signed by Meyerhold.

Yes, she was still acting, Sonia said with a curtness that discouraged further questions.

"In Minsk," Rozanov added. She's good. Isn't she, Sonia?" he prompted. But the absorbed young woman merely shrugged.

Quite a high wind had risen and blew against the tall building, making the floor tremble occasionally and rattling the window. Rozanov began to paint a picture, in words, of an atomic attack on Moscow, all these Stalinist buildings—what secrets they held, of mid-night terror and separation—crashing like a pack of cards.

"It won't happen," said Sonia tonelessly, without looking up from her book. Encouraged by this faint sign of communication, Rozanov launched into the arms race. "Once you start on a certain path," he said, slurring his words, "you can't stop. It's like a narrative, a story. It proliferates. It seeks a dramatic conclusion. So, sooner or later, it will happen. *Puff!*" He blew out his breath and his hands drew a mushroom in the air. "And what bothers me is—if you're about eighty-five years old, like our College of Cardinals in the Kremlin, you know you're going to kick the bucket anyway in a year or two. Why should Brezh-

nev—well, if he's still alive—care a monkey's fuck what happens
to the rest of us? Why not go out in a blaze of drama, if not glory?
And, of course, they'll be safe in their deep shelter, so they'll
actually outlive the little kids—except their own grandchildren
and great-grandchildren, who'll be well taken care of. And think
of the excitement, Ben! Down in their deep hole, playing the war
game to end all war games! . . . Your Reagan too—high noon!
. . . What do you think about Cruise?"

"I don't know much about it," said Findlater, continuing to
stare out at the dark.

"What do you think of it, Marie?" Rozanov asked.

"What?" She turned vaguely from the bookshelves, her
thoughts and her gaze buried in the large book of theatrical
photographs which she was holding.

"This *Cruise* we keep hearing about?"

She lifted her eyes, and smiled at him. "Oh! well, as I told your
. . ." She remembered, just in time Sergei's warning that Nina
was not to be mentioned. "As I told you, we're going to the
Bahamas for ten days. Some sun! Pierre won the cruise as a prize
in a quiz show. Wasn't that lucky?" Noticing Sonia's eyes wander
up from her book, she explained, "Pierre's my boyfriend in
Montreal. We might even get married before we go, I don't
know." Findlater, unable to control the pain in his heart turned
and saw Sonia's eyes resting on him in puzzlement; then she
hastily went back to her book.

"No, Marie!" Rozanov chuckled. "I meant your new nuclear
weapon! Well, never mind!"

Marie shrugged, and also returned to the book she was holding. "I try not to think about that," she said. "Is this Sonia's
mother too?"

Sergei jumped up and walked across to look over her shoulder.
He looked down at the charming portrait and forgot the momentary *déjà-vu* of someone else, earlier that day, responding to a
question oddly. "No, that's Meyerhold's wife," he said.

"Zinaida Raikh. She was an actress. Don't you think she's lovely?"

"She's beautiful," she said enthusiastically. "She looks like you, Sonia."

"Really?" said Sonia in bored tones.

"Yes. Don't you think so, Sergei?"

"Well, perhaps, a little."

"More than a little. Ben, come and look." Findlater strolled from the window, and glanced uninterestedly at the photograph. Rozanov's arm was draped round Marie's shoulder. The lush, exotic lips, wide and glistening eyes, black hair in a chignon: a rose next to the thorns of her husband's brooding, haggard, aquiline face. This woman was *nothing* like Sergei's mistress.

"Don't you think she looks like Sonia?" Marie repeated.

"Not in the least."

"Oh, it's obvious! The mouth, the eyes!"

She closed the heavy book, and put it back on the shelf. Sergei went back to his vodka, and Marie sat down opposite him at the table. Findlater slumped on a chair at the table's end. Sergei refilled their glasses. "Come and join us, Sonia," said Marie.

"No, I must go to bed." The young woman closed her book with a snap, laid it on the arm of the sofa, lifted her feet on to the floor, and stood up. "I'm taking a party round the Tretyakov in the morning, and first I'll have to shop. We don't all have women from the village to help us."

"You mean Agafya?" said Rozanov. "She's dead. She died this evening."

"Oh . . . well, I daresay you'll find someone else." She made slowly for the door. "Nice to have met you. Sergei can show you out."

Findlater, standing up, said, "No, we really should get some sleep ourselves."

"The night is young," Rozanov urged. "Stay just a little while, then I'll run you to your hotel. Please." He gestured to the

American to sit down and drink up. "Marie, you look fresh as a daisy. Stay awhile, won't you?"

"If it's all right with Sonia."

"Of course," Sonia said, hovering by the door. Directing her gaze at Rozanov, she added, in a dead voice: "I hope you weren't thinking of coming back here, afterwards?"

"Actually, I was."

"I shouldn't."

She went out, closing the door; and then they heard another door close softly. Sergei said, "Excuse me a moment," stood up—swayed—rubbed his red eyes—and also left the room.

Faintly, Findlater and Marie heard the tones of domestic strife, unmistakable even in muted Russian; the woman's voice hostile, the man's conciliatory. But the American quickly unleashed his own hostility, taking Marie by surprise. Her cruelty, her crassness—saying he looked years older than Rozanov (whose hair was undoubtedly tinted), that she could fall for *him* . . . speaking so openly about her boyfriend. Okay, he had talked of his wife, but she was dead, he wasn't going on a fucking cruise with her . . . Findlater poured out his wrath, and polished the lenses of his glasses with such force that he snapped the bridge. "Shit! Look what you've made me do!"

"But he *is* an attractive man, don't you agree? Why shouldn't I say so? And he *does* look years younger than he is, admit it. I thought you were above such things—had you been a woman, of course I wouldn't have said you looked older than Sergei; but I didn't think it would bother you one bit. I'm sorry. As for Pierre, I don't see why I shouldn't mention him. I sleep with him, not with you. Why should people think otherwise?"

Putting his half-glasses back in their case, he nodded wearily and closed his eyes; his shoulders sagged. Gloomily he drank his vodka.

She laid her hand on his arm. "Let's not spoil it," she said, "when we've had a lovely time."

He opened his eyes, looked at her wistfully. "It *has* been lovely. We've got on surprisingly well, haven't we?"

She nodded, and said, "It could have been disastrous."

"Yes. But it hasn't, has it?"

"No."

"I'm just—sad that you don't find me attractive."

"I do," she said; "I do find you attractive."

His misty eyes brightened. "Really?"

"Of course. Do you think I'd have agreed to come with you if I didn't? But in the past I've always leapt into the fire—into a sexual relationship straight away; and it hasn't worked. I was told I could only hope to find something real on the basis of a friendship. You see?"

"Yes, I see. I do see. But what about Pierre? *Are* you going to marry him?"

She shrugged. "Maybe. Who knows? I don't expect so."

They sat silent, drinking, listening to the wind and the low quarrelsome tones of the Russians in the next room. Findlater fumbled in his pocket and took out the bottle. "I took this from Sergei's bathroom," he said, with a sad smile. "Lotion!"

"Well, we can still use it."

"Really?"

"Why not? I feel stiff. I could do with a massage. Unless you're too tired?"

"Oh, no! . . . And will you massage me?"

"If you like."

His fingers on the vodka glass trembled. His adoring unspectacled eyes held her gaze for a few moments, then she turned away, smiling, and touched her hair, close to her tiny ear.

The door opened. Findlater stuffed the bottle back in his pocket. Sergei looked sheepish. He apologized for Sonia's tiredness. He sat at the table, gulped vodka, refilled his glass.

"We really must go soon, Sergei," Marie said.

He nodded, glancing at his watch.

They heard the bathroom door shut and lock. The sound of running water.

"The middle of the night," reflected Rozanov. "In the good old days, this was when they came for you . . ." He drank again and fell silent, staring into his empty glass.

"Was there anyone in your family . . . ?" Findlater asked hesitantly.

"My father. Yah. My mother says I cried, though I didn't know what was happening—only that my father was going away with a couple of gangsters. But, funnily enough, I don't remember it at all. It's strange what you remember and forget. I had my tonsils out later that year. I remember my mother, as she kissed me goodbye in the ward, said I would be going to the theatre in the morning and everything would be fine. Well, I couldn't sleep that night from excitement. My only previous visit to the theatre had been marvellous—a children's play. I couldn't wait to go again. But in the morning, instead of plush seats and a curtain and bright lights, there were men in masks and rubber gloves; and one of them shoved something black and rubbery over my mouth and nose, and I had to gasp for breath, and then I passed out.

"That was my second theatre visit! Few things are as good the second time round. . . .

"Meyerhold was arrested in that year too. 1939. The summer. Three weeks later they pulled Zinaida in, then released her after a week. But someone stole into their apartment and—" Sergei, his eyes glittering, made a dozen or more stabbing motions with his clenched fist. "Then, not content with that—" he passed his hand across his throat. "Finally, the eyes. Well, I don't know in which order."

"How ghastly!" Marie exclaimed.

"It was the final unravelling of Isadora's scarf," said Rozanov. "You don't know what I mean? Isadora Duncan. Her two kids drowned in the Seine. She got killed when her scarf entangled in a car-wheel—you know that. Yes. And her husband was Yesenin, who shot himself and also hanged himself. And Yesenin's first wife was Zinaida Raikh. The wheel of fortune. The last unravelling. Not quite the last—Yesenin's son was put in a prison asylum, not long ago. Russia! . . . Shall I improvise for you?"

Findlater glanced at his watch. Marie said, "Yes, please!"

"Then we must really go," said Findlater, and Marie nodded.

"Of course, of course. A short improvisation. Russia . . ." He stood up. Marie asked him if it would be possible to tape it—glancing at Sonia's stereo equipment. She would love it as a souvenir. "Of course," said Rozanov. Stooping over the stereo, he clicked a button to run a cassette back while saying to them: "This room is Leningrad. A couple of months' time. You are two hundred thousand people, crammed into Decembrists' Square. I am—someone yet unknown." He started the tape and stood up.

He closed his eyes, and raised an arm, in a gesture of silencing a crowd. His eyes opened; they burned, glittered; to Marie—Findlater saw only a blur—they seemed like red coals. Lowering his arm, standing to attention, he began to speak in a rhythmical, hypnotic voice, softly, yet somehow giving the impression of addressing a vast concourse. . . .

· 4 ·

FELLOW RUSSIANS! HONOURED GUESTS! HERE IN DECEM-brists' Square I salute with you our brave forefathers, who sought to lift the yoke of oppression from our suffering country.

They lit a spark, which we have turned into a blaze. We must never allow it to become extinguished. We thank God there has been no bloodshed.

I trust you will forgive me, and our other guests will forgive me, if I welcome especially today three people: Alexander Solzhenitsyn, Andrei Sakharov, and Lech Walesa . . . Welcome home, dear Alexander Isayevich! On behalf of the interim government I warmly thank the President of the United States for his fraternal speech; and we wholeheartedly support his pledge that we will, together, tear down the only iron curtain remaining in the world: the iron curtain between north and south, affluence and poverty, plenty and famine, health and disease.

But now I address you, our Russian people, speakers of "the great Russian word", the rich and uncorrupted language of Pushkin, Tolstoy, Akhmatova, Pasternak, Solzhenitsyn, Rozanov . . . Let us throw off all hypocrisies. I was told a few days ago of some workmen who found a brown paper parcel, tied up with string, in the basement of a Stalinist tower-block in Moscow. They opened it, and found the mummified remains of a baby. The police found that the little corpse had been hidden there by an old lady, who still lived in that apartment-building. When they called on her, she said, "I don't want anything to do with it!" She had hidden her bastard child because she was frightened of her mother.

Russia has been like that, my friends. We have lived with our corpses and tried to forget them. It must never happen again. That is why we have placed guards by the statue of Lenin outside the Finland Station. We can't abolish Lenin as he abolished the Tsars, or as Brezhnev abolished Nikita Khrushchev. We have to learn that memory is sacred. We have to learn to live three-dimensionally. We are weary of being cardboard cut-outs. That is why I, personally, dislike the suggestion that we re-name this great city St Petersburg. But it will be for you to decide, through your elected representatives. If there is a referendum, I shall vote against any change of name. It was Leningrad which endured the Terror and the siege. Leningrad has earned its name. The half-million dead, in the Piskaryovskoye Cemetery, do not want the name of their city changed. Leningrad now dignifies Lenin— not Lenin, Leningrad.

In millennia to come people will say, "This great city of granite and water, of Pushkin and Dostoievsky, what a curious name it has! How did it get its name? Who or what was Lenin?"

Leningrad . . . "And by touch, in my sleep, I could find it . . ." Let us not change its name, my friends.

But let us demolish false gods. We no longer want mausoleums in the Kremlin—we want living people, people whose eyes can sparkle with joy and weep at suffering. We ask any Russian who harbours relics of Lenin, gathered during the corpse's removal from Moscow during the war, to return them, so that the man can have a decent burial.

Above all, don't, for God's sake, start to mummify me, or General Kolasky, or any member of the provisional administration! Or of any succeeding elected government. If any city council wishes to honour our bloodless victory, do not erect statues of us, but of beautiful naked women! I mean it! Let the womanly come into our public life, and permeate it, as the Neva spreads its waters through all Leningrad. Let there be fountains and gardens and beautiful nudes! Let there be some grace, humour and eroticism in our newspapers and other media! Away with the boring, bullying slogans! We Russians can learn much from our former serfs, the free and joyous peoples of Estonia, Georgia, Armenia. . . .

And yet, I hope the character of our country will not be too drastically altered. I do not want to see the Nevsky Prospect ablaze with neon signs advertising Coca Cola, Topless Bars, pornographic movie-houses. I understand, and to an extent share, the Patriarch's anxieties concerning the spiritual well-being of our people. Spiritual values—as Alexander Isayevich has warned us—do not thrive easily in freedom. Organized religion is bound to suffer, here, in Poland, the Ukraine—everywhere— from the onset of freedom. That is a cross we must bear.

Because—in the name of God, Who may or may not exist— we've got to *try* freedom! Don't expect life to be perfect. It will be blessedly imperfect. We've had enough of Utopias; of dema- gogues who make our lives miserable with their perfect systems. Utopias deprive us of the right to be unhappy. Under Lenin, Stalin, Brezhnev, we did not have the right to be unhappy—even though, in reality, we were intensely miserable. Now we have taken back the right to be unhappy. Beyond that imperishable right, we can expect only—in the words of our great wartime ally, Winston Churchill—blood, sweat, toil and tears. Many things are going to be worse. Certain prices are bound to rise. Indeed, are already rising—food, housing, electricity. If the State lets you go, like a mother pushing her son out into the world, you must expect bad times, and you won't be able to run to your mama. Some of us will have the freedom to be out of work. Injustices and inequalities will still occur, and perhaps will in- crease. There will be no more delivery vans from the Kremlin, bringing luxury goods to certain privileged people. But some people will earn more than others, because they are cleverer or simply luckier—and they will be able to buy luxury goods, openly. Those who will grumble loudest, or most effectively, will be some of those same people who can afford luxuries. They will start up storms of protest in the free press. They will say, things were more equal under Stalin or Brezhnev! New, angry Lenins, Stalins, Trotskys, will arise!

But don't listen to them! Beware of people who claim to have answers! There is more life in a newly-born kitten than in any *ism*, whether socialism or capitalism—remember that! Cherish kit- tens, strangle *isms*! And continue to live with poetry . . . live poetically, my dear friends! Thanks, at least in part, to the Communist régime, you are among the most literate peoples on earth. Now you can actually read decent books! No more banal, anti-human cant! Tomorrow, there is a lot of work to be done. But just for today, enjoy your holiday! Let your hair down! Go home and fuck your wife or husband! Or go to someone else's home and do it! Be jealous, be confused, start to bear children, Russians! One child per couple just isn't enough! Go with God . . . go and love. . . .

· 5 ·

As Rozanov stopped declaiming and relaxed his body, there were tears in his eyes.

After a few moments he said, in a casual, conversational tone: "Well, my friends, that's the kind of shit our so-called dissidents write. You can see what we have to put up with. I don't know who precisely wrote that shit, but whoever it was . . ." Rozanov stooped and clicked himself off in mid-sentence.

Brushing a shirt-sleeved wrist across his eyes, he removed the cassette, stood up, and slowly carried it to Marie. Saying "I'll treasure it," she put it in her handbag. "Well, it won't happen like that on December 13th," he said. "Quite otherwise . . . I'm sorry about the shit at the end; but you understand? If they find it at the airport it will confuse them, just enough to safeguard me. You'll be okay: they'd just confiscate it. Maybe you should give it to Ben: the customs men are likely to search your bags very thoroughly, Marie, merely because you're a beauty. They'll stare into your eyes as they go through your underwear, try to embarrass you. But they probably won't bother with you, Ben."

The American nodded. There was silence. A distant glug of bathwater.

"We Slavs," Rozanov said, gulping vodka, "gave you your word *slaves.*"

The phone rang, making them all jump. "Who the fuck could be ringing at this time of the night?" Rozanov demanded. "I think I can guess!" He chuckled unpleasantly. "Well, he'll get a shock." He strode to the phone, which rested on a bookcase, and picked up the receiver. "Rozanov," he said curtly.

His face showing amazement first, then rage, they heard his icy voice say: "Who gave you this number? . . . Do you know what time it is? . . . There's nothing to worry about. I sorted it all out before I left . . . Yes . . . Now, goodnight."

He banged down the phone, hissed "Jesus Christ!", and threw himself full-length on the sofa. He thrust a hand into his jeans pocket—removed it again.

"Trouble?" Findlater asked.

"And how! Hand me my glass, will you?"

Marie brought it to him. He gulped. They heard, faintly, the bathroom door opening, a patter of feet; a door closing. "Thank God Sonia was bathing," Rozanov said, lowering his voice. "It was for me. A ghastly woman I slept with last night. A blind woman. I'd never met her before. I only slept with her out of curiosity. Well, it was a nightmare. To pass the time, I told her a story. It was a little—anti-Soviet in places. So, this woman— Olga—starts thinking about it while she's lying in bed beside her husband. She can't sleep. She worries more and more. She sees me being sent off to Siberia. So she has to get out of bed and phone me in the middle of the night! Well, that was her excuse." He gave a bitter laugh.

"But how did she know you were here?" Marie asked.

"She rang my home! Can you imagine it? She woke Nina up! Olga's spoken to my wife before, because she's writing some kind of a thesis on my work and she's rung up a couple of times with questions. She told Nina it was an emergency, and wormed my mother's number out of her. God knows what Nina is thinking. That bitch was out to make trouble. And now she's got Sonia's number." He groaned, and covered his face with his hands. "My fucking mother gave it to her. She covers for me when I'm here."

A wailing drone came from behind the wall.

Almost simultaneously, the phone shrilled again. "Shit!" Sergei cried, jumping up from the sofa and running to grab the receiver. "Oh, it's you, Mother! . . . Everything is okay. She was just some neurotic woman, you know the type . . . You shouldn't have given her Sonia's number . . . Yes, I know . . . You what? The Issahakians? . . . That was quick-thinking of you . . . I'm sorry you were woken up . . . Go back to sleep now. I'll be round in the morning to see you . . . Okay, goodnight now."

He stood uncertainly by the phone. "That stupid cunt!" he murmured. "Olga. She got Mother worried about me—and then Nina rang! Mother told her I wasn't there, that I'd run some Armenian friends of hers home. She gave her this number, pretending it was the Armenian couple's. There are times when I'm glad we don't have telephone directories. But Nina isn't easily fooled. She knows all the tricks, from our own past intrigues. She'll find it hard to believe I'm drinking vodka with an eighty-year-old couple at 3 a.m."

He moved shakily to the table, and sat. "Ben," he said, touching the American's arm, "will you do me a big favour? Nina will ring at any moment. She won't expect me to answer, she'll expect Mr or Mrs Issahakian. I want you to stand by the phone, and grab it as soon as it rings. Do you have a handkerchief you can put over your mouth? Pretend to be Mr Issahakian, and then call me over. He has a kind of heavy, gruff voice, with rather poor Russian. You could pass for him okay."

The New Yorker fumbled in his pocket and pulled out a handkerchief; he stood up and lurched to the phone. "Issaha-kian?" he mumbled.

"That's right. Good. Thank you, my friend."

The hair-drier in Sonia's room had stopped. The wind, too, had ceased, and there was silence in the apartment. Clutching his handkerchief, Ben waited by the phone.

"Don't think too badly of me," Sergei slurred. "There's always, really, only Sonia. Only Sonia. I'll tell you something very personal. Sonia and I haven't slept together for months. We've been quarrelling a lot." He sighed. "I don't blame her. The situation. Hopeless, hopeless . . . But I drive home from here, after a raging argument—half dead, as I feel now—I've had about one hour's sleep in the last two days—and I'll masturbate over an old photo of Sonia! A sexy photo she let me take in the old days. Isn't that an awful confession?" He gave another bitter laugh.

"Don't think Sonia is so innocent. She was sleeping with someone else last night, too; and I bet she enjoyed it a hell of a lot more than I did. A general in the Red Army, called Kolasky. I mentioned him in my speech. He's a kind of a dove. He's been on leave from Poland. I found Polish cigarette-butts in the ashtray by Sonia's bed . . . I could do with a cigarette. Do either of you smoke? . . . Well, you're very wise. I've given up for over a year. But I could do with one now. I'm very tempted to go and get Sonia's."

"Don't do that, Sergei," Marie said.

"Well, I guess not right now. I might wake her up. I hope to God she'll fall asleep quickly. Why the hell doesn't Nina ring?"

His face froze, as he heard footsteps. The door opened and Sonia walked in. Even to Findlater's cloudy vision it was clear that she was transformed. Her hair looked elegantly styled and glossy; her face, without glasses, a red blur at the mouth, looked altogether livelier and more attractive. Her bosom peeped out of a peacock-blue kimono.

There was even the hint of a smile. "I couldn't sleep," she explained.

Findlater dabbed his brow with his handkerchief, then straightened a book he had half taken out, and sat back down at the table. There would be no leaving now, at least for a while.

Sonia touched Sergei's arm as she walked past him to the table. He arranged his mouth into a smile, his eyes flickering from her to the phone.

She helped herself to a drink, then lit a cigarette. "Let's have some music," she suggested, and glided, glass and cigarette in hand, to the stereo. Squatting, she asked, "Did I hear the phone, Sergei?"

"Yes, it was Mother. She'd woken up in a panic, thinking she was having a heart attack. But I reassured her it was only heartburn. She's okay."

He felt his own heart thudding and racing; the room, the people, the sadistic phone, undulated in smoky wreaths.

With an ironic but pleasant smile, Sonia remarked, "Sergei's mother is a hypochondriac. And Sergei takes after her—don't you? He's always imagining he's got a fatal illness! But she's very nice . . . Sergei, have you seen the tape that was here? It was rather good. Some Bob Dylan. I taped it from one of your radio stations, Ben."

"Shit," muttered Rozanov, glancing towards Marie. Marie, reddening, looked down at her handbag.

"I'm afraid I used it to tape something, Sonia," said Sergei. "I'm sorry."

"You *what*?" she stood up, glaring at him. "You taped over it?"

"It was my fault, I'm afraid," Marie said. "Sergei did an improvisation for us, and I asked him if he could tape it." She fumbled in her bag and held out the cassette. "You can't have lost very much, though. Five or ten minutes."

"No, keep it. It's not your fault, it's his . . . Why didn't you check?"

"There was nothing written on it," Sergei said humbly.

"That's no excuse. Why did you think it was in the stereo? Didn't you try it? It's typical! You're very good at giving away other people's things." She turned angrily towards Marie. "He uses people. He doesn't care. He's just a selfish bastard. He wanted to show off to you, and nothing else mattered."

Sergei flushed. "I'm sorry."

"I'll send you a Bob Dylan record from home," said Marie.

"Thank you, but I wanted *this* one." Rozanov watched the loved and hated face concentrate all its years of resentment. Well, at least she will walk out now, he thought sadly yet with relief. But then, to his consternation, her face gradually softened, became human again.

"Well, it didn't record all that wonderfully . . . I'm not very good with machines. I suppose I should have written on it."

She walked to the sofa, scuffling Sergei's hair as she passed. "You're sweating," she said. "Are you getting the flu or something?"

"No. It's quite warm in here." Both the men had stripped to their shirt-sleeves, though Findlater still wore a tie.

"*You* choose some music."

Sonia sat on the sofa, crossed her legs, brushed dust off her silk kimono, took out another cigarette.

"I'll have one," said Rozanov.

"Oh, you're smoking again!"

"Just one."

She offered him the packet, he took one, and she clicked her lighter. "Wonderful!" he said, with a shuddering sigh. Coughing, he lurched across to the stereo, searched in a box of tapes. He wondered if he could dislodge the phone by brushing past it; but that would only make Nina more suspicious. She might call some mutual acquaintances, who knew Sonia, and they'd say, "Oh, that's Sonia Vinokur's number!" At the very thought, the breath cut off in his throat.

A Chopin nocturne filled the room with tranquil sounds. Rozanov walked to the sofa and sat down by Sonia. He closed his eyes and took a deep draw on his cigarette. A long ash dropped on his lap. "Beautiful!" he murmured.

"You don't usually like Chopin," she observed.

"Well, I thought you would like it."

"Why?"

"I thought it would bring back memories."

"Oh, don't be silly!" She chuckled.

"Sonia has a man-friend," he explained in a loud voice to their guests. "That's who she thought was ringing her just now. A very distinguished soldier, stationed on the Polish border. He was here last night. Did I mention him to you? Oh yes. I said he might be here tonight."

"He was hoping," Sonia said. "He was hoping to catch us out."

"Catch you out in what?" Sergei asked innocently. "He's just a friend. There's nothing to catch out, any more. You told me so."

She shrugged.

He picked up a book from the arm-rest. "What's this? *Hot Snow*?" He turned the pages over. "You don't usually read war books, darling. Is it good?"

"It's okay."

"Is Alexei like that? Hot snow?"

"At least he doesn't pretend he isn't grey. Not like some I could mention."

"But is he like that in bed? Hot snow?"

She covered her knees with her kimono . . . She flicked her ash. "Just because a volcano has snow on its peak, doesn't necessarily mean it's extinct."

"What do you mean by that?"

"I don't mean anything. You're being ridiculous."

Rozanov stood up and stumbled round the room. "I'm not being ridiculous. He did fuck you. You've as good as admitted it."

"Not at all. Anyway, it's none of your business." She turned to address the American, who was staring embarrassedly into his glass. "Oh, he'd *like* me to have been fucked! It would give him a perverse pleasure. But I won't give him the pleasure of knowing if I was or not. It's none of his business . . . Anyway, how do I know you were lecturing in Slepnevo last night, and not in bed with some woman? . . . How do I know you weren't fucking that blind woman who's writing about you? Where does she live? Kazan? How do I know you weren't sleeping with her in Gorky?"

Rozanov stopped in mid-circuit of the room, his fingers poised round his cigarette, about to take it from his lips. "That's absurd!" he said. "Why on earth should you think such a thing?"

"Because you're no good at lying. Slepnevo is a very strange place to be lecturing at. Do you know what Slepnevo means, you two?" She glanced at Findlater, slumped at the table, and then at Marie, who had gone to squat cross-legged near the stereo, trying to listen to the low music against the increasingly loud voices. She raised her eyes from her lap, and shook her head. "Does it have something to do with 'blind?' " asked Findlater.

"Yes. Exactly. So instead of lecturing on Gorky in Slepnevo, he was probably screwing a blind woman in Gorky . . . Well, weren't you?"

Rozanov had resumed his pacing, more slowly. "You're crazy."

She chuckled. "No I'm not. I know you. You can't lie. Not completely."

"But *you* can lie!"

"Oh yes, *I* can lie! I can lie very well!"

Rozanov's bagged and blood-streaked eyes glared at her. "Like saying Kolasky was only resting on your bed before dinner."

"Maybe. Maybe not."

Rozanov rolled up his shirt-sleeve. "Look, Ben!" he said, thrusting his right arm at him. "This guy has been teaching Sonia close-armed combat!" He walked unsteadily to Marie, and bent over her. "See that? She's been screwing someone else and then she bites me!" Returning to the sofa, he collapsed on to it. He tried to pat Sonia's thigh, but she pulled away. "Okay, I forgive you," he said. "Whatever you did. I just want to know. Was it a good fuck?" His hand shook. His ash dropped on to her kimono, but she did not notice it.

She rose, and walked to the window. She twitched the curtain aside and gazed out into the blackness.

"Are you in love with this guy?" he asked, more quietly, his voice tremulous.

She turned round to face him. She looked plain again. "Love!" she exclaimed. "You must be joking! I've had my bellyful of so-called love. It doesn't mean anything."

"So what are you doing with him? Playing with him?"

"How do you know I'm not a swallow? Like Nina? . . . You two should meet his wife. Or maybe you have? She sold herself to the KGB, sleeping with foreigners. I bet he hasn't told you that! Or perhaps he has. He goes for swallows. That's what they're called . . . Well, Sergei, maybe you've turned me into one." She moved to the table and absent-mindedly picked up Findlater's glass; gulped the vodka. She faced Rozanov. "How do you know I wasn't ordered to sleep with Alexei? How do you know my bedroom isn't bugged? How do you think I was given such a nice flat and can afford so many nice clothes? Certainly not from *your* money! And certainly not from Intourist!"

She walked back to the sofa and sat down, turned away from him.

"You! A swallow!"

"Why not?"

"Because you haven't got the looks. You're too plain. Your nose is too big. Who ever heard of a swallow in glasses? What's that American verse, Ben?—'Guys seldom make passes at girls who wear glasses?'"

"Piss off." She pushed the fondling hand from her thigh.

"Oh, you might appeal to an ageing general, but you wouldn't be much of a draw to a smart western diplomat, Sonia."

"You're a fucking bastard . . ." She ran her knuckles under her eyes, smudging her mascara. She grabbed her cigarettes and lighter from the sofa, and ran out of the room.

Silence fell. Only the soft piano sounds. Rozanov closed his eyes and leaned back, drawing on his cigarette. Minutes passed. They heard thumping noises through the wall.

Sonia appeared at the door, wearing a black coat and fur hat. "I'm going out," she said. "Just don't be here when I get back, Sergei. And leave your key. I can find a better use for it."

She slammed the door. They heard another door slam.

Rozanov smiled sheepishly.

· 6 ·

THE NOCTURNE ENDED. THE SILENCE WAS SHATTERED BY THE phone. Rozanov jumped up. "Thank God!" he said. "Ben, would you—?" He gestured for him to take the call. Findlater, drowsy, hauled himself to his feet.

"What was the name?" he asked.

"Issahakian."

The heavy New Yorker fumbled in his discarded jacket for his handkerchief, and lurched to the phone. Holding the handkerchief over his mouth, he lifted the receiver. "Hello," he said in his broken Russian, "this is Ikahassian."

"Shit," Rozanov breathed.

The American listened, frowning, then held the receiver towards Sergei. "It's not your wife," he said, through the handkerchief. "But it's for you."

Sergei took the phone. Findlater hovered near. He saw the Russian's face tighten with hostility, then flush. "Do you wish me to get *no* sleep?" he said in a voice trembling with anger. He then grunted a few times, before saying, "I wasn't particularly, at the time, but you can bet your life I am now!" More gently he murmured, "Okay. Just don't bother me any more, please." He grunted again—once—twice; the look of rage returned; he barked "Fuck off!" and put the phone down. Waving his arms wildly, he strode to the window. "It was that fucking cow again! Would you believe it!"

Marie, turning the cassette over, said, "What on earth was she ringing for this time?"

He gave a bleak laugh. "To apologize for upsetting me by ringing before! And to say she hoped she hadn't created any problems! Well, no!—she's only probably cost me my wife and child and my mistress!"

Tranquil Chopin flooded the room again.

"Don't blame her too much," Marie said. "She's blind, remember that. It must be all the worse, not to be able to sleep, when you're blind."

Rozanov was pacing around the room, pulling open drawers, looking under cushions. "She's taken her cigarettes, damn it." He left the room. They heard him roaming around the flat.

"Let's go, Marie," Findlater pleaded. "I can hardly keep my eyes open."

"Not yet."

Sergei came back, smiling grimly yet triumphantly. He waved a cigarette. "Polish! By the bed! And it's got lipstick on it! I guess she must have put it in her mouth, then found better things to do!" He opened a matchbox and struck a match. He breathed out smoke, then he moved to the phone. "I must ring Nina. I don't like this silence. Would you turn the volume down, Marie? The Issahakians wouldn't be playing Chopin. They'd be playing Khachaturian or something." He waited for the music to fade, then dialled. Smoking his Polish cigarette in short, jerky puffs, he waited anxiously.

"Nina, darling! . . . It's me. No, there's nothing wrong. I'm sorry I woke you. It was just that Mother rang and said you were worried, after that crazy woman's call . . . I'm at the Issahakians. I ran them home from Mother's, and got talking. I might stay the rest of the night. I've drunk too much . . . Yes, she's just crazy. It was nothing. I'll explain tomorrow . . . Of course I told her that, but I couldn't be too hard on her: she's not quite right in the head . . . Oh, really? Has he got over it now? . . . No, I distinctly recall putting it back in the bathroom cabinet . . . What a fucking night! . . . Yes, I'm going to see this television guy, and then I'll be right back. You'll keep him home from school tomorrow? Yes, I know—I'll be home by noon: no problem . . . You get some sleep now. Goodnight, dear."

He put the phone down, and walked to the window. He pulled back the curtain. "She didn't ring because Sasha woke up with a coughing fit. He gets bronchitis quite badly. She'd just got him back to sleep and had dropped off herself." He stifled a yawn. "Well, I needn't have picked a quarrel with Sonia. Nina couldn't have been that worried. God, everything's all fucked up."

Marie went to the bathroom, and after a few minutes Findlater followed her. He tussled with her as she came out. "I'm dropping on my feet," he murmured, nuzzling her ear; "we *must* go." She slipped away from him, whispering, "He isn't fit to drive us."

"We could get a cab. Or walk. He said it's not far."

"No. We can't leave him in this state."

Findlater, feeling nauseous, sat on the toilet. He held his head in his hands. Dysentery, on top of everything else. This vodka. Stolichnaya vodka.

When he staggered back to the lounge, he saw they had turned out the lights. Marie was standing by Rozanov at the window; his arm was round her shoulder. "Come here, Ben," he summoned. "The clouds have gone. It's a wonderful night." Resentfully Ben joined them. Without his glasses he saw only cloud. "What does this mean?" Rozanov asked in awed tones. "All those stars? What does God mean by this . . . life? God is a Russian writer. He expresses his vision through riddles. Or *her* vision. . . .

"Without faith in God, life is meaningless, my friends; yet the idea of a God is so intrinsically absurd, even His existence wouldn't make life necessarily more meaningful. Can you imagine being God; waking up one day thinking, Oh, I'm God! It's like growing up knowing you're Tsarevich, only worse. How could He know what it's like to be an ordinary person, a creature? And what responsibilities! Does He ever—as I do sometimes —think, Fuck it, I've had enough! Has he ever thought of suicide? Has he ever thought of throwing Himself out of a window? But if He did—what would there be then? Nothing! But nothing would still be a kind of something! Oh, shit!

"The urge to escape . . . Why not do it right now? Find out at once! Because we're cowards! What do you think, Ben?"

Ben thought that he might be sick any moment. "I've never contemplated suicide," he said. "Even at my lowest. Even when my wife died."

"Ah, wives! I'm sorry, I don't mean to be disrespectful of your wife. Actually I envy you. Not that she died, I don't mean that. But your love for her . . . Freedom! What does it mean? Is it really desirable? Look what marvellous work our unfreedom has created! Forcing us to use invisible ink, which is the best, the most subtle kind of ink, Marie. The ink used by God . . . those inscrutable stars . . . Does freedom make people any happier? Okay, let's say most marriages are unhappy. But in the old days, at least the unhappiness was limited. Nowadays, people think they *ought* to be happy so they rush on to another marriage, another unhappiness, leaving behind them the wrecks of their children's lives. That's why, though I love Sonia, I couldn't go through it again. If divorce weren't possible, she'd know it couldn't happen, and she'd have to make the best of it, or get out. In a way, I would be absolved."

"What's that sign?" asked Marie, nodding her head down and to the left.

"It means 'Glory to Work!' " He chuckled. "But the night comes when no man shall labour. . . ."

"Marie doesn't labour *now*," Findlater remarked; but the jibe seemed to fall on deaf ears, for after a reflective pause Rozanov resumed his theological soliloquy.

"Well, maybe God *is* a woman. I could believe more easily in a woman-God. There are these flashes of great beauty: like those stars, or like coming in and seeing you tonight, my *krasavitsa!*" He pulled Marie closer and kissed her on the forehead. "And then, there is the ugliness. Death. Olga. Her misery—because I am not unfeeling towards it. I am a big event in her life, maybe even *the* big event; yet to me she means nothing. Well, I feel sorry about that. She had a rapturous night, while for me it was sheer hell. The only worse night was when I found myself with a woman who was unbelievably ugly—which Olga isn't—and also deaf. She wore a hearing-aid, which wailed suddenly when I gritted my teeth and screwed her."

He sighed. "I shouldn't get into such situations. I should stick to Sonia, whatever the problems. Well, I do, really. Or she sticks to me. She's bewitched me. I think she is literally a witch."

"It was amazing," murmured Marie, "how she knew about Olga."

"Of course! And it *was* in Gorky! Yes, astonishing . . . but that kind of thing happens all the time . . . She's acutely intuitive, yet also very down to earth. I love that balance in her. She is full of contradictions. Did you see how plain she looked when we first came tonight? Ben, did you notice that? But then, suddenly. . . ."

"Yes," Marie said. "You should have phoned first, Sergei. It's fatal to burst in on a woman when she feels she's looking a fright. That was why she was in a bad mood."

He sighed again. "I wanted to catch her out. To catch them in bed. I raced up, and used my key. It's unforgivable, really. And yet she did come round—for some reason she decided to be friendly . . . only that bitch in Kazan fucked it up . . ." He moved away from them and began to pace around the room. "I wonder where she's gone? Not to Kolasky's hotel—he left today it seems. She's been gone a long time. I hope she's all right. Maybe I'd better take a drive around the streets."

"I'll come with you," the young woman offered.

"Has she done this before?" Findlater asked.

"Often. She usually walks around and around."

"A woman couldn't do that in New York."

"No? I guess not. Well, it's still worrying. There are wolves even here."

· 7 ·

THEY HAD GONE OUT TO CRUISE THE NEIGHBOURING STREETS searching for Sonia. Findlater was left alone in the stillness of deep night, edging towards dawn. The piano music had stopped. He slumped morosely at the table, finishing off the bottle of Ararat cognac with which they had toasted Pasternak: for Rozanov had said it would settle his stomach. He had been sick once, but now his nausea did seem to be settling.

Fighting off sleep, he made shaky pencil sketches on a writing-pad he had found in the bureau: his eyes inches from the page, to bring the blurred lines into focus. They were drowsy ideas for the advertising campaign he would be organizing when he got back home. His first sketch was of Marie, in bed, reaching out to take a glass of vodka from a gentleman friend. Her nipples would be the only colour in the whole advert, except for the caption, STOLICH-NAYA VODKA. He added a Russian fur hat to the girl's picture. A suggestion of something mysteriously kinky. It would look good in *Playboy* and *Penthouse*.

Then he imagined and sketched a glass of vodka, almost filling a page; and *through* the vodka you could see a fur-hatted Russian woman and a crew-cut American walking hand in hand, to a background which blended the Capitol and the Kremlin. And the caption would read something like "EVERYTHING BECOMES CLEAR THROUGH STOLICHNAYA VODKA"; or maybe "PROBLEMS? WHAT PROBLEMS?" and then the name of the product. He could visualize it in the *New Yorker*. Astonishingly, the latest issue of the magazine lay in Sonia's bureau, along with several other English and American magazines and newspapers. Findlater hadn't believed her claim to be a swallow, assuming it to be a thrust in the war between her and Sergei; but it looked as if she took her Intourist work very seriously, and was trusted by her organization with what must be classified material.

It made him think. And, for a woman in her early thirties, she did seem remarkably well off, as she had suggested in her goading of Sergei. Findlater, in his early days, first alone and then with Judy, could not have afforded a Persian rug, nor one or two of the prints, nor the huge collections of books and records. Hell, he would *never* be able to afford a Persian rug. Even without his glasses, he could swear Sonia hadn't bought her clothes at GUM. Nor, for that matter, had Nina; and Sonia seemed to see herself as poorly off compared with the Rozanovs. The American blinked back sentimental tears as he recalled Judy's efforts with the sewing-machine to make her clothes last out another winter. Judy's old blue coat, which he had given to a thrift-shop after she died, would have merged comfortably into the poverty of the women in the Nikolsky Cathedral. Marie, too, stitched and mended; but in her case, sheer beauty carried her through. In the atrociously dressed groups of Western tourists, here and in Leningrad, she stood out like a grand duchess in proletarian disguise. He had felt proud to be with her.

He put on his jacket, feeling cool. Wistfully he touched the absurd bottle through the cloth. He had aimed beyond himself. It was true, he was kind of heavy, as Rozanov's unflattering compliment had proclaimed. Marie was not for the likes of him. He fumbled in his breast pocket for the tattered snapshot of Judy he always carried on him, and as he gazed at her plain face his eyes grew even more blurred. He mumbled a few words to her. He recalled the seven Orthodox corpses, laid out side by side like Snow White's seven dwarfs, in the *mêlée* of the ground floor of the cathedral when he and Marie had decided to push through and see what was going on. Six old people, their gummy mouths sucked in, and one young woman. The mass of mourners behind their coffins, staring at the well-dressed tourists with understandable hostility. Not far off, babies being baptized; a pale sickly boy being blessed. All of life and death, except screwing.

Findlater shivered, gulped Ararat. It was lonely in the flat, even with all the lights on; creepy.

The phone rang, making him jump almost out of his skin. He didn't move. Should he answer? Did phones ring all night in every Moscow household? Could it be Nina? If it was, he couldn't remember the name he was supposed to have. He decided to let it ring. But then, it might be Sergei, or Marie, or even Sonia. He'd better answer it. He stood up and lurched to the phone.

He heard an agitated male voice say, without preamble: "Comrade Rozanov, I'm sorry to have woken you. This is Stiva Kubik. I don't know what to do; so I had to ring you." The American started to interrupt, but the man surged on in a torrent: "You see, I heard my wife call you. I'd been worried about her; she'd seemed disturbed after her visit to her sister's. Well, that's what she'd told me—a visit to her sister in Perm. The first time she called you, I only came in on the end of it; but when she got out of bed again, thinking me asleep, I followed her; and I heard her ask the operator for your number. I was suspicious, so I made a mental note of it. I'm sorry. Well, this time I told her I'd heard her conversation, and everything came out. She became very upset, and rushed out of the house in only her nightdress and dressing-gown. At least, as far as I know: she didn't have time to dress. That's three hours ago, and she hasn't come back. I feel desperate. I can do nothing. I'm blind too, you see—I don't know if she's told you that. I've no one to turn to, except you. I wondered if she'd contacted you again, or even if she was trying to reach you. It's impossible, of course, but she was in a terrible state. Well, you see, I simply don't know what to do. I love Olga, she's all I've got in the world; and I wanted to beg you not to take her from me. I've been thinking—perhaps if you and she could spend a week together . . . Well, it might get her out of your system. I'd be prepared to let you do that. Anything, so long as she comes back to me." The man's voice broke, then he recovered himself. "Comrade Rozanov, can I ask you this: are you in love with her?"

The hectic speech, which Findlater had desperately tried to follow, reached a pause. The American said, "*Ya nye Rozanov*—I am not Rozanov."

There was an intake of breath, audible several hundred miles away, and then the man said, "Oh, I'm sorry. Could I speak to him?"

"I'm afraid he's not here."

"*Gdye on?*—Where is he?"

"He has gone out."

The man gave a gasp: "Oh! That's terrible! . . . Then who are you?"

"*Gost*—A visitor."

At that moment Findlater heard a door open—voices—then Sonia entered the lounge followed by Marie and Sergei. Findlater put the phone down. Sonia, looking brisk, cheerful, as she started to remove her coat, said, "Who was that?"

"Oh, a wrong number."

She shrugged. "It happens." Rozanov, slipping off his jacket, looked relieved; smiling, he patted Findlater on the back and asked if he felt better. The American nodded. Sonia asked if he had been sick, and Findlater said, "Just a little upset stomach."

She fussed around him sympathetically, and seemed an altogether different person from the hurt and angry woman who had gone out two hours before. "You should have had some air, Ben," she said. "It's refreshing out."

"It's lovely, Ben!" Marie confirmed, her eyes sparkling, her fingers straying through her hair, where it covered her pearly little ear.

"Well, let's walk to the hotel," Findlater suggested.

"Oh no! You mustn't go yet!" said Sonia. "We'll put some music on. I'll just put my coat away and have a pee. I'm bursting." She hurried out. The bathroom door slammed.

"Who was it?" Rozanov murmured anxiously, nodding towards the phone.

"I'm afraid it was Olga's husband."

"Shit!" Rozanov sank on to the sofa. He stared at the ceiling for some time before murmuring, "What did he want?"

Sonia came back into the lounge, before Findlater could reply. "Yes, what do we want?" Sonia said to Marie, who had crouched beside the stereo. The young Russian woman squatted down beside her, revealing stretches of black nylon between her high black boots and her grey skirt. "I'm afraid I haven't a very wide selection."

"Who would like coffee?" Rozanov asked. The two women nodded. "With cream but no sugar," said Marie.

Findlater followed him into the kitchen.

"So?" said the Russian quietly, filling the kettle. "What did he say?"

The American, in low tones, told him.

"Jesus Christ, what a fucking idiot!" Rozanov hissed quietly. "He really said that? He wanted to know if I was in love with her? He offered her to me for a week?" He closed his eyes, and shook his head. Sounds of the Rolling Stones came loudly through the wall.

"The guy was very upset about having spewed it all out to *me*,"

Findlater said. Then he broke into a weak laugh. Something had clicked in his fuddled brain: the guy had said "That's terrible!" because Findlater had used a wrong verbal form—not "he has gone out" but "he has passed away. . . ."

"I'll bet he was," said Rozanov. The American, recalling that he'd told the guy he was a *gost*, or ghost, unleashed a wild cackle. "What's so funny?" the Russian growled.

"I'm sorry. It isn't funny."

"Oh, it is." The Russian opened a cupboard door, and took out four mugs. "It's extremely funny. Here am I, really a decent, quiet guy, and there are two fucking women wandering the streets at night, hysterical because of me."

"But Sonia's got over it," Findlater observed. "How did you manage it? Where did you find her?"

"She was walking near Gorky Park. She wouldn't get in the car at first. She was—pretty violent. But then I suggested we take a holiday. She has a week coming to her. I said why don't we go to Armenia? My mother is Armenian, but I've never been there. I've been thinking lately I ought to go. Well, at first she kept saying she didn't want to see me ever again, here or in Armenia; but she got in the car; and as you can see, she's cheered up."

"So all your troubles are over," murmured Findlater, with a touch of malice.

Rozanov grimaced. "For tonight. Unless Olga is actually on her way here! . . . She can't be—can she?"

"I wouldn't think so."

"How could she get here? A blind woman? After I told her to fuck off? . . . But she's trouble, Ben. She'll never let me alone. I know her type. Still, it's sad to think of her out wandering the streets of Kazan." Gloomy, distant, he overfilled a mug, and cursed. He picked up a tea-towel and wiped the tray.

"But how do you know she *is* wandering the streets?" asked Findlater. "Or rather, how does this Rubik, Rubrik, know it, if he's blind?"

The Russian gripped his arm. "Ben, you're right! He can't be sure! She might have slammed the door to deceive him, and got back into bed! Or be sitting right next to him while he phoned, enjoying his agony! Greedy to find out if her husband loves her! Of course! That's it!"

"It could be." Findlater swayed, and clutched at the draining-board. He glanced at the window. The curtains were drawn back; greyness glimmered. He moved to the window and looked out. He saw blurred lights below, and thought he saw movement. Rozanov came up beside him. "Isn't that an amazing spectacle?" he said. "They're building a new office-block. More bureau-cracy—but the actual building of it is amazing, don't you agree? Out at the crack of dawn! Scurrying like ants! All that open space . . . Meyerhold would have loved it. He'd have loved it as his stage. He'd have constructed Elsinore on it! Size! Energy! Meyerhold and Mayakovsky! No number less than one million! Exclamation marks! . . ." He heaved a sigh. "Poor Zinaida . . . I'd like to find the bastard who killed her."

When they returned to the lounge, Sonia and Marie were dancing together. They broke off to take the coffee. Findlater, drinking his quickly, said they really must go. But Marie put down her mug and grabbed him, swung him into a dance. He stumbled around, apologizing for treading on her toes. She merely smiled, and wrapped her arms around his neck. She pressed her body against his. They had never been so close. If only he weren't so exhausted and befuddled. Rozanov was dancing with Sonia, moving lightly for a man who claimed hardly to have slept for two days and nights. Marie whispered in Findlater's ear, "I hope you've still got the lotion." He went weak in her arms, and stumbled again. "You mean, we can still do it?" She nodded: "If you still want to. Or are you tired?"

"No."

"I feel quite wide awake. How about you?"

"Yes," he lied.

The Stones pounded on.

"Perhaps you can give me more than a massage." She looked him full in the eyes, smiling. He began to shake, uncontrollably.

"You're shaking!"

"Do you mean it?"

"Why not? I feel kind of horny." She kissed him gently behind the ear. She had never kissed him before. He felt his knees buckle. She put her tongue in his ear. A thrill, an ache, ran down his nape and along his spine.

The record turned into another; Rozanov tapped Marie on the shoulder and she moved into his arms. The American was glad to sit down. Sonia sat down opposite him. He put up his hand to stop her as she started to fill his glass with vodka, but she told him it would help to settle his stomach. "Okay," he said. His hand was still trembling as he picked up the glass and sipped. "No, that isn't the right way, Ben," Sonia said. "You should knock it back." Picking up her own full glass, she showed him. Findlater knocked back his vodka, then coughed. His head swam.

"Why have you taken your glasses off?" she asked.

"I broke them just now."

"Oh, I'm sorry. I prefer you in them. Are you short-sighted? I have to wear mine for reading and close work, but otherwise I can manage without. Sergei tries to persuade me to have contact lenses, but I tell him it's hardly worth it. Have you ever thought of contact lenses, Ben?"

"I tried, but they didn't suit my eyes. Maybe I should try the soft lenses."

"But why? You look good in glasses. They suit you. You look distinguished in them . . . Dance with me."

He staggered to his feet; dizzy, he almost fell. She put her arms round him and pulled him, stumbling, around the room. He saw two images of Sergei and Marie dancing, their bodies fused. He heard two Russian poets call to him in unison, "Stay on and come to Armenia with us! I've been trying to persuade Marie!" He heard two beautiful raven-haired women say, "It would be *wonderful*, but. . . ."

Then Sonia whispered something in his ear, but he couldn't take it in. When he sought out Sergei and Marie again, there were several couples dancing. His strength gave way; he stumbled; Sonia couldn't hold him; he crashed on to the stereo, ending the music with a grinding scream. He was on the floor, on a spinning, flying Persian rug. Somewhere above him, in the clouds, he heard voices. Then the magic carpet whirled him on, into oblivion.

When he came round, he felt ill. Sick in the stomach, and his head pounding. He didn't at first know where he was. Then he realized he was on the verge of falling off the side of a bed. His shoes and jacket were off, and his tie; but otherwise he was fully dressed. There was no covering: a sheet and a duvet had fallen to the floor.

Something was moving, pushing, at his back. Painfully he eased himself round, and saw that it was Sonia. She was naked; her back was towards him; her buttocks, stuck out, had been the force propelling him over the edge. Lifting his head off the pillow he saw, beyond Sonia, first Sergei and then Marie. They too were naked. All three were sleeping deeply, breathing tranquilly. The limbs of all three were entangled.

With a groan, Findlater hauled himself off the bed, and staggered towards the bathroom. He hung his head over the toilet, and waited to be sick. He knew it would make him feel better. But it wouldn't come. He knew he should stick his fingers down his throat, but he couldn't bring himself to do it.

After gulping water from the tap, he peered in the mirror at his ghastly face. The grey stubble, the heavy jowls, the cavernous eyes, the rhino-wrinkles. He felt a warning stab in his bowels.

After washing his hands, he staggered into the lounge. Blinking, he saw through a mist the collapsed stereo set. His jacket was draped on the back of a chair; his shoes on the floor beside it. He lurched towards the jacket, remembering that there should be a small packet of aspirins in one of the pockets. Marie had used up most of them for her headaches, but he thought there were a couple left. He thrust his hand in the left pocket, but let out a hiss of pain and withdrew his hand sharply. Blood oozed from the ball of his thumb. His hand was also covered in something sticky. Cursing the bottle of body-lotion, broken in his fall, he fumbled with his other hand in the other pocket, found his handkerchief, and wrapped it round his cut thumb. The blood seeped through immediately. It was a bad cut. He tried to recall how long ago he'd had a tetanus injection. It was a long time, too long. He had missed his glasses-case in the pocket. He scrambled around on his hands and knees, and, without warning, vomited on to the Persian rug. He rested a while, then crawled on, avoiding the mess. He found the case eventually. He would have to get new glasses as soon as he got back to New York; meanwhile, he would have to endure in a state of semi-blindness. He couldn't remember when their flight was due to leave.

He hauled himself up on to the sofa, and lay full length, trying to find some ease for his throbbing head, and maintaining a tight grip on his injured thumb, which had also begun to throb. He tasted bile in his mouth. He thought distantly of the scene he had left in the bedroom. Almost without bitterness. She had not even *tried* to make love to him. Hadn't even bothered to undress him. And if Sonia was a swallow, she, too, scorned him as a prey. If the bedroom was bugged, he wasn't worth trying to seduce.

The room was light. A bright grey haze at the window.

He held his wrist close to his eyes.

One forty-five.

He lay quietly. The blood seemed to be seeping through the handkerchief more calmly. The phone rang. He hauled himself to his feet, staggered to the phone, lifted the receiver. It was Nina's voice, high-pitched, hysterical. He thought he caught the words "Sonia," "Is Sergei dead?" "Why haven't you been answering?"

He raised his bleeding handkerchiefed paw to his mouth. A name came to him with surprising clarity.

"Issahakian," he growled. "This is Issahakian."

E·P·I·L·O·G·U·E

EPILOGUE

AT THREE IN THE AFTERNOON, A LARGE AND EXCITED CROWD had gathered for the announcement of the winner, and the awarding of the laurel. The weather, that midsummer day, was the finest of the whole Olympiad; cloudless and hot. Lake Lemminjärvi sparkled like a sheet of silver.

Five of the six finalists sat in a row, to the right of the stage. The empty chair should have been occupied by the British *improvisatore*. The others did not know why he was absent.

The only contestant who was not feeling tense and anxious was the Israeli.

The crowd hushed—the judges were coming, one behind the other, in their green Olympic robes. Tarkiainen, the chairman, walking stiffly with the aid of a stick, was at their head.

The eleven judges—Señora Menendez was in her room, heavily sedated—filed along the front row and sat down. Tarkiainen, helped by an official, mounted the platform and stood before the microphone. The sheet of paper in his hand trembled. His lips trembled. He licked his lips. The silence in the audience grew even deeper.

"Southerland . . ." he began, in his quavery voice, and immediately there was a shriek from somewhere followed by a burst of warm, though hardly enthusiastic, clapping. Many in the audience got to their feet, continuing to slap their hands together. There were some hisses from the grassy slope at the back, where a group of young women set up a chant of "Riznich! Riznich! . . ." But they were quickly hissed down by the people closest to them. The polite clapping went on.

Tarkiainen waved his hand, and one by one the people who had stood up sat back down, and the clapping died away. Then Tarkiainen continued: ". . . Southerland has withdrawn his improvisation, on the grounds that it was not an original composition." There were a few gasps here and there, and a low excited babble. The aged Finn waved his hand again and the noise stopped. The old man licked his lips, and the expectant hush grew quieter still.

"The winner of the laurel crown," Tarkiainen said at last, "is . . ." The piece of paper fluttered out of his hand and came to rest below the platform. He stooped forward, holding out his hand; the official who had helped him on to the stage moved to pick the paper up. He handed it to Tarkiainen. Tarkiainen gazed closely at the paper, as though he had forgotten the winner's name. Then, throwing his head back, he said in a ringing voice: "Kauppinen!"

The audience exploded. Everyone stood; a roar of applause went up. Kauppinen, who was at the end of the row of finalists, jerked his head back, and his mouth gaped open. A blush sprang to his whiskered face. Corinna, immediately to his right, leaned aside to touch him on the arm and said, "Congratulations!"

The Russian, the freckled Australian, the dark Israeli, leaned forward in their seats and turned to their left, to nod and smile their congratulations also.

"Thank you! Thank you!"

Then the Finn, a grin spreading from ear to ear, propelled himself forward in his wheelchair.

He had reached for the stars, and amazingly pulled them down.—At midsummer, when there were no stars.

"Quanto è sterile l'alloro!"—how sterile are laurels! reflected Teresa Bandettini, winner of the Olympic crown at Padua in 1775.

Kauppinen, on the night following his crowning, was already experiencing some of the drawbacks of what is popularly called success. Youthful in spirit, despite his sixty years and his physical disability (caused by a skiing accident in his youth), he was forced to sit at the official table during the Celebration Dinner, with dull officials and their staid spouses, and his own staid wife. With the chairman of the judges and Mrs Tarkiainen either side of him, at times Kauppinen gazed longingly at the next table, where his Russian rival, Markov, was having such a good time, surrounded by four lovely young Finnish ladies.

And yet, there was the ever-present consolation of knowing that he had won! He could still hardly believe it. And as Tarkiainen—who looked like one of those dug-up Pharaohs—related the agonies of the night before, his thoughts kept drifting back to that moment of triumph. So, as the old Professor described Señora Menendez's discovery of the young technician, hanging from a cord, when the lady had gone to his room to ask him to put her equipment right, Kauppinen's grave lips twitched suddenly into a joyous smile. Fortunately, Tarkiainen at that moment was gazing down at his place-mat, Mrs Tarkiainen was talking to the man on her other side, and the couple opposite had gone to dance.

The dinner was taking place in a yacht club, at Sahalahti, a bay a couple of miles from the scene of the Olympiad. The large dining-room was crowded and noisy: the celebrants, a mixture of contestants, judges, officials, journalists, and those who had paid a high price for the chance to get close to the *improvisatori*, to photograph them, dance with them, get their autographs. A succession of musical groups, who had performed at the Olympiad, provided the entertainment.

Markov, surrounded by the four lovely Finns, was in a quandary. Ever since he had confessed to his beloved wife an infidelity in Salzburg in 1970, and been forgiven, there had been an understanding between them that the end of an Olympiad was a very special time, when she might turn a blind eye if he strayed. He had strayed at Havana in '74. Since he had not been granted a visa to attend the Olympiad at Delphi, it was eight years since Markov had been unfaithful to his wife: that is, if one didn't count the brief, extraordinary flurry with Corinna, in the train to Yerevan, on which occasion he had played an almost completely passive role. Now, when he was no longer "in training," as it were, he found himself in love with all four girls who were flirting with him, and he wanted to sleep with them all. At ten the next morning he would have to join Dibich for the drive to Helsinki airport. He expected, judging from the midget's cold stare, a rough ride. Markov wondered if he dared be completely open with the girls, tell them his problem, and ask them to sort out a rota for the night. Say, two hours each, from midnight to eight o'clock.

No, he thought sadly, as he tucked in to glowfried salmon and creamed morels, I shall have to choose. But that's impossible. They're all so fresh, so beautiful; and the three I reject would feel hurt. I shall end up sleeping alone again. . . .

And yet, why can't we be honest and natural? I get phases, like tonight, when I'd love to fuck almost every woman I see. Look at that magnificent, fat, blowsy frau, dancing with the Pole! Krüdner, I think she's called . . . God, I'd love to get it up her, and stifle myself between her breasts! Why shouldn't I tell her so? And, if she wanted it too, why shouldn't we do it? It wouldn't mean I love my wife any the less . . . And that Flamenco dancer! Wonderful! . . . And Corinna, dancing with her young Finn . . . Incredibly beautiful! . . . Why have I not tried to take advantage of what happened in the train? God knows why she continues to go around with poor old Cosmo. Look at him . . . he looks as if his salmon was poisoned. . . .

Then Markov fell to thinking about his wife: wondering if she was okay, with the expected birth just six weeks away. How strange it would be, and rather delightful, to have a baby again in the flat. It would be good to see Anya, tomorrow.

No one here seems to have imagined that there was something of me in Corinna's Russian hero . . . Well, I guess it's because I'm a little younger, and talk about Anya a lot, and don't get drunk . . . God, these Finns! How they can knock it back! But why do they have to get so loud and boring when they drink? . . .

In Moscow, though, they'll be putting two and two together to make five, now Troshin has thrown the spotlight on Riznich's improvisation . . . Did he know it could be bad for me, too? Does he resent me, deep-down? . . . Because I'm creative? . . . Corinna too, maybe—because I'm happily married? . . . Oh well, I might as well enjoy what's left of my last Olympics . . . "Kaija, darling, you're not drinking! Have some more! . . ."

Corinna, wearing the same dress, freshly-laundered, as she had worn for her performance, had been trying to practise honesty but it had gone wrong. Ingmar, her cub journalist, had been in a state of ecstasy after their first dance together; but after the second, during which she had cleared up a misunderstanding, he had run off, close to tears, and left the club.

Her seat was next to a French window. Sipping coffee, she glanced now at the fading light, now at her table companions, to whose remarks she replied pleasantly but briefly. She was happy that Cesare (perhaps at last goaded into rebellion) was dancing for such a long time with a Swedish television reporter; and that the two seats opposite were also vacant. Distancing herself from the increasingly frenzied dancing, by directing her gaze more and more often at the peaceful birches, she felt herself coming to terms with her failure. It didn't matter. She would forget about it. She wished people wouldn't keep coming up to her and sympathizing.

When Lucia Rossi left the dance-floor and came smiling up to sit across from her, Corinna felt torn between the pleasure of at last being able to say hello and pain at having to talk to one of the judges. The embarrassment of the early-morning encounter seemed but a small matter; but Lucia, with a blush, and a nervous striking of a match, plunged in with an apology.

"Don't worry," said Corinna. "I'm sorry we gave you such a shock!"

"But worse for you!" Signora Rossi raised her eyebrows humorously, and unloosed smoke-wreaths from between her small, sparkling teeth.

"Not so much for me. For him, yes—I guess so!"

"Oh dear! . . ." She looked around the tables, and at the dancers. "I don't see him any more. That *was* him, wasn't it? Whom you were dancing with? . . . I thought so, but I wasn't sure."

"He's gone," said Corinna. "I'm afraid I upset him."

"Oh, how was that?"

"Well, it's quite funny, in a way. I've been trying to pick up Finnish while I've been here. I was getting him to practise with me—though actually Swedish is his first language. Do you speak Finnish? Well, Ingmar asked me, *minä nain sinut*: which I happened to know meant, 'Can I screw you?' So of course I said, Great! Yes! Wonderful!"

Signora Rossi smiled. "Ah, Teresa! and you were such a quiet, pure little girl in Sorrento!"

"I know! . . . Anyway, he was thrilled. After I'd danced with my friend, Cesare, we danced again, and Ingmar said he'd told a couple of his friends he was going to screw me, and hoped I didn't mind. You can imagine what I said to him! But actually, as I then found, the phrase for 'Can I screw you?' is *minä nain sinua . . . Minä nain sinut* means 'Can I marry you?' The different ending is a kind of intensive—implying, I guess, 'Can I screw you completely? Can I screw you up?' " (Corinna's experience of marriage had been limited to a month, in her eighteenth year.) "So I had to tell him, No, thank you very much—and he ran off!" She laughed.

Lucia laughed too, as in their carefree days at school. Then, reminded, she asked after Corinna's mother and her brothers and sisters. They were all fine, said Corinna; she had been down south for a holiday in the spring. Her mother was in good health, and refused to move in with Pietro and his wife. She was very independent.

"She never remarried, then?" asked Signora Rossi.

"No. No." Corinna glanced aside, out of the window. Dusk was falling, at last.

"That was tragic, your father's death. My grandmother mentioned it in a letter; and I actually started to write to you, Teresa, to say how sorry I was, but I never finished it. I was settling in my new school and—and one hardly knows how to cope with death at thirteen. But *you* had to cope with it, with your poor father's death; there was no excuse for me."

"I understand. Well, we were different people then. Twenty-two years ago. . . ."

"It was an accident, wasn't it?"

Corinna nodded, and glanced out of the window again. Her eyes clouded. She blinked, several times. "Yes. And I was to blame. A scythe. I was messing around with it. There was no one else in the field." She turned her eyes towards her childhood friend again. "I couldn't stop the blood." She closed her eyes, and breathed very deeply and slowly, her breasts—Egypt and the Bahamas—heaving. Lucia leaned across and placed her hand on Corinna's.

"You poor girl!" she said.

Corinna opened her eyes, and gradually her breathing returned to normal. She turned the conversation to the infinitely less painful subject of the tragic event in the judges' guest-house. She had not known the young Finnish technical assistant, had never even seen him; but everyone who knew him said he had been a fine young man. Did anyone have any idea why he had taken his life?

No, replied Lucia. None of the judges had got really acquainted with him. David Coningsby had talked to him most, and was extremely upset; but he too had no idea why it had happened. They'd heard there was a history of depression, that was all. The tragedy had, of course, cast a gloom over their final judging.

"About that," said Lucia, "—I must tell you what happened."

"I'd rather not know."

"I owe it to you to tell you; and I think it would make you feel better." Her fingers started to rearrange some unused cutlery in front of her, and she stared at the table-cloth. She fumbled for cigarettes and matches in her handbag, and offered one to Corinna, who accepted.

"Go on, then," said Corinna.

"Last night, I had a hell of a job persuading the others to take you seriously. I think they were very tired, and there were the usual objections of pornography and so on. You know?"

"Of course," said Corinna.

"But this morning—it was quite amazing—they'd completely changed. Everyone agreed that yours was the best. Well—almost everyone. Even some of those who had been most strongly against you had come round completely. There were several who thought Markov ran you pretty close. But right from the first comments—by Professor Krüdner over there, actually—" she nodded towards the dance-floor—"who'd been very hostile last night, it was absolutely clear you should win.

"But then, Teresa—Corinna, I suppose I should call you—I put my spoke in. I said that in view of the night's events, a young man's suicide, justice must give way to something even more important: tact, decency. That it was impossible to award the laurel to a work of such darkness and violence as yours, however brilliant it was. And even less could we award it to Markov's: which was either a grisly coincidence, or something much more horrible. Matti—the young man—had listened intently to both of you; in Finnish, I assume. Do you see what I'm getting at?"

"No."

"Well, without the least blame to either of you, it is just possible your works had an effect on him, influenced him to do what he did . . . Do you see? I said we simply couldn't ignore a young man's body lying in a morgue, with his grief-stricken parents coming to see him, and award the laurel to you, or even Markov, as if nothing had happened; as if art had no responsibility."

Stubbing her cigarette, Lucia stretched her hand across again, laid it on Corinna's. "I'm sorry. I'm afraid I persuaded them."

"I understand. I think you were right."

She glanced out of the window, fighting down her anger at the stranger who had cost her the Olympic crown by hanging himself on the wrong night.

"But my argument," Signora Rossi went on, "was that we shouldn't award the laurels at all. We should say, there's been this awful tragedy, and so—that's it. Everyone go home. But they wouldn't hear of that. So it came to a straight choice between the Australian and the Finn. Dibich, actually, had swung overnight from Markov to Kauppinen, for some reason. Perhaps a phone-call from Moscow, who knows? He *wasn't* one of your fans! He fought the Finn's corner, and Jean Moreau, who loathes Dibich, argued for Blake. Well, I ask you! What a choice! I voted against both, but I was on my own."

"Thank you for telling me," Corinna said. "That cheers me up a little."

"I tell you it was a farce," her friend continued. "In the end, it almost divided on ideological lines. Portugal, France, Argentina, Israel and Japan voted for Blake. Señora Menendez wasn't there, she was too shocked. Russia, Poland, Hungary and Iran voted for Kauppinen—and West Germany too, because I hear Krüdner has been having an affair with Wojcicki." She nodded towards the dance-floor, where West Germany and Poland were still closely embraced. "Since I abstained, that left a tie, and Tarkiainen had to come in with the casting vote . . . I shouldn't be telling you this. I've drunk too much."

"You know I could always keep a secret."

Lucia Rossi blushed. "I remember! . . . Thank you. Yours was the best," she insisted, rising from her chair. "Everyone knows it was. I must get back to my table. Let's have lunch together when you're next in Rome."

"Yes, let's."

Signora Rossi gave her a relieved smile, and returned to her table, which she was sharing with Maurice Blake and his wife, and three drunks. Cesare came back to Corinna, and apologized for having been away so long. She smiled at him, and turned to the window.

Midnight. Reflections of arc-lights, red, blue, red, blue; and the red dress of a singer writhing to a Greek band. A bat flew past, above the trees. The high foliage was swaying slightly, against a chiaroscuro of sky and cloud.

She grew lost to the babble inside. Her soul was outside, with the nightingale. Maurice Blake stopped by, on his way to the toilet, to offer a breezy Australian greeting; and she responded pleasantly but was glad to turn again towards the trees and the sky.

Darkened—though it would grow no darker—that light outside was more the spirit of light than light itself; and it struck Corinna as all the more precious, tender, voluptuous. An ache came into her throat; a tremor ran down her spine, and flooded her with ecstasy. Cesare asked her if she felt cold; she half turned, half smiled, and shook her head. She watched the Greek singer and the band for a moment, and smiled cheerfully at someone. But mostly she looked out of the window, at the light, as at a secret lover: to whom she said, with her eyes, as one does amid a crowd of people, Oh, I love you! Forget these stupid people, and our quarrels . . . I love you!